"I missed you so," she whispered.

His heart broke, then regrew three times bigger.

The soft press of her breasts against his body, the rise and fall of her breath beneath his hands. The sheer glory of having her in his arms was well nigh unbearable. It was like the sun had taken up residence in his chest.

And he held her and murmured things, and his hands moved soothingly over her back.

And without thinking, he brushed a kiss over the top of her head.

He felt her breathing stop.

And then her back moved again in a great exhale, and she slowly tipped her head back and looked up at him.

"Liv?" he whispered.

A warning.

The only one he was going to give her.

By Julie Anne Long

THE LEGEND OF LYON REDMOND
IT STARTED WITH A SCANDAL
BETWEEN THE DEVIL AND IAN EVERSEA
IT HAPPENED ONE MIDNIGHT
A NOTORIOUS COUNTESS CONFESSES
HOW THE MARQUESS WAS WON
WHAT I DID FOR A DUKE
I KISSED AN EARL
SINCE THE SURRENDER
LIKE NO OTHER LOVER
THE PERILS OF PLEASURE

Julie Anne Long

The Legend of Lyon Redmond

AVONBOOKS

An Imprint of HarperCollinsPublishers

AVON BOOKS
An Imprint of HarperCollins*Publishers*
195 Broadway
New York, New York 10007

Copyright © 2015 by Julie Anne Long
ISBN 978-0-06-233485-5
www.avonromance.com

First Avon Books mass market printing: October 2015

Avon Trademark Reg. U.S. Pat. Off. and in Other Countries, Marca Registrada, Hecho en U.S.A.
HarperCollins® is a registered trademark of HarperCollins Publishers.

Printed in the U.S.A.

10 9 8 7 6 5 4 3 2 1

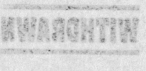

For May Chen, magnificent editor. It's been such a pleasure and privilege to share the triumphs and tribulations of the Redmond and Eversea families with you.

Acknowledgments

Much gratitude to my clever, insightful, and supportive editor, May Chen, who always just *gets* me, such a luxurious feeling; to the hardworking, gifted staff at Avon who are so committed to excellence and innovation, in particular thanks to Tom Egner for the beautiful, beautiful covers, Jessie Edwards for being such a fun and creative publicity partner, and to Shawn Nicholls, so patient with all the technical questions; and to my stalwart agent, Steve Axelrod.

And heartfelt thanks to everyone who has ever tweeted, blogged, commented, written a letter to me, or in any way shared their enthusiasm for the Pennyroyal Green series books. You mean the world to me, and I love and appreciate all of you so much!

The
Legend of
Lyon
Redmond

Chapter 1

◈

The first week of February . . .

SHE'S GETTING MARRIED ON *the second Saturday in May.*

Nine words scrawled across a sheet of foolscap. He stared at them until they blurred into a single gray mass.

When he lifted his head, his ears were ringing and he was as dazed as if he'd literally been dragged backward through time.

For Lyon Redmond, there had always only ever been one "she."

He was momentarily disoriented to find himself on the deck of a ship docked in Plymouth, not on the Sussex downs, waiting by the double elm tree. The one with the "O" carved into it.

A dozen pairs of eyes were on him, waiting patiently for the command that always came.

His crew was a carefully curated, casually lethal lot of men and one woman, the versatile Miss Delphinia Digby-Thorne, she of the many languages and surprisingly useful acting talents—she had once spilled ale all over his sister, Violet.

They had nothing in common apart from mysterious pedigrees, ambiguous morals, and unswerving loyalty. To him.

Unlike, alas, Olivia Eversea.

But then, every last one of them had prospered the moment they'd aligned their fortunes with him. He was cynical enough to know it was all of a piece, the loyalty and the prosperity. He didn't care.

The bearer of this news, a man dressed in footman's livery, took Lyon's silence as dismissal and turned rather too optimistically to leave.

"Hold," Lyon said sharply.

The swords of his men came up swiftly to bar the man's way.

"I'm unarmed," the footman said hurriedly, holding up his hands. "And alone. You have my word."

Lyon smiled a smile that would have had many a man wetting his smallclothes. It bore more resemblance to the curve of a cutlass. "While I'm certain your word is indeed priceless, you've naught to fear. I just cleaned my sword, so there will be no running through of anyone for at least another few hours."

This elicited chuckles from his crew.

The footman gave a wobbly, uncertain smile.

Lyon knew a surge of impatience, which he recognized as shame. He was not in the habit of intimidating clearly unarmed and outnumbered men for the sport of it.

Then again, given how history often treated bearers of bad news, the man was probably fortunate he still drew breath.

"Your name, please."

"Ramsey, sir."

"You're in no danger as long as I believe you are answering my questions truthfully, Ramsey."

"Of course, sir."

But judging from how the footman blanched, he didn't miss the implicit threat.

"Who sent you, Ramsey?"

"Begging your pardon, but Lord Lavay said you

would know when you read the message. I am in his employ. I'm a footman, sir." He squared his shoulders and touched the silver braid on his coat, as if for luck. "And I won the coin toss."

"I was a reward, then, was I, Ramsey?" Lyon drawled, to another scatter of chuckles. "Please describe Lord Lavay to me."

Ramsey furrowed his brow. "Well . . . he's a big gentleman. Perhaps as tall as you, sir. French. He often waves his hands when he talks, like so." He began to demonstrate with a sweep of his own hands, then clearly thought better of it when all the swords aimed at him twitched a warning. "Took quite an injury in a fight not too long ago, but he's fit now."

Lyon studied the footman unblinkingly, searching for the faintest hint of perfidy in the flicker of an eyelash or the tensing of a muscle.

He knew all about that fight and that injury. Lyon and his crew had found Lavay bleeding to death on the Horsleydown Stairs in London.

Lyon was in fact the reason Lord Lavay still walked the earth.

Then again, indirectly, Lord Lavay and his friend the Earl of Ardmay were indirectly the reason Lyon still walked the earth, and they had sacrificed a fortune in reward money to allow him to walk away. Though Lyon primarily had his sister, Violet, to thank for that. Men will do things for women they wouldn't otherwise in their right minds do.

No one knew that better than Lyon.

"I'm glad," he said, at last. Curtly. But he meant it. Lavay was a good man, and Lyon had learned that good men were too scarce, and the loss of one was a loss for all.

Lavay was also the only man in the world who

knew where to find Lyon Redmond right now. And one of the very few people in the world who knew him by his three identities: The real one. The assumed one.

And the one that could get him hanged.

Even if this message was a trap to lure him back to Sussex or into the Crown's custody, it mattered little. Lyon had become a man who could elude or escape any trap, by any means necessary.

In all likelihood this message was Lavay's way of discharging a debt of honor.

"Lord Lavay is a fine man, the finest I know, sir," the footman maintained stoutly, into the silence. "He married his housekeeper. Mrs. Fountain."

This was startling.

"Did he, now? Quite the epidemic of marriage in Sussex lately, isn't there?"

Lyon said this so bitterly everyone blinked as if he'd flicked something caustic into their eyes.

He drew in a long breath.

"And where is Lord Lavay at this very moment, Ramsey?"

"I expect he's still in Pennyroyal Green sir, a village in Sussex, where I left him. You see, given that he's newly married and . . . well, he's quite taken a shine to the place. Right nice town, it is," he extemporized, brightening.

"Is it?" Lyon said with such flat and brutal irony that his crew swiveled toward him in surprise, eyes wide.

He was beginning to alarm them.

He was beginning to alarm himself.

Because for the first time in years time Lyon wasn't certain what he wanted to do.

Damn Olivia Eversea, anyway.

She'd knocked his world off its axis from that first

moment in the ballroom, when she'd turned to him and smiled, and . . .

Even now. Even now the memory of that smile could stop his breath.

He'd last seen Pennyroyal Green in the dead of night almost five years ago. His trajectory since then had been as swift and mindless as if he'd been shot from a cannon. And it wasn't just because of what Olivia had said to him in the garden after midnight, in the pouring rain. Though after she'd said what she'd said, for a time he'd stopped caring what became of him.

No, that fuse had been lit for longer than anyone knew.

No one from Sussex had seen him since.

Though one had certainly tried. He half smiled at the thought of Violet.

And it was this that had broken the speed of his trajectory.

He'd had his own methods for remaining, however tangentially, informed about the lives of those he'd left behind. He'd proved something over the past five years. He'd at first thought it was all for Olivia. But he was no longer certain. He'd tried to purge his life of her, relinquishing even her miniature.

Clearly it hadn't worked.

But what no one knew, not even his crew, was that this was his final voyage. He'd risked this trip into London to track down the source of a little mystery that could devastate Olivia and her family.

He now had his answer.

He was, strangely, not surprised by it.

But he hadn't been prepared to make a decision about what to do next so soon.

Oh, Liv, he thought.

Suddenly it hurt to breathe. Fragments of memories rushed at him, each distinct as stained glass.

Olivia walking along the road to the Duffys' house, then breaking into a run when she saw him waiting beneath the elm tree, her face lighting like a star. As if even a second away from him was wasted.

That was the memory that always came to him in his darkest moments.

And now she was giving herself to another man.

His fingers curled on a surge of emotion. But he stopped just short of giving the message the crushing it deserved.

She. If Lavay had indeed written that word, he might have seen her, or even talked to her, or . . .

He couldn't do it.

He couldn't bloody do it.

And this is what decided him.

He tucked the message into his coat. "You can go, Ramsey," he said. "Thank you."

The footman spun and nearly bolted, silver braid glinting in the sun.

Lyon turned to face all the expectant faces of his crew.

"And we," he told them, "are staying in England."

It was time for a reckoning.

Three weeks later . . .

OLIVIA EVERSEA SIGHED IN the soothing, well-sprung recesses of her family's barouche, grateful for the solitude if only for the duration of the drive from St. James Square to the Strand.

It was perhaps an acknowledgment of how insufferable she'd been lately that her family had *let* her go to Madame Marceau's alone.

The discussion over whether she ought to have

silver trim on her wedding dress, like poor Princess Charlotte, or perhaps even beading along the hem, which would be much more expensive, but wouldn't she just glow like an *angel* (her mother's words) in it, had become absurdly impassioned, and subtle insults may even have flown, and her even-tempered sister, Genevieve, may even have slammed a door. Or, rather, shut it emphatically, which was close as Genevieve ever came to throwing a tantrum.

Minutes of sullen silence later, they had fallen into each other's arms, all apologies.

Olivia knew she was being difficult and prickly and she was somehow skillfully bringing out the worst in everyone she knew, herself most particularly. She was doing all of them a mercy by taking herself off to the modiste's alone.

And she *still* didn't know what kind of trim she wanted.

Did *no* one see the irony in choosing the same trim as the poor doomed Princess Charlotte, who had married the man she *wanted* to marry, rather than the man her father preferred her to marry? She had promptly then died horribly in childbirth, casting all of England into mourning.

Olivia wondered how many parents in England used Charlotte as a cautionary tale. *See what awaits you if you don't listen to me?*

Olivia was satisfied that *she*, at long last, had made a sensible choice from the years of suitors. Everyone in her family approved of him.

She peered out the window as the Eversea barouche rolled through the noisy, colorful, lively throngs of the Strand. Pye men and puppeteers and costermongers and pickpockets wove in and out of gorgeously dressed men and women aglow with wealth and flawless breeding. The Strand's lively dissonance would resonate nicely with her mood and she expected to find it soothing. And she liked Madame Marceau's shop, she truly did. It was a hushed, feminine paradise. It was just that she'd had so many fittings she'd begun to feel a bit like a calf being measured for chops.

She was to have silk petticoats and fine lawn night rails, traveling dresses and walking dresses and riding habits, gloves both kid and cotton, stockings both silk and woolen, ball gowns in silks and satins in glowing, muted jewel tones, along with fascinators and feathers and furbelows. It was a veritable avalanche of finery, or perhaps a *bulwark* of finery, she thought dryly, for surely abandoning it would inspire such crippling guilt that Olivia wouldn't dream of fleeing?

Not only that, but nearly every relative from both sides of her family would be convening upon Pennyroyal Green, Sussex, in May, and there would be not only a wedding, but a *ball*. "Reinforcements" was what she called these relatives, but not out loud.

She was the last of the Eversea children to be married, and she was going to be the wife of a viscount. Her brothers had all married unusual women, not one of whom possessed a title. Genevieve had married a duke—to the quietly gleeful satisfaction of her father, for they had trumped the Redmonds, who acquired a mere earl by marriage—but she and Falconbridge had wed by special license. Olivia was the family's last chance for pomp.

And she knew everyone who loved her would exhale only when she was waving merrily goodbye from Landsdowne's carriage as they went off on their wedding journey.

No one had said as much, of course.

And this was the unspoken source of all the tension.

They had nothing to worry about. Olivia was definitely going to marry him.

The betting books at White's, of course, had it otherwise.

God, but she was infinitely weary of being a *sport* for the wager-happy wastrels at White's. She did not want to be an *event*.

But if she'd learned anything over the years, wanting something and getting it were not always sequential events. Even for Everseas.

She pressed her head back against the plump seat, which smelled vaguely and soothingly of her father's tobacco, then gave a start and fished about in her reticule.

"Blast!" Only two shillings were in there, along with her hussif, her tortoiseshell card case, and, of course, a square of linen folded in sixteenths that she always pretended not to see but that traveled with her everywhere.

It had become a personal ritual, her way of tithing, to say a few kind words and drop a few coins into the cups of the beggars who had appeared weeks ago and lingered near Madame Marceau's shop, and who reappeared no matter how often Madame Marceau tried to shoo them away. They were as intrepid as ants. They knew where to find sustenance, and that was from the affluent women who frequented the modiste.

But Olivia, as usual, always wished she had more to give.

At last "Madame Marceau, Modiste," a gaudy gilded sign swinging on chains, came into view, Olivia sat up alertly. The Strand was even livelier than usual today, apparently: she could hear a *choir*, of all things.

She didn't know the tune, but it was certainly infectious, lilting and lively. Her foot was already tapping before the footman pulled open the door of the carriage, and she was smiling when he handed her down.

A half-dozen men were arrayed before Madame Marceau's, arms slung about each other, swaying rhythmically, their heads tipped back in full-throated song. Another man seemed to be presiding as a conductor, strutting to and fro before them and holding a sheaf of papers in one hand.

He waved one in the air. "Get yer flash ballad here! Two pence! Be the first to teach your friends the song all of London will be singing for centuries to come!"

This was quite a claim, given that one of London's other favorite songs was all about Olivia's brother Colin, and it, like Colin, who had survived the gallows, refused to die.

Years of distributing and accepting pamphlets for the causes nearest her heart—the eradication of slavery and the protection of the poor—had Olivia reflexively stretching out her hand for it.

The man hesitated, then saw the outstretched hand was encased in an expensive blue kid glove and decided to let her hold it.

"Two pence, madame, if ye'd like to take it with you." He beamed persuasively at her.

She didn't hear him.

She was transfixed in horror by the first words on the page.

The Legend of Lyon Redmond

Her breath left her in one painful gust, surely as though a broom handle had been driven into her ribs.

But the worst was yet to come.

Oh, if you thought you'd never see
A bride called Olivia Eversea
Well come along with me, lads, come along with me!
Her pretty self was on the shelf
And at last a-wed she'll be.

Oh, everyone thought
It was all for naught
And she'd dry up and blow away.
But will Redmond return
And make her burn
For the love of yesterday?

Sensation abandoned her limbs.

Where oh where did Redmond go?
Why oh why did he flee?
Is he riding the Nile on a crocodile?
Or did he take to the wide open sea?
Did a cannibal eat 'im?
Is he living in Eden
With Adam and Eve and the Snake?
Did Miss Eversea scare 'im
Into the arms of a harem
Where he lolls about like a sheik?

Shock reverberated through her as though she'd been driven into the ground with a mallet.

And all the while the little chorus behind her sang on.

Someone back there, she thought irrationally, had a lovely baritone.

Chapter 2

❧

SHE FINALLY, BRIEFLY CLOSED her eyes because the air in front of her was spangling ominously.

So this is what it feels like right before one faints, she thought distantly.

She'd never fainted in her life.

Perhaps she ought to breathe. That's what lungs were for, after all, and she currently didn't seem to be using them.

They were words. Just words. Just words.

She inhaled deeply.

Exhaled.

That was a little better.

And still the chorus behind her sang on.

"*Madame,*" the man's insistent voice cut through her daze, which made her realize this likely wasn't the first time he'd said it. "'Tis two pence for that fine composition in your hand."

She opened her eyes.

She was nearly eye level with a sparkling, shrewd brown gaze. The man's waistcoat buttons were severely taxed by the majestic arc of his stomach, and two tufts of hair friskily peeked from beneath his beaver hat. She suspected it was all the hair he had left in the world.

"Two pence, is it? I can see why it's so dear. It's an impressive piece. Quite nimbly rhymed."

The man glowed. "It's my own composition, you know. I'm told I've a gift. It goes on to explain all the other things Redmond might be doing whilst he's away." He leaned over to tap it for emphasis. "Eight verses and counting! I learned about sheiks and crocodiles and the like at a lecture by his brother, Mr. Miles Redmond, the famous explorer."

"*Quelle* irony," she murmured.

"The Redmonds are a very accomplished family," he added proudly, as if he was their personal retainer and the Redmonds kept a staff troubadour to chronicle their lives.

"They are, indeed," she agreed smoothly. "Tell me, *do* sheiks, in fact, 'loll'? You see, I was unable to attend that particular lecture by Mr. Miles Redmond."

"Well, I cannot say for certain. I confess I called upon my imagination for that bit, and the word 'loll' is rather musical, don't you think?"

"It paints a picture. I fear I must take issue with your first verse, however."

He bristled. "On what authority do you speak? Are *you* a poetess?"

"I'm Olivia Eversea."

He froze.

His eyes darted with hummingbird speed over her face.

He made a frantic chopping motion in the general direction of the choir behind him.

They clapped their mouths shut.

The sudden quiet seemed deafening.

And then he whipped off his hat so quickly the ribbons on her bonnet fluttered. He clapped it over his heart and bowed like he'd been felled by an axe.

"Cor, is that so now?" he said when he was up-right again. "Pleased I am to make your acquaintance, Miss Eversea. Ye're prettier than a spring day."

"Clearly hyperbole is your special gift, Mr.—"

"Pickles."

"Mr. Pickles."

She fixed him with stare that distilled centuries of excellent breeding and money and arrogance and intelligence and grace.

To his credit, shamed scarlet slowly flooded into his cheeks.

"I *am* sorry about the 'dry up and blow away' bit," he muttered sheepishly. "I wrote it before we met, you see."

"Of course."

"And I thought it lent pathos."

"It does give the song a certain dramatic structure, as it were," she acknowledged.

Her ears were still ringing from shock and her hands were icy. She probably ought to sit down. Perhaps put her head between her knees.

"A structure!" he breathed. "Yes! You are an insightful woman, Miss Eversea." His face lit with hopeful accord and a plea for understanding.

Olivia gave a start when someone behind her slid the flash ballad from her gloved fingers.

She turned swiftly. It was Lord Landsdowne, her fiancé, looking every bit the viscount in a flawlessly fitting Weston-cut coat, his silver buttons sparkling, his Hessian toes gleaming, his affable, unmistakable air of entitlement radiating from him like beams from a benevolent sun.

She turned a surprised and delighted smile up to him.

He didn't see it. He was too occupied absorbing the little horror in his hand.

And before her eyes his face went slowly, subtly hard.

It occurred to her that she had known him months before they were officially engaged, and yet she'd never seen him angry.

Nor had the words "Lyon" and "Redmond" ever once been spoken aloud by either of them to the other since they met.

She, in fact, hadn't spoken those two words aloud to anyone for years.

Oh, she supposed she'd resorted to the pronoun "he" once or twice, when it could not be avoided. As if Lyon were the Almighty. Or Beelzebub.

And surely this delicacy was ludicrous. Perhaps if she made a habit of tossing his name into idle conversation now and again, it would lose its power and become meaningless and strange, as any word will if you stare at it long enough.

On the other hand, the first night she'd danced with Lyon, she'd lain sleepless, thrumming with some unnamed new joy, and then she'd crept out of bed, seized a sheet of foolscap, and feverishly filled the front and back of it with those two words. They had spilled out of her like a hosannah, or like an attempt at exorcism.

They hadn't lost any of their power then.

"Will ye put your signature to my composition for me then, Miss Eversea?" Mr. Pickles was all humility now. Or rather, three parts humility, one part commerce. "It might very well make me a rich man. I could sell it to the Montmorency Museum to show along with your brother's, Mr. Colin Eversea's, suit of clothes. The ones he was nearly hung in."

Blast. She'd forgotten about Colin's bequest. She sighed.

Someone was bound to fund a Museum of Eversea Ignominy one day.

"She'll sign nothing," Landsdowne said evenly. But his eyes were flints. "I'll give you a shilling to leave here and never return."

Olivia's head jerked toward him in astonishment. He hadn't yet looked directly at her or greeted her, which was both unnerving and intriguing.

Obviously his intent was to protect her honor.

Not to mention his own.

But she'd always found it well nigh intolerable when someone else spoke for her. And this was the first time Landsdowne had done any such thing.

They locked eyes at last, and she watched his soften, the way they always did when they landed on her.

"Oh, where's the harm in signing it?" she coaxed him. "Perhaps if Mr. Pickles becomes wealthy he won't need to sell more of these songs. And far be it for any of us to discourage an entrepreneur."

"Miss Eversea, if I may interject? In the spirit of honesty, I fear I am at the mercy of the muse. My compositions burble forth like a spring from the earth, and riches are hardly likely to discourage them." Mr. Pickles was the picture of contrite humility.

"Then tell me what it will cost to build a dam," Landsdowne said grimly.

"We'll have Madame Marceau fetch a quill," Olivia soothed. "I shall sign it and leave it with her, with instructions to give it to Mr. Pickles after I'm gone for the day."

She'd learned that her smiles were Landsdowne's weakness, so she gave him one. Conciliatory and charming and warm.

And challenging.

He hesitated. As if he was contemplating countermanding her.

She stiffened her spine, as if bracing for a wind.

This was what marriage would be like, she realized. Countless little negotiations, both subtle and overt. Which the two of them, of course, would conduct in the most civilized manner imaginable, because two more reasonable adults had never walked the earth, and a more even-tempered man had never been born. And surely it would be balm after brothers who had dangled from the trellises of married countesses, gone to the gallows only to vanish from them in a cloud of smoke, married controversial American heiresses, and been shot at a good deal during the war.

Nor would Landsdowne ever throw a handful of pebbles up at her window at midnight.

Lyon's face flashed before her eyes then. White and stunned, like a man bleeding inside. His shirt glued to his body by rain, because he'd slung his coat around her.

That image was her purgatory.

She shoved it away, back into the shadows of her mind, the only safe place for it.

No, Landsdowne's courtship had been calm, determined, and relentless. He'd conducted it the way the sea conducts a campaign to wear away a cliff.

His mouth at last quirked at the corner. "Very well, my dear. If you must."

My dear. He'd slipped those words into conversation shortly after they'd become engaged, and he'd begun to use them more and more. It was husbandly and sweet and made her inexplicably as restless as if he'd reached over and fastened a diamond collar round her neck.

Lyon had called her "Liv."

He'd called her other things, too, things that began with "my." *My heart. My love.* He'd used words with the innocent recklessness of someone who had never before been hurt.

They'd of course both learned the harm that words could do.

She suddenly wished for another moment alone. She still felt weak, as if an old fever had stirred.

"Isn't it better to show everyone how little we care about this nonsense?" she murmured to Landsdowne.

His smile became real then. He shoved two pence at Mr. Pickles, who accepted them with pleasure.

Olivia kept the song.

"A pleasure, Mr. Pickles," he said ironically. "And there's a shilling in it for you if you move your little choir a few shops down."

Mr. Pickles accepted the shilling and herded his carolers down the street.

Landsdowne cupped her elbow and resolutely steered her through the pedestrians to Madame Marceau's shop, shielding her with the breadth of his body.

But Olivia stopped abruptly and eased from his grip long enough to crouch before the beggars leaning against the wall. They were so tattered and filthy and abject they were almost as indistinguishable from each other as they were from the shadows. Two of them were bandaged, one around a hand, the other across his face, in all likelihood to hide some kind of disfigurement—war or accident. It mattered not to her.

Her shillings clinked hollowly in the single cup.

"I'm sorry," she said softly to them, "it's all I have today . . . but it might be enough to buy mail coach passage to Sussex. Reverend Sylvaine in Pennyroyal Green can help you find work and food, perhaps shelter . . ."

But it was all she could say, because their un-washed stench was overpowering, and she was ashamed when she needed push herself to her feet again.

She stepped back abruptly against her strong, clean fiancé, who claimed her elbow once more.

But she waited for the beggar, who raised his hand and slowly brought it down in his graceful, characteristic blessing.

She was not typically superstitious, but his bless-ing had become important as she walked into Madame Marceau's for her fittings.

Landsdowne handed her a handkerchief, which smelled of starch and a hint of bay rum and was neatly embroidered with his initials. She applied it to her nose with a relief that shamed her.

And one day it would be her responsibility, nay, her *privilege*, to embroider those little initials into the corner of his handkerchiefs.

Rather like the handkerchief she kept in her reti-cule.

There were initials on that, too.

And blood.

She ought to burn it the way she'd burned the foolscap covered with his name.

"That lot will likely only drink those shillings," Landsdowne muttered dryly.

"They may do whatever they see fit with them." She'd said it a little too abruptly, pulling the hand-kerchief from her nose and handing it back to him.

"The poor are with us always, Olivia."

"Oh, *are* they now? Do enlighten me."

He stiffened.

Which is when she realized she'd snapped at him.

She drew in a breath, blew it out again, and squared her shoulders. She smiled at him apologetically. "Oh, do let's begin again. And forgive my nerves? It's been a day full of startling things and it's scarcely even begun. I'm terribly sorry to be so shrewish."

"There's nothing to forgive," he said instantly. "Or rather, forgive *me*. I was merely making an innocuous comment, and I didn't intend for it to sound like a lecture. And you are an angel, not a shrew. Certainly you know more than I do with regards to the ubiquity of the poor."

"Oh, I'm a novice compared to Mrs. Sneath."

"Everyone is a novice at everything compared to Mrs. Sneath."

She laughed.

"All these wedding preparations would shred even Admiral Nelson's nerves, Olivia. Mine are usually unassailable, and I swear I can hear them groaning from the strain," he confided. "Are you certain you won't allow me to whisk you off to Gretna Green?" It was only half in jest.

"As tempting as that sounds, my mother and Madame Marceau would likely make a widow of me the day they found out. We've had a number of weddings in the family lately, but no pomp, and I think everyone believes they deserve a little pomp."

"Oh, but we deserve pomp, too," he teased gently. "And truthfully, my mother and sisters are both expecting and demanding it, too. Very well. Then at least allow me to take you to Ackermann's for tea, or perhaps Twining's when they've done pinning you, or whatever it is they do to women in there." He gestured at the shop. "They're both on the Strand and we're so close. I knew you'd be here—I stopped by your town house and spoke a bit with your mother and your brother. It was . . . I'd simply hoped to steal some time with you."

"I would love that!" she said quite sincerely. She loved wandering about Ackermann's, poring over the new prints and sifting through the pretty little gifts they sold. She'd found her tortoiseshell card case there. "And please don't consider it stealing time. I shall give it freely and happily."

"Perhaps we can find a new print or two for our town house in Ackermann's. I should like you to impose your taste upon it, since I haven't any of my own."

Our. They were going to be an *our*, too.

She'd have a new home. New furnishings.

A new . . . bed.

A new life.

"Nonsense. Your taste is excellent, if a trifle sub-dued. Be careful what you wish for—you may find yourself up to your ears in embroidered pillows."

"It sounds comfortable. I'll never fear stumbling in the house if I can anticipate a soft landing."

She laughed. "Call for me in two hours? I should have been sufficiently tortured by the seamstresses by then."

"Until we meet again, my dear," he said, with a quirk of one brow, and bowed.

As he turned to go he tripped over the beggar's foot, which was suddenly and inconveniently thrust outward.

Landsdowne swore softly and recovered aplomb neatly, and he was on his way.

Olivia bit back a smile and stepped into the shop at last.

Madame Marceau, whose name was French and purely fictional, and her long, pleasingly homely face pure Plantagenet, clasped her hands in delight when she saw Olivia, and then curtsied, and then wrung the very same hands in despair.

"Oh, Miss Eversea, I am so thrilled we'll be pinning you into your wedding gown today. It will rival even Princess Charlotte's! But you see, we have a bit of a predicament. The girl who assisted me, Mademoiselle Marie-Anne, has abandoned me suddenly—she came into some money and moved to the country like that!" Madame Marceau snapped her fingers. "And I have been called to see to an urgent matter in my other shop on Bond Street. Fortunately Providence has seen fit to provide me with the very competent new assistant just when my need is greatest. I am so sorry to be unable to see to you personally today!"

"Think nothing of it, Madame. I trust your judgment implicitly, and I'm sure your new assistant, Mademoiselle . . ."

"Lilette."

Lilette? Olivia almost rolled her eyes. " . . . Mademoiselle Lilette will acquit herself admirably, as I know you would only employ the best."

Madame Marceau beamed gratefully at this, and the mademoiselle in question appeared from behind her. She was small, pale, pleasingly round girl with soulful dark eyes and dark hair, which was scraped away from her face into a tight, sensible knot. Her severe, high-necked, exquisitely tailored dress implied only the clientele were allowed to shine.

"Mademoiselle Lilette, if you would be so kind as to assist Miss Eversea? I shall return as quickly as possible."

"*Mais bien sûr*, Madame Marceau. If you would follow me, Miss Eversea."

Olivia followed her and divested herself of her pelisse and dress behind a screen and slipped into what would be her wedding gown when she finally decided on the proper trim and all the millions of

measurements were concluded. Mademoiselle Lilette dropped to her knees at Olivia's feet with the
torture instruments of her trade, pins and measure
tape.

A shilling clearly hadn't bought enough distance.
The bloody song started up again outside.

Eight verses wouldn't come close to addressing
the millions of things she'd imagined happening
to Lyon Redmond over the years. She wondered
whether there were any verses about Lyon Redmond dying in a ditch. Certainly a good many
things rhymed with "ditch."

They were on the " . . . did he take to the wide open
sea?" line, the least painful of the lines for Olivia to
imagine, when Mademoiselle Lilette spoke.

"Miss Eversea, if you would hold still, like so, or
your hem will be wavy and not even. Interesting,
non, but wavy is not the style?"

"My apologies, Mademoiselle Lilette." Olivia
obediently froze.

"Such exquisite taste you have, Miss Eversea."

Mademoiselle Lilette's accent was authentically
French and her flattery unsurprisingly rote.

"Thank you," Olivia said, in a tone that meant
Please stop talking.

"So fortunate you are to be marrying such a
grand man, *n'est-ce pas*? A handsome viscount, *oui*?"

"*Oui*," Olivia said tautly.

The song appeared to be rounding on the second
verse now.

Would that her last name was . . . oh, Silver, perhaps, instead. Nothing rhymed with Silver.

Would that nothing had ever happened in her life
that warranted a *song*.

Would that Lyon was here, because she could
think of no one else who would have laughed with

her over that song until tears poured down their cheeks and they gasped for air.

She closed her eyes against an onslaught of fury and yearning so painful it made her nauseous and she nearly swayed.

She held herself very, very still, and the pain washed out again.

She'd learned over the years this was how to manage it. With stillness.

"You must be very, how you say, very in love weez your fiancé?"

Weez? Olivia frowned. What the devil was . . .

Oh—*with*.

The bloody French. They were always on about love love love love love. Suddenly the question made her head ache as if she'd been presented with an algebra problem.

Love. The word had once felt infinite, magical. A word like "Heaven" or "universe."

And now it felt barbed and foolish. She knew an impulse to shrug away from it as if something multilegged had landed on her skin.

"I wish there was a way to disperse the *choir* out there permanently," she muttered irritably.

Mademoiselle Lilette stopped moving and was quiet for a merciful moment.

"Surely we can, how you say, exploit them instead, Miss Eversea," she said mildly.

"Exploit!" Despite herself, Olivia was intrigued. "Go on."

"Perhaps to give all of them, how do you say, *une* pamphlet about the rights and needs of the poor? They will become educated or they will be driven away, perhaps both."

Olivia laughed, genuinely surprised and delighted. "Ah, I do like how you think, Mademoiselle Lilette. You seem a resourceful woman."

Mademoiselle Lilette gave a little modest grunt. "One does not rise from the slums to work for the *magnifique* Madame Marceau if one is not resourceful. *You* must remain still, however, while I pin, for I do not wish to draw blood."

Imperiousness was the province of dressmakers everywhere, it seemed, and for the sake of vanity, well-bred women everywhere obeyed.

"Sorry. The slums, was it?"

"*Mais oui.*" Impressively, Mademoiselle Lilette said this around a mouthful of pins. "The darkest of slums."

"An admirable achievement."

"*Merci.*" She paused to shrug. "But one need only be, how do you say, *tetu comme an anu*, to survive and thrive."

"Stubborn as a mule?"

"*Oui.* And I am."

"I think perhaps we have that in common, Mademoiselle Lilette."

"And they do like to call us the gentle sex. The poor things."

"If only they knew."

They giggled together.

Though Olivia often wished she truly was as strong as everyone seemed to think she was. As strong as she *wanted* everyone to think she was.

"*Oui, c'est vrai.* I, too, admire you, Miss Eversea. I have heard of your work, you see, with the poor and against the Triangle Trade."

Olivia froze, astonished. She craned her head down toward the seamstress. "How on earth did you hear about *that*?"

Mademoiselle Lilette squeaked. "Do not move, Miss Eversea! I am sympathetic, shall we say, to such efforts, and your name is so often mentioned with great respect as someone who supports the cause of slavery abolition. You give to people the pamphlets, *oui*? And attend lectures and ask clever questions? Our paths perhaps may have crossed there. And so much is better now, thanks to the likes of Mrs. Hannah More and Mr. Wilberforce."

"Oh, I scarcely feel worthy of mention in association with Mrs. More and Mr. Wilberforce! And if my small efforts have made any sort of difference, I am gratified. But I suspect those of us who deplore slavery have Le Chat to thank for decimating the illegal Triangle Trade more than my pamphlets," she said dryly. "Everyone has become afraid to sail."

Le Chat was the rather melodramatic name given a pirate who had for a time been the scourge of the sea and the talk of ballrooms and salons. No one knew his true identity—his name might be Edgar, for all anyone knew—but he'd been rather quiet lately, as befit his slinky, enigmatic namesake. Some time ago, the Earl of Ardmay, also known as Captain Asher Flint, and his first mate, Lord Lavay, had been charged by the king to bring him to justice. They had failed to do it, and had thereby forfeited an enormous reward.

Instead, the earl had married Violet Redmond, and Lord Lavay had just married his housekeeper, Mrs. Elise Fountain.

Olivia wasn't certain whether she would categorize these events as rewards or as punishments.

"Oh, but Le Chat is a lawless pirate!" Mademoiselle Lilette exclaimed. "*Oui?* Surely not a hero?"

"Nevertheless, I would like to shake his hand. For he seems to have found the only thing that vanquishes immorality and greed: fear."

"But 'e might ravish you if you shake his hand. It is what pirates do, *non*?"

"Well, I couldn't say for certain, as I do not move in the same circles with pirates."

Ravish. Another very French word.

Another word that belonged to her past.

Though the ravishing had been rather mutual, then.

She only realized she'd stirred restlessly when Mademoiselle Lilette implored, "*Please* be still, Miss Eversea."

"Sorry, sorry. I haven't heard of any new Le Chat attacks. Though I haven't kept up on the news during wedding preparations, which have lasted nearly my entire life, by my calculations. Worth it, of course," she added hurriedly, lest she wound any delicate dressmaker feelings. Ever conscious of how very fortunate she was.

Mademoiselle Lilette clucked soothingly. "You will be so happy when the talk is of how beautiful you look in your dress. Perhaps Le Chat, the pirate, 'e is dead."

"Seems likely. I imagine most pirates go into pirating with the full awareness they likely won't expire in their beds from old age."

"Still, if Le Chat is dead, your work is needed. For every woman should have passions. I am certain your fiancé the viscount admires this quality a great deal and feels himself fortunate indeed."

It was another particularly, irritatingly French thing to say. *Passion*.

Another word that Olivia had managed to dodge for some years now.

Passion was now synonymous with pain and she wanted none of it.

"I don't think my fiancé would consider it a . . . passion," she said carefully.

"No? But surely such a thing is important to you? Your work weez ze poor, and such?"

Mademoiselle Lilette sounded genuinely confused.

"Well, certainly. But I suspect he categorizes it along with embroidery and pianoforte playing. He minds it as much as those things—that is to say, pays little notice. To him, it's just . . . something I do."

"Ah. Rather than something you are?"

The dressmaker made this startling, incisive observation as casually as she'd pinned the next inch of hem.

"*Oui*," Olivia said finally.

Chapter 3

❧

"OLIVIA . . . I THINK THOSE are your brothers."

Colin and Ian Eversea were, indeed, standing in front of Ackermann's Repository of Arts, looking conspicuous, both because they were so tall and handsome and so alike, and because they were having what appeared like an earnest discussion, perhaps even an argument, complete with emphatic hand gestures.

Pedestrians eddied around them, heads turning to admire them as they passed. Her brothers would be turning heads well into their nineties, Olivia suspected. Her heart squeezed a little. She was so very proud of both of them. Both had been a bit wild when they returned from the war, and now both were happily married, Colin to the lovely Madeline of whom he was tenderly protective, Ian to the startling and very pretty American heiress who had caused an uproar in Pennyroyal Green and had, in fact, given even Olivia pause, which was very difficult to do, as Olivia's social supremacy had remained unchallenged for a very long time.

"Yes. Well, it's two of them, anyway." Olivia thought their appearance was a little too coincidental. "You didn't happen to mention to them that we might be going to Ackermann's, did you? When you stopped in at St. James Square."

She knew they were worried about her. They had watched the house fill with flowers every day from suitors who hadn't a prayer of getting her attention. They had seen the betting books at White's fill with wager after wager, making a game of her presumed heartbreak. Presumed, because no one had ever said a word to her overtly about it, and she'd certainly never confessed to such a thing.

Only Olivia and Lyon knew the truth.

Her brothers wanted, above all, for her to be happy.

They liked Landsdowne very much, and she wished they wouldn't tread so gingerly about him, as if they were afraid he would vanish if they made any sudden moves. For God's sake, she honestly did intend to marry the man.

They had married the women they loved.

"They weren't in when I stopped at your town house," Landsdowne mused. "It must be a fortunate coincidence."

She wondered just how "fortunate" it might be.

"Well! Good afternoon, Olivia, Landsdowne!" Ian enthused, when they moved forward to meet them. "What a lovely coincidence."

"Is it?" Olivia said suspiciously.

Hats came off and bows were exchanged.

"Fine weather we're having." This came from Ian.

Colin was standing unusually still and he was uncharacteristically silent. Rather, in fact, like a sentry.

"I suppose," she said, still suspiciously.

"Have you a complaint about it, sister dear?"

"Ian, may I point something out to you?"

"Since when have you ever asked permission to point something out to me, Olivia? Would it be to impress your husband-to-be?"

"Her husband-to-be is already thoroughly impressed," Landsdowne said with charming loyalty.

"I don't think we've ever exchanged banalities about the weather in our entire lives," Olivia said calmly. "Nor have you ever called me 'sister dear.'"

She locked eyes with Ian for a challenging moment.

"Then I have been remiss, for you are a dear sister, and I should tell you so more often," he said smoothly. "We were just inside, and it's an uninspiring lot of prints in there today, wouldn't you say, Colin?"

"Uninspiring," Colin parroted. "Why don't the four of us stop in at Twining's for something hot?"

Her brothers were offering to drink *tea* with her?

"We'd like to take our tea in *Ackermann's* tearoom," she said firmly, and she looped her arm in Landsdowne's and feinted to the right.

In tandem, her brothers gracefully, ever so subtly shifted to the right and blocked her.

"How were the fittings at Madame Marceau's?" Ian tried. "I'm sure your dress is beautiful."

This made her snort in derision. The day Ian was interested in her dress fittings was the day he'd *wear* a dress.

She tried a quick slide to the left, startling Landsdowne, who came along with her just in time.

Her brothers, neatly and in tandem, subtly shifted at the same time.

"Care to share what might be the trouble, gentlemen?" Lansdowne asked, with deceptive mildness.

Which she was beginning to realize was his way of disguising temper.

Her brothers exchanged a glance. Some silent brotherly conversation took place during that glance.

"Olivia." And then Colin said very, very slowly,

as though willing her to understand something, "I genuinely think you don't want to go in today."

It was a tactical mistake. This was Olivia, after all. Telling her what not to do was tantamount to inviting her to do it.

Colin realized this too late. Her brothers, after exchanging another rather fatalistic glance, stepped aside with grim resignation.

She all but burst inside.

Then paused as she took in the space with a swift, sweeping glance.

Nothing was out of the ordinary. Everything seemed splendidly as it should be. She inhaled deeply. Ah, but she loved Ackermann's the way she loved Tingle's Bookshop—for the gentle rustling of fine paper, the pungent scent of fine paper and ink. It was cheerful and airy and brilliantly illuminated by a band of large high windows that poured flattering light down on all the art and art lovers alike.

Her brothers remained silent.

She shot them a triumphant glance.

She gravitated to a wall where a new, dazzlingly colorful print hung in a place of honor.

"Oh, I believe it's meant to be Le Chat." Olivia said this to Landsdowne, who was trailing her protectively and planted himself at her side. "Funny, but I was just discussing him with my modiste."

They paused to admire it.

The infamous pirate was standing triumphantly on the deck of a ship, one booted foot on the chest of a man who appeared to be weeping with fear. His hair waved like a black flag in an apparent breeze, and his penetrating blue gaze was apparent even through his black mask. He was holding a sword to his victim's throat with his left hand. These were the only three things the whole of Europe could agree about with regards to Le Chat: that he had blue eyes ("the very color of evil!" one survivor had declared, which had always struck Olivia as funny, as her own were blue), so vivid they could even be seen in the dark, which was the only time Le Chat attacked; that he spoke like a gentleman when he spoke at all; and that he was left-handed. Or at least used his left hand when he wielded a sword. One merchant claimed to have shot him, but since Le Chat had gone on to attack again, he clearly hadn't managed to kill him.

"That's a handsome print," Landsdowne allowed. "But *he's* a scourge."

"Yes, but a scourge who has all but eliminated the illegal Triangle Trade, from what I understand."

"I suppose even vermin have their uses," Landsdowne said, and she shot him a wry glance. "He hasn't been heard from in a while. Perhaps someone finally aimed into his black little heart when they shot him."

"Seems an inevitable fate for a pirate," she allowed, echoing what she'd told Mademoiselle Lilette. She frowned faintly at the masked pirate.

It was amusingly lurid, but she could see nothing alarming in it, so clearly this wasn't what was troubling her brothers.

"Shall we go now, Olivia?" Colin suggested brightly from behind her.

She turned to scowl at him, and then continued in a slow, suspicious pivot.

She saw nothing but other well-dressed shoppers and couples murmuring to each other as they leafed through merchandise.

And then her questing gaze snagged on a row of vivid prints arrayed side by side along the top of a shelf. The artist was obvious even from where she stood.

"Oh! A new set of Rowlandson prints!"

New Rowlandson work was always a delightful surprise. He had a gift for capturing London's microcosm with scathing wit and acuity.

That was when her brothers went absolutely motionless and silent. Rather as if they were about to witness an execution.

She understood why when she was close enough to read the titles.

The Illustrated Legend of Lyon Redmond

Which rather leaped out at her from the bottom of the prints.

It seemed Mr. Pickles had already been more enterprising than she'd ever suspected, if Rowlandson had been commissioned to do such work.

She drew closer, helpless not to. Landsdowne followed.

In the first print, a man, who she expected was meant to be Lyon—he had a dashing swoop of dark hair over one brow and snapping black eyes, and his outrageously muscular, nankeen-clad thighs gripped a saddled and rearing crocodile, whose tiny legs flailed the air like a stallion. One knew it was the Nile because the artist had thoughtfully drawn little pyramids off in the distance.

Lyon was wielding a riding crop and wearing a beaver hat and a very determined expression.

The funny part was that the expression was really rather similar to Lyon's when he was determined. Which was all the time. Or had been all the time.

"Olivia . . ." Landsdowne's voice was next to her. It was a plea.

She held up a hand. Slowly, as if she had no choice, as though nudged up the gallows stairs, she moved on to the next one.

In blues and pinks and reds, Lyon was depicted lolling—which was indeed a rather lyrical word—on a heap of tasseled pillows, surrounded by voluptuous—the cartoonist had spared no ink and had truly unleashed his imagination—and scantily clad women. Lyon appeared to be smoking a hookah and his boots were tossed carelessly aside.

They all stared at it in helpless, horrified thrall.

"He looks comfortable, doesn't he?"

Her voice was a sort of ironic, distant hush that had the three men exchanging looks of grave concern.

Lyon would never smoke a hookah. Or be so very careless with his boots.

He'd been so extraordinarily disciplined.

"Olivia . . ."

Likely one of her brothers had said her name. She heard it distantly, as if it were merely noise drifting in from the street.

The truth was she was cleaved in three distinct emotions.

Hilarity.

Horror.

Fury.

Rather like the elm tree she used to meet Lyon by, which had been split by lightning but had gone on growing as if hadn't noticed.

The emotions circulated through her like three different drugs, and she felt strangely very separate from her body, rather the way one did when one took laudanum.

But the fury was mostly because *no* one would have enjoyed these more than Lyon, and he wasn't here to bloody enjoy them.

Fury was always the safest emotion when it came to Lyon.

She moved on to the next print.

The next must be the Garden of Eden, because in the center was a lush tree with an apple and a snake in it, and Adam and Eve, both clad in modesty-protecting fig leaves, were flanking Lyon below it. Oddly, *he* was wearing a full set of clothes, as if he'd just stepped out of White's, and his hands were saucily planted on his hips. They were all beaming at each other, even the snake, as if they were celebrating a birthday.

In the center of the next panel a great bulbous black kettle was perched atop a roaring fire, which was rendered in satanic swoops of orange. Lyon was sitting in the kettle, his arms strapped to his sides with vines, and, quite understandably, his mouth was open in a little "O" of distress. What was clearly meant to be a cannibal was sprinkling salt on his head. Another cannibal sat nearby holding a knife and fork, which struck her as incongruous, because surely cannibals ate with their hands?

"And now he looks rather *un*comfortable," she murmured.

Which, ironically, perfectly described all the appalled, silent men behind her.

Ian cleared his throat. "Olivia, we—"

She abruptly held up a quelling hand without turning around.

The next panel featured Lyon standing on the deck of a ship, and he was shading his eyes with a hand, leaning forward, both shirt and the sails of the ship billowing in what appeared to be gale force winds. It was an ironic echo of the Le Chat print. And it was the only scenario of any of them Olivia could imagine being true.

One panel remained. She drew in a surreptitious bracing breath, exhaled softly, and moved on to it.

It featured a lone figure of a woman.

Dread suffused her, but curiosity compelled her. She leaned forward gingerly, as if the print were a wild boar she'd shot but was unsure she'd actually killed.

She was relieved to discover the woman was really rather pretty. Her hair poured in a dramatic black river down her back and she was wearing a fine blue dress, as if the artist had somehow known it was Olivia's best color. Her bosom, unsurprisingly, given the artist's predilections, greatly taxed the dress's bodice.

Something lacy appeared to be trailing from her head to the ground.

"Oh, am I wearing a . . ."

She was about to say "veil."

And then she realized it was cobwebs.

"Mother of *God*," Landsdowne muttered viciously. "These are abominations. I insist that we leave."

"Oh, they're just cartoons," she said almost gently, her voice still rather drifty. Like someone lying in state of grace on her deathbed, beyond caring about earthly things.

The rapt attention four well-dressed visitors were aiming at the prints drew the notice of Ackermann's clerk. He bustled cheerily over.

"Aren't they charming?" he said brightly. " 'The Legend of Lyon Redmond' is an illustrated ballad about a famous young heir who disappeared after a woman broke his heart, and now she's moldering away. I imagine every home in London will have one soon at the rate they're selling. The artist is the eminently gifted Thomas Rowlandson." He pointed at the signature at the bottom.

All four of them turned blackly incredulous gazes on him.

"His eyes are wrong," Olivia said finally, faintly, absurdly. "They ought to be blue."

IT WAS BLISSFULLY quiet in Twining's tearoom. Just the soul-soothing music of teacups clinking against saucers, the *chink chink* of spoons dissolving sugar cubes and stirring in cream, the soft gurgle of brew poured from pots. No flash ballads drifting in from the street through the windows. No decorative prints on the walls making a mockery of her history.

She hoped Landsdowne hadn't noticed the irony of the reclining lion that had always presided over Twining's entrance.

"So," Olivia finally said brightly. "Colin and Ian were right. I *didn't* want to go into Ackermann's."

He snorted a soft, humorless laugh.

The two of them were subdued and dazed. As though they'd barely escaped a trauma with their lives.

Colin and Ian had departed to leave Olivia and Landsdowne to recover from Ackermann's.

"I'm sorry about today," she added. "I suppose London is forever in need of a spectacle. I never anticipated anything quite like this, however."

He smiled faintly at her. "What do you suppose will be next? An operetta?"

She hadn't considered the possibility of an operetta.

"Oh God," she said faintly.

"I suppose you could consider it a tribute. If you were homely, you'd likely be less of an industry."

She quirked her mouth.

Another little silence ensued.

"Olivia, you've been rotating your cup like a roulette wheel. Drink your tea. You need color in your cheeks."

She had, in fact, been fidgeting, and she stopped. The tea in her cup eventually sloshed to a stop, too.

A little silence fell.

"Are you certain you aren't bothered, my dear?" Landsdowne tried.

"Oh, I'm bowed, but unbroken." She managed this with an insouciant sweep of her hand. She felt anything but insouciant, but then she'd been pretending not to feel things for so long it had become second nature.

"It's just . . . when you read that man's . . . shall we say, opus . . . outside of Madame Marceau's, you went a shade or two paler than you already are. And I thought I might need to produce smelling salts in Ackermann's. It was . . . quite concerning."

She hadn't known she'd changed colors.

But speaking of pale things, Landsdowne's knuckles were white on his teacup.

She looked into his face, which was unremarkable if one sought the customary significators of beauty in it—aquiline noses and Byronic curls and the like. But it was compelling in its strength and confidence, and she liked it very much. His gaze was direct and intelligent, his shoulders imposing. One knew instantly he could be trusted with important things. He genuinely cared for her. One knew he would likely never press her for more than she was willing to say or do. He would never test her.

She wondered if this quality was why he, of all the suitors over the years, had won. Because she could go on as she was, sharing only a part of herself with him, and he would never know it.

Lyon had done *nothing* but test her.

"John." She laid a hand gently on his arm.

His face softened immediately and his grip on his teacup eased.

It seemed unfair to be able to transform him with just a touch and a single word. He admired her so much; he asked so little from her. She likely didn't deserve him, but "deserve" was quite the subjective word. It made her doubly resolved to be a perfect wife.

Wife. She was going to be a *wife*.

She leaned back and squared her shoulders, much like Mrs. Sneath did when she was preparing to do something dutiful. "I feel we should discuss 'The Legend of Lyon Redmond.'"

Saying those two words aloud to him as though they were as mundane as "fork" or "biscuit" was one of the bravest things she'd yet done in her life.

"You refer to the flash ballad? Or to the man himself?"

He said it lightly enough. But there was nothing casual about the way he was studying her face.

He was a very astute man.

She managed a faint smile. "Given the events of the day, I shouldn't blame you if you were curious about the origins of the so-called legend. Shall I put your mind at ease?"

"It would be churlish to object to having my mind put at ease."

This was how they spoke to each other: with dry humor and gentle irony. They shared a pleasure in each other's intelligence and view of the world. It was easy and pleasant and safe, and she liked it, because she suspected he would never require more of her than that.

"I confess there was indeed an attraction when I was a bit younger—the legend, if you will, has its foundation in a certain truth—but it did not last long. I cannot tell you why he disappeared or where he is. Whatever took place then no longer has any bearing on the person I am now or wish to be in the future."

Attraction. The word was so pallid it felt like heresy. A scarce few months after she'd locked eyes with Lyon in a ballroom, she'd been lying alongside him in a clearing deep in the woods near Pennyroyal Green, her arms latched around his neck, kissing him as though the two of them had just invented kissing. The pleasure had been narcotic. They only wanted more and more and more.

If her abigail harbored any suspicions about the grass strains on her dress that day, she hadn't said a word.

As for the rest of what she'd just said, Olivia hadn't the faintest idea whether it was indeed true. It didn't matter. Lyon was gone, and Landsdowne was here. She'd said what he'd needed to hear.

"Funny, isn't it, how the 'legend'—I'll use that word—persists." Landsdowne said this idly. "One would have thought the bloods had given up the betting books and forgotten his name altogether by now. Instead, it seems to be sprouting heads, like a Hydra. And I wish I could protect you from it."

"I know, and you're a dear"—there, she'd said the word, too!—"to care so much, and I'm so terribly sorry to concern you. The Everseas have always been a gift to the gossipmongers of London and to the bloods at White's who've had such a wonderful time filling the betting books with nonsense. So many things rhyme with Eversea, you see. And I've been rather a *sport* for so long, like cricket or pugilism, I suppose this is their last opportunity to profit from it. Though your future may be filled with flash ballads about my relatives, as I hardly think my family will breed a sedate generation. Do you mind terribly?"

He smiled faintly. "One day someone will supplant the stories, I suppose. When we're in our dotage. What stories we'll tell our grandchildren."

He said these things so easily now. To make grandchildren they would need to make children, and to make children they would need to make love, and to make love she would need to lie naked beneath Landsdowne's naked body, and—

"I'm glad you think so," she said hurriedly. "Although a dose of 'dull' might be restful upon occasion."

"It's funny about youthful experiences . . . so often the things that happen to us in our youth shape us into our permanent selves. When we're still young and malleable."

"Surely you're not suggesting you're old and calcified?"

He laughed. "I think you'll discover I'm rather limber."

Her eyes flared in surprise, and she looked down into her tea. Heat rushed into her cheeks.

Landsdowne naked. Landsdowne reaching for her. Landsdowne next to her in bed for the rest of her life. Did he moan and make noises and . . .

She tensed and pushed it out of her mind. But she *must* spend more time imagining all of this. Surely the notion was not distasteful. He was tall and manly, he possessed all of his teeth, he smelled wonderful. Surely more time spent dwelling upon it would help her to prepare for that inevitability. Surely it should be something she welcomed . . . one day.

She looked up to find his dark eyes on her intently.

He wasn't smiling.

But she sensed he was imagining precisely the same thing.

Landsdowne wanted her, in every sense of the word.

Perhaps he thought the blushes meant she was modest, and would need to be gently tutored in matters of romance.

If only he knew.

"In the spirit of mutual disclosure, I feel I should ask whether you left a trail of broken hearts behind you on your way to matrimony. You've managed to remain out of the broadsheets, if so, something my family seems unable to achieve."

His eyebrows shot up. He tonged sugar into his tea and swished it about long enough for her to realize he was about to confess something.

He took a fortifying sip.

And then he leaned back and sighed.

"Very well. There is a . . . Well, I've known Lady Emily Howell since we were very young. A lovely girl, very kind, and I admire her a good deal. Our families believed we would one day enter into an agreement. I suppose I believed it, too. And then . . . I met you."

There was a hint of rueful, careful ardor around the word "you."

As if it had been destiny. As if anyone could understand he'd had no choice at all in the matter.

She often thought Landsdowne had viewed her as a challenge. He was wealthy, a bit older, owned property all over England, was known to be fair and yet ruthless in business.

His determination to pursue the allegedly unobtainable Olivia Eversea and her new willingness to capitulate had likely coincided. Their courtship had hardly been the stuff of legends, but many a marriage began on less fortuitous footing.

She smiled but said nothing.

"Lady Emily has been all that is gracious and congratulatory, as a friend would be. Though I expect she is in fact disappointed. I can honestly tell you that I did not court her, and I do not believe anyone assumed we had a formal understanding. And yet."

"And yet," Olivia repeated softly.

"I do greatly regret any pain I may have caused her."

Olivia pictured Lady Emily and her no doubt well-bred disappointment. There would be no hysterics. No foolscap covered in Landsdowne's name, burned at midnight.

When the word that Lyon Redmond had disappeared finally penetrated Pennyroyal Green, and then the whole of London society—it took some time, the way it takes time for damp to make a weak roof cave in—Olivia had stopped eating. It was as if whatever made her human, gave her appetites and needs, had been excised. She had no more need for nourishment than a wickless candle needs a flame. She felt just that pointless.

She hadn't even fully realized she'd stopped eating until her mother began to panic.

And at some point she had begun again, because here she was.

Yet food had never tasted quite the same since.

Lyon had abandoned her.

And Landsdowne was here.

"You're very kind," she said impulsively to Landsdowne. For he was. Good and solid and kind and perhaps most importantly, *here*.

He quirked his mouth self-deprecatingly.

They each took fortifying sips of tea.

"I have a friend who trains and races horses," he said, after a long pause. "It is his passion. He fell off a spirited one and broke his arm badly, and the doctor told him he could set it one of two positions. If he set it the usual way, the way that afforded him the most freedom of movement, he wouldn't be able hold reins effectively ever again. He chose to have his arm set in the second option—in such a way that he could grip the reins."

"So you say we are broken into the shape of our wounds. Or in the shape of the thing that means the most to us, and so we are suited to one thing only."

He smiled at her swiftly. Landsdowne genuinely appreciated her intelligence.

She didn't smile. A chill was slowly spreading in her gut.

"Do you perhaps speak from experience?" she challenged lightly. Suddenly nervous.

He shrugged. "Oh, I don't think so. I just thought it was anecdote worth sharing. That it perhaps merited a philosophical discussion."

"I'm not certain I'm equal to a philosophical discussion at the moment, when I must tell Madame Marceau before next week which trim to use on the hem—the silver or the cream? Or beading? Perhaps Parliament would be thoughtful enough to put it to a vote. Though I'm certain your metaphor doesn't apply to me."

He was quiet, and this time it was he who turned his teacup a few times.

"You haven't yet wed, and you've had countless options."

A fortnight after she'd filled a sheet of foolscap with Lyon's name she'd filled another one: *Olivia Redmond Olivia Redmond Olivia Redmond.* Over and over and over. She hadn't known what else to do with the geyser of emotion she could share with no one but Lyon. It was too new, too potent, and far, far too big to contain or understand.

She'd thrown that sheet of foolscap into the fire, too.

Because as far as her family and his were concerned, it amounted to heresy.

"I haven't wed because I've only lately met you," she told Landsdowne.

It was such a perfect thing to say that he decided to believe it.

He reached for her hand and gripped it. And his was so solid and warm and real and fine, and nothing in her lurched in joy or in any other emotion, and she thought, surely this sort of safety was better, and madness was for the very young.

Chapter 4

❧

About five years earlier, at the
Sussex Christmas Eve Assembly . . .

"No, no, Miles, it's like this."

Jonathan Redmond slouched against the wall of the milling ballroom, shoved his hands in his pockets, narrowed his eyes, and aimed a look down the bridge of his nose at a young woman who was at least five years his senior.

The woman intercepted Jonathan's gaze, frowned faintly, puzzled but indulgent, gave her fan an irritated little twitch, and turned away. Coltish Jonathan, of course, was all but invisible to her at his age.

His brother Miles stifled a laugh. "You look like you just took a cricket ball to the head. It's more like *this*."

He tipped his head back, slitted his eyes, clenched his jaw, and aimed a gaze at the same woman.

And while Miles Redmond, the second oldest, had many splendid qualities, he wore spectacles and hadn't yet quite grown into his nose, and this time the woman remained oblivious.

"You've succeeded only in looking constipated." Jonathan was indignant. "And what woman will succumb to that?"

"How do you know that isn't Lyon's secret?" Miles retorted.

They both laughed.

Lyon Redmond rolled his eyes. His brothers were taking the piss out of him, which he normally rather enjoyed. Taking the piss out of each other was one of the myriad pleasures of having brothers. Affection, if displayed, was usually conveyed via insults and wrestling, which they all found satisfactory and sufficient.

But then, his brothers could laugh.

They didn't have to *be* him.

It was true he did, in fact, have a patented sultry look. It really didn't require much more than simply being Lyon Redmond while aiming appreciative, unswerving attention at a woman for a tick longer than was strictly proper.

It raised a blush nearly every time.

And it was generally agreed among the bloods of the *ton* that given an option, they would choose his life over theirs, if only for a day. Perhaps that day would be spent at Manton's, shooting the hearts out of targets or whipping the foil out of his fencing master's hand; followed by an hour or two in London at their father's secretive and exclusive Mercury Club, where England's wealthiest men devised strategies for making themselves and each other wealthier; and perhaps conclude with a ball much like this one, where most of the women could be counted on to look yearningly past every other man present in the hopes they would intercept one of his smolders.

What Lyon could have told nearly anyone was that even *he* envied Lyon Redmond. Because the Lyon Redmond of current lore was primarily simply that: lore.

It was said he effortlessly excelled at everything. It wasn't true. He focused on what he wanted to master and methodically, ruthlessly conquered it, whether it was cricket or calculus or fencing or shooting or a woman. And while it was true he invariably got what he wanted, he made absolutely certain the effort never showed.

He'd been born knowing the power of subtlety and the advantage of surprise. It was in the Redmond blood, after all.

Which meant he was also discreet about his carnal indulgences.

All in all, given other choices, Lyon would still ultimately probably decide to remain himself.

But he was beginning to feel like a prize bull confined to a gilded pen until such time as his father, Isaiah Redmond, deemed it was time for him to fertilize a carefully chosen aristocratic heifer. The Duke of Hexford's daughter, Arabella, seemed a likely choice. Though Arabella was hardly a heifer. She was stunning and shy to the point of muteness and blushed apologetically after everything she said.

But she wasn't here tonight. This particular ball was far too rustic an event for the daughter of a duke. Lyon was home for good from Oxford, though he had come by way of a lengthy stay in the family town house in London. London's diversions were a startling contrast to those of Pennyroyal Green, whose closest thing to a den of iniquity was the Pig & Thistle and the perennial cutthroat chess game between Mr. Culpepper and Mr. Cooke.

Not that Lyon lingered in any iniquity dens. He cherished his inheritance, and he knew precisely what was required of him in order to keep it.

"Pay attention, you hapless fools," he commanded his brothers. "It's more like . . ."

Dozens of young women were milling about,

most of them in white, some of them titled, all of them glowing and pretty in the way that youth and hope is always pretty, and it was charming and comfortable and as English a scene as one could wish for.

Later, Miles would swear he literally heard the sound of a gong being struck when Lyon clapped eyes on her.

But for Lyon, the prevailing sensation could only be described as panic.

Panic that she might be a vision rather than an actual woman. Panic that she *was* an actual woman, but that he might never be able to touch her, and his entire life would be rendered meaningless if he couldn't. Panic that she would have nothing to do with him. Panic that he wouldn't know what to say if she *would* have something to do with him.

It was absolutely absurd, and all of this would have amused every person who had ever met him, for Lyon, like his father, seemed to have been born knowing just what to say to get people to do just what he wanted.

She was wearing white muslin, beautifully cut and simple, but so were many of the other girls. She was petite. So were many of the other girls.

But she was somehow as distinct as the first wild-flower one happens upon after a long, brutal winter.

An ache started up somewhere in the vicinity of his rib cage.

Her face was like a heart on a slender pale neck—perhaps that's why he'd thought of flowers?

Her mouth, however, made him think of . . . other things.

Her mouth was a sinful pale pink pillow.

His brothers were staring at him.

"Lyon, what the devil is the *matter*?" Jonathan

demanded. "Aren't you a bit young for apoplexy? What on earth are you look . . ."

He trailed off. He'd followed the direction of Lyon's gaze.

Which terminated in a slim, black-haired Olivia Eversea.

"Who is that?" Lyon's voice was distant. A studied casualness.

"You don't recognize her? That's Miss Olivia Eversea. She of the good works, the too-clever-by-half . . . an *Eversea*, Lyon."

Jonathan shot a worried look at Miles.

"No, Lyon," Miles said, and this time he was deadly earnest. "You can't be seri— No, no, no, no, no, n . . ."

Because Lyon was already moving toward her, carried like so much flotsam on the tide.

He wove through the crowd, leaving a little wake of turned heads. He might have even smiled and nodded appropriately, for such was his breeding, and such were his reflexes. Feminine hearts lifted and then broke as he passed.

Olivia lifted her head abruptly when he'd nearly reached her, as if she'd heard that gong. Her eyes flared for an instant.

And then she smiled.

Slowly.

Incandescently.

But with absolutely no curiosity or surprise.

More as though she'd been expecting him.

That smile . . . it was like walking through a door into a world he'd never suspected existed. He understood, all at once, the word "joy," and why it was so small, just three letters. It was as simple and profound as a sudden flame in the dark.

He stopped about three feet away from her.

For a moment or for a year, they stood silent and smiling like loobies, as if they'd already said everything they were ever going to say to each other, perhaps in some other lifetime.

No one else existed.

And yet later they were to discover that dozens were watching all of this via sidelong glances and outright stares and stricken glares.

"Of course," she said, finally, softly.

"Of course?" he repeated tenderly. Already cherishing those two words as the first she'd said to him. They seemed to capture everything about the moment. *Of course. Of course it's you I've waited for my entire life. Of course we're meant to be together forever. Of course.*

"Of course I'll dance with you, Mr. Redmond. It's why you're here?"

He recovered quickly. "Among other reasons."

She tipped her head to the side and looked at him through lowered lashes, a look amusingly reminiscent of his own patented sultry one. "I suppose we can discuss your other reasons during the waltz."

Splendid! She was a flirt!

"Oh, I'm certain the discussion will take at least three waltzes. It might even require a lifetime."

He'd never said anything quite so bold.

He'd never meant anything more fervently.

He was alarmed at himself and hoped he hadn't alarmed her, but he hadn't a compass for whatever this was and he didn't know what else to do besides speak truth.

He held his breath for her response.

She made him wait, and he counted that wait in heartbeats.

"Why don't we start with the waltz," she said.

The words were both a challenge and a promise.

The promise lay in the fact that her words, albeit insouciant, were a little breathless.

Which is how he knew her heart was beating as fast as his.

And then she laid her hand on his proffered arm and led her out to the floor.

OLIVIA HAD NEVER been quite this close to Lyon Redmond, and it was so exotic she felt as though she'd been given an actual lion to dance with. Everseas and Redmonds did not dance with each other. If humanly possible, they did not speak to each other, or about each other, or do business with each other. For as long as she could remember, it was understood that the word "Redmond" would be treated in their house rather as though someone had silently broken wind in company. Its occurrence was distasteful but occasionally unavoidable, and while it could be politely ignored, it was certainly not encouraged or enjoyed.

But he'd appeared before her and a curious thing happened: the entire ballroom had suddenly gone soft at the edges, and it was as though she could see beyond it outward to forever.

She exhaled at length. As if she could finally release the breath she'd been holding her entire life. Waiting for him.

She hadn't yet had a season—she would most *definitely* have a season next year and it was generally assumed she would cause quite a stir and a veritable stampede of suitors, which she rather enjoyed picturing—but she'd heard all the things said about him, of course, and she'd been inclined to believe them. That murmurs soughed through ballrooms when he entered, and one would know he'd arrived by the near wind created by fluttered fans and eyelashes and heads whipping round to get a look. That other young men threw back their shoulders and stood straighter, but they couldn't duplicate whatever it was he brought into a room: a self-possession, an unmatchable elegance, and an arrogance that challenged and awed. Something innate.

Now, however, with his hand at her waist and her hand gripped in his, the two of them were quiet, and something about the quality of his silence made her feel strangely protective.

It occurred to her that arrogance was an excellent cloak for a sort of shyness.

And now they had no choice but to waltz through a room filled with dropped jaws. Hopefully none of them belonged to any of her brothers. They could usually be counted upon to be off causing dropped jaws of their own. Her parents weren't here tonight. They had clearly assumed that nothing was more benign than a Pennyroyal Green assembly and that Olivia would be the last person to do something untoward.

Her head reached to about Lyon Redmond's collarbone.

If she tipped her head up and he tipped his down simultaneously, and she stood on her toes, by her calculations their lips would meet effortlessly.

She'd never had such a thought before in her entire life.

The backs of her arms began to heat.

His face was a glorious geometry of angles meeting planes meeting hollows that seemed specifically designed to make hearts pound and breathing more difficult, as if the observer had suddenly been thrust into a different altitude. Olympus, perhaps.

Really, he was untenably handsome and alarmingly masculine.

But his blue eyes were warm and bemused.

"It just occurred to me that I may have absconded with you, Miss Eversea. Was this waltz already spoken for?"

"Of course it was. But I'll apologize to the gentleman in question apace," she said airily.

"'Apace'?" He was amused. "Would it be the man who is glaring at us? I can see the whites of his eyes as we sail by."

"That would be Lord Cambersmith."

"Good God, that *is* Bumble! I didn't recognize him in grown-up clothes."

He lifted his hand from her waist to wave merrily, and Bumble reflexively waved back before he realized what he was doing and dropped his hand to resume glowering.

"I used to go fishing with his older brother. Do you think he'll call me out?"

"Would you shoot him apace?"

"I would try not to," he said with mock regret. "It's just that I never miss, and I should hate to ruin his grown-up clothes, given that he is so lately in them."

She smiled up at him. The two of them were being insufferably and uncharacteristically selfish but neither could seem to care at the moment. Nobody else in the world seemed important.

"Well, he wouldn't be within rights to call you out, and he won't, anyway. I've known him almost since birth. He hasn't any sort of claim on me."

A hesitation.

"Has anyone else?"

A blunt, bold question. Low, and gruff again.

"No."

Though she sensed she had just been claimed.

Another little silence, as the truth of that settled in.

"And you, Mr. Redmond? Did you disappoint a particular young woman?"

"Dozens of them, likely. There are only so many waltzes during any given ball."

This was so arrogant she laughed, and he smiled down into her eyes, teasing her. He was laughing at himself.

His smile faded and he grew serious and almost diffident.

"I will apologize to Bumble, and feel I must apologize to you, too. I can't remember the last time I so egregiously abandoned my manners. It's just that I . . . that it seemed important to reach you before you could disappear."

That little hesitation charmed her. "Disappear?"

He paused again. "The way dreams do, when you wake in the morning."

The words were gruff. She knew them to be truthful, because she sensed they'd caused him a great measure of embarrassment.

This was first indication that the matchless Golden Boy Lyon Redmond, who towered over her and had shoulders for miles, could be hurt.

Just let anyone try, she thought fiercely.

She accidentally ever so slightly squeezed his hand.

He returned the pressure subtly.

Never let me go. An irrational thought, especially since she suddenly wanted the waltz to end so she could dash off, run and run like a firework let loose. Or find a corner and think about all the things she felt right now, all of them confusing, all of them dazzling, all of them filling her a trifle too full. She was not impulsive, and she always liked to know the why and how of things, and she did not know how she had come to be dancing with him. Only that she would rather be nowhere else in the world than here, in his arms, in this ballroom.

"You've been away for some time, Mr. Redmond," she said finally. When it seemed he still couldn't talk.

"Oxford."

"What did they teach you there?"

"Quite a number of things. Latin, cricket, how to get rich. Or richer."

"Truly? Is there a professor of wealth, then?"

"They all are, if you listen properly. It's how one applies what one learns. And the friends ones makes."

She hadn't the slightest objection to wealth although she often found its unequal distribution and the results thereof unfair and intolerable, and she was fascinated by this point of view.

"How do *you* intend to become richer?"

"Steam engines. Clever investing."

"Steam engines?"

"Or rather, railroads. I do believe steam engines are the future of transportation. Imagine, if you will, Miss Eversea, a Great Britain united by rail from end to end. One day you may be in Scotland in a matter of hours. Or Bath. I've also ideas for importing and exporting. I do think the day of the canal will be finite, and—is this inappropriate waltz conversation? Ought I to be complimenting you on your . . ."

A swift glance that took in her coronet, her necklace, the soft fair swell of her bosom peeking very modestly above the lace she'd chosen so carefully for that particular gown.

He said nothing.

But that look poured down through her like hot honey and fanned out through her veins and she knew she was flushing.

"Thank you," she said, finally, as surely as if he'd spoken.

He laughed again, sounding delighted.

It turned heads, that laugh.

He lowered his voice conspiratorially. "The redoubtable Mrs. Sneath is watching. I just saw her turban twitch. I believe it's because her eyebrows went up."

Olivia laughed, too, charmed to her toes, then stifled the sound, too conscious that the two of them ought not be enjoying themselves so instantly and thoroughly.

"She *is* redoubtable, isn't she? And fearsome. I spend a good deal of time with her on the Society for the Protection of the Sussex Poor. My job is to take a basket of food for the Duffy family once a week. On Tuesdays."

"The Duffys . . ." he frowned faintly. "They live in the house at the south end of town, beyond that big double elm tree. The house that's all but falling down."

"Yes!" She was peculiarly delighted that he knew this. The elm had been split by lightning and had gone on growing as if it hadn't noticed.

"Mrs. Sneath certainly accomplishes things. And has since I was a boy."

She was suddenly sorry she'd seen him only from a distance when she was a little girl, or the back of him when she was in church, and that she hadn't hoarded every single glimpse to pore over in her mind later.

It occurred to her that they likely knew all the same people and all the same places, but had seen all of them from different perspectives. Their families included.

"I should like to be like her when I am older," she said.

"You haven't a prayer of being her when you are older," he said instantly.

She bristled. "And why? I admire her *immensely*. She does so much good."

He was unmoved by her little flare of ferocity, when she'd seen other men blink in the face of it.

"Oh, I think she's remarkably, admirably effective. Like a general, she identifies needs, rallies the troops, and goes after addressing them quite unsentimentally. But I think it's in part a redirection of her energies due to disappointment. Her boys are mostly grown and I think her husband bores her. I do not believe for an instant, Miss Eversea, that you are destined for that sort of boredom."

She smiled slowly. The observation about Mrs. Sneath's marriage seemed faintly scandalous, but it reminded her that for all her intelligence, he was still older and more seasoned and he'd seen more of people and the world. She had never thought about it in such terms, and she suddenly wanted to think about every adult she knew in a new light.

Poor Mrs. Sneath.

Lucky her, to have a thrilling life ahead of her.

Lucky her, to be claimed by Lyon Redmond.

"A prophet, are you, Mr. Redmond?"

He smiled again, and his smile made her breath catch in her throat. "Merely very observant."

They were silent again for a time.

"Speaking of investing, Miss Eversea, I think I'll go to Tingle's Bookshop tomorrow at about two o'clock to see if he's got in any books about Spain. Tingle keeps them near the history section, which, as you may know, is the remotest, dustiest part of the store. In the very back. I suppose it's because many of his customers don't often venture toward those shelves."

She understood at once.

"Spain is sunny," she said inanely.

"Yes," he said shortly. She sensed he'd unnerved even himself.

They were quiet a moment, and then:

"I hate waltzes," he finally said, so darkly she gave a start.

He noticed her widened eyes and smiled faintly, tautly. "It's just that they are far, far too short."

She was suddenly too shy to answer.

The music ended.

But her heart was still waltzing.

He bowed, and she curtsied.

He led her off to the edge of the ballroom, returning her to her friends, as if restoring a figurine he'd stolen to its proper shelf.

Chapter 5

꧁

The next day . . .

At twenty minutes to two o clock, Lyon all but flew from his bedroom.

He halted in his doorway, yanked open his desk, and snatched a sheet of foolscap he kept under the rosewood box, the one with the false bottom, a delightful puzzle of a box. He scrawled two short sentences, sprinkled it with sand, willed it to dry *immediately*, which it mostly did, and then folded it and shoved it into his coat pocket.

He paused in a mirror to ensure his cravat was straightened, which proved to be a mistake. Just as he had one hand on the banister—he liked to use it to launch himself a few stairs at a time—a voice stopped him like a wall.

"Lyon . . . a word, if you please?"

Lyon glanced over his shoulder and saw just his father's hand and forearm. Both were thrust out the door of his study and making beckoning motions in the air.

Bloody hell. Summoned to the Throne Room, as he and his siblings liked to call it. He often had pleasant enough visits with his father, but an actual summons seldom boded anything good and was rarely comfortable, particularly for poor Jonathan, who could, rather amusingly, do no right, and not even for Lyon, who could generally do no wrong but was as conscious of the need for rightness as a horse is of its harness.

He inhaled deeply, exhaled gustily, resignedly pivoted, and strode into the room, aware he was usually a welcome presence and his father sometimes merely liked to beam proudly at him and discuss the latest work of the Mercury Club, which Lyon usually rather enjoyed.

But as he entered, his eyes avoided the clock.

It was his enemy right now, and perhaps time would slow if he pretended it did not exist.

"Good afternoon, Father," he said cheerily.

"Have a seat."

Damn. If sitting was required, then something serious was afoot.

Lyon did, pulling out a chair and arranging himself casually in it, crossing his legs and swinging one polished Hoby Hessian.

He could see the reflection of the clock in its toe. Its pendulum kept swinging traitorously.

"Did you enjoy your first ball in Sussex?"

"It's definitely pleasant to be back. Very different from London. I should like to stay a bit longer and rusticate, if no one objects. I've missed the country a good deal, I realize."

It was his way of preparing his father for the fact that he didn't intend to leave Pennyroyal Green anytime soon.

"We always enjoy having you about, Lyon. Did anything else interesting happen last night?"

"Saw a few old friends."

"Such as young Cambersmith?"

"Yes."

All at once suspicion flared bright and hot and he was, in an instant, on guard.

"His father mentioned that you danced with Miss Olivia Eversea. Stole a waltz right out from under his nose." His father sounded faintly amused.

Just the very words "Olivia Eversea" made the back of Lyon's neck warm and tightened the bands of his stomach.

He would not look at the clock he would not he would not.

"Yes. I believe I did. Among other girls." Whose names he could not remember even if someone had pointed a pistol at his head. "Isn't it funny that Cambersmith would tattle?" He smiled faintly.

His father was silent. Never a good sign.

Lyon and his siblings had more than once jested about his father's green eyes. They suspected he could see like a cat right through to any secrets hiding in what he no doubt (affectionately, one hoped) considered the black little hearts of his sons, as well as his one quite lively daughter. He'd always seemed to know who'd gotten jam on the banister, or who had accidentally shot the foot off the statue of Mercury in the garden, or who had stolen a cheroot from the humidor.

His father steepled his hands and tapped the tips of his fingers lightly together.

Which was peculiar, as his father was neither a fidgeter nor a procrastinator. He preferred to deliver orders and news the way a guillotine delivers a nice sharp chop. Swiftly and surgically.

"Did one of your brothers or friends dare you to dance with her, or . . ."

Lyon blinked, genuinely surprised. "I'm sorry?"

"You're sorry for dancing with her?" His father sounded faintly relieved.

"Forgive me if I'm being obtuse, sir, but I don't understand the question. Why would anyone dare me to dance with a young woman who doesn't want for partners and would hardly be likely to refuse

me? We *are* Redmonds, after all." He said this half
in jest.

It was the sort of jest his father typically enjoyed.

It rang flatly in the room.

Lyon dancing with an Eversea was aberrant, and
they both knew it. Because Lyon was dutiful, and he
had been raised with the notion that the Everseas
and the Redmonds quite simply did not dance with
one another, any more than cats and dogs enjoyed a
good waltz.

"Why, then, did you dance with her?"

Lyon stared back. He saw only his own reflection
in his father's eyes.

He wickedly contemplated saying, *Because she
is my destiny* just to see whether his father was too
young for apoplexy.

He'd never even known he was capable of thinking such words. Let alone believing them.

And then all at once it wasn't funny.

He decided to try cajoling. "Come. You've eyes in
your head, Father. And you were young once. It was
an impulse, I suppose."

His father would likely disinherit him at once
if he'd said, *Because she reminded me of the first wild-
flower in spring.* His father considered excessive use
of metaphor a character flaw.

His father smiled, faintly and tautly, a smile in
which his eyes did not participate. "I was, indeed,
young. Once."

It was as ironic a sentence as Lyon had ever heard.

Something about it stirred a faint memory, a suspicion he'd had for some time. Because he was, as
he'd told Olivia Eversea, indeed observant, and he'd
seen his father's eyes linger ever so slightly on a particular woman more than once.

He cautiously echoed his father's faint smile with

one of his own. Over the years he'd learned to modulate his emotions, his expressions, his word choices, all in order to ensure his father remained indulgent and proud, because that's what ensured a comfortable life in the Redmond household.

"And yet you're not typically impulsive, Lyon."

"No. I suppose I'm not." He knew better than to expound.

Lyon was in fact demonstrably the opposite of impulsive. He hadn't squandered his allowance in gaming hells, impregnated the servants, or appeared in the broadsheets for cavorting on Rotten Row with notorious aristocratic widows.

Though he had indulged in an aristocratic widow or two. Sometimes he thought God had created aristocratic widows for the sole purpose of indoctrinating handsome heirs into carnal pleasures. But he was both discreet and discerning.

From the moment he was born Lyon's responsibility as future head of a dynasty had been impressed upon him, the way a signet ring grinds into hot wax.

He was coming to realize his learned carefulness was something of a useful skill.

He was also beginning to understand the grave cost to himself.

So he said nothing more.

But God help him, he darted a swift look at the clock.

His father usually missed nothing. But if he noticed that glance, he didn't remark upon it.

"Lyon . . . you should know how proud I am of you. A man could not ask for a better son."

He said this so warmly that despite himself, Lyon nearly flushed. His father's pride and approval was as potent as his censure, and his three sons, despite themselves, had lived for it their entire lives.

His brothers usually had to make do with whatever splashed off Lyon and landed on them. (Their sister, Violet, occupied her own category. Every one of them doted on her, his father included, and she was in danger of becoming hopelessly spoiled.)

"Thank you, sir."

"Your future with the Mercury Club is brilliant. The world is your oyster. You have not only your family name to thank for this, but your focus and intelligence and discipline. There will, in fact, be an opportunity in a few weeks for you to accompany me to London to present your ideas for investment to the members of the club."

Yesterday this would have been dizzying, gratifying news. It was everything he had always hoped for.

But oddly, now a trip to London sounded like a trip to purgatory. Heaven, as far as he was concerned, had a population of two.

"Thank you, Father. I should be honored."

"You are poised now to make a magnificent marriage, as I did, one that will bring a wealth of blessings and stature to the Redmond family for decades to come. I know your suit will be welcome by one young lady in particular, and her family will welcome us to London, too."

Lyon was wary now. The name of some girl would likely be produced any moment. A girl with a title and a fortune and a father with connections that Isaiah could charmingly exploit in the service of building the fortune.

In all likelihood, Lady Arabella.

Yesterday Lyon would have been curious to hear the name. He'd, in fact, had several names in mind not too long ago. Yesterday, Lady Arabella would have seemed a perfectly reasonable, indeed, desirable choice. It was a choice he understood, and he'd been raised with the knowledge that making a spectacular marriage, and conferring the associated kind of honor and influence upon his family for generations to come, was his duty.

He knew, definitively, that it no longer mattered what his father said.

Lyon now knew who and what he wanted.

And before yesterday, he hadn't even known what it was to truly want.

"I always hoped to marry as well as you did, Father."

Lyon thought he saw a flicker in his father's eyebrow region. He could have sworn something about that sentence had touched Isaiah on the raw.

Isaiah finally merely nodded once. "Nothing makes me happier or more proud than knowing I can count on you to do the right thing, son, for your actions are a reflection of your fine character. I am absolutely certain you will never disappoint me or bring shame to our family, and this is such a comfort to me and your mother."

It was as though he could will these things into existence by merely stating them.

Lyon had always been fascinated by the fact that Isaiah could persuade nearly anyone of anything. He'd watched his father subtly but relentlessly ply wit, charm, and strategy in meetings at the Mercury Club, over drinks at White's, milling about with port and cigars after dinner parties. He studied people for weaknesses, strengths, fears, and proclivities, and he used them to his advantage the way conductor shapes a symphony. Lyon had witnessed one wealthy investor after another succumb to his father's tactics, none the wiser. Thusly the Redmond fortune and influence grew and grew.

It was an extraordinary talent, his father's intellectually driven intuition, and Lyon had always been secretly proud of it.

But now that Isaiah was employing the same tactics on him, it seemed faintly sinister.

Lyon's skin itched. As if strings binding him were chafing.

It was not the first time he'd had these sorts of thoughts. Almost two bloody o'clock in the afternoon would not go down in his personal history as the hour of his epiphany.

But it had finally come completely into focus, and with it came an interesting sort of calm.

Lyon was a separate person from his father.

He did not like to be told what to do.

And, like his father, he intended to get what he wanted.

"Thank you, Father. Your opinion means the world to me."

His father said nothing. He pressed his lips together thoughtfully.

The clock ticked inexorably on. It was now *bloody hell* two o'clock.

Lyon shifted slightly. The message he'd shoved in his pocket rustled.

He finally could no longer bear it. "Will that be all, Father?"

"I hope so," his father said. And smiled faintly.

IT HADN'T BEEN difficult for Olivia to persuade Genevieve to accompany her into town to Tingle's Bookshop the following afternoon. Genevieve *loved* Tingle's Bookshop, and Tingle was fond of the Eversea girls. They were two of his best customers, after all, between Olivia and her pamphlets and love for a good horrid or adventure novel, and Genevieve and her predilection for florid romances and biographies of great artists and the occasional indulgence in a London broadsheet, which usually made both her and Olivia giggle.

But Olivia rose late, because visions of waltzes had kept her feverishly awake all night. And Genevieve dawdled at home, because she was attempting, and failing, once again to curl her hair, and Olivia thought her head might launch off her neck from impatience as the clock raced toward two.

It was a quarter past two by the time they arrived.

They burst in the door and both paused on the threshold to inhale at once the singular perfume of leather and paper and glue that characterized Tingle's. It was a roomy shop, serving all of Sussex, and it was partly sunny, so that people could admire the gleaming of gold-embossed bindings and comfortably flip through a page or two of books that had already had their pages cut, and partly softly dark, to keep the fine covers from fading.

A few other people were in the store, two older gentlemen and a woman, and all were absorbed in the separate little worlds of their books.

Tingle looked up, beamed, and bowed as if they were princesses. "If it isn't the Eversea girls! What wonderful timing. Miss Olivia, I've a new pamphlet for you."

Mr. Tingle lived to serve his customers.

Olivia seized it delightedly. "Oh, wonderful, Mr. Tingle. So very kind of you to remember to get it in for me."

"Oh, it's no trouble at all, my dear. And Miss Genevieve, I've a shipment of books I *know* you'll want to see," he said, twinkling. "It's in the back, however." He beamed at them. "I'll be just a moment."

He ducked into the back of his shop, and they

could hear him rustling about and whistling cheerily and tunelessly under his breath.

Olivia drifted, as casually as she could make it
seem, over to the section of history books. Her blood
was ringing in her ears, since her heart was circulat-
ing it rather enthusiastically.

"*History* books, Olivia? Wouldn't you rather have
a look at the horrid novels? I thought I saw *The
Orphan on the Rhine* on the shelf. You want that one,
remember!"

"Shoo," Olivia muttered beneath her breath to
Genevieve, who had attached herself to her hip.

"I beg your pardon?" Genevieve was startled.

"Er, my shoe. I believe there's a pebble in it."

"Oh. Well, perhaps you ought to take it off and—"

"Oh look! Mr. Tingle has returned with your
books, Gen!"

"Ohhh, lovely!" Her younger sister whirled and
all but skipped to the front of the store.

Olivia took a deep breath and rounded the corner
of a shelf.

Mr. Redmond was standing there idly, his long
form looking as at home there as he did in a ballroom, one leg casually bent, and he was studying
the spines of the books as if he had all the time in
the world to do precisely that.

A book was already tucked under his arm.

She stared at him.

He didn't even turn. "Well. Good afternoon, Miss
Eversea."

His voice was scarcely above a murmur.

"Why, good afternoon, Mr. Redmond. Have you
an interest in history?"

"As a matter of I'm positively fascinated by the
events of the past. Specifically, the events of last
night."

"Last night . . . do you mean the first time you stole a waltz?"

He smiled. "I still refuse to feel chagrin."

"You did indeed do me a charity, for Lord Cambersmith would have trod upon my foot. He always does."

"You see? I am a veritable Robin Hood of the ballroom."

"Didn't Robin Hood give to the poor?"

"Oh, but I did. I gave to poor me, who had heretofore gone my entire life without dancing with you."

She stifled a laugh at that.

He turned. "I have already made a purchase." He gestured with the book beneath his arm. "I just wanted to make certain I didn't leave the shop before I ascertained there was nothing else in the store I wanted."

"Very thorough of you," she said, her voice just barely above a hush. "I should hate for you to forgo something you want."

He approved of that saucy little sentence with a slow smile she felt in her solar plexus.

"What's that in your hand, Miss Eversea? Have you brought me a love letter?"

Olivia stifled shocked laughter. Then reflexively whipped the pamphlet behind her back.

"I'm terribly sorry, was that too bold?" He was all mock somber contrition.

"Hush. No. I'm difficult to shock. I've a number of rather lively brothers, you know. One becomes inured to being startled."

"Oh yes. Everyone knows about your lively brothers, Miss Eversea. Very well. Difficult to shock, is it? Have a care, or I may consider that a challenge."

"I personally find challenges invigorating."

"Bold words from a woman who doesn't want to

show me whatever it is you're holding, because she's afraid of what I'll say about it."

Damn. This was precisely true and she blinked at being skewered with the truth.

He raised his eyebrows in a challenge.

"It's true. I *don't* want to show it to you," she admitted. Quite pleased with him, perversely.

"Oh God. Is it because . . . is it because it's a . . . poem?" he said with such crestfallen trepidation she burst out laughing and then clapped her hand over her mouth.

"If you'd *told* me you liked poetry I would have stayed up the entire night to write a poem about you, Miss Eversea. And I never thought I'd say that to a soul in my entire life."

"Fear not. It's not a poem. And I shouldn't wish for you to endure that ordeal. Particularly because nothing rhymes with Olivia."

"Nothing rhymes with 'beautiful,' either. But for you I would undertake the challenge."

Her breath snagged in her throat.

She'd heard that sort of compliment a dozen or so times before.

But somehow the way Lyon Redmond said it made her understand precisely what he saw and felt when he looked at her, and what he saw and felt were very adult, very complex things, indeed. "Beautiful" was not a word to be taken, or delivered, lightly.

The backs of her arms heated, and she prayed it wouldn't turn into a blush.

"You *are* very bold, Mr. Redmond," she managed finally. A little subdued.

"Am I?" He sounded genuinely surprised. "I've never been accused of such a thing. I thought I was simply being truthful."

"Truthful, and a bit of a rogue."

He smiled slowly, crookedly, pleased with that assessment, apparently.

"What will you do, Mr. Redmond, if you ever succeed in genuinely scandalizing me?"

"If I do, you'll forgive me straight away." He said this with a little shrug that was both thrilling and irritating.

She gave him an insincere scowl.

"Come, show me what it is." He nudged his chin in the direction of what she was holding. "I shan't judge."

She didn't want to introduce a discordant note into these giddy, stolen few moments of his company.

But she remembered his own truthful bravery of the night before.

And she loathed artifice.

She drew in a bracing breath and sighed it out.

With resignation she turned it around and held it up so he could read the title.

" 'A Letter to His Excellency the Prince of Talleyrand Perigord on the Subject of the Slave Trade,' " he read aloud softly. "William Wilberforce."

He looked up into her face again.

"It's . . . an antislavery pamphlet." He sounded faintly confused.

Her heart sank.

He studied her, a question in his eyes, but none of the other things she dreaded: censure or mockery or condescension or boredom or that blank, dull complacency of someone who utterly lacked intellectual curiosity.

He simply waited for her to expound.

"You see, it's just . . ." she faltered.

And now she was abashed.

"What? What is it?" he urged softly, and stepped

closer to her. She recognized it was an unconscious reflex to protect her from whatever was distressing her, to put himself between her and danger or upset.

And it was odd, but she immediately felt sheltered.

Now the back of her neck began to heat, too, and she was worried it would migrate to her face in seconds, and she would be in the throes of a full-blown scarlet blush.

She looked up at him. His eyes were so warm.

"It's just that I cannot bear it."

She'd never confessed this to anyone, in so many words, anyway. Her family thought Olivia was clever—too clever by half, much of the time—and vivacious and witty, occasionally cuttingly so. Everyone had a role in their family, and this was hers.

But all of these qualities also nicely disguised how much she actually *viscerally* suffered over the world's injustices. How they settled into an aching knot in her stomach and made her restless, and were only eased when she did something, anything about it. She had never tried to truly explain it. It would have confused and distressed them and upset the natural order of the Eversea household, and they would have tried to soothe her out of it, for they hated her to be uncomfortable, when she knew it was a permanent condition.

"Cannot bear it?" he repeated gently.

Her cheeks were hot now. "The Triangle Trade . . . these merchants . . . this illegal practice . . . they buy and sell *people*. They tear them from their homes and families and sell them. Can you imagine your freedom and your home and your life stripped from you? For *profit*. It's . . . really quite unbearable to contemplate, and there's so little I can do to help. And you see . . . so I read and share pamphlets when I can, and, and, help out with Mrs. Sneath and . . ."

He was clearly listening intently, but his expression was difficult to decipher. A mix of thoughtfulness and schooled inscrutability. He was listening, but he was also thinking something else altogether.

Shining through all of it, like the sun rising, was a sort of blazing tenderness.

Every jagged uncertain place in her was instantly soothed. She should not have questioned him. Of course he understood. Somehow she'd known he would.

Oh, I'm afraid of him. But it was a dizzying, gorgeous sort of fear, like standing on a mountaintop and seeing infinity in every direction.

"Why didn't you want to show me?" He was puzzled, gently.

"Well, it's not considered ladylike, is it? Crusades and good works and the like. Or rather, it's an activity for spinsters and bluestockings and young women who haven't dowries, and I'm not one of those. Or for very strident women with booming voices who frighten men. Who do you think of when you think of crusades?"

"Mrs. Sneath," Lyon said promptly. He looked fascinated.

"And she booms, doesn't she?"

"She *does* boom."

"My parents don't precisely deplore my interest, but they've taken to changing the subject when I broach it. I do have other topics of conversation. And other interests. I do not always run on and on about it."

Ironically, she felt as though she was running on and on about it. More truthfully, she was babbling. His gaze, unblinking and unabashedly admiring and very blue and intent, had sent her thoughts careening off their track.

"The slave trade is an evil practice, a blight upon all humankind. And I can't think of a lovelier quality than compassion. Promise me you will never feel ashamed of it, Miss Eversea."

She was speechless.

"Promise me," he insisted fervently.

"Very well," she said shyly, and gave a little laugh. "But truly? Doesn't that sort of thing bore you?"

"I'm finding it difficult to conceive of a circumstance in which you would bore me. I imagine you're simply *filled* with surprises."

"Careful, Mr. Redmond, or I may consider *that* a challenge."

"Even when you're sleeping, I'm certain you're fascinating or at least entertaining. Perhaps you snore or mutter things, like Colonel Kefauver at White's, who talks in his sleep. About tigers eating the natives and the like."

She ought to have laughed. But her mind's eye was instantly flooded with an image: she was opening her eyes to the light of dawn, and turning her head on her pillow.

To finding him lying next to her, his blue eyes on her, warm and sleepy.

She dropped her eyes, all of her aplomb hopelessly lost.

The silence that followed was filled with the comforting sound of the pages of books being turned, the faint merry lilt of Genevieve chattering with Mr. Tingle.

"Mr. Redmond, I think this is one of the instances in which I may need some time to forgive you for cheek," she finally said, softly.

He was silent for the time it took her heart to beat twice.

"Was that enough time?" he whispered.

It was, indeed, but she wasn't about to let him know. She simply looked up again through her eyelashes.

He hadn't gotten any uglier while she was looking down.

Though now he looked faintly worried. There was a faint little shadow between his eyes. Her impulse was to take his face in her hands and smooth it away.

She'd never had that kind of impulse in her entire life.

Let alone for someone at least a foot taller than she, like Lyon Redmond.

She sensed he carried more burdens than anyone knew.

"I'm sorry if . . ." he whispered, finally. "I'm not normally so . . ." He made a helpless gesture. "It's just that I . . ."

She shook her head sharply: *Don't be.*

She knew what he meant.

And suddenly neither of them could speak again.

The initial giddy rush of words ebbed into a velvety silence. Olivia knew a temptation to close the gap between them and lay her head against his chest.

As if she'd done it dozens of times in her life.

"May I . . . may I have this pamphlet?" he asked suddenly.

"You *want* to read it?" She was skeptical.

He nodded somberly.

So she hesitated, then held it out to him, ceremoniously, with both hands, and he took it as gravely as if it was coated in gold leaf.

It wasn't until their fingers were a hairsbreadth from touching that she noticed his hands were trembling, too.

And as she relinquished the pamphlet, his thumb lightly, deliberately skimmed the back of hers.

A bolt of pleasure traced her spine. Her heart flipped over in her chest.

The first touch of his skin against her skin.

Illicit and far too bold.

And not enough.

Oh, not enough.

She knew it was just the beginning.

"Take this," he whispered urgently, and thrust the book he was holding into her hands.

"Olivia, Mr. Tingle said he'd—"

Olivia leaped backward as if Lyon was a bonfire and whirled on her sister, who had just flounced innocently around the corner.

"For heaven's sake, Genevieve, you gave me a fright!" she snapped, and tucked the book beneath her pelisse.

Genevieve froze like her father's pointing hunting dog, her eyes perfect saucers of astonishment. "I merely turned a corner, Olivia," she pointed out, reasonably, because Genevieve was nearly always reasonable, except for the fact that she longed for hair that curled and hers simply wouldn't. "It was *you* who jumped like a trod-upon cat. Wasn't that the Redmond heir? Lyon?" She lowered her voice to a whisper. "Did he spook you?"

She said this sympathetically. As if the Redmonds were goblins out of folklore or ghostly highwaymen, like the legendary One-Eyed William, the highwayman who had once allegedly haunted Sussex roads. As if they could be stirred into mayhem, like the devil, unless they were spoken of in whispers.

Then again, Lyon had indeed vanished like a ghost.

And there might be something to the bedeviling theory. She surreptitiously skated her forefinger over her thumb. Her hand still buzzed from his touch.

As if he'd been the fuse that had set her cells permanently alight.

Olivia shrugged. "I suppose it could have been him. I was absorbed in my pamphlet."

Genevieve studied her gravely. "Olivia, you're somehow very, very pink and very, very white at the same time. Those are not your usual colors."

"You've been looking at too many paintings, Genevieve. I'm certain everyone has begun to look like a Gainsborough to you."

Genevieve laughed. "There is no such thing as too many paintings."

Olivia smiled at her. Genevieve was a dear. Funny, lovely, quiet. She was suddenly tempted to reach out and hold on to her, as if she were receding out of sight. This was the first time she'd had a secret from her sister.

"Did you find a book you liked, Genevieve?"

Genevieve gestured mutely with a little stack cradled in her arms. All of them, in all likelihood, about art or artists. Stacked atop it was a broadsheet. "Do you think Papa will mind if I buy all of them? Did you find what you were looking for, Olivia?"

There was neither sight nor sound from behind the bookshelf.

"I believe I did," she said.

Chapter 6

✌

OLIVIA AND GENEVIEVE RACED home from Tingle's and arrived there just in time to deposit their books in their respective bedrooms and slide into their chairs for dinner. It was a relatively informal affair most nights, with footmen creeping in and out only very occasionally. Jacob Eversea liked to preside over his table and do the carving, especially when he could saw into a good roast of beef, like tonight.

"So what gossip did you bring back from last night's assembly?"

Their father addressed this to the table at large.

Interestingly, no one leaped to answer the question.

"Very fine music," Olivia said a little too brightly. "Everyone looked very pretty."

"The oldest Redmond is back in town," Marcus said idly. "That was new."

"Our Olivia danced a waltz," Chase said. "I saw her sailing by as I danced."

Et tu, Chase! She shot him a swift glare, then ducked her head lest that glare incriminate her.

She hadn't known they were watching.

More specifically, no one else in the world had existed when she was dancing with Lyon Redmond, and if pressed, she wasn't certain she could remember anything that came after.

"Did you now, Olivia? With whom? Practicing for your season next year?" said her father. Her poor, innocent father. He was prepared to indulge or tease her.

Olivia stared at him, robbed of speech, suddenly.

"Lyon Redmond," Colin volunteered. "As it so happens."

"And we saw him in Tingle's Bookshop today, too," Genevieve added, brightly. "Over by the history tomes. Lyon Redmond."

That's when everyone seemed to freeze mid-chew.

"In Tingle's, you say?" her father finally said, idly, reaching for more roast beef.

Olivia suddenly wasn't certain where to aim her eyes. She felt as if Lyon Redmond was imprinted on her corneas and everyone could see him.

She applied herself to her peas, which were bobbing in a little pool of sauce. They friskily eluded the tines of her fork, which gave her an occupation.

"Yes!" Genevieve continued brightly. "And Olivia spoke with—*OW!*"

Genevieve scowled at Olivia and reached down to rub her kicked shin.

"As Genevieve was saying before a twinge overcame her—perhaps too much beef gives you indigestion, Gen?" Olivia added with pointed sweetness, "I spoke with Mr. Tingle, who then referred me to another book and gave me a new pamphlet."

A sort of collective, sighing groan rumbled around the table. It wasn't that they were an uncharitable lot. It was just that the word "pamphlet" had that effect upon her family. She had waxed evangelically on the topic more than once, and they were indulgent but puzzled by what they perceived as a passion that had sprung from nowhere, and would likely be cured, like an ague, when she married.

"Pamphlet" ought to frighten them off the topic of Lyon Redmond.

Her father drizzled gravy over his meat. "A bit of a coincidence that Mr. Redmond would be in the bookshop at the same time as you two ladies were in it."

He flicked a swift look at his older daughter.

Olivia went still.

She didn't dare look at her mother, because her mother could read her like a bloody book.

Her father, Jacob Eversea, was usually so merry and affectionate they often forgot he was also unnervingly astute. The Everseas were wealthy for a reason. *He* was the reason. His instincts for investments were uncanny and occasionally, if rumors were to be believed, unorthodox.

Olivia was fairly new to both subterfuge and guilt and found both of them uncomfortable. The latter had, in fact, rendered her mute. Genevieve was still nursing hurt feelings and a smarting shin and was unblinkingly inspecting her sister's face as if she suspected she was instead an impostor wearing an Olivia costume.

Genevieve, alas, was no imbecile.

So neither of them replied to her father.

And the silence was teetering on the brink of becoming damning.

Help came in the unlikely and oblivious form of Ian. "The diversions in Pennyroyal Green, apart from riding and shooting, begin with the pub and end with the bookshop. Where else is Redmond to go? Church?"

"I do wish you wouldn't say 'church' quite so in-credulously," their mother said dryly. "We do own the living, you know."

"A pity none of us went into the clergy."

This elicited a scatter of uneasy chuckles that rapidly dwindled. Olivia, like her mother and her sister, wouldn't have minded in the least if any of her brothers had gone into the clergy. Her brothers had all instead gone to war. Chase and Ian had been gravely wounded. Colin, with his talent for survival, had been relatively unscathed. All had served with honor and bravery. It was a miracle they had all re-turned.

She was freshly reminded that idly discussing *anything* around the dinner table with her entire family now, whether it was Lyon Redmond or church or cricket, was a luxury she would never again take for granted. These people, so rarely together all at once now, meant more to her than anything else in the world.

They *were* her world.

She was suddenly flooded with love and resent-ment for this very fact, and she was inclined to for-give them for anything, including tattling on her.

"I don't know what on earth would keep Red-mond in Pennyroyal Green, anyway," Colin added. "I heard at the Pig & Thistle that he's meant to go to the continent on Mercury Club business. Or marry Hexford's daughter, as White's betting book has it. After all, when a man is accustomed to throwing money about and women falling all ov—"

Her father slowly turned toward Colin and shocked him into silence with a glare so arctic it was a wonder the candles weren't snuffed.

"This is a dinner table," Jacob said mildly to his frozen family, after a moment's stunned silence to allow his point to settle in. "Why should we ruin a fine meal with such talk?"

"Fair enough," Colin said, after a moment, subdued but undaunted. "What do you say we get up a cricket match tomorrow? Run down to the Pig & Thistle in a bit, recruit a few men?"

And they were off and talking cricket, and all the forks and knives were moving again.

Olivia couldn't take her eyes from her plate.

Hexford's daughter. As in the *Duke* of Hexford. That would be Lady Arabella. Olivia knew her. Shy girl, pretty, so very, very wealthy. On the marriage mart, Arabella was the equivalent of winning the Sussex Marksmanship Trophy.

She was remembering the worried shadow between Lyon Redmond's eyes when he thought he'd alarmed her. The little step he took toward her to protect her. The impulse to lay her head against his chest, as if she could transfer her every worry to him through her cheek.

She'd danced perhaps four waltzes in her life and countless reels and quadrilles, but not once had she noticed so acutely the fit of her hand in another's. Not once had the heat of a touch lingered at her waist.

Such talk.

Wicked, laughing blue eyes.

His trembling hand.

A whisper of a touch that had turned her blood effervescent and hot, and ignited a craving that made her understand at once everything and nothing about the matters between men and women.

Such talk.

As if the mere idea of him or any Redmond was enough to turn the roast beef.

She had never questioned it. Children were trusting and malleable when they loved and were much loved by their parents, and Jacob and Isolde Eversea were in general bastions of kindness and wisdom and authority, in turns affectionate and strict. The Everseas had dozen of friends all over England, all of them, at least the ones she knew about, respectable. Olivia had certainly never witnessed any marked tendency toward arbitrary enmities.

So surely the objection to the Redmonds was based in some truth?

But then there was a legend, after all. The trees in the town square, the two ancient oaks entwined, said to represent the Everseas and Redmonds. Who were now so entwined they both fought for supremacy and held each other up, and could no longer live without each other.

Some called it a curse.

"May I be excused?" she said suddenly.

"Olivia, darling, are you feeling well?" Her mother was worried. Olivia usually polished her plate and then returned for more.

"She has a new *pamphlet*," Genevieve explained.

"Right, right, a pamphlet, right," everyone murmured.

She dashed up to her room. She'd given the pamphlet to Lyon. Thank God no one in her family wanted to read it.

She snatched up the book on Spain he'd shoved into her hands, eager to touch something that he'd touched. She hadn't yet opened the book.

Oddly, she wasn't terribly alarmed or surprised by the notion that women fell all over him. Of course they did—one need only look at the man to see why. Certainly she was beginning to truly understand the power of her own beauty, and she knew the notion of her marriage settlements bestowed her with an extra frisson of allure.

But her beauty was the least of who she was.

And she knew instinctively this was true about Lyon Redmond, too.

She turned the cover of the book over, reveling in the feel of the crisp new spine, in that little surge of pleasure that came with opening any new book, almost no matter what was inside.

A slip of foolscap promptly slipped out and tumbled into her lap.

Her heart gave a little leap and she snatched it up.

Meet me next to the double elm tree on Wednesday at three p.m. Say you're going to visit the Duffys.

Her jaw dropped.

And then she gave a short laugh, dumbstruck by the sheer audacity of it.

He'd obviously written that message *before* he'd left home for Tingle's books.

It was *far* too presumptuous. It assumed she was comfortable with lying, which she definitely was not, that she didn't mind being told what to do, which anyone who knew her knew she minded *immensely*, and that she wanted to see him again.

Which she wanted to do more than nearly anything in the world.

She read it over again, her heart thundering so hard it was a wonder someone in her family didn't hear it and shout a complaint up at her.

It had clearly been dashed off quickly. His letters leaned forward eagerly and his "L's" and "D's" made daring vertical leaps. Elegant and handsome, impatient and determined, and unequivocal, like the man himself.

It was too much. It was too fast. It was too new. She was held fast in a tangled skein of emotions and she did not know how to begin unraveling it, when heretofore her existence had been wound as neatly as the embroidery silks she and Genevieve tended carefully, and occasionally squabbled over.

She thought of her beloved family downstairs, even now probably sprawled together about the fire, reading to one another, playing chess, embroidering flowers onto samplers, a bit of quiet before her brothers ventured out to the Pig & Thistle. They all would eventually marry and have homes of their own, and this moment in time was precious.

Was it like that in Lyon's house tonight, too?

She doubted it was quite that peaceful.

Was her appeal for him the appeal of the forbidden?

She didn't think so.

She frowned faintly. She felt . . . *pushed*. Or perhaps "tugged" was a more appropriate word.

Her reflex when pushed was always to dig in her heels.

But still, she drew a finger over those letters, tracing them, and as she imagined him writing them, a surge of tenderness surprised her. He was a man, with a man's intensity and desires; she would warrant he knew all about sensual hunger and how to get it satisfied, and that few women if any would ever say no to him. She would chew and swallow this sheet of foolscap if Lyon Redmond was a virgin.

But there was also almost an innocence to his honesty. She knew he was a bit at sea here for the first time, and she was the only other person in the world who knew how he felt.

Oh God.

How could she possibly be equal to any of this? To him?

He could be leaving for the continent.

Or marrying the daughter of a duke.

She held her breath, as if preparing to pull a

splinter, and with a lurch of almost physical pain, she consigned the note to the fire.

Where it burned down to join the ashes of the sheet of foolscap she'd burned the night before.

She'd written the words "Lyon Redmond Lyon Redmond Lyon Redmond" until there was no more room to write it.

HE'D NEVER ANTICIPATED he'd actually need to wait for her, so he didn't bring a book, not even *Marcus Aurelius*, which usually traveled with him everywhere.

He did bring her pamphlet, which he had already read three times, as if it were her heart in publication form. Which, in a way, he supposed it was.

His own flesh crawled at the notion of slavery. But his response was more intellectual in nature, perhaps even selfish: the idea of losing his own freedom stopped his breath.

But clearly it reverberated through Olivia's very soul.

All he knew was that she suffered over such things, and the notion of her suffering at all made him so peculiarly uncomfortable and furious he thought he might do anything at all for her to ease it.

He admired her fiercely, and this made him restless. In part because her passions, so native, made him realize now that for years he hadn't been so much dutiful his entire life as numb.

He leaned against the double elm tree and looked up through the leaves. He'd done this at least a dozen times in his life—he could probably walk the whole of the town with his eyes closed and not get lost, so familiar was every landmark and texture of the town. He peered upward and tried to enjoy the contrast of the jubilant green of the spring leaves against the blue sky. It was rather like stained glass.

This required the kind of patience he no longer possessed.

He'd shaved with particular care that morning, and he was confident the man who looked back at him from the mirror was polished and regal. He'd tied and retied his cravat three times, before deciding simple was best primarily because his hands were oddly clumsy with nerves. Anyone who knew him well, Jonathan or Miles, would have laughed to see him so at the mercy of a woman, when it was generally understood that it was always the other way around.

Though perhaps it would have been less funny when they learned this particular woman was Olivia Eversea.

At half past three, he sorted through the contents of his coat pockets. Two pence, an old theater ticket, a tiny folding knife, and his gold pocket watch engraved with his initials, a gift from his father on his sixteenth birthday. He cherished that watch. It had made him feel very adult. He'd become someone who needed a watch, for he had places to be and things to attend to.

He flipped the pocket watch open, and then closed. And open, and then closed. Not feeling terribly adult. The click seemed deafening here in the quiet woods, and seemed to emphasize how very foolishly alone he was out here beneath the elm tree.

At four o'clock he walked thirty feet up the rutted dirt road and peered, and saw nothing but a squirrel, who was then joined by another squirrel. Lucky squirrels, whose assignation was a success.

He watched the shadows of everything around him lengthen, even his own.

At four-fifteen, he carved the letter "O" in the elm tree with his knife. Because he thought perhaps if he wrote it somewhere it might ease a bit of the restlessness, the fever. Because it felt as though a knife were at this moment carving it into his very soul.

It did not.

He wasn't certain he'd ever waited two hours for any *human* before, let alone a woman.

He was a determined man. He stood on the road and *willed* her into appearing on the horizon.

She did not.

Finally, desolation sank through him, so black and weighted for a moment he couldn't imagine moving ever again. They would find him centuries from now, planted like the tree. Pining like a fool in the direction of Eversea House.

This mordantly amused him. He had never cared enough to be desolate before, and the feeling was so new it almost did him in.

Almost.

It was the very notion of newness that revived him. Desolation was at least *interesting*.

Today was only one day.

And he was going to get what he wanted.

Chapter 7

That Sunday . . .

THE ENTIRE EVERSEA FAMILY crowded into their usual pew in the Pennyroyal Green church, which had been polished by centuries of other Eversea bums, to politely pretend to be interested in what the vicar had to say. They each had their own strategy for staying awake during the sermon. Olivia and Genevieve often made a game of guessing who had a new bonnet, or at least new bonnet trim.

"One day we'll have a *fascinating* vicar, mark my words," their mother told them.

"I shouldn't hold my breath," Jacob Eversea muttered in reply.

"Look at who's here. I thought he was leaving for the continent." Her brother Colin whispered this to Ian, nudging him.

Olivia followed the direction of Colin's chin nudge.

And she froze.

The shoulders were unmistakable. And when he turned, just a little, to speak to his mother, that profile made her breathing go jagged.

Her heart shot skyward like a bird released from a cage.

It seemed insanity now that there had been a small part of her that had wished him away, because that would simply be easier. It was so very clear that *everything* was better when he was near.

Olivia didn't hear a word of the sermon, but anyone watching her would have thought she found the vicar's message transcendent, so unblinkingly rapt and aglow was she. She'd never been happier to be wearing the blue striped muslin and the bonnet with the blue ribbons, because everyone said it was the precise color of her eyes.

And that familiar sound of dozens of people at once, shaking out crushed skirts, waiting for old limbs to thaw or creak into motion, and the crowd moved en masse out of church, slowly, pausing to mill and exchange greetings.

She had just shuffled with the crowd to the edge at the churchyard fence, and she paused to look up, her heart hammering. The trees surrounding the church had leafed almost overnight in a joyous explosion of green.

Suddenly a voice was in her ear.

"Drop your prayer book."

She instantly did just that.

She and Lyon Redmond both simultaneously then dropped to a crouch. Anyone observing would have thought he'd simply solicitously stopped to pick the book up for her. The Redmonds had exquisite breeding, after all.

"I waited *two hours*," he said on a whispered rush. It was both faintly accusatory and awestruck. And a little amused.

She bit her lip. He was so handsome she literally *ached*. As if all of her senses were flooded with him.

"I do *not* like to be told what to do. Especially if I'm being told to lie. I never lie."

"Never?" He was so genuinely astonished that she couldn't help but smile.

"Well, I'm bad at it. And one ought to have a code, after all."

"I agree. One *ought* to," he agreed, somberly.

But his eyes were dancing.

She tried and failed not to smile.

"I do apologize, Miss Eversea. I see now that I assumed too much. For instance, I assumed you might wish to speak to me again. Do you?"

Clever, clever wicked man to demand an answer in a way she couldn't dodge. Because she'd just self-righteously announced she never lied.

"Yes."

"Shall I come to call?" He said this evenly. But impatiently, as they could not crouch here forever.

Their eyes locked.

God only knew how the Everseas were discussed in *his* household.

He'd made his point without saying another word, and furthermore, he knew she understood.

She was aware of the hum of cheerful voices, a child shrieking in what sounded like mad joy, because it had been released from the purgatory of sitting still on a hard pew while a man in a long dress droned on and on.

It was a very peculiar view she had at the moment, a word comprised only of skirt hems and boot toes and Lyon's blue, blue eyes.

"You should know that I don't make a habit of lying, either, Miss Eversea. I apologize if the note caused offense. I merely thought the gentlemanly thing to do would be to arrive at a plan that would allow us to see each other again, and then present it to you. Because I wanted to see you again, and *my* code is to get what I want."

It was so thrillingly arrogant her heart all but keeled over in a hard swoon.

"It was very efficient of you," she admitted. "Well done."

He shook his head slightly, as if she were a delight, lips pressed together, eyes sparkling, and she smiled at him, grateful her bonnet disguised her flushed cheeks from the rest of the world.

What a joy it would be to speak with him endlessly, because somehow she knew that she could. To use a normal conversational voice, not a constrained hush. To laugh out loud. To savor his presence without looking over her shoulder or anywhere else but at him.

Which reminded her she really ought to look over her shoulder.

If anyone in her family had yet noticed she was missing from their milling little throng, they hadn't thought to look down yet. Thankfully her brothers were all very tall, and the ground wouldn't be the first place they looked for their missing sister.

She half wondered if Lyon Redmond had thought of this, too, when he'd told her to drop her prayer book.

She was very clever, a quicksilver, incisive sort of clever. But she had the suspicion that Mr. Redmond was one step ahead of her.

It irritated her, even as she liked it very much.

"Mr. Redmond . . ." she said finally.

"Lyon," he corrected on an almost irritable, impatient hush, as if he'd done it dozens of times before. As if they hadn't enough time for two words when one could do.

"Lyon," she repeated gently, as if he'd given her a little treasure.

He smiled at her as if she'd just knighted him.

A fraught few seconds during which they locked eyes, and the milling legs of departing churchgoers began to thin and they would be exposed crouching face to face on the ground outside the churchyard.

"I will bring a basket of food to the Duffys on Tuesday afternoon," she whispered in a rush. "About two o'clock. I'll be alone."

"Wouldn't it be a coincidence if we met on the road going south?"

"It would at that," she agreed breathlessly, then launched herself to her feet, and whipped about and walked away from him without saying another word.

It was all she could do not to leap up and click her heels as she hurried back to her family.

"I dropped my prayer book," she explained, though thankfully her family looked mildly puzzled by this announcement, as no one had really noticed she was gone. "It just leaped from my hands. It's my favorite book. I should hate to lose it. By dropping it."

"I think our Olivia just had a religious epiphany. She's glowing like a lamp." This came from Chase, who was studying her oddly. Though that could be because she was babbling about her prayer book.

"How could she have an epiphany after *that* service, when I could swear the vicar dozed off for a second or two while he was speaking? And if he can sleep during the service, why can't I?"

Colin presented this logic to his mother, who snorted and looped her arm through his, as if this alone could rein in her irrepressible son and prevent him from climbing the trellises of married countesses.

"We are Church of England, daughter mine, and we do own the living, as you know, so please don't entertain any ideas of becoming a nun," her father said dryly, and looped his arm in hers.

"Olivia would annoy all the other nuns. She'd have to be the *best* nun," Ian teased.

She laughed, even though it was absolutely true: she quite loved winning. But she was prepared to find everything funny and beautiful at the moment and she would not look back she would not she would not she would *not* to see if Lyon Redmond was watching her.

Genevieve was walking ahead of them, and glanced at Olivia over her shoulder. "I don't think *those* are the ideas she's entertain—*OW!*"

Olivia stepped on the back of her sister's shoe and pulled it off. "I'm so sorry, Genevieve! Clumsy me."

Genevieve shot her an aggrieved look and Olivia returned it with a daggerlike one.

"Come here, my love, where you cannot be stepped upon by your sister," her father commanded, teasing both of them.

Genevieve skipped backward and took his other arm.

A fortnight ago, this was the definition of perfect happiness for Olivia. A beautiful spring day, tiny purple wildflowers already peering through the little fence surrounding the churchyard full of ancient leaning stones covering Eversea and Redmond ancestors and other familiar Sussex names; her family, together, bantering, bickering, teasing, arms linked, walking the familiar path to home. Her father, tall and broad and handsome and only a little soft in the belly like any properly contented man, cigar smoke and wood smoke practically woven now into his favorite Sunday coat. His coat was the smell of love and safety to Olivia. Her mother, whose heart-shaped face and blue eyes were so like her own, sending her a quick and wry and loving look that said, *We know our men need us to keep them civilized.*

Her life was stitched together by countless Sundays just like this one, and other beloved little rituals she'd known since she was a child.

She pulled her father's arm snugly against her ribs as if to keep herself anchored to him and to the ground, even as she couldn't quite feel the ground beneath her feet. Even as she knew something was pulling her away.

She was going to see Lyon Redmond again.

She did not look back.

So she didn't know that Lyon stood for an infinitesimal moment of utter stillness to watch her go, as if marshaling all of his senses to remember it.

And it was this very stillness that caught the eye of his father, because it was the sort of stillness an arrow has after it strikes its target.

He followed the line of Lyon's gaze, and saw a dark-haired girl with a slim back and a light step, linked arm in arm with Jacob Eversea. A girl so achingly familiar he nearly swayed with a vertigo comprised of years.

Jacob Eversea. The man who lived the life that could have been Isaiah's.

And then Isaiah's beautiful wife, Fanchette, linked her arm in his, and he turned a reflexive fond smile on her.

He led his own fine family, Lyon and Miles and Jonathan and Violet, in the opposite direction, toward Redmond House.

ON TUESDAY AFTERNOON, at fifteen minutes to two o clock, Lyon waited alongside the double elm tree, vaguely embarrassed now that his earlier desperation was permanently commemorated with a carved "O." Poor tree.

But then he saw a dot of white in the distance and his heart seemed to acquire a thousand extra beats.

And when she saw him, she broke into a run, her face suffused with light, for all the world like a shooting star.

Suddenly the "O" seemed entirely inadequate. He ought to carve an "H" in front of it and "sannah" after it.

He tried to appear nonchalant and manly and arrogant, all the things the world believed he was. But he met her halfway before he even knew he was walking.

They both stopped, mutely delighted.

She smiled and pushed a tendril of loosened hair away from her eyes, and for a moment they said nothing at all.

"Let me take that for you," he said at last.

He slid the basket from her arm.

"It's heavy," she warned. "Bread and half a wheel of cheese, and some fruit and other things in jars. It's an awful lot of food."

He gave it a little heft to demonstrate how strong and manly he was. "There are an awful lot of Duffys."

"There are, and there are bound to be more, because he won't stay off her."

She froze and clapped a mortified hand to her mouth, blushed scarlet when she realized what she'd said.

He gave a shout of laughter.

But even *he* almost blushed.

"A pity they're not Church of England," he said. "They're a trifle less enthusiastic about that sort of thing."

"Are they?" She sounded genuinely curious and faintly disappointed.

"Well, not all of them."

As, of course, the two of them were Church of England.

They stopped, both dizzied and nonplussed by the sudden veering of the conversation into the Duffys' bedroom.

"We really oughtn't be talking about this sort of thing," she said dubiously. Abashed. She'd said it more because she thought she ought to than because she believed it.

She set out down the road. It was lined with elms and ashes and ancient hawthorn hedges, which rustled with birds and other tiny living things. It had seemed so desolate when he waited for her. And now it was paradise.

He wanted to rescue her from embarrassment. "If we avoid all the things we ought not do, Miss Eversea, neither of us would be walking along this road, enjoying a spectacularly beautiful day in the presence of someone charming. And if something worries you, I should like to know about it. We're friends, are we not?"

"Most definitely."

She said this so fervently he was literally charmed down to the soles of his feet.

Their initial giddy burst of conversation spent, and for a moment no one spoke. They simply walked. The things they felt free to say aloud had not yet caught up to the things they felt about each other, and the silence was filled with happiness and impatience.

"I truly didn't mean to say that," she said suddenly. "I shouldn't like you to think I'm so careless. It's just that I do worry, you see. The Duffy children are darling in their way but so often ill because there isn't enough to eat and they are not very strong, and

Mr. Duffy works when he can but he also drinks when he can."

"I think most men drink when they can. Have a look inside the Pig & Thistle on any given night." Though he suspected Mr. Duffy did more than his fair share.

She laughed. "Most of the men we know, surely, but within reason, at least in polite company. Outside of polite company, God only knows what happens. My brother Colin once threw his boot at his door when I knocked on it too early in the morning. He'd been at the darts and the ale at the pub very late."

"My father would murder me if I drank to excess in any sort of public fashion. Or threw shoes."

She darted a quizzical, sympathetic look. "Murdered? For throwing shoes?"

He laughed. "Perhaps not literally. It's just . . . I've always been held to a rather strict standard of behavior. I don't suppose I objected. There are benefits associated with it, after all," he said ruefully. "Such as, my father doesn't withdraw my allowance."

In the little silence that followed the two of them freshly realized how very constrained Lyon's position was.

"Aren't you ever *tempted*?"

He considered what to say. "I have spent much of my life learning how to resist temptation."

Which caused a funny, awkward little ripple in the conversation, given that they privately considered each other temptation on legs.

He hurriedly added, "Which I suppose is a fancy way of saying, yes, indeed, I've been tempted, but I've learned the easiest way to manage my father is not to throw shoes. Or dice. Or tantrums. Cricket balls are allowed."

She was watching him rather avidly, a tiny crease of sympathy between her eyes.

"A very good deal *is* expected of me, Miss Eversea." He was only half teasing. He wasn't certain if he knew how to explain the magnitude of his role as Redmond heir.

"Ah, yes. People often speak of you in hushed and awestruck tones. Lyon Redmond. The apple doesn't fall far from the tree, and so forth. Will be a legend one day."

He laughed, and it tapered into a happy sigh. She was so very surprising. So forthright and confident and *happy*. Very unlike poor Lady Arabella.

"I fully expect I *shall* be a legend one day," he said gravely, only half jesting.

"It's rather a tradition of the Everseas for the young men to find their own ways to fortune. My father went out to sea more than once and came home wealthy. I can't imagine my father threatening murder. He does have rather a *look* he uses when he wants to make a point."

Lyon knew the Eversea brothers had allegedly found their ways into the bedrooms of married countesses and the like.

"My father has a look, too," he said, rather grimly.

She cast him a sidelong glance. "I thought you were meant to go on a tour of the continent on behalf of your father's business straight away. Or marry the daughter of a duke."

His head whipped toward her in surprise. "Where on earth did you hear that?"

"One of my brothers heard it at the pub."

"I was a topic of discussion in *your* household?" And now he was astonished.

"Not for long," she said revealingly. "It was shot down like the season's first grouse."

He gave a short laugh. "Your house sounds like anarchy compared to mine. I don't think I've ever heard the word 'Eversea' spoken aloud voluntarily."

"It's not anarchy!" She whirled on him in a passionate defense. "We all have *beautiful* manners."

And while he was certain this was true—whatever debauchery Ian and Colin Eversea got up to, he was certain they said "please" and "thank you" before, during, and after—he felt a surge of almost painful tenderness. She of course would always passionately defend the people she loved.

It was a quality he shared with her.

It was also the thing that could divide them, if they lingered on it. The history between their families was complex and sensitive, much of it still not fully known to either of them.

He wanted no complexity to intrude on this idyll.

He reached out and nearly laid a hand on her arm, a reflex to soothe and reassure.

He withdrew it swiftly. It was definitely one of the "ought nots."

Oh, but the day she was in his arms . . .

It was not an "if" but a "when."

And he suspected they both knew it.

"I didn't mean to imply any insult, Miss Eversea, so do forgive me . . . I suppose it was my clumsy way of saying that our families are likely very different. My mother is a placid sort, loving and tolerant, and Father . . ." How on earth to summarize Isaiah? " . . . I admire him a great deal," he decided, though it strangely felt less sincere to say this than it would have mere days ago. The admiration was shot through with a rather dark awareness now. "I am acutely aware of the grandeur, if you will, of the family name, and that great things are expected of me, and that every move I make reflects upon every member of my family, him most especially. Or rather, it's very much how he sees it. My good fortune is immeasurable. I both know this inherently and am essentially told this rather frequently."

He said this dryly.

She took this in thoughtfully, and a little silence passed. "I imagine the consequences would likely be dire, should you diverge from your proscribed path."

She was startlingly astute.

Simply walking with her along this road to the Duffys constituted a divergence from his proscribed path.

He paused, and chose his next words carefully. For regardless, he had loyalties of his own.

"My father has ways of making his displeasure known. And yes, he has plans for me."

She turned to watch him, her face somber and yet so vivid, so intelligent and sympathetic. He sensed all at once that she wanted to touch him, too, for the same reasons he'd wanted to touch her. To soothe.

And the idea of touching her made him restless, indeed.

It occurred to him that perhaps it hadn't been entirely sensible to meet her alone in the woods. Because within a hundred feet of where they now walked, off the road, there was a small clearing, carpeted in moss and enclosed by hedgerows and trees, and he knew from now on when he lay in his bed at night he would imagine lying her gently down on her back there, and leaning over her to—

He hurriedly cast about in his mind for an erection discourager, and settled upon the image of Mrs. Sneath.

Olivia was an innocent, but hardly naïve. And the air between them was as full of sparks as the hours before a lightning storm, and it seemed almost dishonest not to discuss it directly. A bit like not saying the word "rain!" even as the sky opened up and poured.

Someone, one of her tall brothers, ought to have walked with her, he thought perversely. Lyon wanted to protect her from himself even as he contemplated ravishing her in a clearing. A paradox.

Into the silence birds sang competing arias, and the trees shook their new leaves like tambourines.

"He'd like me to address the Mercury Club in London soon. To present my thoughts about steam engines and introduce some investment strategies."

"I'm certain you'll acquit yourself as well as your father does."

"I shall do it better."

He said this so simply, and with such easy conviction, that she gave a delighted laugh.

"Is it what you want to do? Investing, and the like? Just like your father."

He hesitated. "I've been groomed for it. I'm good at it. But I've lately learned a good deal about what I want."

He let that statement ring a moment. *What I want.* Like something being wrought on an anvil. What he wanted was her.

She flushed with pleasure.

"Have you been to London, recently, Miss Eversea?"

"Oh, not recently, but I suspect shall have a season next year. I should have had one last year, but I managed to catch an ague instead."

And he already knew what her season in London would be like: men swarming her like bees swarmed flowers. A rogue surge of jealousy swept in, which was absurd, given that it was jealousy for something that hadn't happened yet.

"To your earlier question, Miss Eversea . . . I was indeed meant to go on to the continent straight away. But I have decided to stay in Pennyroyal Green."

They both knew that statement for what it was: a confession.

He did not mention the daughter of a duke. She didn't ask again.

At the quiet heart of the storm of sparks around them was a strange, peaceful certainty. *This person was meant for me.*

They walked on, or rather floated on, silently, as if the moment was a small wild creature neither one of them wanted to frighten away.

"Well, *I* should like to tour the continent," she said finally and gave a little skip, reaching up a hand to touch a leaf on an elm tree as if it were an old friend, which it likely was.

He did like to watch how she moved. He'd once watched a dandelion spiral in a breeze, and she seemed that natural and graceful.

"Would you?" he said, somewhat mistily.

"I've always wanted to go on an ocean voyage. To see the water *all* around! How magnificent! And pluck an orange straight from a tree that isn't growing in a hothouse. And dig my bare toes into warm golden sand. The closest I've come is Brighton. And reading *Robinson Crusoe.*"

He laughed. "I've long wanted to see Spain. I want to build a house of my own there, with a view of the sea, in a *sunny* country."

"Not England, in other words."

"We're hardly the tropics, are we?"

"Though today is paradise, isn't it? Imagine a land where the weather is comprised of day after day just like this one." She tipped her head back and took a deep, spring-filled breath.

"You're describing Spain."

"I'll read your book, then!" she said enthusiastically. "I haven't yet, you know. I only read the message that fell from it. Tell me, what sort of house will you build there?"

"Graceful lines. Perhaps a bit Moorish. White. Simple. Large rooms with vast windows, and from every angle you'll be able to see the sea. Filled with light and fine things, but not a *lot* of things."

He was describing the opposite of his family home, Redmond House. Which was ancient and handsome and lush, all dark woods and hushed hallways and frighteningly dear things they'd never been allowed to touch as children.

"That sounds heavenly. I hope I see it one day."

There was a funny little silence. Because that sounded rather like a declaration, too.

He could sense her deciding whether to ask her next question.

"Does your father know you would like to have a house in Spain?" She said it almost gently. Carefully.

This girl understood so much so quickly.

"No," he said.

It seemed odd, suddenly, to realize that Olivia Eversea already knew his heart better than his father did. Better, in fact, than anyone else in the world.

He had been waiting for this opportunity to exhale, it seemed, his entire life. And with her, he felt more himself than he'd ever been.

She'd already begun showing him that there was much more to himself than he'd ever dreamed. Not entirely comfortable, but wholly seductive.

The Duffy house was now in view and Lyon consciously slowed his steps. But no matter how slow they went, they would eventually arrive.

"Perhaps you best stop here," she said, a bit awkwardly.

He slid the basket from his arm to hers into a fraught silence, because there was far too much to say and it seemed there would never be enough time. And their arms brushed, briefly, and yet deliberately across each other, and it really was only like throwing kindling onto the fire.

That little touch rendered both of them mute for a moment.

"Miss Eversea . . ."

"Olivia."

"Olivia."

He said this gravely. Accepting it with the ceremony such favor deserved.

And he smiled slowly, which made her flush to her roots.

Her eyes were a shade bluer than the sky, and her lashes, when she lowered them, cast a shivering shadow on her cheek.

"Olivia, I . . ."

He stopped. He could have finished the sentence in a million ways.

"I usually bring a basket to the Duffys every Tuesday, after the meeting for the Society of the Protection of the Sussex Poor," she said in a rush.

And then she whirled and dashed off, stopping once again to stretch up to touch a leaf. "We meet again, spring!" she said.

He gave a short laugh and watched her go.

And then he whirled around and though he mostly walked nearly all the way home, he occasionally leaped a few low fences just for the devil of it.

And he stopped just once, to touch the "O" he'd carved into the elm tree.

Chapter 8

Six weeks before the wedding . . .

"HERE ARE FOUR SHILLINGS." Olivia dropped them one at a time into the cup shared by the beggars against Madame Marceau's wall. "I hope you will buy something hot to eat with it. Do consider going to Sussex, if you would like to work and live quietly. This should be enough for mail coach fare."

She stepped back abruptly.

"This may be the last you see of me. Farewell."

The bandaged beggar never lifted his head or spoke, and she wondered again if he even could. Perhaps he couldn't even hear. But he raised his hand and brought it down in a slow blessing. It was like watching a curtain lower on a portion of her life.

Madame Marceau was clever and busy and she congratulated herself on the hiring of Mademoiselle Lilette, for she and Olivia had established a rapport.

Mademoiselle Lilette was whistling softly as she pinned. As it so happened, she was whistling "The Legend of Lyon Redmond," and it was just too much today.

"Mademoiselle Lilette, may I ask you not to whistle that song?"

"I am so sorry. Do forgive me. It is very lively, the song, *non*?"

"Oh yes," Olivia said blackly. "Very lively indeed."

A prickly, raw little silence ensued.

"Forgive me, Miss Eversea, if the subject is a *peu difficile*, but you are the only woman I know for whom a song was written. He was a lively man? As lively as the song? This Lyon Redmond?"

Was he *lively*? She did not want to think about Lyon during the final fitting of her wedding dress.

No, he wasn't lively.

He'd been life itself.

She never talked truthfully *about* him. She only talked around him, in generalities. No one had known him the way she had.

Suddenly she wanted someone to know.

"He was a surprising man. A . . . vivid . . . man who was also very disciplined. He was very clever and alarmingly quick. He was tender-hearted. And he did so want to see places. He had a wonderful laugh. He would . . . he would have enjoyed the song. I hope—"

She stopped.

"You hope?"

She'd nearly run out of ability to speak about him.

"I hope he did." Her voice was husky now. "See places."

She did, God help her. He might have died in a ditch. Or he might in fact be riding the Nile on a crocodile. She had entertained every imaginable scenario over the years. She imagined him again on the deck of a ship. It gave her some small measure of comfort, even as a hair-fine filament of anger ran through the picture: no matter where he was, he wasn't here, and he had gone without her.

"Was he brave? Was he good?"

Mademoiselle Lilette seemed a trifle too curious.

But Olivia closed her eyes. She couldn't find it in her to mind at the moment.

And she, as she'd once told someone else, never lied.

"Yes." Her voice was thick. "Very brave. And very good."

She didn't know how long her eyes remained closed.

She opened them, because when she closed them she saw his face again in the rain, in the dark.

She slid Landsdowne into place in her mind's eye instead. His dear face and dark eyes.

"I had a great love, once," Mademoiselle Lilette volunteered softly, hesitantly.

Ah! Perhaps this was the source of the questions. "What became of him?"

"I do not know. He disappeared one day." She snapped her fingers. "Like that. I have never married."

"Oh, Lilette . . . I am so sorry." Olivia's heart squeezed painfully.

"*Merci*, Miss Eversea. You are very kind."

There was a little silence.

"Surely one day . . . you are still young . . ." Olivia ventured.

"Perhaps. But my heart, she cannot seem to see anyone else."

Oh God. Olivia wondered what her life would be like if she'd ever dared explain that to her family that way: *My heart, she cannot seem to see anyone else.*

And then had quietly retired from life. There! Done with that nonsense.

Instead she'd endured years of bouquets and wagers in betting books. She'd dodged suitors neatly, charmingly, and had managed to hide the greater part of herself for years.

Until her cousin Adam Sylvaine, the vicar, had given her the miniature she'd once given Lyon. He'd said he was not at liberty to tell her how it came into his possession. All she knew was that Lyon had somehow relinquished it, and he'd once vowed he never would.

It had broken the spell. She had decided then to do something to rejoin life.

And life for any woman typically meant getting married and having a family.

"I'm sorry that you lost him, Mademoiselle Lilette. Truly."

She reached down a hand, and found Lilette's hand coming up to squeeze hers.

"Mais bien sûr, I am strong."

Olivia couldn't see it, but she sensed a Gallic shrug from down around the area of her hem.

There was a hush, honoring lost loves.

"Mademoiselle Lilette . . ."

"Oui, Miss Eversea?"

She was almost afraid to ask the question. She'd never known another soul she could ask, and she was half afraid of the answer.

And finally she did.

"How did . . . how did you go on?" Her voice was nearly a whisper. "When you knew he was gone?"

She had never met another soul who could possibly *answer* that question.

Mademoiselle Lilette was quiet for a time.

"I have my passions, too, you see. If you are a passionate woman, you find things to care about, for you cannot help yourself. As you have, yes? For the strong, we do go on."

Olivia couldn't speak. It had taken all of her nerve to even ask that question, and she hadn't yet found her voice again.

"Your heart is healed, *non*, Miss Eversea? The song, it is silly nonsense, and you should not let it trouble you. You will be happy, Miss Eversea, you will see. You are marrying a fine man."

Olivia was not willing to discuss the condition of her heart. "One of the finest of men I've known."

"And you are fortunate."

"I am fortunate."

"And only the grandest of women are sung about."

Olivia snorted at that. "There I fear our opinions must diverge. I wish more than anything for a little time away from songs and wagers and prints and all this nonsense. It's everywhere I turn. If only I could escape for a week or two to catch my breath . . . so I can be married with a clear mind."

"Perhaps a trip to the country?"

"*Another* country, perhaps," Olivia said mordantly. "My home is in the country, in Pennyroyal Green, Sussex. I would have to go very far to escape the nonsense, as we've agreed to call it. It seems to have saturated London and its environs. Then again, my mother might not even notice I've gone and I've hardly been very helpful lately. My nerves are making me shrewish."

She was still talking when she noticed Mademoiselle Lilette was motionless for some time.

"Miss Eversea?"

"Yes?"

"We are *fini*."

Well, then. She and Mademoiselle Lilette were the first to see her stand up in her wedding dress.

The seamstress turned her around by her shoulders ceremoniously and aimed Olivia at the mirror.

The dress was a masterpiece of gossamer, flowing simplicity. The tiered sleeves were short and ever so slightly puffed and trimmed in silver lace. They looked as dainty as little fairy bells perched on her shoulders. A train flowed behind her like mist—a *train,* not cobwebs—and silver ribbon gleamed at the neckline, the hem, the waist. The hem was caught up in little loops of silver ribbon, with just a scatter of beading. She was to wear white kid gloves.

She hardly recognized the girl who stared back at her. White-faced, dazzled. Haunted.

"I would certainly marry me," she said.

Mademoiselle Lilette smiled.

"You are beautiful, Miss Eversea. Surely it is all anyone should require of you right now."

It was time to think about Landsdowne.

And how his dear, strong face would look when he saw her in the dress.

Perhaps her *heart* could not see anyone else. Perhaps her heart had indeed been permanently blinded.

But she had decided that making someone else happy was the next best thing to being happy, and she knew she could do it.

And perhaps one day she would not be able discern Landsdowne's happiness from her own.

About five years earlier . . .

ANNIE, JENNY, PATRICK, MAEVE, Jordy, Christopher, Michael, and the baby, who likely had a name, but was a girl and would be called "the baby" until another one was born, which, given that these were the Duffys, was an inevitability.

Lyon knew the names and all their little dramas by heart.

Rather the way he'd come to know his ceiling at night.

For almost three months he'd met Olivia just once a week, for just shy of two hours, unless one counted church, where he could hardly look at her, let alone speak with her. He didn't even make excuses anymore. He simply disappeared from the house about the same time every Tuesday. He hadn't tried very hard to be convincing, but he'd managed rather skillfully to dodge his father, the only person he truly needed to convince.

He knew she liked marmalade better than blackberry jam, that she preferred coffee to tea unless the tea was very black indeed, and she didn't take sugar in either of them, just like him, and that she preferred to take breakfast in the kitchen rather than the dining room because she liked the way the sun came in that particular window in the morning, gauzy and bright, and that she yearned after a pair of white kid gloves trimmed in gold that were in Postlethwaite's window. He knew that she'd had a kitten who'd died when she was nine years old and she'd never forgotten him, and that she was worried about her brother Chase, who seemed rather quiet lately, and about Colin, who was conducting quite the stormy and obvious courtship of Miss Louisa Porter, that her favorite flower was red poppies, that she had named the immense holly tree outside her bedroom window Edgar, because it seemed to fit, that her heroes were Mrs. Hannah More, Zachary Macaulay, and Mr. William Wilberforce, who were passionate, tireless abolitionists and crusaders for the poor. And, of course, Mrs. Sneath.

His ambition was to be her hero, too.

He admired her almost helplessly. It was the first time in his life Lyon had felt he'd needed to *earn* anything. Sometimes when he was with her he felt as though he were walking a narrow fence rail, arms balancing him, worried that the next moment would be the one she decided he was unworthy.

But his native confidence always returned.

It was so very clear she felt the same way.

Conversation spilled from them, sparkling and effortless, ricocheting from topic to topic. They found each other an infinite source of delight.

But every moment with her seemed to enhance his awareness of her, until it was so acutely sensitized he found the smallest things erotic. The bend of her elbow. The skin of her wrist when she turned it up. He longed to trace the faint blue veins with a single, delicate finger, and press his lips against her pulse. That shadow between her breasts that made his head light, because all it did was make him imagine them bare. The pale, tender strip of skin between her bound-up hair and the collar of her pelisse. The way her slim back flared into her hips. The whorl of her ear. He imagined tracing it delicately with his tongue, and how she would moan softly. When they stood near each other the space between them pulsed with heat, until it seemed patently absurd that she wasn't pressed against him.

And he lay awake and suffered.

This kind of consuming *want* was entirely new to him. He was accustomed to appetites, not obsessions, and there was usually an aristocratic widow available to satisfy an appetite. And he certainly knew how to satisfy himself alone in bed at night. But he could do neither, because they were so far from what he really wanted it would have been like eating wood shavings simply because no food was available.

His restlessness had driven him out to the Pig & Thistle at night, where he watched Jonathan win dart games, and had begun conducting a half-hearted flirtation with a charming teacher from

Miss Marietta Endicott's Academy who took some dinners at the pub. It distracted him slightly, but alleviated nothing.

Lyon simply wasn't a rake or a rogue. One didn't seduce well-bred young ladies, particularly one's neighbors, and most definitely not an Eversea, if one was a Redmond. Even stealing a kiss from her was fraught with a statement of intention.

But the silences between their giddy rush of conversation had begun to grow longer and more tense. They stole little touches here and there—a brush of their fingers when he handed off a handkerchief, or when she slid the basket onto his arm to hold. It was so absurdly not enough that it bordered on torture.

He understood why Romans didn't feed the lions before they set them upon the Christians. Hunger made one furious and untenable.

He was off for a good gallop one morning after a sleepless night, when he slowed his horse to a walk and then pulled him to a halt in front of Postlethwaite's. He stared at the window.

Then slid from his horse's back and tethered him.

He hesitated briefly. Then he pushed open the door, and the bells danced and jingled merrily. This morning the sound shredded his nerves.

"Why, Mr. Redmond, good morning!" Postlethwaite bowed. "What brings you to my fine establishment?"

"Good morning, Mr. Postlethwaite. I'd like to purchase the white kid gloves in the window. The ones trimmed in gold."

He was conscious that he was speaking in a rush and perhaps too adamantly.

"A gift for a lady in your life, eh, Mr. Redmond?"

Clearly Postlethwaite was familiar with the syndrome.

Lyon said nothing. His nerves were wound too tightly and he needed this transaction to happen very quickly indeed.

Postlethwaite was pulling them from the window and reaching out to hand them to Lyon to inspect when the bell of the shop jingled again.

Lyon pivoted.

And froze.

There stood his brother Jonathan, just as frozen as Lyon.

Jonathan's gaze darted from Lyon. To the gloves. To Postlethwaite. Back to Lyon.

A damning little silence ensued.

"I saw Benedict tethered outside," Jonathan ventured, quietly.

Lyon found he couldn't speak. He could only imagine what his expression was, given the three hundred things he was feeling at once. He couldn't seem to arrange mild disinterest over his features.

"I won't say anything," Jonathan said quietly and surprisingly gently.

Lyon couldn't even nod.

"I'll just wrap those gloves for you, shall I, Mr. Redmond?" Mr. Postlethwaite said discreetly.

"Thank you," Lyon said stiffly. Still looking at his brother.

Neither he nor Jonathan had yet blinked.

"Now, young Mr. Redmond," Postlethwaite said brightly. "Are you looking for something, too?"

"Thank you, Mr. Postlethwaite, but I was looking for my brother. Father wants a word with you immediately. Something about London?"

SHE LOVED HOW he spoke of his family: the warmth in his voice when he spoke of his sister, Violet, who was about Olivia's age and was *quite* a handful. His admiration for his clever, quiet brother Miles and his affection for Jonathan, who was rather like a puppy but who looked so like Lyon that Olivia knew he would someday be devastating. She knew his horse was named Benedict, that he had once rescued and raised a baby sparrow, that his favorite color was blue, like her eyes and his, that he'd won the Sussex Marksmanship Trophy three years running and a half-dozen fencing competitions at school. He was left-handed. He had two middle names, Arthur and James, which she'd discovered when he'd handed her a handkerchief one day to clean off a bit of jam, and she'd rubbed her thumb over his embroidered initials. As if she could imprint them on her soul that way.

She learned that he loved scones, very strong unsugared coffee just like she did, and reading while stretched out in chair farthest from the fire in their main room, because he could tip his head back and see, on clear nights, the Starry Plough, and she knew that he had accidentally shot the foot off the statue of Mercury in his father's garden when he was a boy. He read and read and reread *Marcus Aurelius*, and sometimes he read to her from it as they walked, when she asked. His favorite quote was "Accept the things to which fate binds you, and love the people with whom fate brings you together, but do so with all your heart."

How she loved that sentence. *Love the people with whom fate brings you together, but do so with all your heart.* And she loved the little silence that followed when he'd read it to her, because she knew he was thinking about her, and wanted her to know it.

He was relentlessly, fiercely intelligent, and willing to rousingly argue in a way she found exhilarating, since she was so accustomed to being cleverer than nearly everyone, and he would not simply *let* her win. Not even when her temper flared.

Though he was delighted when she did win.

Every new thing she learned about him was like being handed a jewel, which she would turn round and round in her hands, studying its every facet.

She wanted to trace with a finger the lines of his face, his lips, his jaw. To slide her arms around his waist and tilt her head up and touch her lips to his. To *breathe* him in. Sometimes he would say something, or the light would catch him just so, and just like that her throat would knot and she would lose her ability to speak, as if everything she felt had rushed her senses all at once.

And then he would fall silent, too.

She knew his reciprocal silence was recognition. And if *she* burned, she could only imagine how he burned. For of course he knew much more about such matters than she did. Her pillow was probably shocked at the attention she lavished upon it at night.

She occasionally regretted he was a gentleman. The fact that he was meant she was safer, and luckier, than she deserved to be.

But it all meant she felt faintly feverish much of the time. It was a pleasant sort of sick that apparently left her looking even more beautiful, or at least more interesting.

"You look as though you're in the throes of an opium dream, Olivia," her brother Ian accused over breakfast, four weeks after Lyon had first joined her on her walk to the Duffys. Her parents had breakfasted hours ago. Olivia, who had tossed and turned and scarcely slept for weeks, was late to the table lately, so she usually breakfasted with whatever brother happened to be home and slowly recovering from a night of doing too much of everything, primarily drinking.

"How on earth would you know *that*? And what's wrong with it, if I do?"

"Interesting," Ian mused. Studying her curiously.

"What is?" she said irritably.

"You just responded to me in full sentences. I haven't heard one of those from you in a while. And you're so *very* fond of sentences."

He was teasing her, but Olivia was startled. She was vaguely aware her conversation had become somewhat drifty and monosyllabic lately. It was just that conversation that wasn't with Lyon suddenly seemed a waste of time. She'd talked to these people her entire life. She was only able to talk to him for about two hours every week.

All her senses seemed forever occupied with him, but she had gone so long unable to talk *about* him that a hair-fine fissure of something she couldn't quite identify—it felt a bit like anger but might also be fear, or frustration, or some blend thereof—had opened up in her joy. She was swept up in a current and forever adjusting her sails.

But both she and Lyon knew this could not go on forever.

Olivia, who never could bear to be told what to do, knew he would need to dictate whatever happened next. And Lyon was so much more comfortable treating the future like a plaything, for speculation was how men like him and his father grew wealthier.

"How on earth would you know about opium dreams, Ian?" she countered swiftly.

"Er, just a guess," Ian said hurriedly. "Reached for a metaphor. You forgot to correct my grammar a moment ago, so I wondered if something was amiss. You seem a bit distracted lately." He pushed the coffee over to her. "This ought to help."

Olivia poured some coffee and closed her eyes and inhaled its heavenly vapors.

When she opened them again Ian was frowning at her. "If I didn't know better I'd say you were nursing a *brute* of a whisky headache."

She snorted. "Naught is amiss. Perhaps I've simply given up on correcting your grammar, exhausted from the fruitless effort."

"Ah, Olivia," her brother teased. "Never give up on me."

She smiled at him then and he pushed the marmalade over to her so she could set about painting her bread with it.

Suddenly Genevieve darted into the chair opposite her, startling both her and her brother. "Olivia, will you come with me to Tingle's today?"

"Er . . . Oh. Um. I cannot. I must to go to the meeting of the Society for the Protection of the Sussex Poor, and then to the Duffys. It's Tuesday."

A little furrow appeared between Genevieve's eyes. "But that's not until one," she pointed out gently.

"I've things to do until then," she said swiftly.

An interesting silence ensued, and Olivia realized that Genevieve and Ian had gone still and were studying her unblinkingly.

"Like . . . gazing dreamily off into space?" Genevieve exchanged a swift speaking glance with Ian, who ducked his head. Perhaps suppressing a smile.

Olivia scowled. "Correspondence," she said loftily. "Regarding my pamphlet."

She had, in fact, started a letter to Mrs. More some time ago, so this wasn't entirely a lie. She *might* even finish it this afternoon.

"Very well," Genevieve said at last, still frowning

a little. Less daunted by the word "pamphlet" than Olivia would have preferred.

Another funny little silence ensued.

"What's that in your hand, Genevieve?" Ian gestured with his chin.

"Oh, it's a broadsheet from London." She brandished it. "I thought I'd read it whilst I had a cup of coffee."

Ian tipped the pot and a sad brown trickle dribbled into Genevieve's extended cup. Genevieve eyed it disconsolately.

"We can always get more," Ian said complacently, and the housekeeper was moving to bring in another pot as he said it. "What's the latest gossip?"

"Why, are *you* wondering whether you're in here?" Genevieve fanned the broadsheet open.

"I shouldn't be," he said vaguely. "This month anyway."

Olivia cast her eyes heavenward in mock dismay. In truth, she enjoyed all her siblings thoroughly, though of a certainty her household *was* more anarchic than the Redmonds. She also knew instinctively it was a happier one. How fortunate they were to sit here together and laugh and talk and know they "could always get more," more coffee and marmalade and conversation that would amuse and irritate, such a contrast from the terrifying squalor in which the Duffys lived.

All at once it seemed freshly inconceivable that she couldn't tell her siblings about Lyon, because sharing the things she loved with people she loved was not only of the chief pleasures of her life, it was fundamental to who she was.

How odd that Lyon could make her world feel so infinite and simultaneously shrink it.

This paradox had begun to feel just a little bit like a vise.

Genevieve cleared her throat and crackled the paper as if preparing to orate.

"Let's see . . . Lord Ice—that's what they call the Marquess Dryden, isn't that funny?—is said to be searching for four black horses with white stockings. How very dramatic of him. The Silverton sisters have returned after a season abroad and are cutting quite the social swath . . . And Lady Arabella, Hexford's daughter is supposedly about to become engaged, and she's been in London for a round of social engagements. We saw her once, do you remember, Olivia? She's blond and so pretty."

"Better a Redmond leg-shackled than one of us," Chase said with near-religious fervor, around a bite of fried bread.

Olivia slowly lowered her coffee cup to the table. As if she were suddenly falling and falling and afraid it might shatter when she landed.

"Does it say to whom Lady Arabella will wed?" She could scarcely feel her lips form the words. They sounded bright and brittle in ears.

"All I can tell you is that the betting book at White's has it that it's Lyon Redmond," Ian said, on a yawn.

Accept the things to which fate binds you, and love the people with whom fate brings you together, but do so with all your heart.

How could she have missed it? She was besotted, that's why. The word "bind" was synonymous with "chained." Which, coincidentally, suddenly seemed to be wrapped around her heart and squeezing the breath from her.

Did "fate" indeed bind Lyon to a duke's daughter and a life the duplicate of his father's?

His future had been stamped upon him since birth, for all the world as if he was a minted coin.

There was no rule that said love would supersede his sense of duty.

Then again, there was no rule that said it wouldn't.

"It's just a stupid broadsheet," she said so vehemently that both Genevieve and Ian gave a start.

She pushed herself blindly away from the table without saying another word.

LYON LEANED BACK against the elm tree; his heart was pounding so absurdly hard it was a wonder it didn't rustle the tissue-wrapped gloves he'd tucked into his coat. He had never before really given a gift to a woman who wasn't his mother, and this gift seemed perfect and yet woefully inadequate all at once. Because he wanted to give her the world.

He did *not*, however, want to give her the news he needed to deliver.

As usual, when she appeared, the world seemed to flare into double its usual brightness, and he stepped out to greet her, to bask in the light he usually saw in her face.

She kept walking right on past him as if he was the elm tree. Or invisible.

Well, then. Something was clearly amiss.

He fell into step beside her, and reached for her basket. She pulled her arm away abruptly. And *still* didn't look at him.

His second rather profound clue that something was definitely wrong.

"Olivia," he tried.

She sped up just a little, as if the sound of his voice were instead the whine of a mosquito she was attempting to outrace.

He kept pace with her. "Olivia, I can't stay today. I need to go to London for about a month. I leave tomorrow."

And that's when she finally stopped. She looked

at him. Her face blanked in shock and disbelief, for all the world as if he'd shot her.

Scarlet flooded into her cheeks.

And then her mouth set in a thin line, and she whipped around so quickly her skirts nearly knocked her down.

But she kept walking.

Much, much faster now.

"Olivia, please *talk* to me." He felt ridiculous scurrying alongside her.

She ignored him. Her jaw was as hard as an axe blade, and her nose, while not necessarily pointed skyward, was definitely elevated. For the first time in his life he understood the term "high dudgeon."

"*Olivia.* For God's sake. *Stop.*"

She halted abruptly and whirled on him. "I thought I told you that I don't like being told what to do."

He was utterly unfamiliar with whatever mood this might be, and he was very unaccustomed to flailing. At least she was speaking to him. He thought he'd best take advantage of the moment.

"I'm sorry," he said carefully. "It's just that I . . ."

He paused.

"Yes?" she prompted tersely.

"I shall miss you whilst I'm there. In London."

It wasn't remotely close to how he truly felt, which was all manner of desolation. And he'd said it stiffly. It was rather impressively difficult to speak into the face of whatever formidable mood she was in.

She didn't soften in the least.

"Then why are you going to London?" She sounded like a magistrate.

"To give the presentation to the Mercury Club. The one I told you about. About steam engines."

Her eyes bored into him. "And the Duke of Hexford will be present."

He fell silent a moment, wary now. "Yes," he said finally.

"And Lady Arabella will likely be there, too. In London."

He sighed.

Damn.

How . . . ? Ah. The bloody broadsheets had likely said something about it. Either that, or London gossip had wormed its grimy little way into the Eversea household.

"Not at the Mercury Club meetings, no."

He understood an instant later that this was a very wrong thing to say. Olivia's pride or feelings appeared to be ferociously wounded, and teasing was not the way to balm it. He hurriedly amended, "It's just that I cannot keep making excuses for why I remain in Sussex, and I particularly can't forestall this meeting. It was planned long ago. I simply haven't a choice, Liv."

She stared at him, head tipped as if he were a specimen of some sort pinned to a board.

"No choice but to ride with Lady Arabella in public. And dance with Lady Arabella in public. And walk with her. And talk with her. In public."

"Lady Arabella doesn't talk much. Mostly blushes and agrees with things."

"She sounds *delightful*."

He paused to think again, frowning faintly. This angry version of Olivia was very impressive indeed—her eyes snapped sparks, her cheeks were scarlet against cream, her every word was hung with icicles. She was utterly beautiful, and he was tempted to tell her that, too, but he suspected it wouldn't be at all well received at the moment.

He knew deep hurt when he saw it.

And it was killing him to be the cause of it.

"Some might concur," he said gently. "I, on the other hand, infinitely prefer speaking to you. No matter what. No matter when. I even prefer having *this* deucedly awkward conversation with you, with your eyes blazing and your fists clenched and just moments away from stamping your foot."

There was a surprised little silence, during which he could tell she was tempted to laugh.

Ah, but she was stubborn.

"But you *want* to go to London." She said this flatly. Sounding, however, a trifle mollified.

"I've wanted to speak to the Mercury Club investors, yes. But no. I don't want to leave now."

He'd just said a good deal, and they both knew it.

And a little silence, a detente of sorts, fell.

But for the first time the things they'd left unspoken and undiscussed, because they would have robbed them of the sweet fleeting pleasure of each other's company, rendered them unable to speak.

Perhaps he ought to let something else do the speaking for him. He took a deep, steadying breath.

"Olivia . . . I . . . I wanted to give you something."

His hands seemed ridiculously unwieldy and twice their usual size with nerves when he reached into his coat. He fumbled about in there, but finally got hold of the gloves.

He handed the tissue-wrapped bundle to her silently.

His heart took up that absurd pounding again.

She looked up at him quizzically, silently. Her lovely eyes were still blazing with temper and hurt, but he thought he detected a bit of softening.

He held his breath as she carefully parted the tissue and removed, slowly, as if in amazement, those beautiful, long-coveted kid gloves.

She went still.

And then she looked up at him, her face utterly stricken.

Which was all wrong. Terribly, terribly wrong.

"But . . . these are . . . these are the gloves from Postlethwaite's," she said faintly.

"Yes," he agreed cautiously.

He could hear her breath shuddering in and out.

"Are these . . ." Her voice cracked, and she drew in a long breath. "Lyon, are these a parting gift?"

He was shocked. "No! Good God, no! They're just—I wanted—"

"An apology for going away to see Lady Arabella?"

"No! Olivia—"

But she couldn't hear him.

"But I can't *keep* these, Lyon. What am I to do with these? I can't wear them in public. I can't do anything at *all* with you in public. How will I explain how I came to have them? What were you *thinking*?"

She was trembling now with hurt and fury and thwarted longing, and tears were beginning to glitter in her eyes. If he'd ever been tempted to become a rake, now would a good time to start: he could sweep her into his arms, kiss her senseless, and make her forget the reasons she was hurt. It would certainly absolve him of trying to explain himself.

But he quite simply couldn't do that either to her or to himself.

Because he would still have to leave her and go to London.

He drew in a breath. Counted to three silently. "Olivia."

He said it so calmly, so portentously, that she at last went still and looked up at him, breath held. Willing him to say something to make it better.

He took a moment to marshal his courage.

"I want to give you the moon. But I was forced to make do with gloves."

She made a little sound of pain. As though he'd shoved a needle into her.

Her face suffused with misery.

Too late he realized how that must have sounded to someone whose heart and pride were abraded: as though the moon was no longer on offer, and this was a consolation prize.

"Olivia—"

"Give them to Lady Arabella." She shoved them back at him.

He took them, stunned.

She turned on her heel and ran as if she couldn't get far enough away from him fast enough.

Chapter 9

❧

Five weeks before the wedding . . .

ONCE OLIVIA'S TROUSSEAU WAS complete, peace of a sort descended upon the Eversea town house. All the Everseas apart from her mother and Colin had dispersed to Pennyroyal Green or to other parts of England, Genevieve into the waiting arms of her husband.

The next day Olivia was painting her toast in marmalade—it was her tradition to spread it neatly out to the corners before she took one bite—when a footman brought in a tray of correspondence.

"For you, Miss Olivia."

Olivia frowned faintly at the address written on the front of the letter.

She slit it rapidly and read the few lines.

She lay it down on her plate and stared at it, one hand over her mouth, eyes wide.

"Oh. Oh my goodness. Oh my. Oh my. Oh my. Oh my."

Her mother dropped her knife with a clatter. "Olivia, good heavens, tell me nothing has—"

She laid a hand immediately on her mother's wrist. "Everything is fine, Mama. Everything is more than fine. Everything is *wonderful*."

Her mother had survived losing a baby, sending

sons off to wars and to the gallows, and children off to matrimony with aplomb and extraordinary strength, grace, and humor. But Olivia remained a grave concern, and her mother tried not to show how *much* of a concern. Olivia knew she'd in part gotten her own stoicism from her mother.

"No, Mama, something *splendid* has just occurred. I've been invited to visit Mrs. Hannah More in Plymouth. And Mr. William Wilberforce will be there, too. For a fortnight! At a small gathering in a house in Plymouth!"

This was met with blankly bright expressions from her mother and Colin.

"*Hannah More.*"

"Oh yes, yes. Hannah More. You may have mentioned her a time or two," her mother said carefully.

"Or fifty," Colin amended.

Hannah More. The poet and playwright and crusader for the rights of the poor and the abolition of slavery. She was a remarkable woman. She was one of Olivia's heroines.

"She will be a guest in the house of a fine family in Plymouth along with William Wilberforce. Oh my *goodness*. And they've heard of my work on behalf of the poor. It says so right here." She tapped the letter. "I spoke with her very briefly once after a lecture and she must have never forgotten." She sighed happily.

"A fortnight, Olivia! *Now?* You're going to be married in May! In just a few *weeks*."

"Oh, May is it? I best make a note of that," Olivia said.

Colin laughed and her mother swatted him. "Don't encourage her!"

"Mama, my trousseau is complete and it is beautiful beyond my wild imaginings. I'm so blessed in family and friends and I can't imagine wanting for clothes until I'm in my dotage. Unless you need my help in preparing the house for guests . . ."

"We've servants enough for that, but you'll need to see to setting up your own household."

"I've a lifetime to do that. And please understand, Mama—*this* is the opportunity of a lifetime. She's elderly now, Mrs. More, and I may never have an opportunity to meet someone I admire so greatly. Believe me, nothing but this kind of invitation would persuade me to leave now. But it's that important to me. And I'm not a little girl."

"I suppose," her mother said, after a moment. "And you may be too busy with babies to go soon."

"Er . . . That may well be true," Olivia allowed carefully, startled.

Her mother looked pleadingly at Colin, seeking an ally.

Olivia took a deep breath. "Mama . . . It's just that everywhere I turn I see . . . or hear . . . something about me. The songs, the betting books . . ."

She was flushing now.

Her mother's eyes widened and she instantly took her hands in hers and squeezed.

"Oh, my poor sweetheart. You never say anything. You never let it show how much it troubles you. It's all right, you know, to not be so very, very stoic."

It wasn't all right. Olivia wouldn't quite know where to begin if she decided to fall apart. "Stoic" was what helped her survive to this point in her life.

And she'd only ever felt free to fall apart in front of Lyon.

But her mama's tenderness was balm.

"It's ridiculous," Olivia said firmly. "The songs are ridiculous. That's all. Please do not worry about how much it troubles me. And yet I'd like to go away to a quiet place, and marry without those songs in my head. I don't see how that's unreasonable."

"She should go." Colin said firmly. In utter seriousness. He'd seen Olivia's face in Ackermann's.

And this was one brother who knew a little something about being haunted by a song.

"But who will accompany you?" her mother said finally, swayed.

"I know just who I should like to invite as a companion. She has an interest in Mrs. More's work, too. A very solid young woman with a practical head on her shoulders. You've met her, Mama—Mademoiselle Lilette."

"Oh yes, the pragmatic seamstress. I did like her. And surely absence will merely make Landsdowne's heart grow fonder," her mother said.

"It's only a fortnight, Mama. And Landsdowne will be so occupied with the arrival of his mother and sisters that he'll be *more* than delighted to see me when I return, believe me."

"YOU WANT TO go . . . away? *Now?*"

Landsdowne went motionless. They occupied the same settee in the Eversea town house sitting room, but a foot or more of tufted velvet remained between them.

He settled his teacup down carefully on the table and eyed her warily.

"Just for a fortnight, John, and just to *Plymouth*. It's scarcely even 'away.' As benign a place as ever graced a map. No betting books in Plymouth, at least that I've heard of."

She handed the letter over to him. His eyebrows went up. "Ah, Hannah More is indeed an impressive woman. I suppose it takes one to recognize another."

She could tell he was struggling with diplomacy, and she smiled at him, grateful and relieved.

"Flatterer."

"I don't suppose *anyone* can get up to any mischief in Plymouth," he teased.

"I'm not prone to getting up to mischief at all. It's mischief that dogs *me*."

"August personages, all of them, to be certain." He tapped the letter. "I can't pretend they hold any particular fascination for me, my dear, but I would love nothing better than to accompany you. It's just that my mother and sisters have arrived, along with . . ."

"Lady Emily and her family?"

It was a fortunate guess.

"They were childhood friends." He quirked the corner of his mouth. "And now I am at pains to make all of them comfortable and welcome in my house before we all proceed on to Sussex."

Olivia had met his mother once before. A solid woman possessed of little intelligence but a good deal of warmth. She was primarily harmless and seemed happy enough to welcome Olivia into the family.

"It's just . . . I would like to start our life together without . . . a song ringing in my ears. And I think the company of wise, kind, elderly people who neither know nor care anything about me apart from my interest in abolitionism will be soothing. I feel so terribly crowded in London, and by all the speculation. Believe me, nothing but this kind of invitation would persuade me to leave. It just seemed like *serendipity*. And then I'll return, and you will be wed to a woman who is happy and peaceful and will excite no comment or gossip for the rest of her life."

He was watching her thoughtfully.

"You do understand?" she asked, almost desperately.

"I suppose I do. I *shall* miss you, even if it's only a fortnight. You're the only one who can commiserate with me over the wedding madness."

She smiled faintly. And then she reached out and cupped his cheek tenderly in her hand, because she wasn't terribly certain she would miss him, and she wished that she would.

He covered her hand with his and turned his head to press a hard, hot kiss against her palm, startling her. It was a fierce kiss. As if intended as a brand. He didn't meet her eyes.

It made her realize how hungry he'd been for a gesture from her.

Another man would have simply reached for her before now, propriety be damned. After all, they were going to be sharing a bed for the rest of their lives.

He was perhaps too careful with her.

He *had* kissed her passionately when he proposed. And not since then. Since then, they had walked about like a pair of horses in harness, clearly heading in the same direction with the same objective, but seldom really touching one another.

She knew she hardly encouraged the touching.

Still, he ought to have attempted more of a seduction, she thought traitorously. Uncertain whether she was glad or not that he hadn't.

"It won't be madness for much longer, John."

Five years ago, while Lyon was in London . . .

"PERHAPS A DOSE OF castor oil, Olivia?" her mother suggested gently, looking up from her embroidery.

"Perhaps a dose of whisky?" suggested Colin, looking up from the chessboard, as his father, his opponent, snorted.

"Perhaps a simple?" Genevieve said wickedly. "I think a simple would help." Because their cook's simples were noxious and her mother believed in them fervently.

"Why does everyone want to *dose* me?" Olivia said blackly, dropping her book in her lap, covering it surreptitiously with her hands. It was about Spain. She didn't need to field a dozen questions about why she would want to read about Spain.

The evening was chilly and they were all gathered in the drawing room.

"You've the look of someone needing purging," diagnosed her brother Chase, who had his aching leg up on the stool in front of the fire.

"I'm merely thinking about the Duffys. The baby has been very fussy lately and I think she has taken ill and it's quite worrisome."

The eyes of nearly every member of her family were upon her, deciding whether they thought this was true or not. Colin finally shrugged, because what else could it be?

And Mr. Duffy had been drinking nearly all of what he earned, which was scant to begin with, and Mrs. Duffy had the haunted look of a woman who would sooner fling herself off a bridge than spend another day in that house. And for a short hour of the week Olivia tried to be a rudder of sanity amid their chaos. She was so grateful to escape when she did. And yet she could not resist going through that door every Tuesday any more than a sailor can resist the sea.

She hadn't realized how much talking with Lyon about them had helped.

Olivia had thought she was happy before Lyon. Certainly she had naught to complain about. And then when he became a part of her life, it was like a secret passageway had slipped open in a mansion, revealing an infinite number of beautiful new rooms just waiting to be explored.

For about a week after he'd left she'd been practically *incandescent* with hurt and righteous, wounded pride. This had somehow inured her to his absence.

But he'd been gone three weeks now.

And now the entire landscape of her life seemed barren and stripped. The light had gone out of her days, and she was learning to navigate this newly dim, newly cramped world, and apparently not doing it gracefully, if everyone thought she needed to be purged. Perhaps she did. For if love made her sick, then heartbreak was an entirely different kind of sick.

It was just that she'd never been *stormy* or delicate. That nonsense was for other people. Her emotions ran fierce and deep as did her suffering, when she suffered, but she'd always had all of that firmly in hand. They'd never before buffeted her, or seeped blackly through her very soul so that every part of her felt so leaden she could scarcely raise the corners of her mouth. She'd never been *obvious*. Until now. She loathed melodrama, and irony of ironies, she was the heroine of one and couldn't seem to stop it.

The worst part was the guilt: Lyon had bought her a beautiful gift, and when she'd shoved it back at him . . . Olivia would have gladly ordered a horse-whipping for anyone else who had put that shocked, stricken expression on his face.

It was intolerable to know that she was the one who had done it.

And what if he never returned? She would have nothing to remember him by.

And what if he was set upon by cutthroats or his horse tossed him into a ditch?

Her parents had commissioned miniatures of all their children a year ago, and Olivia kept her own on her night table. She decided to carry it with her from now on. If she ever saw him again, this was what she would give to him, if he would accept it after she'd behaved so horribly.

By the third week of his absence, the solid, leaden misery had shifted enough to allow the pendulum of her emotions to swing between two poles: that she'd acted like a fool and a child; and that she was in the right, and had every right to savor her hurt and indignation.

None of this, of course, changed the fact that he simply was gone.

"I'll have a little of that whisky," she said to Colin.

"No you won't," everyone said at once, and she almost, but not quite, laughed.

Because he would be gone for at least another week.

The possibility remained that he would never return.

And he might be someone else's fiancé if he did.

And to add insult to injury, her mother made her drink a simple.

LYON HAD SLEPT beneath the roof the London Redmond family town house hundreds of times throughout his life, but it was the first time he'd become so intimately acquainted with the ceiling.

And the first time he'd resented it so thoroughly and irrationally.

His head ached abominably. The night before he'd departed for London with his father, he'd shoved those beautiful white kid gloves into his coat pocket, and had gone to the Pig & Thistle and gotten uncharacteristically drunk.

And outside, on the way home from the pub, he gave the gloves to that schoolteacher in exchange for a kiss in the dark outside the pub.

And it was a sweet kiss, but it tasted of betrayal.

And now he had self-loathing to contend with, yet another emotion in the buffet of emotions he'd been presented with since he'd first laid eyes on Olivia Eversea in that ballroom.

His soul felt flayed.

The notion that Olivia should feel hurt or ashamed or abandoned, that she should think for a moment that she could bear being apart from him, tortured him at night, and London, which he had always loved, had become excruciating. Time was, once again, his enemy.

To survive, he'd mastered a permanent faint, interested smile. It was as effective as a mask, and he soon discovered it was all that seemed necessary to be considered charming, because he was Lyon Redmond, and everyone was predisposed to think him charming, anyway.

He accepted invitations to dine with old school friends; he spent a pleasant enough few nights at White's, where the waiters greeted him with real pleasure and deference and where old Colonel Kefauver still alternately snoozed, talked in his sleep, and told alarmingly violent stories of his days in India. And would, Lyon thought, until the end of time.

One evening at White's he and his father had settled in at a table with drinks, and when his father pored over the newspaper, Lyon wandered over to the betting book and flipped idly through a few pages.

He froze when his name leaped out at him.

N. Gracen wagers Lord Fincher fifteen pounds
L. Redmond is engaged to Hexford's daughter by
year's end.

Wagers on his proposed wedding to Lady Arabella already.

Though no one was taking much of a risk at fifteen pounds.

But Arabella was a prize, and anyone's willingness to concede her to Lyon was a way of conceding his own supremacy. Lyon was a prize, too.

At one point in the distant past, perhaps six months ago, this would have brought immense satisfaction.

And now he just felt like a prize bull kicking the walls of his pen.

The bloods at White's were *fools*. They would wager on anything.

And as he stared at that, he could feel the blood leaving his face.

He must have been white with fury when he turned.

His father was watching him. And he raised his glass in what appeared to be a toast.

AT HIS FATHER'S request, he persuasively presented his ideas about steam engines and railroads to a group of England's wealthiest men in what must surely be the longest, glossiest table in all of England.

He knew his father envisioned Lyon at the head of it one day.

Lyon, in fact, had envisioned *himself* at the head of it.

And he did lose himself for moments at a time in the enthusiasm of the investors. He loved clever minds and innovation and the idea of risking for rewards. The discussion grew lively and detailed and Lyon basked in their genuine admiration for his ideas about steam engines. He'd committed his own discretionary funds to the eendeavor.

"The apple doesn't fall far from the tree, old man," was the consensus, as the club lingered over drinks later.

The tree being Isaiah, of course.

Which Lyon supposed was a compliment. He wasn't completely unmoved by it, either.

Isaiah certainly glowed as if it was.

But every bit of it, even this anticipated triumph at the Mercury Club, had begun to feel like an interminable dream.

His real life only existed in about hour increments, and only on Tuesdays.

AND HE RODE in Rotten Row with Arabella, who sat a mare beautifully, and who was so accustomed to stares that she never blinked when heads whipped toward them as they rode past. The row was crowded thanks to the weather, and they were seen and remarked upon and he could anticipate precisely what the broadsheets would print about it.

"What a magnificent couple," he heard someone murmur appreciatively.

And when he delivered her home again she smiled and blushed with something like apology. For she knew she was too quiet and too shy, and that Lyon was brilliant. Arabella would likely never resist whatever destiny her father planned for her, and suddenly this made Lyon pity her so achingly that he gave her hand a kiss farewell.

He found his father at home when he returned,

settled in his favorite chair, one that Lyon could remember always being there, a great enveloping leather behemoth. He was reading a newspaper.

"How was your ride with Lady Arabella?"

"Charming," Lyon said shortly.

He waited another moment, in the hopes that his next words would sound more casual than desperate.

"Father, if you can spare me, I need to return to Sussex."

His father looked up from his newspaper and studied him for a moment.

"Oh? You need to? Why is that?"

"A chestnut mare I've been coveting is at last available for sale. I've put some of my allowance aside for the purchase of her."

He'd prepared the lie as he was riding with Arabella, who was riding a chestnut mare. And Lyon had sunk his funds into the latest Mercury Club endeavor and was awaiting the return. He was hardly currently in a position to buy a mare.

His father lowered the paper all the way into his lap and regarded his oldest son calmly. And it was a moment before he spoke.

"A mare, is it?"

There was something ironic about the words that had the hairs prickling on the back of Lyon's neck.

"Yes." He was aware the word was faintly defiant, but he couldn't seem to help it.

More silence.

"Very well, Lyon," his father said at last, in a tone Lyon found difficult to interpret. "Go home to Pennyroyal Green. See to your mare. And tell your mother I'll be home in a week."

OLIVIA TOOK A deep breath of clean, free air before she crossed the threshold into the Duffy household, much like a diver preparing to enter a murky sea. Her only responsibility was to leave the food with a quick, charitable smile and then depart—it really was all her parents had given her permission to do—but she never could. It wasn't as though they were chickens in a barnyard, for heaven's sake. She didn't know how any human with a heart or conscience could look about the Duffy house or into Mrs. Duffy's face and not offer some momentary respite.

She'd grown fond of the children, some of them noisy little heathens, some of them angels, all of them, truly, some blend of each, all of them vying for a scrap of attention from their exhausted, beleaguered mother and their indifferent, hapless, usually absent father. The children scarcely were allowed to be children, anyway, pressed into service as nannies and cleaners as soon as they could walk.

Olivia tried to give each of them a word of praise, a special greeting, a question that told them that she recognized them as separate little individuals, not a mass of hungry open mouths. Everyone, she fervently believed, had a right to be loved, to be fed, to be clothed and sheltered. But her attentions were like a drop in an ocean of need.

She settled the basket of food on the begrimed table, whipped open the curtains, and slid open a window, which let out a little of the foul air but revealed the crusty remains of porridge on the stove and the fine layer of dirt that coated everything, children included. The fire was low, and wet clothes draped on the hearth seemed on the brink of mildewing.

Mrs. Duffy immediately began to unpack the basket as her children clamored around her.

"Scones today, Mrs. Duffy," Olivia said brightly.

"Thank you." Mrs. Duffy swiped a strand of lank hair behind her ear. Whatever pride she might have laid claim to had gone down beneath a wave of hungry mouths to feed and soiled baby clouts long ago. She accepted whatever charity she could get.

Had Mr. Duffy ever looked at Mrs. Duffy with a face lit with awe and hunger?

Had Mrs. Duffy's heart ever leaped when she looked at Mr. Duffy?

"Shall I hold the baby for you, Mrs. Duffy, whilst you feed the others?"

Wordlessly, the drawn and weary Mrs. Duffy handed over the baby, a pretty little thing who had once been generous with her laughter, delighted at the newness of the world, even the dusty, grimy, shrill world of the Duffy house. Now she was listless and frighteningly too warm. She'd been unwell last week, too.

Olivia's gut clenched. She looked up, desperate to leave here, desperate to do something to make it better and knowing whatever she did would matter for only a few minutes.

"Oh, sweetheart," she murmured to the baby, who fussed. "Do you think a doctor ought to see her, Mrs. Duffy?" she whispered.

"Of course she needs a doctor, Miss Eversea."

Mrs. Duffy smiled a tight, bitter, faint smile, so resigned that it chilled Olivia's very bones and made her feel abashed and very young. The Duffys could not afford a doctor. Or a headstone, either. The baby, when she died, would likely be buried beneath a wooden cross somewhere behind the house.

Mrs. Duffy would have to keep on living here.

And Olivia could leave.

"I'll see you next Tuesday," she whispered.

She kissed the baby between the eyes and handed

her back to Mrs. Duffy, who hoisted her up like the burden she was, not the person she could become if she survived to adulthood.

And Olivia seized her basket and left the house.

She fought back tears as she gulped in huge breaths.

She now understood that Lyon was a grace note on top of all the other blessings in her life. Suddenly not even Lady Arabella or the broadsheets or his father mattered in light of this. What mattered were the moments she had with him.

She was frantic to see him one more time, if only to tell him how grateful she was.

Chapter 10

❧

IT WAS TUESDAY AT three o'clock, not two o'clock, by the time Lyon was in Pennyroyal Green again. Not even he had yet been able to alter the laws of time, but his horse was fast and the roads were good and he'd all but run from the stables to the elm tree, still dusty from the road.

He stood next to the "O" he didn't dare turn into "Olivia" with his knife. He didn't need to. The word was carved on his heart. But if he was lucky, very lucky—and when wasn't he, for he excelled at making his own luck—he would be able to intercept her returning from the Duffys.

And when her familiar petite form came into view, he closed his eyes and said a silent hosannah.

He opened them again, and stepped out from the tree slowly, so she wouldn't be alarmed.

She didn't see him. Her head was lowered, eyes on her feet, rather than on the sky and scenery as usual.

His heart lurched. Something was off. It was a bit like watching a kite struggling to get airborne.

She stopped abruptly when she saw him, and clapped one hand to her heart.

And for a long moment neither said anything at

all. But her face said everything, and he was certain the brilliance he saw there was a reflection of what she saw in his.

"I thought you were going to be gone for a month," she said softly.

"I invented an excuse to come home."

"I thought you wanted to be in London."

"All I ever want is to be wherever you are."

He literally saw her breath catch when he said it. She moved closer, slowly, as if his expression, his very need for her, was spooling her into him.

Her lovely face was still a trifle guarded.

She lowered the now-empty food basket on the ground.

The silence was taut, their joy in each other all tangled in a net of tension and recrimination and frustration, of responsibility.

"Did you see her?" she asked. But she sounded more abstracted than accusatory.

"If you mean did I see Lady Arabella, yes. I saw her. I danced with her. I rode with her in Rotten Row."

She watched him unblinkingly.

"I thought about you every moment of every day, Liv. I saw you everywhere. In trees, in clouds, in the faces of women who walked by, in the puddle of gravy on my roast beef . . ."

She tipped her head and studied him with those blue, blue eyes, deciding whether she thought this was true. There was a glimmer of what might be amusement about the corners of her mouth.

"She means nothing to me. I was like a man in Newgate. I made a mark with a nugget of coal on my bedroom wall for every day I was there."

This made her smile faintly. "You did not."

"I even wrote a poem: 'For Olivia, Who Would Not Accept My Gloves.'"

She smiled in earnest.

"I have learned that everyone else in the world is boring except you."

"It has taken you this long to realize it?" Still, it was a shadow of her usual sparkle.

Now he was truly worried. He stepped toward her, stopped just shy of touching her, but close enough to catch a hint the lavender she likely stored her clothes in.

"Liv," he said softly. "Something is very wrong. Please tell me."

She drew in a breath.

And then it was like a cloudburst.

"Oh, Lyon. I'm sorry I behaved like such a *child*. It's just . . . the gloves were so beautiful and thoughtful, and I . . . I've been wretched thinking about how I hurt your feelings. And I thought—"

"It's my fault," he interjected hurriedly. "I just didn't think it through. I never, never meant to hurt you. And all I wanted—"

"—I *thought* . . . what if I never *see* him again? What if he had a carriage accident or rode his horse into a ditch and lay there, broken and alone?"

He gave a startled laugh. "That's quite a vivid picture, but I'm a very good rider."

"Don't laugh! And I'd been so beastly to you, and you wouldn't have anything to remember me by, as you lay in the ditch alone. So . . ."

She fished about in her apron pocket, and then drew in a steadying breath. "Before another moment goes by I wanted to give this to you. If you'll accept it. Hold out your hand."

Eyebrows raised, he hesitated, then did as ordered.

She settled something into his palm. And then bit her lip, waiting for his response.

He looked down. From his cupped hand, her sweet face looked up at him: the blue eyes, the soft clouds of dark hair, lovely and so vibrantly alive. The miniature wasn't nearly as beautiful as the original standing before him, of course, but the spirit of her was captured so perfectly in strokes of paint he was too moved to speak. It was the best, most perfect thing he'd ever been given.

He was a grown man, but he didn't quite trust himself to look up yet.

A little hush had fallen over them.

He cleared his throat. "I shall cherish it forever, Liv."

His voice had gone a bit husky.

He closed his hand gently around it, and tucked it into his coat.

"I should hope so," she said, sounding a bit more like herself. But her voice was husky, too.

He looked up then. They smiled at each other, and his world and hers began to restore itself to rights, but she was still shadowed.

"Liv," he said abruptly. "There's something you're not telling me."

She went still.

And then alarmingly, she brought her hands up to her face and covered it.

And then she took a deep breath, sighed it out, and when she swiped her hands down again her grief was plain and frightened him.

"Very well. I may as well tell you . . . Lyon . . . it's just . . . it's the Duffys' baby. She's so ill. I don't think she's going to live. And it's so heartbreaking. She needs a doctor. And they don't even have enough money for the rent this month. That's not unusual, of course. Except that they're so late they'll likely be evicted and then the baby will die for c-c-certain."

She drew in a shuddering breath.

His gut clutched. By now he felt as though he knew every Duffy intimately and was invested in their collective well-being.

He produced his handkerchief and gave it to her just as the tears welled, and the wheels of his mind began turning. Relieved that he'd found the source of what was troubling her, because now he could set about fixing it.

"I'm so terribly sorry to be so weepy, Lyon. It's just been difficult to witness. She's such a pretty baby, doesn't fuss at all, and she hasn't a prayer of a decent life, really, even if she does live. I've asked my father for help with them before and he's been indulgent with me but they're hardly the only poor family in Sussex and he says they'll simply come to expect it and he can't feed everyone. I can't ask him again."

"Sounds very much like my father."

Lyon was, at his core, pragmatic. He agreed with both fathers. Some families navigated poverty with dignity and resourcefulness. The Duffys, thanks to Mr. Duffy, weren't one of them.

Still, he couldn't stop himself from doing what he did next. It was more reflex than thought, born of need.

He thrust his hand into his pocket. "Take this." He pressed his pocket watch into Olivia's hand.

"Your watch? Why?"

"Take it," he insisted. "Give it to their landlord. He'll be able to pawn it for a year's rent, at least. Instruct him to return the balance, if any, to an attorney in London named Bartholomew Tolliver, to be held in trust for the children. Good sort, Tolliver."

She stared down at the watch, dumbstruck.

"But . . . your initials are on it . . . Lyon, you love this watch . . . was a gift . . . I can't . . ."

"It was a gift to me, and now I'm giving it to you. If I had a sack of guineas in my coat pocket right now, I'd give that to you, but I don't. If I could, Liv, I'd feed all the hungry myself, and wipe out the Triangle Trade forever for you. But the need is now and urgent, and we have a solution. Take the watch. I'll have another watch, one day."

And still she hesitated. "But Lyon—"

"Olivia."

She looked up at the tone in his voice, her eyes widening.

"You must allow me to *give* you something." He said this slowly, a subtle anguish thrumming through all of those words.

She closed her fingers over it.

"I don't know what to say," she whispered.

"Say thank you."

"Thank you." She looked down at it, running her thumb gently over the satiny metal he had opened and closed countless times. He'd cherished that watch. And somehow he felt only relief that he could ease her troubles.

She looked up at him, smiling faintly. "It's round. Like the moon."

"So it is."

He smiled at her, too.

"What a ninny I am, Lyon. I didn't mean to cry."

"Ninny?" He was incensed. "What 'ninny' walks into a house, gets their heart shredded, and still goes back, over and over again because she's needed? You're a *tigress*."

And that's when the tears spilled again in earnest.

He didn't remember doing it, but one moment she was glowing up at him, tears beading her eyelashes, the next his arms were circling her and she was clinging to his coat. She tipped her forehead against his chest. He cradled the back of her head with one hand, and slid the other down her spine to rest in that sweet small scoop right before the curve of her arse, and murmured things he'd never dreamed would ever pass his lips.

"Oh, Liv. Liv. My heart. My love. Please don't cry. Please don't cry. It will be all right."

She wept a little, quietly, for a time. And at last heaved a sigh.

And then he simply held her.

It was as perfect a moment as he'd ever known. It seemed an astonishing privilege to be the person who could comfort her.

He'd never known there was much pleasure in simply quietly breathing with another human being.

"I missed you so," she whispered.

His heart broke, then regrew three times bigger.

The soft press of her breasts against his body, the rise and fall of her breath beneath his hands. The sheer glory of having her in his arms was well nigh unbearable. It was like the sun had taken up residence in his chest.

And he held her and murmured things, and his hands moved soothingly over her back.

And without thinking, he brushed a kiss over the top of her head.

He felt her breathing stop.

And then her back moved again in a great exhale, and she slowly tipped her head back and looked up at him.

"Liv?" he whispered.

A warning.

The only one he was going to give her.

But she rose up on her toes to meet his lips as they lowered.

He brushed his lips across hers so softly, and even

that much was playing roulette with his control. A heaven of petal-softness and give, her mouth.

He tightened his arms around her. His limbs were suddenly awkward, thrumming as he unleashed, just a little, what felt like a lifetime's worth of desire.

His lips sank against hers more determinedly, this time claiming. He parted them with a little nip of a kiss.

She made a little sound. A sort of gasp that was both surprised and wholly carnal.

It went to his head like bolted whisky, that sound.

He kissed her again, and this time he touched his tongue to hers, then twined his with it softly, exploring, teasing, arousing. Her head tipped back into his hands, to allow him to take the kiss deeper, and, oh God, she kissed him back as if she'd been born knowing how.

He took his lips from hers briefly to breathe.

"Did I do that correctly?" she whispered.

"God, yes," he rasped.

"Can we do it a—"

He took her mouth before she could say "again." Fiercely now. She met him with full hunger. Desire was a thing with claws and it spurred him on. His hands wandered her shoulder blades beneath her muslin, the warm satin of her skin just a fine, fragile layer of fabric away from his hungry hands, and he wanted to tear it away like a savage and bury himself in her.

She wrapped her hands around his head and pulled him close. Her mouth was honeyed sweetness and he was dizzier, drunker with each kiss, pulled deeper and deeper into a maelstrom of need.

He backed her up against the elm tree. And now they were nearly climbing each other, the kisses swift, rough, plundering.

They paused between each kiss to breathe raggedly against each other's lips. He heard his own breath like a distant storm in his ears.

Her hands slid down to his waist and she pulled herself tightly against him, and his cock was so hard her slightest movement sent an agony of pleasure through him. He hissed a breath in through his teeth.

"Liv." He bumped his lips softly against hers.

Her eyelids were heavy, and her breath came hot and swift between her parted lips. She moved against him, seeking her own pleasure, not quite knowing how to find it.

He knew if he hiked her skirt he would find her wet and hot, and he could slide his fingers between her legs, and he could make these woods echo with his name as she screamed it.

He was losing his mind.

She arched against him.

"Liv . . . I . . ." His voice was a shredded rasp. "You mustn't . . ."

Her head went back and her eyes were closed, and he could see her pulse in her throat, and her breath came swift and hot through her parted lips as she pulled him harder against her body, her hands sliding down to his hips.

"Oh God. Oh God."

His voice was in shreds. He buried his face in the crook of her neck and bit his lip hard as his release tore through him. Wave after wracking wave of unimaginable pleasure. He soared out of his body, somewhere over the Sussex downs.

The shame and glory of it.

Despair and euphoria each had one end of him and were tearing him in two.

He hadn't come in his trousers since he was thirteen years old.

And yet he'd never felt so frightened, and somehow infinite and powerful.

What in God's name was he going to do?

They breathed for a time.

"You're shaking," she whispered.

He rested his forehead against hers and closed his eyes. He couldn't yet speak. Their breath mingled, hot and swift, then spiraled whitely in the cold air.

He finally opened his eyes. Hers were blue, still kiss-hazy, worried.

"I'm sorry, Liv. I didn't mean for this to become so . . . so . . ."

"Shhh," she said. "I'm not sorry."

He gazed down at her. Her lashes were still a little damp.

He drew a finger softly, softly, slowly around the contour of her lips. The sweet peaks up top, the luscious, eloquent curve below.

He knew from now on every time for the rest of his life he saw mist on a windowpane he'd trace that shape there.

"You probably know . . . you should know there's more, Liv . . . for you. It's . . . rather extraordinary."

"More?"

"If I were to touch you in . . . certain places . . . in certain ways . . ."

He had never had a more torturously awkward conversation in his life.

And now she was scarlet.

He suspected he was, too.

"I hate to leave you unsatisfied. It's just . . . we mustn't ever . . . we must be so careful . . . you do understand that it's dangerous?"

She nodded.

Perhaps she understood. Perhaps she didn't.

She would definitely understand the next time.

"Dangerous," she repeated softly. Her pupils dark, her gaze dreamy.

"Yes. So . . ." He kissed her lips, softly, lingeringly. "So . . ."

" . . . dangerous," she whispered, her mouth opening to his again. Slow, slow, this time.

As if they had all the time in the world.

Chapter 11

❧

OLIVIA HADN'T KNOWN A universe could be created from a kiss. She wanted to *be* Lyon, to crawl inside him. But one did have to breathe between long kisses, and when she did she opened her eyes and tipped her head up . . .

Long enough to notice there was, in fact, a purple streak across the sky.

The sun was lowering. It was shockingly late.

"Eeep!"

Without another word she seized her basket and bolted like a rabbit freed from a trap, running as though her very life was at stake, likely losing a few hairpins along the way.

She consciously slowed to a walk as the Eversea house at last came into view.

As did her Father, who was out as if for a leisurely stroll, a hound at his heels. When normally he would be inside preparing for dinner.

She stopped abruptly.

"Good . . . evening, Papa."

Damn. It was, indeed, evening.

"Walk with me for a bit, daughter?"

Her heart lurched in dread. Her palms began to sweat and she longed to swipe them on her skirt, which was likely rumpled. She didn't dare.

"I was at the Duffys, Papa. I brought food to them." She gestured with the basket.

"Ah, yes. It's what you usually do of a Tuesday. You stayed for a good long time today," he said mildly.

"I did."

" 'Tis safe enough here in Pennyroyal Green, but a father worries, you know. Perhaps you ought to take a dog with you. This hound, for instance."

The hound smiled and panted up at them hopefully, trotting along and sniffing things.

"A dog would only fight with the Duffys' dog. Or mate with it, and goodness knows how many breeds went into the making of the Duffys' dog as it is."

Her father laughed and she blushed.

"Sorry, Papa. I won't be late again. You don't need to worry. I'm sorry to worry you, if I did."

He *didn't* need to worry about her being late again.

But did it show? Her flushed cheeks, and goodness knew whether her hair was in disarray, and her lips felt permanently branded by hot kisses. She wanted desperately to be alone to touch them now, to savor the feeling of Lyon's mouth there. To relive it again and again. She didn't dare do that now.

If her father noticed, he didn't say a thing. Perhaps he attributed it all to her running.

"You look a good deal happier now than you did just a day ago, Olivia."

"It must be the simple mother forced, er, encouraged me to drink last night."

"Ah," her father said.

They walked in silence, and Olivia was grateful for his company now that it was nearly nightfall.

"You know, I walked with your mother on this very road when I was a boy. You look so much like her when she was a girl. And she was a *stubborn*, thing, my goodness. So witty. So clever."

He said this with relish. He was proud of all of those things in his wife and in Olivia.

Olivia laughed. He took the basket from her and looped it over his own arm and took her arm in his.

"I was her brother's best friend, did you know?"

"Uncle George? Oh yes, I think I knew."

"Indeed, your Uncle George. We were boys together at school."

She smiled, picturing her father as a young man. Dashing and handsome and full of himself. Her mother's brother was a Syvlaine and father to a half-dozen cousins she didn't see as often as she'd like to.

They walked as dark mauve cloud bunting draped over the sky, and she wondered if Lyon was home now. She slipped her hand into her apron pocket and closed it over the watch. The Duffys' landlord was honest and beleaguered and lived very near them. She would need to cajole a footman into taking it to him.

And what did he do when he got there? And was he thinking about her?

She smiled faintly. How could he not?

"Did you . . . did you fall in love with Mama straightaway, Papa?"

He turned to her and smiled faintly. "I did indeed. I understood all that Cupid's arrow nonsense at once." He clapped a hand to his chest. "In it went, and never left."

"Did Mama . . . ?"

"Did your Mama . . . well, it seemed to me that every young man in Sussex was in love with her, but then I was looking through the eyes of love. Do you know Mr. Tingle was captivated with her?"

"Mr. Tingle from the *bookshop*?"

"Oh, he's married happily now to the woman who was right for him. There was a viscount, even an earl, who sent flowers to your mama. Sylvaines are a very good family, but not as wealthy then as they are now. A learned family, a good one. But not exactly in line to the throne."

Olivia laughed. "One day, Papa. There are certainly enough of us and we may marry royalty yet."

"Oh, you and Genevieve will most certainly marry brilliantly," he said, almost complacently.

Guilt seized her ability to speak again.

"There was even Isaiah Redmond, if you can imagine that. He courted your mama."

Ah.

Unease settled in her stomach. She resented the sensation greatly, when she wanted to fly home on winged heels and relive, over and over, how it felt to be in Lyon's arms. Perhaps she'd employ her pillow in helping her remember tonight.

Her father was a subtle, subtle, clever man. And she began to suspect this was an agenda disguised as a stroll. And as surely as they were traveling this road to Eversea House, her father was leading her on a road to some kind of realization.

She and Lyon had been so very careful, until today. Surely no one had seen them when they met?

"I was at sea for a time, traveling, you see, making my fortune in my own way, as all Eversea men are wont to do. The fortune you enjoy today, darling daughter." He gave her a playful little nudge. "When I returned, there was a bit of competition for her hand. Including Mr. Redmond."

"It sounds like Mama was spoiled for choice. I am ever so glad she chose you. You're clearly the best of the lot."

"Ah, flatterer. That makes two of us."

"Though Mrs. Redmond is certainly very pretty, too."

"You ought to have seen her when she was young."

It was odd for Olivia to imagine all of these people as young men and women. They were so content now, Mama and Papa. Had they ever suffered torments of longing? Had there been a subtle war between all of them? It was nearly impossible to imagine Lyon's cold, elegant father suffering throes of anything, apart from greed. Let alone her own mother not instantly falling in love with her father, who was a delight. Though perhaps she had.

"You know . . . Money makes many things possible, Olivia. I love it desperately, if you must know. To me, money is possibility. Infinite possibility. Acquiring it, managing it, growing it . . . it's a skill, it's an art, it's not for the faint of heart. Above all, it's safety. It keeps my loved ones safe, and for that I am eternally grateful. And you know, my dear, there is indeed a difficult history between our family and the Redmonds, and one day you may hear more of it. We are not faultless. There are more than a few rogues in Eversea history, but we are survivors, above all, and we shall always, mind you, *always* thrive."

He glanced at her, as it to ascertain she was truly listening.

"But as much as Everseas love money, the Redmond family care more about wealth than *anything*. It will always win. And they do not care who is hurt."

The unease had tightened into a cold, hard, knot. She resented the intrusion of doubt into her paradise, and yet, there it was. Joining that minute kernel of doubt that had, perhaps, been there from the start. Her father had always seemed to know best. It was a constant in her life.

And what did it mean for everything that came before if he was wrong now?

She didn't speak.

Her father was quiet awhile.

"We should like to give you a season in London this year, Olivia, since you were unable to last year. Would you like that?"

"Yes, Papa, that would be lovely, thank you," she said abstractedly.

The season seemed so very far away. And she'd just kissed and been kissed (and kissed and kissed) for the first time, and it was all the wanted to think about. That, and the next time she would kiss Lyon.

THE FOLLOWING MONDAY, when Olivia finally wandered downstairs after a feverish, near-sleepless night, she found, to her surprise, her entire family sitting around the breakfast table, chewing, chatting, yawning. The light was pushing into the kitchen in the way she loved, through the sheer curtains, and as she slid into her accustomed spot and the coffeepot was pushed over to her, and she smiled sleepily and gratefully.

She was about to reach for the pot of marmalade when she found a little folded sheet of foolscap next to her plate.

"What could this be?" she said brightly.

"It arrived for you this morning along with the rest of our correspondence," her father said. "Mrs. Sneath sent it over."

She unfolded it quickly.

Dear Miss Eversea,

I've decided another family would benefit from your commitment and charming presence. Miss Putney will now see to the

Duffys. I should like to meet with you to discuss the O'Flaherty family on Tuesday at two o'clock at the vicarage.

Yours in charity,
Mrs. Sneath

Little cold prickles of foreboding rained over her.

She didn't dare look up from the message. Not yet. Not yet.

The O'Flahertys lived quite a distance away from the Duffys. Nowhere *near* that elm tree.

She didn't know how to let him know. And she imagined Lyon waiting and waiting for her . . . and when she didn't come . . .

The notion was unbearable.

The timing of the message could, of course, be entirely coincidental.

Or her father, in his own subtle way, had set out to make a point, and had put in motion a plan to protect her.

But they couldn't *possibly* know anything for certain about her and Lyon.

Then again, she wasn't precisely looking anywhere but at Lyon when she was walking. Or kissing him. For all she knew the entire town had been watching them through field glasses.

Surely not.

She thought she detected a hush in the kitchen while she was looking down. As if everyone had frozen to watch her reaction.

But when she finally, slowly looked up again, everyone was chewing, or reaching for jam, or holding a sore head (Colin).

Regardless, they didn't know Lyon.

Lyon was determined.

And Lyon was a planner.

And if they thought it would be this easy to keep them apart, if indeed this was the intent . . . they didn't truly know her.

"What does Mrs. Sneath want, Olivia?" her mother asked.

"She'd like me to visit a new family!" she said brightly. "I'm very much looking forward to it."

THE CHURCH SERVICE that Sunday was interminable, made slightly less interminable by the presence of a particular pair of shoulders and a beautiful fine head for Olivia to stare at throughout the service.

She might have imagined it, but she thought they vibrated from the strain of not turning about to look at her.

And when at last they had been set free from their weekly duty, and everyone had stood and shuffled out of the church, she paused a moment, as if peering fondly in at all her buried ancestors, and dumped her prayer book from her hands.

She dropped to her knees.

Lyon Redmond, who just happened to be strolling by at that precise moment, dropped to his to pick it up for her.

"Mrs. Sneath moved me to the O'Flahertys," she whispered. "Two o'clock on Tuesdays."

He said nothing. He merely picked up her prayer book and placed it back in her hands, then touched his hat once when she muttered thanks.

It took superhuman discipline not to open her book during the walk home. It took superhuman discipline not to *run* all the way home, for that matter.

But once there, she scrambled up to her bedroom and gave her prayer book a good hard shake.

A little strip of foolscap fluttered out.

Meet me at three o'clock tomorrow by the stand of oaks near the O'Flaherty's. I know a clearing.

She clutched it to her with a delighted laugh. Somehow he had found out. He had, as always, been prepared.

"I WAS SO worried you thought I abandoned you," she said breathlessly, as she ran to greet him. He took her hands in his, because they could now.

They could and oh, how they would, touch each other.

"I knew you wouldn't, Liv. I knew something must have happened. So I paid Mrs. Sneath a visit, and we had a little chat about the virtues of charity. I made a small donation, and then I told her that my sister Violet was interested in volunteering to deliver food baskets. She was so shocked and dazed by this possibility that it was easy enough to winkle from her which families needed help and which young ladies were doing the helping."

She laughed, imagining poor Mrs. Sneath, who would consider Violet Redmond a challenge and a project. "Did you think I was frightened off by all the kissing?" she teased.

"Good God, no. I knew you wouldn't be able to resist coming back for more."

She pulled her hands away and gave him a playful little shove, and he dodged her, grinning.

And then he took her hand gently in his, lacing his fingers through her fingers, so casually intimate, so precious an act, they fell silent.

And he led her to the clearing. The point of a clearing was to be alone, and it seemed such an obvious statement of what they intended to do once they got there that this kept them silent, too, tense and eager and abashed.

People rarely ventured into this part of the woods, but Lyon, as a boy, had explored nearly every inch of them.

"Voilà, Liv!"

And they ducked through a hedgerow.

She gasped. "Lyon, it's like a fairy ring!"

They were now all but entirely enclosed by ser-endipitous shrubbery, and elm and oak tree–filtered sunlight poured down on them. Beneath them was a lovely, seductive cushion of moss and fallen oak and hawthorn leaves, perfect for sprawling.

"I discovered it when I was a boy. I always knew the knowledge would one day prove useful."

He whipped off his hat and shook off his coat. He sank down onto the soft carpet of moss. He folded his coat neatly and gave it a pat, and she delicately knelt upon it.

They were both a bit too shy to set upon each other at once.

"Here. Put your head in my lap," she ordered him.

"Very well. If you insist."

He did and it was bliss to be cushioned by her thighs.

"This is perfect, Liv."

She stroked his hair away from his forehead again and again and softly again, and he sighed with pleasure.

"Let's stay here forever," she said.

"All right," he murmured.

"I'll decorate. We'll make it look like your house in Spain."

"Very well," he agreed, drowsily happy.

"Mrs. Sneath tells me the Duffys' baby is well again, Lyon. She's going to be just fine. They were able to get a doctor in to see her and pay for better food, it was your watch was responsible, I'm certain of it, though the landlord has been all that is discreet and of course neither Mrs. Sneath or Mrs. Duffy have a clue who their anonymous benefactor might be. And Mr. Duffy vows he's going to find permanent work, Mrs. Sneath says."

"Thank God." He meant it. About the baby. Though he had no faith at all in Mr. Duffy.

He opened his eyes.

The angle of the sun was such that he could see the shadow of Olivia's nipples against her sheer bodice, pushed up by her stays. Just inches away from his eyes.

The blood roared into his head and into his groin and he closed his eyes again and thought of Mrs. Sneath and he didn't hear a word Olivia said after that.

"Lyon?"

She must have asked him a question. She could have said a dozen things he hadn't heard.

He opened his eyes again.

She was gazing down at him with some concern.

"Olivia. Lie down beside me."

His voice sounded abstracted in his own ears. As if it was coming from under water.

He rolled from her lap and stretched out on his side, and she stretched out on her side next to him, and smiled softly.

For a moment that seemed suspended in time, they simply gazed into each other's eyes, untenably happy.

And then he tentatively reached out and softly trailed a finger along the tender inside of her arm, following the faint blue road of her vein. Her skin was a satiny miracle, glutting his nerve endings with pleasure. All the weeks of restraint had taught him to savor minutely. To be a connoisseur, and not a glutton. To see every part of her as infinitely desirable.

The day they made love, the earth would shake so hard new continents would form.

He skated his nails all the way along her arm and watched the gooseflesh rise. Her eyes went dark and huge and fascinated.

And then he leaned over and placed a hot kiss in the bend of her elbow.

She sighed and closed her eyes.

And then he moved his mouth to kiss the thumping pulse in that tender, satiny secret place beneath her ear.

And he watched her nipples go erect, and her hips shifted and she drew her knees up restlessly, hunger building.

He leaned over and covered her glorious pillow of a mouth with his, taking a slow, slow, deep, searching kiss, and she threaded her fingers through his hair, skating her nails softly over the back of his neck, which made him mad with lust and sent little rivers of flame through him. He moved his lips to her throat, and he dragged them lower, and lower, until he touched his tongue to that alluring shadow just above where her breasts swelled softly.

She drew in a sharp breath and arched, and he knew what she wanted, but he couldn't. He would have literally killed a man for the privilege of pulling down her bodice and closing his mouth over her nipple.

He didn't dare. He didn't trust himself. He knew the logic of lust, and once he saw her naked breast he would have convinced himself that mounting her was the next most reasonable step, and he knew Olivia was passionate enough to get lost in the moment.

And she trusted him. This was the thing he cherished the most.

And while it was faintly absurd, as if they needed to treat all the most delicious parts of their bodies as if they were injured, or covered in thorns and therefore to be avoided at all costs, it was also more erotic than anything he'd ever before experienced.

He was already shaking.

"Oh God, Liv," he whispered.

He slid his lips back up to hers, then moved them to her throat again, then traced her ear with his tongue until she whimpered softly, her body rippling. She sighed his name, beseeching. He pulled her body against his, and slid a hand down to her hip, and cupped it, pressing her hard against him, letting her feel his stiffening cock at the join of his legs. He thrust subtly against her, and her head went back on a gasp.

The lust was electric in the back of his throat.

She wrapped her arms around his head, and their lips met and parted, feasted and caressed, as they folded their bodies tightly together and side by side found a rhythm, a graceless, deliberate, grinding friction comprised of thrusting and circling hips that became faster, and harder, more painful, more exquisite.

Her breath was in tatters. "Lyon . . . Lyon, I . . . Lyon, *please* . . . Oh God . . ."

Oh, to feel her hands on his cock.

Or her mouth on his cock.

Her sweet, soft mouth on his cock.

It was this that made him thrust against her harder, more swiftly. And that was when she screamed softly, hoarsely, her release whipping her upward with its force, her fingers digging into his arms.

He went rigid then as his own release broke over him, wave after glorious wave of it. He heard her name in his voice, a tattered groan of raw pleasure.

And then they were floating in that ether of bliss that was the aftermath.

He closed his eyes, spent. She curled into his arms and their chests rose and fell in tandem.

And when he breathed, in came the lavender and sweetness and sweat that was Olivia, and it was inconceivable that he wouldn't wake like this every morning for the rest of his life.

He opened his eyes at last. To find her eyes still dark and dazed and dreamy, a soft smile curving her mouth. She was watching him.

He gave a short pained laugh. "Liv, my love. You may be the death of me."

She said nothing.

She knew this wasn't actually funny.

For either of them.

The lightness between them been usurped by this fraught hunger. It would only build and build upon itself the more they were together, and would only make them eventually hate each other if they couldn't fully satisfy it, or do something reckless—even more reckless than this—and regrettable.

But oh God, the pleasure while they were doing that regrettable thing would be unforgettable.

Possibly even worth it.

And that, as Lyon had said earlier, was a very dangerous way to think.

"I lie awake at night, Olivia, and all I think of is you," he murmured, his voice lulled, amazed. "And how I'd like to touch you, and where I'd like to touch you. Imagine what *this* is like with no clothes on."

"I do. Every night."

He closed his eyes and made a sound, half laugh, half groan. "You *are* killing me."

They held each other, and as that feverish desire ebbed for now, they were left to contemplate the fact that they were on the precipice of a change they simply could not avoid. And like any precipice, it was dangerous and alluring.

"I'll speak to my father tonight," he said finally.

It almost sounded like he was handing down a sentence.

She stopped breathing.

She gently pulled out of his arms and sat up, and folded her arms around her knees, tightly, and stared at him, biting her lip. Emotion sliced through her, some hybrid of joy and terror. Hope and foreboding were awfully similar.

"Truly, Lyon?"

He sat up abruptly, too.

"Yes."

"But . . . your father . . . what if—"

"Tonight," he insisted.

He made the word "tonight" sound synonymous with "forever."

And his code, after all, was to get what he wanted.

And then he kissed her, and any doubts and fears about ramifications bowed down to pleasure.

Tonight. There was nothing but infinite possibility in the word. It was the word that divided them from this moment and the rest of their lives.

While she was kissing him, it was easy to believe they would have everything they wanted, for how could destiny array itself against their happiness, despite what their families might think? What possible *sense* could there be in that?

Chapter 12

✤

LYON MADE HIS WAY home in a peculiar state of mind, or rather state of heart, split like the elm tree into equal portions of bliss and unease. A seam of hope ran hot and bright through him. He could not imagine a life in which he didn't lie in bed night after night for the rest of his life next to Olivia Eversea. An objection to their match would be like arguing in favor of a world without a sun.

And surely he could persuade his father of this. After all, he'd experienced more than one miracle in a span of months: he'd met and kissed and loved and was loved by Olivia Eversea. In light of this, even winning over Isaiah Redmond seemed possible. And yet Lyon was a Redmond, and his father's son. He'd been born with a sense of duty and destiny, and facing his father's certain censure was hardly something he relished.

So be it. He would happily endure whatever he needed to endure to make Olivia his.

As he walked, a gray front of clouds moved in and crowded out the last of the blue sky. There ought to be a rousing storm this evening.

Once home, he did a cursory knock of his boots in the entrance to shake off any dirt, and was five feet into the foyer when his father's voice floated out from the sitting room.

"Ah, here he is. Lyon. Where have you been?"

Lyon closed his eyes, cursed silently, then followed the voice.

He froze on the threshold of the room.

His entire family was arranged over the furniture on one side of the room, all wearing their best clothes and sporting their most impressive posture.

And Lady Arabella sat on the largest settee, a dark brown velvet.

She smiled when she saw him. And then blushed the shade of her dress, which was pale pink and trimmed in cream satin at the bodice. She was wedged between her parents, the Duke and Duchess of Hexford, who looked rather like sentries guarding a fragile artifact.

"Your Grace. Lady Hexford. Lady Arabella. What a pleasant surprise, indeed."

He took off his hat and bowed elegantly.

And when he did, an oak leaf clinging to his hair floated in an almost leisurely fashion down to the carpet.

Every eye in the room watched its progress to the carpet.

Then every eye went up to his face.

A funny little silence ensued.

"Forgive me," he said at last, evenly. "I was out riding."

"It certainly looks that way," his father said.

Which sounded very much like an innuendo.

Bloody hell. He hadn't had time to pause in a mirror, though he'd done a cursory review of his trouser front before he'd bid good evening to Olivia and was satisfied it was free of stains. He could blame a flush, sated expression on a vigorous hour or two on horseback, but the other men in the room had likely seen similar flushed, sated expressions in their own mirrors at one point or another. They would draw their own conclusions.

He doubted anyone would interrogate the groom about whether he had actually taken out his horse.

"The duke and duchess and their lovely daughter will be staying with us for a few days. Isn't that wonderful news?" his father pressed.

"Wonderful," Lyon parroted. And smiled the smile he'd perfected in London.

Another funny little silence ensued.

"Do forgive me," he said finally, "but I'm feeling a trifle at a disadvantage. I should like to take a moment to make myself more civilized and then rejoin you. Before I shed additional flora on the carpet."

This won him a collective merry laugh, and allowed him to retreat.

He could have sworn his brothers were watching him sympathetically.

THE EVENING WAS interminable, but his breeding was such that he endured it convincingly. He charmed over dinner. Arabella was seated at his right side, naturally, and he was attentive, armed with a stock of benign questions that could be safely asked and answered, such as did she enjoy the country? Did she think it might rain this evening? Yes, and yes, as it so happened. She seemed frightened of having opinions and never expounded, and pursuing exposition made him feel like an inquisitor, so he finally stopped.

After dinner, over brandy and cigars, he leaned back against the mantel next to his father, and asked,

"Do you have about thirty minutes or an hour to spare this evening? There's a matter of some importance I'd like to discuss with you."

His father didn't look at him. He was occupied with lighting a cigar. "Certainly, Lyon. I shall be up late reviewing some correspondence. About eleven o'clock?"

"Thank you."

Hi father turned his back on Lyon to say something to the duke, but Lyon scarcely heard the conversation after that. Eleven o'clock. The hour the rest of his life would begin.

A LITTLE LATER, everyone reconvened for a time and then dispersed, his brothers to shoot billiards, his father to chat with the duke, Violet to chat with his mother and the duchess. He was, by unsubtle collective design, left alone in a room with Arabella.

He spoke to her very gently. He couldn't seem to find the stamina to torture her with further questions. If there was a subject that could arouse her to animation, she was guarding the secret of it jealously.

But he was feeling tenderly toward her, because he was so in love with Olivia he felt charitable toward the entire world. He hoped Lady Arabella would find someone to love one day.

But she did seem eager to agree with everything he said, so he found himself conducting a monologue about gaslight for an hour, before he suggested she might be tired, another thing with which she gratefully agreed.

And by half past ten, a hush had settled over the house.

Lyon sat briefly in his favorite chair and peered

out for a glimpse of the Starry Plough. But a ceiling of gray clouds obscured all stars.

He wasn't much of a believer in omens.

And once he made a decision he never veered from it.

He sat suspended in a little hammock of time spanning his old life and the life he knew would be his by midnight tonight.

And so when the clock chimed eleven, he took himself upstairs to the Throne Room.

"THANK YOU FOR your time, Father."

"Of course, Lyon."

His father gestured to the chair and Lyon took it. His father, of course, sat at the great polished boat of a desk, so shining Lyon could see two Isaiah Redmonds in it, which was definitely one too many.

Lyon inhaled and then exhaled at length. He'd decided how to begin, and what to say, and had just opened his mouth to speak.

Isaiah casually reached into a drawer to retrieve something and laid something gently, very deliberately in the middle of his desk.

Lyon leaned forward to peer.

And froze.

All the sensation left his limbs.

It was his pocket watch.

His father then slowly leaned back in his chair. And watched him, waiting for this realization to fully sink in.

Lyon slowly raised his head and met his father's eyes.

His father was regarding him with the mild interest he might focus upon a chess opponent. It was, of course, all bluff.

He even gave his fingers an idle drum on the desk. As if everything was oh so inconsequential. As if the most profound and beautiful significant thing to ever happen to Lyon was merely another problem to dispense with in the hours after dinner and before bed.

The silence rang in Lyon's ears.

All of his senses felt scraped raw.

The tick of the clock was deafening.

"A pawnbroker recognized the initials," his father volunteered finally. "He knew only one such family in Sussex who would possess both such a fine time-piece and these particular initials. He told me it came to him through the landlord of the Duffys, and it was given to the landlord by Miss Olivia Eversea. He thought I should like it returned. And so, Lyon, I have purchased this watch twice over. Brandy?"

It was a moment before he could speak. "No thank you."

He hated the fact that his voice was hoarse.

His father splashed a little brandy into the bottom of a snifter, then cupped it in his hand.

"When did you purchase it?"

Lyon heard his own voice as if he were speaking underwater. He wanted badly to clear his throat, but didn't dare. Isaiah Redmond was a wolf. He could scent weakness, and he would capitalize on weakness, and methodically, slowly, tear his son limb from limb.

A cascade of new realizations about his father were arriving too late.

"Two weeks ago, Lyon."

Two weeks.

His father had held on to that watch for two weeks, waiting for just the right moment to spring it upon Lyon.

It was both fascinating and horrifying. In a peculiar way, he admired it immensely. It was an eminently effective way to knock Lyon off balance.

His father pushed the watch over to Lyon. "Here. Why don't you put it back in your pocket where it belongs, and we'll put the episode that prompted it behind you. We can begin to make marriage plans for you and Lady Arabella. It will be a magnificent match."

Lyon ignored it. "I don't want it, thank you. It was given to me as a gift, and I in turn gave it as a gift."

"To Olivia Eversea," his father mused.

"To Olivia Eversea."

He let the watch lay where it was.

His father furrowed his brow as if this was faintly interesting.

He took a sip of brandy and rolled it thoughtfully in his mouth.

Lyon waited. In a detached way—for detachment was the only safety in this circumstance, and his only hope of possibly outthinking his father—he was curious about what his father would say next.

"Son," he said. "Even the best of men occasionally thinks with his cock."

Lyon stopped breathing.

He surreptitiously, slowly released the breath.

Christ, that was shockingly well played.

"With all due respect, sir, I assure you I am not thinking with said appendage in these circumstances."

"Then I must assume no thinking at all took place."

The words were utterly contemptuous. As if Lyon was not his son. Or even a man deserving of any kind of respect.

"On the contrary, I've given more thought to the

matter I'd like to discuss this evening than anything else in my entire life."

"In your *entire* life," Isaiah repeated wonderingly, indulgently. "My goodness. All twenty-some odd years of it?"

"Yes."

"Then I have failed you completely."

"No, Father. You have not."

Another little silence.

"Very well, son. Why don't you apprise me of this 'matter,' as you call it?"

And all the while the watch lay there between them, a damning little centerpiece.

"I wish to marry Olivia Eversea."

The silence in the aftermath of those words, the words he'd thought since the moment he'd laid eyes on her in the ballroom, went on so long it seemed to develop a texture.

"And?" his father finally said.

"And because your respect and regard mean the world to me, and I have come to you to ask for your permission and blessing."

More well-nigh unendurable silence. The second hand traveled around the clock twice.

Lyon said nothing. It was a battle of wills.

"If you're wondering at the silence . . ." Isaiah said slowly, at last, "it's because I'm finding it difficult to find just the right words to convey my disappointment and disgust."

"I have faith that you will find them, Father."

Isaiah Redmond's eyebrow twitched upward, as if this interested him.

"And you want my . . . blessing, do you?" It was a detached sort of curiosity, as if Lyon had lost his mind utterly and Isaiah needed to find a new way to communicate with him.

"Yes."

His father was very, very good at whatever this was.

"Have you impregnated the girl?"

An ugly, goading word. It was part of what Lyon knew would now be a relentless strategy to diminish and degrade him, pummel him, break him down, until Lyon confused his own will his father's; saw his love affair as callow, sordid, silly, ephemeral; and did exactly as his father wanted.

Unfortunately for Isaiah Redmond, the apple really *didn't* fall far from the tree.

Lyon's will was very like his father's.

Absolutely immovable.

And when Lyon loved, it was forever.

"Of course I have not, as you say, impregnated the girl. She's very well-bred, as am I."

Another pause.

"Does her . . . Do her parents know of your intentions?"

An interesting hesitation there.

His father had tried to make the question idle, and had failed.

That catch in his voice was revealing.

And suddenly Lyon knew the suspicions he'd had for years were confirmed.

"No," Lyon said.

His father nodded once. He seemed almost relieved.

"If she isn't pregnant, then why in God's name do you want to marry this girl when you could marry the daughter of a *duke*?"

"Her name is Olivia," he explained patiently, enunciating each word painstakingly. "And I want to marry her because I am in love with her."

His father's face spasmed in contempt. "In *love*." He spat the word with scorching incredulity.

The muscles banding Lyon's stomach tensed as if someone had thrust a torch into his face. And yet he was proud that he didn't even blink.

"Yes."

"In *love*, as you say, with a woman you respect so thoroughly that you sneaked about with her for months, perhaps rutting with her in the woods now and again. I do wonder what this says about the young woman's character. And you would throw your brilliant future and your *family's honor* away for a girl like this?"

Rutting with her in the woods?

Lyon's shock must have shown.

"You were seen pawing *someone*, Lyon. Some weeks ago."

"I must request that you not in any way impugn Miss Eversea's character, which is unassailable, and her family is as fine as ours."

His father gave a short laugh, then sighed. "Oh, son. You should hear yourself."

"And I should think you'd admire stealth and strategy, Father. After all, I learned it from a man who repurchased a pocket watch and kept it for two weeks, all the while apparently spying on me, waiting for just the perfect moment to produce it."

He wasn't helping his cause. His father had more practice, after all, and Lyon's temper was beginning to burn through the fabric of his control.

And yet he had the satisfaction of seeing Isaiah go still.

How about that, he'd managed to surprise his father.

"Son," he said with insufferable pity. "You were hardly stealthy. You might as well have hung a sign around your neck."

And just like that, the gauze was ripped away.

And Lyon could feel the hot color pour into his cheeks.

Of course they weren't stealthy. Of course he'd walked about in a haze of happiness and torment. Distracted, happier than he ought to be, absent for mysterious hours of time, remaining in Pennyroyal Green where the diversions consisted primarily of the pub and the bookstore, outside of hunting season. Of course his valet had in all likelihood seen his stained shirttails. And of course someone had likely seen him, at least from a distance, before he had the wisdom or the lunacy to take Olivia into that clearing. They had thought they were careful.

How could anyone who was as in love as they were be discreet enough? It in all likelihood radiated from the two of them like beacons.

He loathed himself for not doing a better job of protecting her.

"Then the sign would have read, 'I am happy for the first time in my life,'" he said valiantly.

Isaiah leaned back in his chair and studied him again.

"You are not the man I thought you were, Lyon." He said this almost thoughtfully.

"No," Lyon agreed. "Thankfully, I am not."

"No," his father continued as if he hadn't spoken. "You are a *fool*."

The volume of that sentence escalated until "fool" was spat like a dart.

Lyon didn't flinch.

"If you pursue your . . . Why don't we call it 'association'? A better word than it deserves, surely . . . with Miss Olivia Eversea against my wishes under any circumstances, you will immediately be cut off from all Redmond funds. You will no longer be welcome under this roof, and you will be forbidden contact with your brothers and sister. I will ensure you will never be received in proper company again, or welcome in any clubs in all of England."

Lyon stopped breathing.

He surreptitiously pressed a palm against his thigh, as if to brace himself against the hard landing of a long, long fall.

Just like that. His punishment for simply loving one woman was to be denied everything else he loved. Forever.

Oddly, it wasn't entirely unexpected. But hearing it conjured desolation that was like looking down into an abyss. No Miles, no Jonathan, no Violet. Sundered, like that.

"If you *wish* to maintain ties with your family and fortune, you now have two choices. Beginning tomorrow, you will either go to the continent and stay for one year, you will do the business of the Mercury Club, and when you return you will marry appropriately. In this way we can mitigate any damage to your reputation, and you may one day restore yourself to my good graces. Or you can propose to Lady Arabella this week and be married next spring."

Lyon abandoned strategy and pride.

"Father . . . I hope you know I have always valued your love and respect above all things. I have strived my entire life to make you proud."

His father remained coldly silent.

"I love Olivia." He tried to keep his voice even, but there was the slightest hint of a break on her name. "And she loves me. I know you could come to love her, too, if you knew her. It's . . . I swear to you if . . . Surely you were once in love . . ."

He knew this was tantamount to the lamb leaping for the knife, revealing this vulnerability. But *he* still had a heart. He would prefer to be honest than to gain the most important thing in the world to him through strategy, which was clearly what ran in his father's veins instead of blood.

Somewhere behind that cold facade was a man who had taught his sons to fish and hunt and swim and ride. Who had praised their accomplishments, commiserated with their failures. Who had carried him on his shoulders, and been strict but fair, thoughtful and even amusing, always an object of fear, but also of admiration and respect. Who, Lyon was certain, loved them.

If only Lyon had known how conditional all of this paternal love apparently was.

"Father, I swear to you, I didn't have a choice."

"For God's sake, *of course you had a bloody choice!*"

Isaiah was shouting now. He was all fury.

And Lyon was absolutely motionless.

Just like that.

He was beyond fear. Beyond anger.

He'd made his decision.

And he was grateful now that he possessed precisely the weapon that would bring his father to his knees.

"All of this. All of this because *you* made the wrong decision," Lyon said softly.

Isaiah hesitated. "What in God's name are you talking about?"

"I am aware that you watch the back of Mrs. Eversea's head in church every Sunday, rather than the vicar."

He'd just given voice to a truth so buried that no one who suspected dared speak it.

Lyon instinctively knew it was a brutal thing to say, and he welcomed it as a weapon.

He had the sublime, visceral satisfaction of watching scarlet slowly flood his father's cheeks.

So this, at last, was his father's weakness.

Isolde Eversea. Another man's wife.

His father had once had a heart. He knew *all* about love.

And he had burned his own love down to the ground many years ago by marrying the wrong woman.

"Ah," Lyon said softly. "I believe I understand now. You didn't have the courage to fight for the woman you loved. You made the wrong choice. And look at you. Look at what you've become."

Lyon's head went back hard.

It was a moment before he fully realized he'd been struck.

He tasted blood, coppery in his mouth.

And in seconds, the initial numbness gave way to burn in the shape of his father's handprint.

It was the last mark Isaiah Redmond would ever leave on him.

Lyon stood up slowly.

His father stared at him, eyes almost unseeing, splotches of vivid color high on his face.

And Lyon could have sworn he saw fear there, too.

Good.

And Lyon turned on his heel and was gone.

It was the last his father ever saw of him.

Chapter 13

❧

WHEN THE FIRST PEBBLE hit her window, Olivia thought perhaps it had begun to hail. The little painted porcelain clock next to her bed said it was a quarter past one in the morning.

The cold was fierce and the sky was a solid, sullen shade of slate when she'd pulled her curtains closed for the evening.

The color of dread.

Surely it could also be the color of hope? Surely good things had happened on other rainy days throughout history?

But the cold outside had leached from the room whatever heat had managed to soak into the floors, and not even her low-burning fire could penetrate it. It was merciless and thorough, as if it had a point to make.

The first little click was followed by another.

Followed by a scatter of more.

It wasn't how hail behaved, and insects didn't go about dashing themselves to death on windows on freezing Sussex nights.

She slipped out of bed, pushed her feet into slippers, and reached for a pelisse. Fur-lined, an elegant, much-loved birthday gift from her parents.

Every time she shoved her arms into its furry embrace she was reminded of how loved and fortunate she was.

She opened her window a crack. And peered down. It was nearly black in the garden, but she could make out the glow of one of the stone benches scattered about the ground.

Her breath caught when she saw the outline of a man, his face tipped up at her window.

Lyon!

"Olivia, come down."

"What are you *doing*? It's freezing!"

"You must come down at *once*."

She'd never heard that tone in his voice. Urgency and desperation and command.

She had the presence of mind to light and seize a little lamp before she bolted down the stairs, skidding a little on the way. The house was absolutely silent and dark, but every shadow and corner of it was familiar, and she likely could have done it with her eyes closed.

She darted through the kitchen and bolted out the door. She could feel the cold through her slippers.

She ran to him.

He seized her by her arms. "Liv. Run away with me, Olivia. We can go tonight and be in Scotland inside of two days, and then we can be married."

Her breath left her in a shocked gust.

"Gretna Green," he continued in a feverish rush. "We can leave tonight, be there in two days, and then we—"

"Lyon, have you been drinking?"

"No," he said firmly, as he shook out of his overcoat and draped it over her, then pulled her close to him, so she could benefit from whatever heat remained in his body. But he was vibrating with a suppressed fury that frightened her. "I have never been more clear in my entire life."

"The lamp," she rasped.

He took it from and leaned over to place it on the bench.

And as he did it illuminated his face.

She gasped.

"Lyon, you've blood . . . There's blood . . ."

He touched the corner of his mouth. "I'm sorry. I came straight here from . . ."

He stopped abruptly.

She thrust her hands into his coat pocket and came out with the handkerchief she knew would be there.

"Oh, Lyon." She tenderly, gingerly touched it to the corner of his mouth. His beautiful, beloved mouth. He didn't even wince. "How did you . . ."

And then realization sank through her with guillotine brutality.

"He hit you."

She had her answer when he said nothing.

And a red haze of rage, like nothing she'd ever before experienced, moved over her eyes.

How dare, how dare *anyone* hurt him?

His face was white and tense in the lamplight, but she still saw a flicker of shame. An expression that never, ever should have shadowed Lyon Redmond's face.

Her heart cracked, and in poured terror that made her shiver, and that's when the sky broke open and the rain began to fall.

This was the end. Of everything.

She suddenly knew it with absolute certainty.

How on earth could she have prepared for this? For the ghastly pain that she knew was about to follow and swallow her whole.

His voice was steady, but there was an abstracted, stunned quality to it.

"I told him that I wished to marry you. And I asked for his understanding and his blessing and told him he would grow to love you, too, for who wouldn't?"

"And he hit you."

"He hit me for another reason altogether, but the two events were related, yes."

"Tell me why he hit you."

"I can't."

He said this in a way that brooked no argument. She knew quite clearly that he would not tell her.

She couldn't bear picturing it. Proud, clever, bold Lyon laying his tender heart bare to his cold father. Suddenly their love seemed as fragile as the Duffys' sickly baby.

How sordid it must have sounded to his father, the man who could not abide weakness, the man who needed always to be in control. A secret love affair, this sudden engagement request. Callow, foolish, careless. How could any words capture the grandeur and torment and sweetness and *rightness* of it? Let alone the careful, formal ones Lyon would have been forced to use before the merciless green gaze of his father. How little of consequence the two of them must seem to someone who owned not only much of England, like her own father, but essentially owned his son, too, and was accustomed to making everyone do precisely what he wanted.

"And then?" she said hoarsely.

"Oh, he forbade a match." He sounded almost mordantly cheery. "He said he would cut me off from all funds and every member of my family, and ensure I would never be received in any decent home or club ever again."

The guillotine, indeed.

And Isaiah Redmond could do it, too.

"And he *hit* you. Because of . . . me?"

"Not because of you. Because of me. I've been hit before, Liv," He sounded almost reasonable, and there was a hint of black humor in it. "Not by him, of course. But I'm male. It's difficult to avoid hitting and being hit on the way to manhood. It's all part of it."

"But it's different when you can't defend yourself."

He said nothing because he knew she was right: Lyon would never in a million years strike his father.

Then again, he was a different man from his father.

And the fear iced her limbs and a surge of panic that threatened to become anger. Fear that he was not different enough, because he had not been allowed to be.

"P-Perhaps . . . perhaps your father simply needs a little more time . . . perhaps he reacted badly because he was surprised . . . perhaps . . ."

"Oh, my father was not surprised," Lyon said with bitter irony.

And now her cheeks were ablaze.

Of course. Love's blindness had clearly extended to the lovers themselves. People had noticed something was different; how could they not have?

Olivia had been walking about in a radiant haze for months now. And her family, delicately, had attempted to point it out. To warn her.

Perhaps even Mrs. Sneath knew.

"Olivia, I've been given two choices: he's going to send me to the continent tomorrow, or I'm to propose to Lady Arabella this week. So you see, don't you, that you must come with me tonight. We'll leave Sussex, marry, and make our own life. It will be heaven, Liv."

She was speechless. The roil of emotions he always caused stormed through her.

And it was this perhaps that brought home to her the reality of their circumstance, which was dire. Lyon had been exquisitely bred, and could ride and shoot and fence and dance and charm. He was brilliant and gifted. He was her very heart.

But she was in love with a man whose father hit him simply because he *could*.

And could cut off his allowance.

She knew her silence was damning.

"You *must* come with me. You must trust me to take care of you, Liv. Will you trust me?"

She stiffened in his arms.

"Liv?"

And then he stiffened, too.

"What the devil are you afraid of?" His voice was low and taut. It emerged as an accusation.

With a tinge of fear.

As usual, he'd looked right into the heart of the matter: he knew she was afraid.

He likely knew what he was asking was utterly unreasonable, but there was nothing else he could do.

And Lyon, as he'd told her, was a man who got what he wanted.

She was terrified of losing him. But she'd never anticipated needing to abandon everyone else she loved without warning, especially since she'd only lately had all of her brothers back. And suddenly she hated him as much as she loved him for forcing her to make this decision, now, in the pouring rain, in the dark.

"What am I *afraid* of? You're asking me to leave everything and everyone I know behind right now.

But how on earth would we survive? What kind of life will we have?"

"I *will* take care of you, Liv."

He was so certain she almost capitulated.

But fear had momentum.

"*How?* What way? What on earth do you know how to do? Shall I go out to work? How on earth will we live on nothing at all? I've seen how the Duffys live, Lyon, and it's hardly life at all. If they loved each other ever, it was killed long ago."

"If you think for a *moment* that will be our fate, you don't know me at all." And now he was coldly angry.

"But I *do* know you. I do. And you . . . you're your father's *creature*."

He froze.

"How can you say that?" he said hoarsely.

Panic was crescendoing. She hated herself for half believing her hateful words. She hated him for not recognizing how *afraid* she was now. For not realizing that she was wholly unprepared to abandon her family. If only she'd had time to *think*.

She wanted to cling to him and comfort him and be comforted. But there was no comfort to be had anymore, from anyone.

"What else do you know how to do?" she said furiously. "You've invested your money with the Mercury Club. If he cuts off all resources, how will we survive? What can you actually *do*?"

She was aware that she was hurting him but she couldn't help herself. She heard her own shrill, cruel, frightened voice as if it belonged to someone else entirely. She only now fully understood that this was what had given the serrated edge of sweetness to their every moment together: that it was impossible. It had always been impossible.

In the long silence that followed, neither of them noticed the rain. He didn't deny any of it.

"What if loving you is what I do best?"

He managed to measure out the words calmly, laying them before her one at a time. But she could hear the anguished dignity thrumming in each one.

It sounded like a test.

She closed her eyes.

Damn him.

How she loved him. And entwined with her love was fear that she didn't think she deserved someone who loved as bravely as he did. She was furious with herself and with him for causing each other so much pain.

She opened her eyes. She looked at him, standing in the rain, amid the wreckage of their dreams, and said:

"Then I pity you."

He jerked. As surely as if she'd sunk a blade right into his heart.

And then . . . and then she'd never seen anyone so still.

His face was ghost-white even in the lamplight.

She shook his coat from her shoulders and seized the lamp and then she ran back into the house, her feet skidding along the wet ground, as if fleeing the scene of a murder.

It might as well have been her own.

Chapter 14

❧

One month before the wedding . . .

MADEMOISELLE LILETTE HAD BEEN thrilled to be invited to be Olivia's traveling companion for her trip to Plymouth. Madame Marceau was able to spare her—in another stroke of serendipity, the modiste who had disappeared had reappeared, begging for her job back if only for a few weeks just when Madame Marceau needed her most—and she relented.

And so Olivia and Mademoiselle Lilette set out for Plymouth.

Plymouth was about a day and a half away from London by stage. Mademoiselle turned out to be the perfect traveling companion—resilient, uncomplaining, not a prattler.

The farther away from London they went, the cheerier Olivia got. Interestingly, the farther away from London they went, the quieter and more tense, more watchful and taciturn, the usually loquacious Mademoiselle Lilette became.

"Are you nervous about meeting Mrs. More?"

Olivia asked her. "I'm a bit nervous. I've been such an admirer of hers for so long."

"*Oui*," Mademoiselle Lilette said shortly "I am nervous."

MRS. MORE WAS coming by way of Bristol, and they had arranged to meet her at an inn called the Hungry Gull near the harbor in Plymouth, then travel on with her to the home of their hosts via a much better-sprung and sweeter-smelling convey-ance than the stage, according to the message they'd received from her.

It was well after midnight by the time they ar-rived at the inn. Olivia and Mademoiselle Lilette gratefully stretched their legs and inhaled. The air was cold and briny and pungent with tar. A thrilling smell. The smell of adventure, she'd always thought. Olivia inhaled great draughts of it, as if she could save it for later.

The masts of ships rose tall and shadowy against the blue-black sky, their sails furled and quiet for now.

Given that the hour was late, they were surprised to find the innkeeper remarkably alert and waiting for them inside. He was, in fact, all but pacing.

The taproom was empty, but clean and warm, and a lively fire still burned. All other guests of the inn must have gone up to bed.

He was plump and brisk and polite. "You must be Miss Eversea and her companion! Welcome, welcome. Mrs. More has only just arrived as well, and she would have joined you for a bit of a repast here—we do still have a bit of stew in the pot from dinner—but her knees aren't what they once were. She has asked if you would mind terribly going up to her room when you arrived, so that you all can dine together there. 'Tis the third one on the left once you reach the top of the stairs. We'll bring up your trunks to your room for you."

"Thank you so much, sir," Olivia said, and fished about in her reticule for a few pence.

He waved them away. "'Tis me job."

Olivia untied her bonnet and gratefully rubbed at her bare neck. She smoothed her palms against her skirt. Her heart was hammering with anticipation. She turned to Mademoiselle Lilette, brows raised.

"Well, shall we?"

"*Oui, mais bien sûr,*" Mademoiselle Lilette answered tersely.

Olivia bounded up the stairs, invigorated by the prospect of good intelligent company, Mademoiselle Lilette right on her heels.

The third door on the left was ajar a few inches.

She looked back at Mademoiselle Lilette, who shrugged.

"Mrs. More?" Olivia said tentatively.

There was no reply.

Now she was concerned. Mrs. More was an elderly woman, and she perhaps had nodded off, or worse, expired, or perhaps she'd fallen, and was injured.

"We best look inside," she whispered to Mademoiselle Lilette, who simply nodded.

Olivia gave the door a little push to open it farther.

The small dim room seemed comprised of a leaping fire and heat and not much else. A rocking chair, empty and still, was positioned in front of the fire. A bureau was in the corner, and a narrow bed was against the wall.

Mrs. More was nowhere in sight.

Mademoiselle Lilette hovered in the doorway, as if reluctant to enter.

Olivia took another step into the room.

And then another.

She gave a start. Then froze, clapped her hand over her heart.

The short hair on the back of her neck began to prickle, uneasily.

For a man was standing in the corner, so motionless she might have mistaken him for furniture. The firelight reflected off the gleaming toes of his boots gave him away.

Those were the toes of a gentleman of significant fortune. She would have wagered everything on it.

She whirled around.

But Mademoiselle Lilette was standing fully in the doorway.

For all the world as if she was blocking it now.

Olivia swiveled around again.

The man remained perfectly still. But something about the shape of him . . . Her scalp tingled. It was a very primal thing, and she felt it at the base of her spine. It did interesting things to her breathing.

She cleared her throat.

"I beg your pardon . . . I'm so sorry to intrude . . . I was told I should wait for Mrs. More in this . . . in this room. Perhaps I've the wrong room . . ."

Her words trailed like vapor when the man slowly straightened to his full height and took a slow step forward.

Into the firelight.

Realization penetrated. Rather like an arrow.

She stopped breathing.

Her lips parted.

And finally a tiny, arid sound emerged. Part raw pain, part shock.

"Liv."

Quiet. Gruff.

His voice.

Nothing.

Nothing could have prepared her to hear her name, in his voice, again.

She couldn't move.

Her mouth parted again. But absorbing the impact of him had required all of her capacities. She couldn't say a word.

Instead she began to tremble.

He stepped toward her swiftly. And it was so very him, that instinct to protect and to shelter her, that her knees nearly buckled.

But he stopped himself and remained about four feet away from her.

As if she was flammable, or might be holding a broadsword.

She remained precisely where she was, too.

And neither of them said a word.

But now he was lit only by leaping firelight. His face was all amber and shadows, the hollows, the angles, hard clean line of his jaw, the rise of cheekbones. The same. The beloved, beautiful face was the same. It hurt, it hurt, and it was glorious to see it.

And yet.

And yet there was an air of both implacability and impatience about him, as palpable as the heat from the fire. He'd always been arrogant, but this was different. This was authority. As if the experiences he'd had since he'd left were layered down like rock strata and he was now immovable.

The set of his shoulders—broader now, a distinct horizontal shelf tapering down into his lean torso—called to mind something feral. A wolf, perhaps.

That sizzle along her nerve endings at the mere sight of him reminded her of how little she'd felt anything at all since he'd gone.

The way his clothes fit, their quality . . . it was clear they were staggeringly expensive. He almost looked as though he could have stepped out of White's an hour or so ago.

But something was different.

His hair, black and always prone to waving, was long enough to be pulled back into a short queue. And his face was sun-browned.

It made his eyes so.

Damned.

Blue.

And when he suddenly became brilliant and convex she realized her own eyes were welling with tears.

He produced a handkerchief with magical immediacy and thrust it out.

Their hands did not touch when she took it. Instantly, an old reflex, she ran her thumb over the corner, and there they were: "LAJR."

Lyon Arthur James Redmond.

"It's shock. That's all. Just surprise." She sounded remarkably calm in her own ears, but she might have been hearing someone else speaking through glass.

So those were going to be the first words she said to Lyon Redmond after all these years. *It's shock. That's all. Just surprise.*

Mundane and not at all true.

"Is that so? Are you certain those aren't tears of joy?"

He'd never spoken to her in that tone before. All dark irony.

He'd never spoken to her with anything other than affection.

"Humans either faint or weep when shocked. If we emitted a lavender scent instead I'm certain I would have done that."

He laughed at that, sounding startled, because who wouldn't? It was an absolutely ridiculous thing to say.

That laugh.

The sound she'd once loved more than any other sound in the world.

And suddenly all of it . . . her name spoken in that quick, gruff voice, his handkerchief with his initials in the corner that she used to run her thumb over and over, because they were precious because they were his . . . all the things that were the same about him and the things that were different about him . . .

All of it, *all* of it made her blackly furious.

She thrust the handkerchief back at him, because she wanted to kick him.

He took it with a surprised grunt.

Good God, his abdomen was hard as a rock.

He was motionless a moment, staring down at the handkerchief as if she had indeed shoved a sword in.

And then he looked up at her and folded it neatly, deliberately, and placed it back in his pocket.

As if to demonstrate his total composure in the face of her loss of it.

And then he looked up slowly and studied her. Almost dispassionately. Measuring her as he would an opponent.

She wondered if he knew how much he looked like his father when he did that.

Once she could all but read his every emotion. But that was because he'd trusted her. Somehow over the years Lyon had learned cold, hard inscrutability, that air of looking at someone through a magnifying glass.

She supposed she had herself partially to thank for that, too.

She stood and withstood his scrutiny, wondering what he saw.

How had she changed, or had she?

He'd once traced her lips with a single finger, as if he wanted to imprint the memory of her on his soul.

Perhaps since he'd left, a dozen other women had diluted the memory of her.

Her shoulder twitched, as if it sensed her intention to whirl on her heels and flee.

But she couldn't seem to complete the motion any more than a tree could uproot itself and take a stroll across the Sussex downs.

He seemed to sense her impulse to flee.

"Olivia."

It was her name, all right, but it was another tone she'd never before heard him use. No ardor, no cajoling, no playfulness, no tenderness.

It was quite distinctly a command.

Very nearly a warning.

And this was when sense finally jostled aside the confusing tide of dammed emotion: he might have been torturously vivid in her memories and dreams.

But he was, in fact, a stranger now.

And he didn't like her.

"Yes?" she said. She attempted to mimic his cool tone. She was still shaking. She hid her trembling hands in her skirt.

"I should like to talk with you at some length. I think perhaps we have some unfinished business."

Well, this was unassailably true.

Still, she wasn't certain how to reply.

"Perhaps you have one or two things you'd like say to me?" A glimmer of mordant humor there. Still, the prevailing tone was detached irony.

"Perhaps," she managed. Her voice was still a thread.

"Then perhaps you'll agree to a conversation. But not here. I'd like to conduct it on my ship."

"On your *ship*?"

"Yes," he said. Almost impatiently.

"Your . . . ship."

"Yes."

The arrogant bastard didn't bother to explain why on earth he would have a *ship*.

"So . . . Mrs. More isn't here at all."

"No." There was a flicker of something like intolerable amusement in that word.

"So you lied. And tricked me."

"Yes."

He was almost brutally monosyllabic and completely unapologetic.

And that's when she fully understood:

Lyon was furious, too.

Blackly, coldly furious.

And somehow, perversely, this heartened her. It was better than that impassivity.

She looked into his face, searching for some clue as to who he was now. There was no evidence of the young man she'd last seen standing as motionless as the dead, his face leached of color, the rain plastering his hair to his face and his shirt to his chest because he'd given his coat to her.

"One must have a code, as you once said to me, Olivia. And while I prefer not to lie, I also prefer to get what I want. And what I wanted was to speak privately to you without anyone else knowing. And I knew just how to do it."

Every word as coldly delivered as if she was up before a magistrate.

Her own fury ramped and then wavered in the face of his, which was as palpable as a wall.

It wasn't as though he didn't have the right to his.

"On your ship." She matched his irony.

"On my ship."

"You couldn't have . . ." Her voice was faint again.

She didn't finish the sentence because she already knew the answer.

"What? Called upon your father, hat in hand? Sent flowers? Shouted objections from the church congregation while they read your banns Sunday after Sunday? No, Olivia. I won't be doing that. But I do want to speak to you. If you are agreeable to this, it will be on my ship. And it will be now, or never."

Now or never.

Just like that night five years ago, when he'd forced her to decide her future in one minute in the pouring rain, in the dark.

This coldly, unnervingly confident man was the same Lyon.

And yet he was not.

That impulse to comfort her. Her name in his voice. Gruff with emotion. She recognized those.

Were all of those simply reflexes born of old memories?

My heart, he'd once called her. *My love.*

She'd been his heart. And he'd been hers.

And he'd left her without a heart when he disappeared.

Perhaps now she could get it back. Along with the whole of her life.

"It's docked very near. You'll be escorted safely. It's a short enough walk. You're free of harm from me and, I assure, you, from any cutthroats or other unsavory personages. And it must be now."

That's when she saw the sword at his hip beneath that beautiful coat.

He was wearing a *sword*. The way any other man would wear a watch fob.

She blinked, and felt another little prickle of warning.

Who was he now?

What was he now?

God help her, she wanted to know.

"Very well," she said. "I'll go."

Chapter 15

H~E DIDN'T SAY,~ "T~HANK~ you."

He simply nodded shortly in acknowledgment, then made a mockingly elegant sweeping motion with his arm. "After you."

She whipped around and all but fled down the stairs, her footsteps echoing.

Mademoiselle Lilette, whom she'd only now remembered, was waiting on the stairs.

"Thank you, Digby," he said shortly to her, as if she were a subaltern who'd completed an assignment.

Digby?

Olivia's head whipped around.

Mademoiselle Lilette was staring straight ahead. For all the world as if she were a soldier and Lyon was the commander.

As for the innkeeper, he was nowhere to be seen.

Olivia gave a start when a phalanx of men silently appeared from the night and fell into step with them, and Mademoiselle Lilette joined them.

The gray dawn light glinted off the swords swinging at their hips.

She doubted they were armed only with swords. These were trained men, disciplined and deadly. That much was clear.

But they weren't soldiers.

They looked like mercenaries.

She was politely, matter-of-factly helped into a boat by men who climbed in after her, and rowed out over an inky black sea that gently moved and heaved.

Lyon sat in the prow, ahead of her, like he had in church so many years ago.

He did not look back.

She'd never before been aboard a ship, and the strange, elegant, imposing bulk of it was fascinating. She craned her head and then gave a start as she met the downturned, shadowy gaze of a man in the crow's nest.

"If you'll come with me, Olivia," Lyon said politely. "You can wait for me in this cabin while I attend to a brief bit of business."

Only an insane woman would consent to follow him below deck.

But in for a penny, in for a pound.

She followed him down a steep flight of stairs, though a narrow passage, to what were clearly sleeping quarters.

He pushed open the door of a cabin, and waved her in.

"It's safest if you wait for me here. Please don't leave. I've some business to attend to on deck and I'll return . . . apace."

He'd chosen that word deliberately, she was certain.

It was very nearly a monk's cell of a room. But it was carpeted, if not in Savonnerie, then something fine and Persian in origin, and the bed, nailed to the floor, looked clean and was crisply made with a blue woolen counterpane. A little desk with an unlit oil lamp sitting atop it was pushed against one wall, and a map of the Mediterranean was pinned above it.

Pinned across from that was a print from "The Legend of Lyon Redmond" collection.

The one of him in the cannibal pot, his mouth a little "O" of alarm.

She whipped her head toward him, astonished.

Humor briefly glimmered about his mouth. "I thought it was funny."

He closed the door and left.

She leaped up and tested the cabin door. She wasn't locked in.

And so she decided to stay where she was, as ordered, because she could think of no other options.

This wasn't where Lyon slept. Somehow she thought she would have known it. There was nothing of him in here. No shaving soap or brushes, no books, no trunk of clothes. It was clearly a cabin for guests.

And apart from pacing restlessly, which was one of her options, the other was to sit and wait. Perhaps pray.

Perhaps remember.

She sat on the edge of the bed. She hadn't a prayer of sleeping, but while her mind had never been more alive, her limbs were weary as the devil.

She leaned back and closed her eyes. Lyon. She thought of the last time she'd opened them to see him next to her. In that clearing, on the heels of new and shattering pleasure, beneath his hands, against his body.

Her eyes snapped open. She did *not* want to dwell on that now.

And then she frowned.

She was motionless. But she thought perhaps she was dreaming.

And then she saw the chair ever so slightly shift.

The ship was moving.

The bloody ship was moving!

She leaped to her feet and bolted out the door with a slam, raced through the passage, clambering, skirts hiked in her hands, up the stairs to the deck.

She whipped her head about frantically. The sails were full and the dock was already alarmingly farther behind them.

She found Lyon instantly, speaking to a member of his crew.

He saw her and went still, and said a single word to the man he was speaking with. It looked like "Go."

The man did just that, and rather rapidly.

He strode over to her. "I thought I told you it was safest to remain where you were."

"But . . . the ship is moving." As if it was something they had accidentally overlooked, and could now rectify.

"Yes."

"The ship is *moving*. Away from the harbor." Her voice escalated in disbelief.

"Yes," he said, sounding bored. He glanced skyward, the way one might look at a clock for time, then at the rigging, and he nodded to a man at the wheel, some secret signal, affirmation of some sort.

"You're . . . leaving me with me aboard?"

"Yes."

"I . . . *you* . . ."

He simply regarded her with a sort of insufferable patience and one eyebrow cocked, as if waiting for a slow child to finish a sentence.

"You can't . . . My God . . . Lyon . . . you can't . . ."

"Leave with you aboard?" He completed. "Well, clearly I can."

She was speechless.

"Are you kidnapping me? Will I be held for ransom?"

He snorted derision at that.

Her words abandoned her yet again. It was so utterly astounding. The temerity was shocking and, yes, rather piratical.

She stared at him.

"Yes?" he prompted mildly.

"I'll scream," she tried. They were, after all, still within earshot, more or less, of the dock.

"I wouldn't."

He said this so simply and grimly that she decided against it immediately.

And all of these quite terrifying and efficient-looking men obviously considered him their commander.

And one woman. Digby. Formerly known as Mademoiselle Lilette, aka that bloody traitor.

"What sort of madman *abducts* someone?" She almost spluttered it.

Then again, perhaps she ought not say those sorts of things to a madman.

And he didn't look at all mad. She'd in fact seldom seen anyone look quite so lucid.

"May I point out that you were invited, and then voluntarily boarded, this ship?"

"But I never thought you'd . . . You didn't say you would . . ."

"You used to be infinitely quicker, Olivia. Perhaps you're keeping slower company these days."

"You never said the ship would be *sailing*."

"Funny, isn't it, that the things we don't say can become more important than the things we do say."

She fell abruptly silent.

He evenly held her gaze, as they were both hurtled back to a night in Pennyroyal Green.

"You will be returned to London in a week or so, unharmed. And no one will know where you were." His voice was gentler now.

Olivia covered her face with her hands to her cheeks, then brought them down with some effort and shook her head with incredulity.

She began pacing the railing like a caged animal. Back and forth. Back and forth.

Lyon watched her. If she had any notion to fling herself over, he'd snatch her back easily enough. He could likely pick her up in one hand by her scruff.

It made him strangely restless and angry.

She was too thin. The fine bones of her lovely, lovely face were etched more sharply, so that she looked like something brittle and porcelain a maiden aunt might keep on the mantel.

She finally stopped pacing and whirled on him.

Still. And after all these years. The muscles of his stomach *still* tightened when he looked at her. Bracing to withstand her beauty, or whatever elemental thing about her that made him feel that sweet panic of need.

She whirled on him. "You've lost your mind. You're a . . . you . . . you . . ."

"Before you choose that next word, you might wish to have a care how you address me. After all, you don't know who I am anymore. Or who I've become. If I'm a madman, I might do anything, after all. I've grown accustomed to simply taking what I want."

"Try 'taking' anything from me, and you may lose an eye."

"Don't flatter yourself. All I *want* is a reckoning."

She fell abruptly silent again.

They locked eyes.

And before his gaze, he watched acceptance and acquiescence set in, and something like peace.

And guilt, too.

She knew precisely what he meant.

Ah, that was Olivia. She had a quicksilver intelligence. And her sense of fairness was unshakable.

He'd never needed to explain anything to her. He'd all but forgotten what a luxury this was, and how it felt. The world had simply felt larger and safer and kinder with her. It had made infinitely more sense, and it had never been the same without her.

She was biting her lip thoughtfully.

He'd bitten that lip before, too. Softly, softly, as her hands had wound in his hair, as they'd discovered ways to give and take pleasure from each other.

A gull screamed into the silence.

The ship moved inexorably on.

"A week, Olivia," he said, more quietly.

She gave her head a rough shake. "How did you . . . Where have you . . . What have you . . ."

He held up a hand. "Later."

She literally growled.

"You *planned* all of this."

"Yes," he said simply. "Of course I did."

She pulled her pelisse more tightly around her shoulders.

He contemplated shaking off his coat and draping it over her, and he once would have done it reflexively.

Now it seemed too intimate an act.

But even now he couldn't bear for her to be uncomfortable.

He leaned against the rail, near her but at a safe distance, and together they watched England shrink. All the sounds of the Plymouth dock were now fading. Soon it would be the elements, only. Sun and wind and sea.

What a relief it had once been to move away from land to something bigger than him. The sea could have killed him more than once. It had certainly tried more than once. And it still might win in the end. But he'd harnessed it, and there had been immense satisfaction in that, given that the rest of his life had resisted his command.

"Olivia?" he ventured gruffly into the silence.

She turned swiftly to the sound in his voice.

"Yes?" she said tersely.

"Why are you marrying Landsdowne?"

She didn't answer immediately. She wouldn't look at him. She looked up instead. The sunrise was a truly flamboyant one, all streamers of scarlet and apricot. It was tinting her skin golden and left a sheen of red on her dark hair.

"Do you mean, why am I marrying him rather than choosing a life as a walking, breathing, yet ever-withering shrine to your memory?"

That was certainly bitterly said.

But Olivia was the only woman he'd ever met who would have said something like "ever-withering."

Despite everything, even now, it perversely charmed him. The things she said, the things she noticed, the expressions that flitted across her achingly lovely face—she had never, ever been dull.

"Were you withering without me, then, Liv?" he said softly.

"I didn't say that," she said tautly.

She was still looking determinedly away from him. "I inferred."

There was a sort of tension at the corner of her mouth that might have become a smile. In other circumstances it would have.

"No, Lyon," she said evenly, with a sort of muted infuriating patience that was nothing like the Olivia he knew. A schoolteacher sort of patience. "I was not withering. You are not the sun and the moon and the stars. Life can and did go on in your absence."

"The *nerve* of life," he said softly.

She stole a swift glance at him again, her eyes flaring, as if she, too, was remembering the things about him that had set him apart. Made him uniquely him.

Made him uniquely hers.

Then she looked determinedly away again.

"And you are, of course, madly in love with Landsdowne. Which is why you're marrying him."

It wasn't as easy to say that aloud as it probably seemed to her.

"Love" was always a word he'd all but enshrined when he'd left Pennyroyal Green. There had been pleasure since then, some of it extraordinary, some of it memorable, all of it mindless, in the arms of other women.

But that word had belonged only to Olivia.

She said nothing.

"Ah. So lies still don't quite trip effortlessly off your tongue. At least that much hasn't changed about you."

It was a thrown-down gauntlet. Because Olivia wouldn't be able to resist discovering what precisely he thought was different about her.

She opened her mouth as if to retort. Then closed it.

"I'm too old to do anything 'madly,'" she said finally.

And it wasn't quite an answer.

"Is that so?" he said idly. "And yet you used to do everything madly."

He rested his arms on the rail, still close to but not touching her, and they both looked out at the sea, the ever-widening blue gap between them and English shores.

"You felt everything madly. You believed in things madly. You *argued* madly. I had to stay on my toes with you."

She swiftly turned her face up to him, delight glimmering tantalizingly, lighting her face, a haunting hint at the Olivia he'd known. At the way she used to look at him.

It was swiftly, deliberately shuttered.

She turned away again.

"And you kissed . . . Liv, oh God, but you kissed madly. Or you did, once upon a time. Perhaps you've forgotten how. Perhaps I was imagining all of that. Perhaps it was all a dream."

Before his eyes, pink flooded her cheeks. She reached up a hand to touch one, as if to soothe the heat from it, then dropped her hand.

She still wouldn't look at him.

He turned away from her, and in silence they gazed out at the heaving sea, gilded in early morning sun. The slap and rush of the water against his ship, the wind whipped and cracked in the sails, a sound he had come to love.

"Has he kissed you?" he asked bluntly. His voice sounded thick in her own ears.

"You've no right to ask."

He made an irritated sound. "Dodging and rhetoric are boring, Olivia, and you know it. Has he kissed you? Yes or no."

"Yes. Of course."

Of course.

He looked at her.

And even now, jealousy began a slow, scalding spill through his veins.

Olivia was almost always right, of course.

He had no right to his jealousy.

But then, by that same reasoning, his lungs had

no right to the air he breathed, and his heart had no right to beat.

And now she was watching him, and she knew, she knew just what the words had done to him, and there was a flicker of triumph in her eyes.

"Was it everything you dreamed?" he murmured. "That kiss?"

The tone was dangerously silky.

She watched him, incredulously. In her eyes glittered the beginnings of temper.

"What did you discover when he kissed you, Olivia? Did you discover that one kiss is much like another? Did you discover that mine were mundane, very ordinary indeed? Did you shiver when he kissed you? Because as I recall . . . you shivered when I kissed you. As if a river rippled right through you. As if the pleasure was almost more than you could bear. I could *feel* it in your body when my hand was at the small of your back."

"Stop it." Her voice was low and taut and frantic.

"I remember that you made this little sound when I first kissed you. A sort of . . . It was an astonished, hungry, *joyous* sound. That night, I lay in bed and I thought about that sound over and over. I thought I would die just for the privilege of hearing it again. I thought I'd discovered the reason I was born. To kiss you, and to hear your pleasure in it, and to know that it would only lead to more pleasure for both of us."

"Stop it." She was breathing roughly now and the hectic color was back in her cheeks.

He continued in a relentless tone of casual reminiscence. "Kissing you . . . well, I knew, suddenly, what a roman candle must feel like. One moment lightless, the next soaring, dazzling. The difference between living and not living."

"*Stop it.*"

"Did Landsdowne make you feel that way, Olivia, when he kissed you?"

"Stop it!"

It echoed shrilly.

Stop it stop it stop it.

Frightened seabirds flapped away from their perches.

Suddenly Lyon was ashamed.

He blew out a breath and turned back to the water, peculiarly drained and thwarted.

This was going badly. Clumsy fits and starts, attacks and feints.

What *was* he doing? What did he hope to gain?

He hoped to gain a life, he reminded himself. He hoped to get his heart back, if it could be had.

Another futile silence tacked itself down around them, dark and resentful.

Seconds stretched into a minute, then two.

"I suppose you've been celibate."

Her words had a certain studied casualness.

Which sparked a tiny flame of something like hope in him.

"Of course not." He shrugged.

It was absolutely true, but the shrug was meant to hurt her.

He didn't expound and she didn't ask. Olivia was intelligent and her imagination would torture her better than any Catherine wheel, if indeed she found the notion distasteful.

She was absolutely still and silent. But her knuckles were white on the railing.

She was imagining it. And suffering.

And perversely, it both elated and destroyed him.

It simply wasn't in him to hurt her. The point of his life had always seemed to be to keep her from harm.

And for a moment, his nerve and resolve wavered. He could return her now, and say good-bye, and she might know hurt again, but he wouldn't be the one to hurt her.

"He loves me," she said suddenly, quietly. Defiantly. "Landsdowne does."

"The poor fool."

"He *does* love me, Lyon."

It was the first time she'd said his name since he'd seen her again, and he hated the context.

It infuriated him, her calm certainty. The warning. His name, in her voice, which had once been so beloved. "Oh, no doubt. No doubt. And you must of *course* protect the man you love from being hurt."

He was aware of a faint bitterness in his voice.

She whirled on him hurriedly. "I didn't say I love—"

They both froze, eyes locked.

The moment so taut and fragile one could have tapped a *ping* from it.

"Yes?" he said tersely.

At last she dropped her gaze again.

And was stubbornly silent.

The breeze had freed more of her silky black hair and it lashed and danced around her head like a dervish. Mesmerizing, the dark hair against the brightening blue of the sky. He remembered the feel of it in his hand when he'd cradled her head to take a kiss deeply. The textures of her had long haunted him: the generous give of her lips. The silken slide of her skin when he'd dared to explore so far, and no farther.

"I don't think you should underestimate him," was all she said, finally. Her voice quieter now.

"I wouldn't dream of it. After all, people you underestimate might surprise you and do things like, oh, absconding with you a few weeks shy of your wedding."

"He'll come after me if he discovers I'm gone."

"He won't discover it. I've made certain of it. But If he does, I'll be ready for him," he said simply. Amused. "And I'll hand you back if that's what you want."

A hesitation.

"Lyon—"

That *tone*. So reasonable. So condescending. Almost placating.

It infuriated him.

"Enough." His voice cracked like a musket shot.

She flinched, her eyes widening.

"Don't you want to *finish* this, Olivia? And if you can swear on all you hold dear—whether that's your own lovely head, your family, the ground your ancestral estate rests upon, the esteem of Landsdowne, if indeed you *do* hold that dear—*if* you know with the same certainty you know the sun will rise tomorrow and that Everseas and Redmonds will remain at each other's throats through eternity that you don't love me anymore—I will send you back now. Say the word. Can you swear that you don't?"

Love.

That word. It was a cannonball fired over battlements.

He'd used it so much more easily than she had.

Then again, men were always more comfortable with weapons.

Her eyes had seemed to him so beautiful and changeable, so full of promise and tenderness and mystery, a little dangerous when they crackled with temper. A man could get lost there. Or found there. Like the sea.

And maybe that was why he was so at home on the sea.

She closed them.

And gave her head an almost imperceptible shake: *no*.

"That's what I thought," he said, with grim satisfaction.

He turned swiftly.

"But—"

"I need to speak to my first mate about our course. Don't try to throw yourself overboard. You're being watched, and my crew isn't accustomed to handling anything gently."

Chapter 16

❧

SHE WAS STUNNED AND furious and exhausted but she still couldn't help it: she opened one eye, and then the other, just so she could watch him go.

But then, it had always required a superhuman effort not to watch Lyon Redmond.

Now she saw a critical difference. When she'd met him that night in the ballroom, there had been a remote self-awareness about him. As though he balanced a burden no one could see, as though he was walking an invisible line drawn for him beyond which he could never go.

Now he walked as if he owned the earth and everyone on it and gave not one damn what anyone thought, including her.

She'd forgotten how *relentless* he could be. Absolutely merciless in the pursuit of a truth.

She hadn't forgotten how easily he could surprise her into laughing.

And just like that, in came another tide of anger for all that he was now.

And all that she'd missed.

And all that *he'd* missed.

She turned toward the water reflexively and tensed in shock, her palms digging into the railing, her knuckles curled in a painful grip.

No land in sight.

Dear God, no land in sight.

Just endless, heaving, glassine, blue-green in every direction. A veil of silvery foam, like the train of a royal bride, trailed the ship. The air was briny and winy, every breath she took exotically delicious and wind-scoured, and it stung her cheeks and sent her hair lashing at them like a cat-o-nine tails.

The sails cracked and billowed as the wind swelled them, and pushed the ship ever more swiftly forward.

Damn.

Damn him anyway.

Because . . . it was glorious.

He'd remembered. He must have remembered. All of the things she'd said she'd wanted. To see the ocean. To sail on a ship.

She closed her eyes against a violent surge of emotion. Something soaring and brilliant was burning through her shock and fury and fatigue. A bit like a beautiful, half-remembered song heard through castle walls.

"Good morning, Miss Eversea."

Her eyes snapped open.

Mademoiselle Lilette was leaning companionably against the rail of the ship.

"Oh, good morning, whoever the bloody hell you might actually be," Olivia drawled.

"Oh, that *does* sting a bit," Digby said with infuriating cheeriness. "Something tells me that's the first time you've strung 'bloody' and 'hell' together, Miss Eversea, and it suits you right down to the ground. I'm *actually* Digby." She curtsied. "Mrs. Delphinia Digby-Thorne."

Digby's accent was now English. But then again, perhaps she excelled at accents. She might be a native Portuguese, for all Olivia knew.

Olivia turned and eyed her balefully. "Where did you learn to speak French, you fraud?"

"Fraud?" Digby clapped a hand over her heart. "I'm wounded. I'm more in the way of a skillful actress, and no one accuses actresses of fraud when they practice their craft. And I learned to speak French rather like you did, I suppose. They do want young English ladies to learn such things, don't they? That, and sewing, and the like. I suppose you can say that's where our similarities diverge."

This Digby was insufferably at ease and regarding Olivia as if she were an achievement of which she was particularly proud. And Olivia's cheeks felt warm again at the thought of how much she'd confided in Digby.

"You are also a spy."

"Well, yes," Digby said, sounding mildly surprised at hearing the obvious pointed out.

"A good one."

"Yes," Digby agreed, modestly.

"Did you even ever lose a great love?"

"I've had plenty of loves, but none of them great until the man I married. I am recently wed to the captain's first mate. Mr. Magnus Thorne. And I intend to keep *him* forever."

Olivia snorted.

"How did you . . . How did he . . ." Olivia made a frustrated gesture in the direction of London, no longer visible.

"He learned Madame Marceau had the making of your trousseau, and he bribed her assistant to disappear and *I* serendipitously appeared when Madame Marceau's need was most urgent. The previous girl was settling into enjoying her retirement in the country and can afford to marry well or not at all, whatever pleases her. And the captain coaxed her back again with another payment when she was needed. The captain can do that sort of thing, because he's rich. Very, *very* rich," she said with relish and awe. "I simply followed his directions and my own instincts, which ultimately made it possible to intercept you. It's generally the right thing to do, following his instructions, that is."

Olivia stared at the woman, who was small and dark and round and lush in a way that would appeal to nearly any man. She had merry and too-knowing dark eyes. As Mademoiselle Lilette, she had clearly powdered her skin, for now a few golden freckles were apparent, and her hair had been clearly scraped and flattened into submission in order to play the role of modiste, as it was apparent now that it was riotously curly.

"'Intercept,'" Olivia quoted sardonically. "Is that how one refers to kidnapping and deception these days?"

"Nevertheless, it's an accurate word, one must admit."

"And how did you come to know . . . the captain . . . Digby?"

So strange to refer to him that way. The *captain.* Her brothers had returned from the war wearing new mantles of calm and authority, an air of abstraction that sometimes settled over them when they were silent. They had seen things, and done things, of which they would never speak, and it was this that separated them from their sisters, and somehow bound them closer to each other. It was the lot of men, it seemed, to see and do a lot of things of which they could never speak.

And yet Lyon's air of authority was something else altogether.

As if he made his own laws.

She wondered if anything could hurt him now.

"Well, his reputation rather preceded him," Digby said, "and I greatly admired it. I needed a job. I convinced him I would be a useful employee. And so I have been," she said with great relish. "For he wanted you here, and here you are."

Olivia stared at the woman, a thousand competing questions clamoring to be asked. "What do you mean, 'his reputation' . . . ?"

"As ship captain, exceptionally successful and wealthy merchant . . . and revolutionary, of a sort. Though the last bit isn't as commonly known."

Merchant?

Revolutionary?

Lyon *Redmond*?

Was she dreaming?

"You left out possibly a madman, Miss Digby," she said shortly.

Digby tipped her head. "Have a care, Miss Eversea. I suppose he's many things, but mad isn't one of them. There is method in all he does. I won't hear a disparaging word. I would do anything for him."

Olivia fixed the other woman with a stare. "And have you?" she said softly.

Digby blinked in shock.

And then gratifyingly, the insufferably confident woman flushed.

"Firstly, Miss Eversea do you really want to know what I think you're insinuating? And secondly, do you believe you have the right to the answer?"

Digby's self-possession was both enraging and amusing, in large part because it was like looking in a mirror. And as much as Olivia would have loved to engage in a good fight right now, her sense of justice was muscular.

"Excellent points, Digby. No, and no."

Digby's eyes flared briefly in surprise. Then she,

too, nodded shortly. "If you need any assistance, I'm at your disposal, Miss Eversea. I'll show you back to your quarters, if you'll follow me."

"Wait . . . where is this ship going?"

"Spain," Digby said shortly. "It's but a day or so across the Bay of Biscay."

Spain. Of course.

She wondered what she would find there.

And suddenly she was certain she knew. And a tiny, rogue, inappropriate filament of joy snaked through her.

"And Digby . . . what did you mean by 'revolutionary'?"

Digby paused, considering.

"Miss Eversea . . . You're aware your name is on the ship."

Olivia's mind blanked in astonishment. "It's on . . ."

"The ship is called *The Olivia*."

Olivia was speechless.

Digby must have seen something in her expression for her own softened.

"Men do have their romantic fancies, Miss Eversea. If he says you're worth his time, then I'll believe him, and reserve judgment. I've come to like you, but my opinion matters not. And I'll leave it to him to tell you what he's been doing since you last saw him."

"Very well," Olivia said softly.

"I will tell you this, Miss Eversea. The captain never did want anything more from me than my loyalty, more's the pity, and that's the honest truth. Though what woman wouldn't be willing to give him anything he wants? He's a remarkable man. Now come with me. You'll want sleep."

HER TRUNK HAD magically appeared in the cabin while she was on deck.

She snorted at that. He'd been confident he'd be able to get her onto the ship, that much was clear.

But then, he did know her.

Tempering her anger at the elaborate deception was the reminder that the only reason it had been at all successful was because he did, indeed, know her. Better than anyone ever had.

And it merely emphasized how truly lonely she'd been since he'd gone, even surrounded by friends and loved ones.

And the bastard had managed to glean a bit about how she felt about him, too.

She almost smiled at that.

Had he been lonely, too?

Olivia was certain she wouldn't sleep at all.

But what seemed like moments later, she woke with a start, with the sense that a good amount of time had passed. When she saw Lyon simmering in a pot across from her on the wall, she remembered where she was.

She rolled over and peered down.

A chamber pot was thoughtfully situated next to her bed, and a message was folded and propped like a little tent next to it.

She leaned over and read it.

In case you must puke.

It was tidy, even, ladylike printing, nothing like Lyon's. Digby must have been in.

Thoughtful of her.

She rose tentatively then took a few steps on the gently heaving floor of the ship. She didn't seem to be afflicted with seasickness, thankfully. She took a few more steps, and she still felt quite steady.

There wasn't a mirror, so she felt about the back of her head and smoothed her hair as best she could, patted her dress, and then opened the door a few inches.

She leaped back with a gasp as an enormous man glittering with metal—in his ears, at his hip, and, alarmingly, in the hook where his hand ought to be—turned to her.

"Ah, ye're awake now, are ye, miss? Stay here. Ain't safe on the deck. I'll get the captain. Lock yer door."

He shut the door emphatically.

If a man like that said it wasn't safe on the deck, she would take his word for it.

What kind of world did Lyon live in now?

She locked the door.

A few minutes later she heard footsteps outside, and then several smart raps on the door.

"Olivia, may I come in?" Lyon's voice.

And her heart, the traitor, gave a leap at the very sound of it.

She slid the bolts and pulled open the door.

He filled the doorway Large, hard, and shockingly beautiful, particularly since he was wearing what amounted to evening clothes.

Apart, that was, from the sword.

Most of the men she knew didn't wear swords to dinner.

"What time is it?" she asked.

"It's nearly dinnertime. Accordingly—" He raised a bottle of wine in one hand and a sack in the other, which she suspected contained some kind of food. "We'll reach harbor by late afternoon, perhaps closer to sunset, tomorrow."

He withdrew a loaf of bread, a wedge of cheese, a knife, a plate, and two glasses, all of which he arranged without ceremony on the little desk.

She sat on the foot of the bed, hands folded primly, while he settled in at the desk.

She watched him slice away at the bread and cheese and arrange them somewhat artfully on the plate.

"Why is your ship called *The Olivia*?"

"I had to name it something, and *The Mrs. Sneath* hadn't quite the same ring."

She laughed.

Before she remembered how angry she was with him.

His head turned toward her quickly, and his expression was almost hungry.

But then her smile faded, and silence settled in again.

He placed the bottle of wine in the center of the little desk and extracted the cork with alacrity, then glugged a bit into two glasses.

He handed one to her.

He lifted his. "*À votre santé*, Olivia."

She took a sip. A shockingly excellent wine that launched her eyebrows.

"Spanish," he said shortly. "I export it."

A fascinating sentence to be sure, and it inspired a thousand more questions.

"How did you come to have a ship?"

"I bought it."

She stared at him. "It's going to be like that, is it?"

"Like what?"

"Curt, petulant answers that tell me nothing, really."

"Petulant?" The word seemed to amuse him.

"It's precisely the right word. You can do better."

He inhaled, then exhaled gustily. "Very well. I bought it with money I earned by working on this very ship. Supplemented by money I won from men foolish enough to play five-card loo with me. I worked, gambled, and invested."

He leaned back to study the effect those words had on her. His arms were crossed before him. There were faint lines about his eyes.

How had he gotten those lines?

Five years without him. He'd gotten older, bought a ship, exported wine. And now he had lines about his eyes.

And she had seen none of it.

The muscles of her stomach tightened with something like panic, for all that she'd missed. All that he'd done without her.

The panic subsided and became that unspecific, simmering anger again.

"But what made you . . . want to buy a ship?"

"From Pennyroyal Green I went to London and got work on a ship, because I wanted to go as far away as possible from England."

They both knew the reason for that, and the statement rang by itself in the silence for a moment.

"And . . . did you?"

He hesitated.

"I went very far indeed." He smiled slightly. It wasn't the most pleasant smile. It contained memories of things he'd seen and possibly things he'd done.

And, in all likelihood, women he'd made love to.

He'd been doing this while she was in Pennyroyal Green deflecting suitor after suitor and instructing the footman where to put flowers delivered by men who hadn't a prayer of gaining her attention.

Because they weren't Lyon.

Once they'd been able to talk about anything and everything, endlessly. He needed only speak about anything in order for her to find it fascinating.

But another chasm of silence opened up. There were too many things to say. And they had lost the knack of talking to each other.

"You were a member of a ship's . . . *crew*?" Someone of his refinement and breeding would have been painfully conspicuous.

Then again, Lyon had won the Sussex Marksmanship Trophy and more than one fencing competition.

"They'll take any able-bodied man willing to work on a ship, Olivia. They taught me. I learned. I worked. I fought. I won. I didn't need to know how to do anything that I didn't already know how to do."

He said it very deliberately. Very evenly.

But it was very much a reference to that night in Sussex. *What do you know how to do?*

In five years he'd risen from menial labor on the deck of a ship to owning and commanding one.

But then, she didn't suppose she ever truly doubted him.

She was quiet. She had a million questions for him.

She dismantled her bread, then realized what she was doing and put it in her mouth instead.

He watched approvingly. "Eat more than that. You've gotten thin."

Her eyes flared wide.

His voice was gruff.

He'd likely been pondering how thin she was while she was wondering about the lines near his eyes.

She contemplated countermanding him. But she knew concern when she heard it, and her reflex was to take his troubles away.

So she obeyed him. The bread was crusty and coarse but delicious, and the cheese was fine. She'd never eaten with an audience, but he watched in absolute silence as she devoured two more slices and sipped her wine.

He handed her a napkin. She dabbed at her lips, then folded her napkin and looked up at him.

"Olivia?"

"Yes?"

"Why Landsdowne? Why now?"

She met his eyes.

"Why shouldn't it be him and why shouldn't it be now?" she said evenly enough.

He drained his wine and then stood, and looked down at her a moment.

"Because you don't love him," he said idly.

She sucked in a startled breath. "How *dare* you."

"I think you would be amazed at what I now dare."

They locked eyes again. The air shimmered with dangerous emotions and unspoken things.

She didn't know how they would ever be spoken.

"We'll reach shore soon enough," he said finally. "Don't attempt to leave the cabin again. None of my crew were gentle born and even if they were, months at sea without a woman tends to erode gentlemanly impulses."

He said this so easily. As if it was the most natural thing in the world for someone of his breeding to command a crew of dangerous men apparently united in a struggle to control their animal desires.

She glanced at the print on the wall, the one in which he was simmering in a pot.

And she thought of that other print on Ackermann's wall.

Of a man with blue eyes, holding a sword in his left hand, hair rippling in the breeze.

"If you need something to pass the time . . ."

He reached into the sack and carefully placed a copy of *Robinson Crusoe* down on the desk, and followed it with *The Orphan on the Rhine.*

She stared down at them. Stunned.

And suddenly, unaccountably deeply moved.

They'd been purchased at Tingle's, she was certain of it.

She looked up at him, remembering that day. How simply standing near him had been magical. Like falling and flying all at once.

He would have done *anything* for her. She'd sensed it even then.

She suddenly didn't dare look up. And then she did.

And saw in his eyes that he was remembering that day, too.

Both the beauty of it . . .

And how it had all then been sundered.

"Take your pick." He smiled faintly.

And then he was gone.

SHE MUST HAVE fallen asleep again over her copy of *Robinson Crusoe*, because she started when there was a sharp rap on her door.

Olivia leaped up and smoothed her skirt and peered out.

It was Digby.

"It's time to disembark, Miss Eversea. We've arrived."

DIGBY LED OLIVIA up to the deck while a pair of truly intimidating men passed them, touching their hats, to fetch her trunk.

Olivia emerged blinking; the dazzling lowering sun seemed to be aimed right into her eyes. She craned her head backward. A few shreds of clouds were scattered over a sky that had been brilliant but was now beginning to give way to the indigo of sunset.

Her namesake, *The Olivia*, was anchored in a little inlet created by the golden, curving horseshoe of a beach.

A caress of a breeze fluttered the hem of her dress, played in the hair that had escaped its pins. It was so serene something in her eased, and for an instant she forgot she'd been tricked into coming, and was simply grateful that she was here, wherever this was.

And then Lyon was at her elbow, and her traitorous heart gave that leap. Recognizing to whom it had once belonged. She yanked it back again. It wasn't his to command anymore.

Or so she told herself.

"Cadiz," he said simply.

THEY WERE ROWED ashore in a longboat. His crew managed to beach the craft and assist her to the beach without dampening overmuch, and she managed mostly to preserve her modesty. God only knew she didn't want to display too much stocking-covered calf to any of those female-deprived men.

She shook out her skirts and patted them and murmured thanks.

Lyon was standing on the beach, stark as the needle of a compass in dark trousers and boots and white shirt, speaking to members of his crew in what sounded like fluent Spanish and pointing toward the foot of a cliff.

She watched as one of his crew ferried her trunk away and deposited it where Lyon was directing, at the foot of what appeared to be a little road that wound up the cliff.

The men saluted Lyon and piled into the boats again and shoved them back out into the inlet.

Leaving her entirely alone on the beach with Lyon.

"Shall we?" he said simply, and without waiting for a reply from her, set off across the beach.

She turned toward the ship and froze.

The crew was raising the anchor. Her heart lurched.

"Lyon . . ." she called.

"Yes?" he called over his shoulder. He didn't stop.

She scrambled to follow him, grateful for her traveling boots.

"Why aren't they coming with us?"

"They weren't invited."

"What are they doing?"

"Leaving."

"Where are they *going*?"

"Away," he said shortly.

"What do you mean, *away*?" She hated the sound of her voice. She'd been shrill more frequently in the last two days than in the whole of her life.

"They'll be back in a few days."

That did it. She stopped and threw back her head. "Arrrrrgh!"

He whirled around and froze.

Her roar echoed around them.

Which is when she realized how very, very quiet it was. And how very, very alone they likely were.

"That was an interesting sound," he said carefully, finally.

"Lyon Redmond. Do not make me raise my voice again. I don't like the sound of it when it's shrill. Do *not* order me about. You will inform me and engage me in conversation as if I am a guest, not an enemy captive. You will not stride ahead of me and force me to scramble inelegantly to catch up. I am now here voluntarily and you will treat me at all times with civility, unless you've forgotten how."

In the silence the wind filled his shirt like a sail and whipped his hair up off his sun-browned forehead. And in truth, he looked more pagan than civil at the moment. He was perhaps a little too accustomed to people doing his bidding.

Despite it all, his beauty knifed through her.

"Very well," he said finally, with a surprising, utterly disarming tenderness. "I apologize for being insufferable. And I accept your terms."

She was speechless.

"Have you any other terms?"

She gave her head a shake, because she didn't trust herself to speak over the sudden lump in her throat.

"May I point out *you're* now issuing orders?" he added, teasing her gently now.

"Duly noted."

She wanted to smile. She almost did.

He wanted to smile, too, she could tell. He almost did.

And yet neither of them could yet completely give way, because the weight of years held them back.

He turned away from her again.

"Look up there, on that rise."

She shaded her eyes with her hand and followed the direction of his pointing finger. She saw a low, gracefully sprawling house of creamy white stone, surrounded by lush greenery—flowering trees, spreading oaks, and needled pines.

A serene house, simple in line, but possessing both a sort of peace and grandeur.

The view from every window would be spectacular—ocean and sand and hills.

Precisely as he'd described to her so many years ago.

Her breath hitched.

She looked at him.

"It's my house," he said.

Every word of that sentence thrummed with a sort of quiet, steely satisfaction.

Her heart skipped. *"Your* house?"

He wasn't looking at her. And that's when she realized his terseness may well have been because he was nervous about showing it to her.

"One of my houses," he replied shortly, one of the more intriguing sentences she'd ever heard.

He slid her a sidelong glance. Inscrutable. "Shall we?"

Chapter 17

❧

H<small>E STRIPPED OFF HIS</small> coat and handed it to her, wordlessly.

Startled, she took it. Folded it gently over her arm, and resisted the urge to hold it to her nose and breathe it in to see if it still smelled just like him.

Then he pushed up his sleeves and hoisted her trunk to his shoulder, carrying it without apparent effort.

She followed.

The path wound gently up, but she was a country-bred girl quite accustomed to walking, and it posed no difficulty at all. He didn't seem inclined to speak, so to occupy her time she watched the fascinating play of muscle in his back and buttocks as he climbed.

The path concluded in a wrought-iron gate joining the surrounding low white stone wall.

She pushed the gate open and stepped forward.

Her breath caught.

They were in a little courtyard. Beneath their feet a checkerboard of muted rose-red and darker red tiles stretched out in either direction, wrapping around the house. A white tiered stone fountain was the centerpiece.

One wall of the courtyard was hung entirely with a tapestry of green vines starred everywhere with white jasmine. The wall adjacent was a flamboyant spill of scarlet blooms.

Before she knew she was doing it, she moved over wonderingly to touch one, a reflexive response to beauty.

"Bougainvillea," he said shortly.

"It's so beautiful," she breathed. "I've never seen one outside of a hothouse. But they belong in the sun, don't they? They're like the skirts of Spanish dancers."

She turned to find him smiling at her.

"All you need is a blue flower growing somewhere and you'll have the British flag," she added.

He laughed. "The Spanish would love *that*. Speaking of things you won't see outside of a hothouse— and no, I'm not referring to you—turn around and take a peek around that corner."

She did as ordered. A few steps over the red stone, she peered around the corner of the house.

And there it was.

Her jaw dropped. She stared as if she'd just accidentally stumbled upon the queen lounging here in the middle of Spain.

"Go ahead. You always wanted to."

It seemed whimsical and dreamlike, growing right there out in the open, covered all over in luscious, sunny globes of fruit.

She approached it as if it were an exotic creature, and reached up and gave a tug.

And an orange tumbled into her palm.

She closed her eyes and held it to her nose and breathed in deeply. The singular scent, sharp and sweet and citrus, was heavenly.

The English weather would have killed that orange tree straightaway if it had the temerity to grow out in the open. Which is why all their English trees were so sturdy, and so many of them ancient.

Like the two oaks in the center of Pennyroyal Green, for instance, said to represent the Redmonds and Everseas. They had grown for centuries, stubbornly thriving, holding each other up, competing for resources.

She gave a wondering laugh, and whirled.

She caught some fascinating expression fleeing his face.

"Pick a few more," he said evenly. "We'll eat some, we'll drink some."

She pulled a few more from the tree with an air of wonder, and filled her arms with them.

He settled her trunk with a little grunt and then slid a hefty key into the heavy arched door, and turned the knob.

She gasped.

The entire house was made of light.

And then she blinked and discovered why it seemed that way: a series of three soaring arched windows that allowed in sea-scoured sunshine, which spilled through nearly the entirety of the main room. A heavy table of slabbed wood, weathered to a silvery finish, was pushed in front of the windows, and in the center was a large glass bowl of the palest shade of aquamarine. It was like a drop of the sea had been captured in Venetian glass.

The creamy pale walls rose and met the high ceiling in rounded corners, and the floors were tiled in huge, satin rose-red stone, edged with tiny, intricate blue and yellow mosaic.

Arched doorways led into dark, cool hallways, off which, presumably, were bedrooms.

A settee—ivory brocade, French, and possibly Chippendale, and yet somehow right in this room for all of that—was angled before the fireplace, flanked by a pair of sleek ormolu chairs upholstered in more brocade. A low oval marble table, its wooden legs intricately turned, sat between all of them.

It was like stepping into his dream. One of the very first things he'd shared with her.

"The oranges can go there."

He pointed at the blue bowl, and she spilled them from her arms and stood back to admire them.

Beautiful things, not a lot of things, he'd once said. That's what he would have in his house.

She remembered, because she remembered everything about him.

They were both silent.

She held still, suffused with wonder and a peculiar peace and sense of *rightness* in this house. It was a strangely familiar sensation.

And then she recalled the first she time he had felt that way:

It was when he first approached her in the ballroom. As if the fences surrounding her world had been kicked down.

In retrospect quite ironic, given their association had been confined by the clock and hedgerows and their family's expectations.

"It's so beautiful, Lyon. The house is like stepping into your dream."

"Perhaps literally. Since it was one of mine."

On the surface, it was an innocuous enough sentence.

And she could feel the war in him between his desire to take pleasure in her pleasure, and whatever dark, unspoken thing thrummed through both of them at the moment.

She of course had been his dream, as he had been hers.

On a shelf above the table was a row of books.

She moved toward it slowly.

For there was his copy of *Marcus Aurelius*.

Nearly tattered now, the gold embossing nearly worn smooth from being tucked inside his coat countless times, packed into trunks, cupped open in his hands.

She paused before it with a sense of vertigo. She hesitated. Then gingerly, tentatively, she reached out and gently touched it. As if it might vanish, along with this room and Lyon, like a mirage.

Marcus Aurelius. One of the very first things she'd learned about him.

How she had cherished everything she'd ever learned about him. Almost as if she'd known her time with him would be finite. That someday he would be gone, and all she would have would be a scattering of memories, like figurines kept in a curio cabinet.

And just like that, suddenly, the anger swept in again.

For all that he'd missed.

For all that she'd missed.

For leaving her.

And now showing her what his life had been like without her.

She wasn't certain if this was rebuke. A way to show her how very, very wrong she'd been.

Or if he was showing her what could have been.

Next to *Marcus Aurelius* were all the volumes written by his brother, Miles Redmond, a naturalist and now a famous explorer, a coveted guest at London dinner parties for his tales of his travels in Lacao.

"Miles was almost eaten by a cannibal." She said this almost lightly. "Did you know?"

He betrayed not a flicker of surprise, but then he seemed to have mastered inscrutability.

"He wouldn't have gone down easily. A bit sinewy is Miles."

She turned to look at him.

His face was still and hard. His arms were crossed. A bit like armor.

She moved farther down the shelf, examining the spines of the books.

"Violet has a baby now. She married the Earl of Ardmay. She's a countess."

She chose this one deliberately. She glanced over her shoulder.

He still didn't blink.

"She nearly died giving birth, I heard," she added, almost casually.

And now he was absolutely motionless. But he was whiter about the mouth now.

She was certain he knew precisely why she'd said it.

She sensed a sort of coiled potential in him that boded ill, something was being wound tighter and tighter. His face was taut, his mouth white at the corners.

But she couldn't seem to help herself from winding it tighter. She wanted it to break. *You weren't there. I needed you I missed you. You missed it. You missed it all.*

"Did you know Colin nearly died on the gallows?"

"I knew." His voice was soft and taut.

She had sat with her family in their London townhouse that horrible morning and prayed.

She had longed for Lyon then. If only he could have come home to her.

But he hadn't.

Colin had lived. Colin generally had that sort of luck.

She turned abruptly away from him again, toward

what appeared to be a tiny sculpture of some sort at the end of the shelf that caught her eye.

"May I?"

He nodded curtly.

It was a bird. A lovely, fragile little thing, scarcely heavier than a dandelion. She plucked it up and perched it in her hand.

"It's an origami crane," he told her. "Origami is the Japanese art of paper folding . . . a sheet of paper cleverly, intricately folded into different shapes. Animals, flowers, and the like. It's funny how one ordinary thing can so easily be transformed into something extraordinary."

She looked up at him searchingly. She knew precisely why he'd said that.

"A woman gave it to me. For luck, and to remember her by."

And she knew why he'd said *that*.

The little crane in her hand suddenly might as well have been a viper.

And now it was clear that every word they were exchanging, no matter how seemingly civil, no matter how seemingly mundane, at its core hid seething fury and accusation and hurt.

Perhaps love was in there, too.

Perhaps they were forever inextricable now.

She put the origami crane down quickly.

Now she would like to set it on fire.

"I could do with some air. Why don't we have a walk on the beach, Olivia?"

He seized his coat and turned without waiting for her reply and was out the door.

She followed just as swiftly.

HIS STRIDES WERE punishingly long. She ran to keep up with him. He didn't apologize, and he didn't slow down. And she didn't ask him to. She *wanted* to run.

"Where are your other homes, Lyon?"

"I've a plantation in Louisiana. Sugarcane. One in New York. A home in the south of France."

"But not England."

He didn't reply.

Their feet crunched down along the path, until the sand of the beach silenced their footsteps, and she followed him out to the shoreline.

They appeared to be utterly alone. No ship. No sign of other people. No birds.

"I could buy nearly any house I wanted in England now. If I wanted to be in England," he added coldly. Ironically. Sounding abstracted.

The sun had nearly dropped into the sea, and the vivid sunset colors were now fading to the color of old bruises, and giving way to the blue-purple of night. The air was still soft and warm, but there was a nip at the edges of it now.

"Do you remember, Lyon, how dull the vicar once was? My cousin Adam Sylvaine is the vicar now. And he's quite good. The church is crowded every weekend. It helps that he's gorgeous."

He smiled a small, taut smile. And said nothing.

"They called him when they thought your sister was going to die from childbirth. In the dead of night. An Eversea in your house. He did say that Jonathan offered him a brandy."

He was rigid as a monument now. His arms folded even more tightly across his chest. As if he were trying to hold something in.

"And Jonathan married a very surprising woman, and he set London upside down in the process. He began his own investment group. *And* he's running for Parliament. Did you know he's interested in child labor reform? Jonathan Redmond, of all people. Your brother did that."

Lyon remained motionless, apart from a breeze that lifted his hair from his collar. The sea was blue-black now, apart from a wedge of light laid down by the full moon. It was calm, throwing lace foam up onto the beach at sighlike intervals. That's where his gaze was aimed. Away from her. As if she was a source of pain.

"I find myself wondering, Olivia, if the point of all of this to imply that I don't know any of these things—for I do, or much of—or that I simply don't care? Or would it be both?"

He said it very, very slowly. Dangerously slowly. His voice contained a warning for anyone sensible enough to heed it.

It was shaking with fury.

But she couldn't stop herself. Her need to goad him had momentum.

"It doesn't matter, does it? You missed it. All of it. All of these things. All . . . because . . . you . . . *fled*."

He turned very slowly then.

She had the sense to take two steps backward, away from him.

Because fury came off him in waves. As if she'd opened the door to a furnace.

He was staring at her as if he'd never seen her before.

"Fled," he said carefully. As if he was learning a new language.

She stood her ground.

But he'd stolen her voice, so she simply nodded.

"Fled," he repeated. The word was incredulous and scathing. "Interesting choice of word coming from a coward."

The contempt in his voice was scalding.

It ripped her breath from her lungs.

"I'm a—"

"Co-ward," he enunciated, with intolerable specificity. As if teaching her a new word.

Her mind blanked in shock.

"How. Dare. You. When *you* were the one who *ran away.*"

He gave a short amazed laugh. "Ah, Olivia. Look at you. You should remember how you can't intimidate me with your temper. *I know you.* And I speak the truth. Furthermore, I think you know it, too."

"You *know* me? Do you think you still do? You have a lot of bloody nerve."

But this was bluster. Because it was true. And in all likelihood he knew this, too.

He'd always been one step ahead of her, after all.

And they were now hurtling headlong toward something she had hidden from herself for years.

The truth.

She couldn't stop it now if she wanted to.

"I do have a lot of bloody nerve," he said calmly, relentlessly. "And I do know you. I always thought you were so brave. You were so passionate about the rights of the poor, the downtrodden, the voiceless. A woman who says what she thinks. I admired you painfully for *caring* so much. I wanted to be worthy of you. When in the end you were only in fact a frightened . . . little . . . girl."

The words were cold and brutal.

She could feel her very soul shriveling away from the attack.

She was hoarse. "You don't know what you're—"

"And you're still afraid, I'd warrant. You're afraid of wanting what you think you shouldn't want. Of how powerfully you feel about things. Of how very, *very* much . . ." He stepped toward her, and she stood her ground. " . . . how very, very much you wanted me. In *every* sense of the word. It killed me, Olivia, that you had the courage to fight for everyone else except me. If I was my father's creation, then you are *your* family's creation."

"Lyon . . . You don't under—"

He didn't hear her. All of this, like a volcano, had clearly lain dormant for years.

"I would have given you the moon. And I could have, too, Olivia. I asked for your faith that night. And you returned it with *scorn*. Because. You were. Afraid."

It was unbearable.

"Lyon . . . Please . . . you must understand . . ."

"I believed you saw something fatal and irredeemable in me, and I quite simply couldn't bear it, Olivia. Now I know that you were just a coward. It really wasn't more complicated than that."

The silence was ghastly. It was filled with the roar of their breathing. As if they were grappling gladiators who had finally sprung apart.

Her hands went up to her face and her lungs felt like a furnace as she drew in a ragged hot breath.

The fact was that he was right. Everyone was right about her.

All the rumors and legends were right.

She *had* broken his heart.

And in so doing, she had willfully, perhaps permanently, broken her own.

And everyone else's who loved him.

All because she'd been too afraid to fight for him.

Chapter 18

❧

"LYON . . . YOU HAVE TO understand . . . I never dreamed you would leave," she said brokenly. "I didn't mean for you to *leave*. You shouldn't have gone. You shouldn't have gone. You shouldn't have actually *gone*."

Her voice spiraled in anguish, the anguish she'd never shown anyone, let alone herself, lest it rip her to shreds.

She dropped to her knees and covered her face with her hands.

She drew in a hot, ragged breath. And then another.

And the sob that clawed its way out might as well have been a shard of her own heart.

One ugly, wracking sob followed another.

Old tears. Too long held back.

She had never, never wept for him since he left.

After a moment she could feel him drop to his knees next to her.

"Oh, for heaven's sake. My girl. My sweet girl. For heaven's sake. Don't cry. Please don't cry. I didn't mean to make you *cry*."

He said it so softly, almost panicky. He was flailing.

It was *almost* funny.

No one else called her that. No else had ever thought she was *sweet*.

No one knew how tender she really was.

No one else had ever been able to really hurt her.

No one else could save her from herself.

And all of this made her throw herself backward on the sand, fling one arm across her eyes, and weep with abandon.

He said nothing.

Perhaps she'd appalled him speechless.

She lay there on the sand, and she didn't care that her hair would be full of it, or the back of her dress would likely be ruined, or that her dignity was in shreds, and she wept as though it were the end of the world. As though she'd just lost him all over again.

At some point gentle hands tenderly scooped up her head.

She submitted as he thrust a folded coat beneath her as a pillow.

The coat smelled just like him. And just like everything about him, it comforted and stirred.

She heaved a great ragged sigh and sank back into it.

The sobs seemed to be done with her.

She finally peeled her arm away from her eyes.

And blinked, surprised.

It was full dark. Somehow the entire night seemed cleansed. The stars had an almost stinging brilliance.

She felt peaceful and empty and borderless. She might as well have been sand or sky.

Which was how she knew heartbreak had comprised nearly the whole of her for so long.

Now that she'd released it, she didn't know who she might be.

She lay still in the emptiness.

She let her head loll to the side. There Lyon was, mostly in shadow now, his arms wrapped loosely around his knees, staring out at the water, his profile etched in shadow.

No other soul on the planet would have skewered her so completely. There was a peace in being so known and understood, even if that meant being excoriated.

"You were right," she whispered. "About all of it. I was—am—a coward."

He turned to her swiftly. And then he gave a short, humorless laugh.

"Before you do any more self-flagellation, Olivia—not *all* of which is unjustified—the truth of the matter was that I *had* to leave Pennyroyal Green. With or without you. And I only realized that recently. Perhaps in the end . . . perhaps in the end it was all for the best."

His voice was quiet, too, and almost drifting. That's when it occurred to her that he'd said what he wanted to say to her, and perhaps he, too, was feeling empty and cleansed.

But who were they now?

And were they finally—as he'd said—finished?

How could anything that took them away from each other be all for the best?

But she knew, too, that once Lyon had spoken to his father about her, Isaiah Redmond would have made good on his threat to ruthlessly clip Lyon's wings: stripping him of his allowance, bullying him into a marriage Isaiah considered appropriate, threatening him with the loss of everything he loved unless Lyon did precisely what Isaiah wanted him to do.

It would have been intolerable for Lyon and intolerable to witness.

"Yes. I see what you mean, Lyon. I do believe you are right about that, too. You had no choice."

To her surprise, he laughed, a genuine laugh. It tapered into a pleased sigh.

"Oh, Liv. I could almost *hear* your brain rifling about to arrive at that conclusion. I never did have to explain anything to you. It was always such a luxury . . . You have no idea. Being with you . . . it was like . . . like slipping out of tight shoes. Only infinitely more thrilling, of course."

She smiled. God, she knew what he meant. Before him and since he'd gone away, she'd either contracted or ever-so-subtly contorted her very being to accommodate nearly everybody else.

She was only ever wholly herself with him.

It was a bittersweet realization.

"And you weren't completely wrong about me being . . . my father's creation," he added. His voice was thicker now.

"I'm seldom *completely* wrong," she murmured. "And your father managed to create a few magnificent things. You, for instance."

Somehow she could feel he was smiling. Just something about a change in the air. As if his mood was her personal weather.

He sighed companionably, and then unfolded his long body and languorously stretched out beside her, his hands clasped behind his head to pillow it.

He did all of this slowly, as if to emphasize how very tall, how very strong, how very dangerously male he was.

That few inches of space between them almost pulsed. And yet it might as well have been the whole of the Atlantic Ocean.

"Lyon?" Sobbing had scraped her voice raw.

"Mmm?"

"I'm so, so very sorry I hurt you."

Words she had longed to say for so long.

He said nothing.

She held her breath.

For so long the peace they'd created began to gather into tension again, began to ring in her ears.

Forgive me, she silently begged. *I need your absolution.*

"I thought you despised me." He'd been gathering his thoughts, clearly.

"I never—"

"And you know . . . I always thought I would die before I hurt you. I would certainly want to kill anyone else who'd dared to hurt you. And yet at the same time *I* wanted to hurt you. I wanted you to care that I was gone."

He stopped talking.

His breath seemed held.

"Oh God. Lyon. I cared."

Cracked, whispered words. Yet they managed to contain the desolation of the years without him, and her whole heart.

He sighed, and tipped over on his side, propped his head on his hand, and stared down at her. His face was all shadows and moonlight.

"I'm sorry, too," he whispered.

And that was done, then.

They let his words hover softly in the air for a while.

"I would have found a way for us, Olivia."

"I know. I don't think I ever truly doubted you. It's just . . . you were older than I was. More experienced. Always a little quicker. Sometimes . . . it was too much. Sometimes I felt . . . caught up in something, a little pushed. I just wasn't ready to make that kind of decision that night."

He took this in with a long breath.

And he sighed. "I was so certain of the rightness of it, I suppose. Of my own *rightness*. I was so very arrogant. Young and invincible and all that."

She smiled. "What did we know about love?"

And there it was. The word. Somehow it was easier to say now that they were utterly empty of pretense or defense. She'd lost her fear of it because it was simply truth, something that just *was*, like the sand below them and the sky above them.

"Love is like a loaded musket," he mused. "And yet it's available to everyone. It's always . . ." He mimed thrusting out a gun. " 'Here you are! Try not to kill yourself or others with it.' They oughtn't allow young people near it."

But they were still speaking of love as if it were separate from them, as if it were part of the scenery, a reminiscence, not a thing that belonged to them now.

She laughed. "Ah, but the species would never perpetuate if the young weren't idiots."

He parted his mouth as if he meant to say something. And then stopped, and gave his head a little shake. "The things you say, Olivia. I just . . ." He gave his head another little shake.

Too filled with the pleasure of her to say anything.

She smiled at him.

She listened to him breathing for a moment, and the lick and sigh of waves rushing up to the beach and slipping back out to sea. That was all and that seemed enough forever. It seemed all she'd ever needed.

She'd never said "I love you" to him aloud then. She'd always regretted it.

She was so weary of disliking herself. She was engaged to marry a fine man, who said he loved her, and she'd begun to envision a life with him, a life grand, consistent, respectable, soothing, and safe, surrounded by family, friends, eventually children. A life, and a man, any woman would be proud and privileged to claim.

A man she could imagine one day loving.

She didn't want to hurt Landsdowne, or anyone ever again, herself included. She was so tired of pain. Perhaps she was simply tired of *feeling* so very much.

But she couldn't not touch Lyon now any more than she could keep her heart from beating.

Her fingertips landed softly on his cheek. Uncertain of their welcome.

She felt rather than heard his breathing arrest.

The soft peace of the previous moment was gone, just like that.

And all was portent and anticipation and wariness.

She couldn't see the expression in his eyes any more than she could see the expression in hers.

She dragged her fingers softly along the line of his jaw. She knew it as well as her own. It had seemed the most magical thing in the world to watch his desire for her kindle on his face, simply because she touched him.

Back then, they could only have that much and no more from each other.

Perhaps this would always be true.

Still. Her fingers trailed down his throat. And his pulse thumped swift and hard.

And just like that, she could feel the serrated edges of desire settling around her.

And then his face lowered. His lips touched hers.

Hesitantly.

So softly.

And perhaps, like her, wary of fresh pain.

But their bodies contained the memory of each other in their very cells. And when their lips met, hunger and celebration rushed in and swept out sense and caution.

They knew how to do this. He'd taught her, after all, and she'd inspired him.

Her mouth parted beneath his, and then . . .

Oh God, the incomparable, heady sweetness of his mouth, the heat and satin. The remembered pleasure. Surely no drug could be more decadent.

Desire roared along her nerve endings and her fingers laced through his hair and she was lost.

"*Liv.*" Half sigh, half groan, all surrender.

He lowered himself alongside her and they eased into each other's arms. The fit of his body against hers was so right, so familiar. But there was a new ferocity in him that was both dangerous and seductive. The wall-like chest against her was a reminder that this was not the Lyon of yesterday. That perhaps she didn't know all she needed to know about him now.

But she did know that she wanted him.

His hand slid down to cup her hip and he pressed her against his now-hard cock. Pleasure cleaved her, and he rose over her to take the kiss more deeply, and they clung, the kiss devouring, nearly punishing.

And then suddenly he pulled his mouth away from her.

Pushed himself up on his arms, drawing in a long, shuddering breath.

He rolled away, lying flat. Away from her. Arms at his sides rigidly, as if to discipline them for wrapping her in them at all.

And they both lay, dazed and once again separate, which seemed wrong, suddenly. She felt unmoored, between worlds.

Even logic and gravity succumbed to Lyon.

Every bit of her body was thrumming as if she were a struck gong.

He finally broke the silence.

"I'm not a boy anymore, Olivia. I don't intend to spill in my trousers ever again."

It was coarse but quite honest.

"Understood."

He turned his head to look at her, in something like amazement. And then gave a short laugh.

They lay in utter silence, each of them tense as pulled-back bowstrings, until at last she became aware of other things besides Lyon, such as the fact that it was growing cooler.

She gave a start when he sprang to his feet.

He looked down at her for a moment, as if he was admiring a kill, and then thrust out his hand.

She seized it and he pulled her to her feet, with a mock effortful grunt.

"Excellent! You're already a little heavier, Liv, from the delicious shipboard food."

"Beast," she said, without rancor.

When she was upright, she discovered the world was still spinning a little.

There was no intoxicant in the world like Lyon Redmond.

He dropped her hand abruptly and bolted off, his heels kicking up little sprays of sand.

"Where are you—what are you—"

He pivoted and ran backward a few steps, eyes on the sky, and then stopped abruptly.

"Stay right where you are!" he commanded.

He stretched out his arm like a triumphant acrobat landing, and ceremoniously turned up his hand.

"Now look up, Liv. Look at my hand."

She did.

And lo and behold, the bright orb of the moon was right there, nestled in his palm.

"Ohhh," she breathed.

It was beautiful and perfect and magical.

And an illusion.

And then he wound his arm and pretended to bowl the moon to her, a la cricket.

She ducked, flinging her arms over her head.

He shook his head and sighed, gustily and funereally. "We're going to have to work on your catching, Eversea, if you're ever going to be a decent wicket keeper."

He dropped his arm, leaving the moon in the sky, and strode forward.

She laughed and scrambled to catch up to him, her bare feet sinking into the silken sand, and she found herself savoring every step, because every step brought her closer to him.

He remembered to stop to wait for her.

AH, CEILING, MY old friend, Lyon thought mordantly. *We meet again.*

He wondered if ceilings would always remind him of Olivia.

They'd silently gone their separate ways into separate chambers once in the house.

And he'd stripped out of his clothing and climbed into bed, and waited in vain for sleep, and it was just like old times.

He was a little older, perhaps a little wiser, infinitely more jaded. He'd been stabbed at and shot at, and he'd done a fair amount of stabbing and shooting. He'd amassed a fortune through a piquant blend of ruthless opportunism, lawlessness, and idealism, and he'd earned his sense of near invincibility, not to mention the calluses on his hands and on his heart.

And yet here he was, lying perfectly rigid, like a man attempting not to jar a grave wound. As uncertain and burning, burning, burning with untenable lust as if he was a boy again who had just touched his first breast.

And all it had taken was a few moments in her arms.

He was darkly amused at himself, and at everything, really.

In some ways this suffering was truly operatic, the stuff of legends. Tragic, consuming, all the doomed and star-crossed lovers nonsense, etcetera. She was his Achilles' heel, his Chiron wound that would never heal.

On the other hand, surely nothing could be more mundane. For there would *be* no myths, no operas, no plays, no flash ballads, if men and women before the two of them hadn't performed this particular fruitless pas de deux over and over since the beginning of time.

He'd thought that he'd wanted to show her his house in Cadiz to prove to her how wrong she'd been. To show her what she *could* have had.

Now he knew it was because he simply wanted her to know that he was worthy of her. Which is all he'd ever wanted.

And she was right. He hadn't quite seen it before, but he *had* pushed her. He knew how precious her family was to her, especially since she could have lost her brothers in the war. She'd had enough uncertainty in her life. And yet he had demanded of her that they go forward into uncertainty, together.

He had simply thought love was enough.

He shifted restlessly in his bed.

He could have taken her tonight.

Her perhaps ought to have taken her tonight.

He could still take her tonight. She was lying only a few rooms away.

He knew how to use Olivia's own passion and sensuality to get what he wanted.

But what then?

He had enough honor and breeding to not relish cuckolding a man like Landsdowne. Or to deflower a woman who was engaged to another man.

But when he peered beneath the veneer of that rationale he knew the truth:

He might have survived being shot and stabbed.

But Olivia Eversea was still the razor who could slice his callused heart to ribbons.

She always had been.

He wondered if she always would be.

And God help him, he wasn't certain he was brave enough to live through that again.

So when he finally slept, he slept alone.

Chapter 19

✌

MORNING POURED THROUGH THE window, sea breeze scoured clean, the light so pure and brilliant everything in the room merged into a single soft glow, the walls, the windows, the curtains, the floors.

Everything apart from a gleaming jar of marmalade and the shining handle of the knife protruding from it.

Lyon was sitting at the table, a small stack of fried bread on a plate next to him, steam rising from a cup next to his elbow.

She slid into the chair across from him and propped her chin on her hands.

He poured a cup of coffee from a surprisingly fine porcelain pot and pushed it over to her.

"It will singe your eyebrows off." His voice was still gravelly from sleep, and it affected her senses as surely as if his fingers had played with the short hairs on the nape of her neck.

He watched, waiting for her to taste it.

"*À votre santé.*" She raised it in a toast, took a sip, and winced.

"Eh?" he said happily.

"Eh!" she approved, and took another bracing

sip. "It's marvelous. It's what I always imagined lava tasted like."

"Turkish," he said shortly. And smiled faintly.

She smiled at him. A pair of mauve shadows curved beneath his eyes, and she suspected she sported a matching set. Clearly neither of them had slept well, if at all. They had metaphorically set each other's bodies on fire and then gone their separate ways to smolder in their respective beds.

She wondered if he'd memorized his ceiling the way she'd memorized hers. She'd probably lost any weight she'd gained on this journey by tossing and turning violently.

But he'd been very right to stop that kiss last night.

"You look piratical," she said. And dangerous. And appealing. And human. And vulnerable.

And the black whiskers made his eyes seem even bluer.

His eyes flared an instant at her choice of words. Which had not been idle.

He smiled swiftly and swiped a self-conscious hand over his chin. "*You* look . . ."

His eyes finished the sentence for him.

If one could make love with a single look, he'd just done that.

He reached for a slice of fried bread and slid the plate over to her, along with a jar of marmalade. Her favorite.

"All the luxuries of home," she said. Her voice was a little faint, after that look.

She seized the knife and spread the marmalade over the bread as if she were one of Genevieve's beloved painters.

He watched her, bemused.

She paused to admire her handiwork before she took a bite.

"Does it have to be completely covered?" He sounded fascinated.

"Yes," she said easily.

He smiled at that.

They knew each other so well, but there were so many other things they didn't know, the homely humble things.

She bit into it. Heaven. Bread and marmalade had never tasted so marvelous.

When she finished chewing she said, "I should like a bath."

He paused mid-chew and studied her with faint surprise, then flicked a glance over her, as if to ascertain whether she was indeed dirty.

"I'm a woman," she pointed out. "The tolerance for sand in my various crevices is no doubt lower than your own."

"Fair point."

He watched approvingly as she tore into her bread again like a starved wolf. She'd never been this hungry in her life.

"I know just the place," he said at last. Sounding mysterious.

"The *place*?"

"I haven't a bathtub yet, per se, and as you likely have noticed, no household staff to see to it if I did have one. You see, when it's just me and I want to thoroughly bathe, I . . ." And he gestured with his chin out the window.

"You aren't going to tell me to wade into the ocean!"

"I'm not going to *tell* you to do anything. You made it clear how you felt about that." He said this with a sort of relish. "I'll just show you."

He took another bite of his own bread, then studied her face.

He put the bread down.

"You'll love it," he said gently, and with total confidence. It was both irritating and hopelessly magnetic, as usual. As if she were a mare who spooked easily, and the whole point of his life was to lead her to things she loved.

"JONATHAN HAS HIS own investment group, you say?" he said suddenly. "I've had my ways of staying abreast of the news, but I hadn't heard this bit."

They had set out into the beautiful morning. He'd thrown a few things into a knapsack, cheese and bread and a little bottle of wine and a couple of rolled-up blankets, and he was swinging it in his hand and whistling some unidentifiable tune. It meandered so much she suspected it was his own invention, which made her smile.

That brilliant blue sky above them was the very color of happiness, as cheerful as a carnival canopy. The sun was gentle but brilliant, the air softly humid, and she wondered at the fact that she hadn't thought to bring a bonnet, or wear stockings. She'd seized her reticule, more out of habit than from necessity, though it contained a comb. How quickly she'd taken to becoming a heathen.

"*And* they say he'll be running for Parliament," she reminded him. "He's passionate about child labor reform."

Lyon shook his head in wonderment. "There must have been a woman involved."

"Why do you say that?"

"Because women are why we do anything."

She thought about this. "A generalization, surely."

"But sadly, it bears up under analysis."

He shot her a mischievous look, knowing analysis was very nearly Olivia's favorite thing.

She smiled, enjoying being known.

"Jonathan may not have done it at all if you hadn't left Pennyroyal Green."

He looked at her sharply then.

And fell into a silence that had stretched on long enough to take on something of the feel of a brood.

She knew, no matter what, that he had missed his family, too.

"Are we waxing philosophical this morning, Olivia?" he said finally.

"It's generally how I wax, when I do."

He laughed.

She wondered if for the rest of her life the sound of his laugh would make her heart launch, because it made every single thing about life better, the way salt or marmalade did.

They mounted a gentle rise, which was when she became aware of a rushing sound, a constant, soft roar, distinct from the pulse of the ocean breaking on the beach and rolling out again. As they crested the rise, he reached for her hand.

"We'll be heading down in a bit, and the ground can be a bit shifty here, so . . ."

She gave him her hand. It was engulfed in his, and she suddenly felt shy and solemn and girlish.

"Don't trust my agility?" she said lightly.

"Oh, it's not that. I just don't want to go tumbling to my death unaccompanied."

She laughed, and then gave a little gasp as he tugged her forward and then down a fairly steep slope, flexing his arm expertly, effortlessly, for all the world like a rudder on a ship. His strength was both shocking and humbling and innate. She might as well have been gripping a steel bar.

With a little jump they landed on a narrow strip of golden beach.

"All right, then," was all he said.

She couldn't speak.

They were nestled in a sort of basket made of towering stone and sheer cliffs.

A turquoise jewel of a pool shimmered at their feet, spreading in a gently wavy oval for perhaps fifty or more feet, then curving, like the tail of an apostrophe, into another smaller pool that disappeared beyond an enormous outcropping of rock. Its surface shivered, delicately disturbed by the waterfall at its far end, an endless pour of foaming water about as tall as Lyon and about the length of two landaus, if she had to guess, across. She couldn't see its ultimate origin; it spilled from another craggy hill out of sight above them; and it ended by tumbling down staggered ledges of stone before it emptied into the pool.

Behind it was a soft and shadowy recess of stone. Flat from the looks of things.

It looked for all the world like a lacy white curtain over a stage.

"Eden."

She hadn't realized she'd said the word aloud. It was more like an exhale from the very depths of her soul.

"Precisely what I thought when I first saw it."

They admired it in silence for another moment.

"And now you take off all your clothes and stand beneath the waterfall and wash."

Her head whipped toward him.

He extended his hand and opened it ceremoniously. In it was a bar of soap. It looked very white against his browned hand.

She stared at it.

Then looked warily up at him.

"It's French, the soap is. Have a sniff."

"I believe you," she said dryly. "The sentence prior to that one is what gave me pause."

Another silence. During which they locked eyes, and a good deal was thought very loudly but not spoken.

"I'll stay in here." He made a sweeping motion at the little curving portion of the pool that disappeared behind the outcropping. The little tail of the apostrophe. "And perform my own ablutions. It's quite shallow throughout, and I daresay even you can stand up in it. I won't be able to see you and you won't be able to see me. Though if you stand behind the water you ought to be somewhat veiled, regardless of where I am."

She turned toward the waterfall. Then back to him. Then back to the waterfall. Then back to him.

"Do you . . . need some assistance? With laces, stays, and so forth?" he said almost stiffly. "Or would you prefer to keep the sand in your crevices as a souvenir of your sojourn here?"

"I can manage," she said tautly.

"Intrepid as always."

She snorted softly.

"I'll keep guard, and I'll protect you from any encroaching seagulls or vengeful mermaids."

"Vengeful, are they?" She at last gingerly reached for the soap.

She was reminded of the time she'd handed a pamphlet to him. That first touch of his skin against hers, illicit and cherished. The fuse that had lit all of it.

His hands were still long and elegant, but brown and hard now. But now there was a faint scar across one. They looked well-used. As though he'd spent the past few years wielding weapons. And other quite dangerous things.

Did he ever tremble now? Or had he seen and touched enough women to shave the edge off wonder forever?

"Oh, mermaids are a jealous species," he said softly, as if he could hear her thoughts. "They often make very cutting remarks about other beautiful women."

She was so enchanted by the image of fuming aquatic maidens smacking their tails indignantly she immediately forgot to be nervous.

It was also the first overt compliment he'd given her since she'd first laid eyes on him again, and it was absurdly potent enough to make her blush.

She couldn't remember a time she'd changed color in the presence of Landsdowne, or any other man, really.

Apart, perhaps, from when she'd gone pale upon reading "The Legend of Lyon Redmond."

Which made her think of Landsdowne, and his hands, strong and square and aristocratic, the signet ring gleaming as he stirred sugar into his tea and confessed to maybe, possibly, mildly disappointing another woman when he became engaged to Olivia.

And here was Lyon, who was incapable of doing anything mildly, yet again offering her something new, something she might or might not be equal to, something that might or might not be wise.

"Take this, too, because you'll need to dry off." Lyon thrust the rolled blanket at her, and she tucked it beneath her arm. "You can walk right up to the waterfall, and tuck yourself behind it. You'll see."

And then she suddenly reached up pulled her ribbon loose and gave her head a good shake, giving her hair up to the breeze, which immediately began tossing it about like a new plaything. And then she kicked off her slippers and lunged to seize them up in one hand, hiked her dress to her calves in the other—let him admire *that* view—and set out toward the waterfall.

"For all you know, *I'm* covered all over in iridescent scales," she said over her shoulder.

"Good God, I hope so. Then all my dreams will have come true."

Her laughter trailed her, unbridled and musical as that waterfall.

IT WAS THE one thing that had been missing, he realized. That sound more than nearly anything meant "Olivia" to him.

He stood and drank it in.

She sounded free and *happy.* An innocent sort of happy. It was like birdsong after a rainstorm, when birds all sang their fool heads off, throwing their hearts into it.

She should always be this happy.

And then he noticed something on the ground nearby, a scrap of shining fabric.

She'd dropped her reticule.

He picked it up, and a comb and something folded into a tight, white square tumbled out and unfurled on the way, fluttering to the ground.

He picked it up gently, frowning, and ran it through his fingers.

And then all at once he knew what it was.

His thumb found "LAJR" embroidered in the corner.

How had she gotten it? The handkerchief was spotless, apart from a tiny drop of blood.

And then he remembered: it was from the night he'd left Pennyroyal Green. The night his father had hit him.

She'd kept it this long.

And she'd carried it with her folded in a tight square.

He closed his eyes, and once again, his chest exploded with light, like the first time he'd held her in his arms.

Perhaps this was all they would ever have—an hour or two of bliss here and there, strung together like jewels by interludes of longing and loss. Perhaps they were destined for nothing more than a few pockets of time, tucked away into their lives, hidden from everyone and everything the way this cove was hidden from the rest of the beach.

Still.

He watched her go with bemused wonder at fate, his lungs constricting a little with yearning. That ever-present desire that always had its claws in him and seemed to doom him to restlessness.

She loved him. She always had.

He knew it as surely as he knew the color of his own eyes.

And he was just as certain then he'd been born loving her, as surely as he'd been born with blue eyes. It was that simple. That permanent.

And if it was a curse, then he didn't know what a blessing was.

Now he knew what must do, for her sake and for his.

OLIVIA TRIPPED DELICATELY along the beach in her bare feet until the damp sand butted up against cool silvery-gray stone, its jagged edges polished through who knows how many centuries of rushing water. She took a step up, easing past the waterfall into the recess behind it. It was deep enough so that the smooth back wall of the arcing cave was dry, if cool, and the damp, earthy, mineral smell was a perfume. She inhaled deeply.

She peered out through the curtain of water.

On the shore was a little stack of clothes and a pair of boots and a blanket spread out neatly, which meant Lyon had adroitly stripped and must already be in the water.

Men. Bless their heathen little souls.

And in for a penny, in for a pound.

She could accomplish this quickly if she didn't pause to mull. It was an easy enough thing to slip her dress off over her head once she'd finished with the laces, and after that, she slipped off her shift. She folded all of it neatly and stacked it against the stone wall.

And just like that, she was entirely naked outdoors and about to step beneath a waterfall, which wasn't a very English thing to be or do.

Though she wouldn't be at all surprised if one of her brothers had done it once or twice.

She stood, simply enjoying being nude, unfettered by anything that defined her, like fine English clothing. The air was warm and dense and velvety, a caress, and it turned mundane acts she'd never given much thought to—raising her arms, walking in bare feet, giving her head a toss to pour her hair down her bare back, shake her hair down her bare back—into sensual ones.

She stepped beneath the water and gasped, and then she laughed in shock.

The contrast between the cold water and the silky air was a brand new kind of bliss. She held the soap beneath the water and rubbed it between her palms.

Too vigorously as it turned out.

"Damn!"

The stones amplified her voice as if she were on stage at Covent Garden.

The soap leaped for its freedom from her grasp and landed with a splash in the pool below and immediately began sailing away.

LYON DUCKED BENEATH the water and burst to the surface swiftly. A quick little baptism, an attempt at clearing his head.

It was a mercy to surrender his thoughts and tension to the cool buoyancy of the water. He floated on his back, watching a gull ride the breeze above him just because it could.

Then again, the gull had its own hunger to contend with, and it lived for its next meal.

Freedom—from anything, really, whether it was the past, one's family, from a seemingly hopeless love—was really rather an illusion, he'd learned.

Something bright and white caught the corner of his eye, and he blinked.

A bar of soap was drifting merrily by.

He shot out an arm and seized it, then stood upright.

He knew in a flash what he had in his hands:

Leverage.

The thing with which to bargain.

Also: potentially a terrible mistake.

He could let it go sailing out to the ocean.

He could tuck it into his knapsack and pretend he'd never seen it.

He could have done a dozen or more things more advisable than what he did next. He raised his voice.

"Did you . . . perhaps lose something, Olivia?"

A silence. A telling and almost palpable hesitation, during which he could practically hear the gears of her mind clicking away over the sound of the waterfall.

Let your body have the say, Olivia.

"Did it . . . find its way to you?" The acoustics were such she scarcely needed to raise her voice. It was pitched a little higher. She was tense, too.

"It drifted on by en route to Le Havre, and I seized it."

In the silence that followed it felt as though the world itself held its breath.

"Do you want it?" he asked.

The words were gruff. He didn't bother to disguise the tension in his voice.

So much hinged on her next word, and he didn't know which answer he wanted most.

It turned out to be:

"Yes."

Chapter 20

❧

H<small>E WENT TO HER</small> immediately and without another word.

He never second-guessed decisions. It was a quality he'd inherited from his father, born of arrogance and privilege, tempered through one test after another over the last few years.

He swam into the larger pool and stopped abruptly.

His breath whooshed out when saw the suggestion of her body, veiled by the pouring water. Her head was tipped back to allow it to run the length of her, as if she were a fountain carved of marble.

And he'd held her body close to his before, through layers of muslin. He'd often thought over the years that it wouldn't matter what Olivia looked like beneath her clothes. She could be sporting the head of a girl and the body of a rhinoceros and he'd still feel that frisson.

She was most definitely sporting the body of a woman.

Through the water he saw her in profile: a suggestion of a small, up-curving, rose-tipped breast, a waist that flared eloquently into a round white arse, long slim white limbs.

The impact was as total and instant as a lightning strike. It sizzled along his spine and he thought his head might pop off away from his body and join the circling gulls.

And he was on shore and out of the water swiftly, soap in hand, before she even saw him.

SHE TURNED WITH a start when he appeared.

They stared at each other, like Adam stumbling across Eve for the first time.

Or very like that first time in the ballroom, when time had stopped and they had stared.

"No scales," was all he said, finally.

She couldn't speak. When she saw him, the blood stampeded to her head and her ability to form words had clearly been trampled in the process.

A new sort of logic asserted itself. This sudden weakness in the face of extraordinary male beauty was perhaps an evolutionary thing. The point of which was to stun the female into helpless, willing submission.

Nude we ought to look vulnerable, a little absurd, she thought. But Lyon looked as right out of clothes as an actual lion did in its own skin, and he looked as comfortable standing there as he would be in a ballroom or the deck of a ship.

Then again, she didn't know why anyone would bother with modesty if they looked like him. His lean body was everywhere gradations of sun-touched gold, darker on his arms and legs and face, his hips and lower on his belly paler. He seemed etched from muscle, shining hard quadrants on his chest, downright lyrical slopes of his shoulders, vast enough to turn his torso into a veritable "V," to the lean bulge of thighs, to the concave scoops on each side of his buttocks, each just about the size of the palm of her hand if she had to guess.

There were a few worrisome scars on him, one that was most definitely from a musket ball.

But there was his penis, of course, already beginning to curve toward his belly out of a nest of black curls from merely the thought and sight of her.

Olivia had an epiphany born of lust: *He was only overwhelming when I resisted.*

If I surrender to what we both want, everything is simple.

She knew he thought her beautiful, because it was reflected in his face. But more thrilling was the intent she saw there. It was primal and absolutely implacable.

He intended to take her.

She wanted very, very badly to be taken.

There was no thinking or right and wrong. There was only now. But suddenly fear and exhilaration seemed of a piece.

"Perhaps you need help with washing the back of your neck, Olivia? I imagine it feels sticky."

She stared at him mutely. All of her faculties were engaged in absorbing how he looked nude, and with luck it would be branded on her brain forever.

And he moved to stand behind her. As it were the most natural thing in the world. She closed her eyes. She could feel the heat of his body, and the press of his swelling cock against her buttocks. Her heartbeat ratcheted.

He lifted her heavy wet hair gently, as if she were indeed a wild animal who might balk or bolt.

And he applied the soap to the back of her neck with feather strokes of his fingers. Quicksilver rivulets of sensation communicated to her groin and her nipples ruched tighter and every other part of her body stirred, clamoring for the attention he was giving to just a few square inches of it.

Her breath came more swiftly, in ragged gusts.

He cupped his hand in the flow of the waterfall and trickled the water from his fist over her neck.

And then he slowly slid his hands around her waist, laid his lips against her throat where her pulse beat, and opened them into a slow, scalding kiss, drawing his tongue along that tender, hidden place beneath her ear.

And blew a soft breath over it.

She moaned a soft, long, low, carnal animal sound.

It was the sound of begging, and he knew it.

He immediately abandoned any notions he might have had about subtlety and lost whatever grip he had on his own desire, and God only knows what became of the soap.

Because his hands were on her now, callused and hot as they learned and reclaimed her, sliding over her wet skin to her hips. He pulled her harder against his body, and she arched into him like a shameless cat, savoring the glide of her skin against his, teasing his cock. His hands journeyed up her rib cage and cupped her breasts, reveling in the satiny weight of them, and his breath, his tongue, his lips in her ear, on her throat, sent fresh shock after fresh shock of pleasure through her. He left little bonfires of sensation everywhere his fingers touched, until she was burning and restless and comprised of need.

He thumbed her nipples, and she gasped. He did it again, harder, and again, until she was rippling against him, urging him on.

His hands slid boldly and swiftly over her belly, down her thighs, over the damp between her legs, his fingers sliding into her cleft, an inexorable and determined exploration.

"Olivia," he breathed slowly in her ear, and gooseflesh arose over her arms, and just like that, her name became a part of her seduction.

His hands delved between her legs again, and his fingers dipped into the heat and damp and pulsing ache of her, stroking and circling, hard and skilled and very strategic, and she moved against him, with him.

"Lyon . . . Lyon please . . . *please* . . . more . . ."

And then he suddenly spun her and she found her back against the slick cool of the stone, and his mouth fell on hers hard. Their groins fused as she arched into him, her hands latched around his neck, and she savored the friction of her nipples against his burnished skin. He slid his cock against her, teasing her, teasing himself, bringing both of them to the very brink of madness.

A devouring kiss was broken when her head thrashed back.

Her voice was a raw scrape. "Please . . . Lyon . . . I want . . ."

She didn't know what she wanted, but he did, and she trusted him.

He scooped a hand beneath her thigh and he guided his cock into her with a swift thrust.

Her knees nearly buckled but he wasn't about to let go of her.

And it was a wordless, nearly savage coupling, of years of longing and anger and love and every other thwarted emotion. She wrapped her hands around his head as he buried his face in her neck, and then she slid her fingers and dug them into his shoulders, clinging, her eyes never leaving his until his lids closed and his breath rushed hot from between his parted lips. And then she slid her hands to his hips and gripped, wanting to feel every thrust, rising to meet him as his cock drove into her again, again, and *oh God* again. The world was the rush of the falls, the sound of their bodies colliding, the roar of their breath, the exquisite pressure of an ever-building need she thought might kill her before it was met.

Until she shattered into glittering fragments, the bliss blinding and indescribable.

She nearly crumpled as a raw and nearly silent scream shredded her throat. She heard it from somewhere outside her body.

He held her fast, relentlessly racing toward his own release, his breathing a storm now.

And then he went rigid. It was her turn to hold him fast when his release wracked him again and again, and his cry was one of almost pain.

She fancied she could still hear their voices mingling and echoing over the water.

HIS SHOULDERS MOVED in a great sigh, and she savored the rise and fall of them, and the feel of his smooth, hot skin beneath her palm. His back was a fascinating network of muscle beneath satiny skin.

They clung to each other like shipwreck survivors.

His face was tucked into her throat, and her hands moved over his back gently, soothing him as the storming rush of his breathing and hers became more even.

There were a lot of things she ought to be thinking.

But with every breath she drew in and breathed out, all she could think was *at last at last at last.*

LYON FELT *AMAZING.*

Newer, cleansed, deliriously good, suffused with well-being and love for all mankind.

All because of a petite girl who could be so fierce and relentlessly clever when she was clothed, but when naked was all delicate pink and cream and saucy, almost whimsical curves, and who made love like an animal.

The contrast delighted him.

He hoped he hadn't bruised her.

He was fairly certain *he'd* be sporting bruises where her fingers had dug into his hips and shoulders. He knew a sizzle of very masculine satisfaction at that thought, and at the sound of her scream, and at the way she'd clung to him in order to withstand the pleasure.

"You are positively beaming," she said finally.

"I ought to be mourning. You never did get to finish your bathing," he said sadly. "And now we've lost the soap."

"Perhaps it's even now on its way to Le Havre."

"Depending on the currents," he said.

They stared down in the little pool pensively for a moment.

And then the devil came over him. And he kneed her in her white round arse.

With a little shriek and a lot of flailing she tumbled into the pool and disappeared beneath the water.

She shot to the surface with the ferocity of a geyser and whipped her hair out of her eyes, incensed, eyes flashing sparks he could almost feel on his skin. "You . . . you . . . wretch! You *beast*!"

Moments later her face transformed. "Ooooh, but Lyon, it's lovely!!"

He laughed.

She swished her arms about her, savoring the feel of the water, her limbs silvery suggestions beneath the clear water, her nipples peaked and shell-pink and tantalizingly, mesmerizingly bobbing right at the water line.

And he leaped into the water, capsizing her again. They spluttered to the surface at the same time.

"I'm a fisherman and I want a mermaid to ravish!" he declared on a growl.

"*Never!*" she vowed passionately, and pushed with her toes off the bottom of the pool with surprising strength and shot like an otter away from him.

He lunged after her.

She shrieked and dodged him again, eluding him with selkie skill until they were both giggling like children set free after a winter locked in a cell.

Of course he was going to win. They both knew it. Either because he was faster or because she was going to let him.

And about five minutes later he finally maneuvered in front of her, seized her, and gathered her against him.

He held her loosely in the circle of his arms, which felt like bands of iron and ironically made her feel weak again with desire.

Wet skin against wet skin, her nipples chafing against his hard chest. Blue eyes met blue eyes.

"I've got you." Rather a statement of the obvious, on his part.

"And so you have. Deal with me gently, kind sir."

"Not on your life," he murmured.

"Perhaps we can . . . strike a bargain for my freedom."

Her hands slid down his chest and dipped below the water and reached between his legs.

He went still, his eyes intriguingly and instantly abstracted. "I see you've found my harpoon."

"And so I have," she murmured.

"What do you intend to do with it?"

"Perhaps I'll do this with it."

She closed her fingers around his already swelling cock and stroked upward, sliding her fingertips over the satiny dome.

"Excellent . . . suggestion." He sounded as if he could barely breathe.

And suddenly everything was quite serious, and the rush of the waterfall, the ragged rhythm of his breath against her lips, seemed all of a piece, elemental, part of this place.

Kisses that began as slow and languid became thorough and claiming, growing ever deeper, ever more hungry, each one paring away a layer of control, exposing again the raw need that had pulsed between them from the very beginning and was very clearly never going to be fully sated.

"Oh God . . . please don't stop, Liv," he whispered hoarsely against her lips, and then took hers again. He covered her hands with his and pushed them down to show her just how he wanted to be touched.

She didn't mind at all being told what to do. His pleasure was indistinguishable from her own.

His head went back hard and the cords of his neck went taut and his breath was hot and swift. His throat moved in a swallow.

She kissed him there, too, then drew her tongue along the glowing skin of his throat.

He slid his hands beneath her buttocks and lifted her up, and thrust into her again, and her head went back on a gasp as he filled her.

It was glorious and strange and it made her savage with need.

"My *God*, Lyon," she moaned again.

She locked her legs around his waist, and he moved her over him, slowly, tormenting, teasing both of them, the water buoying them as they rocked together, until they were colliding swiftly, her head dropped back.

"Liv . . . Liv . . . oh my God, *Liv*."

And just like that they were both in the throes of release, their screams echoing, water rippling out from them.

HER LEGS STILL wrapped around him, he carried her effortlessly toward the shore, then tipped her backward on the beach onto the blanket he'd spread, then sprawled flat out next to her.

They lay there in a stupor of contentment for a time.

She absently traced the lines of him. Drew her finger around that round scar. She recognized a musket ball wound when she saw one.

Someone had shot him.

He had lived.

She suspected she knew why he'd been shot, and how he'd been shot, and was amazed to find that the reason didn't bother her in the least.

She would find out soon enough, because she intended to ask him.

"May I confess something?" She said this dreamily.

"Certainly."

"I should like to bite you."

"Bite me? What have I done to deserve such ill treatment?"

His voice was as languid as someone who'd drunk a half bottle of laudanum.

"It's just that your skin is so smooth and a delicious color, like toasted bread, or a biscuit. Just a little nip."

He smiled dreamily. "I'll allow it."

"Is it in the book of rules, then?"

"Oh, there's no official pamphlet, or anything of that sort, if that's what you're wondering. But all manner of things fall under the rubric of sex. If it can be imagined, someone has likely tried it and enjoyed it. Or died trying."

"Really?"

"Really."

"You're not jesting."

"As enjoyable as it would be to tease you, no. I'm far too replete to make anything up at this point."

"I like everything we've done so far."

"Good God, so have I." He stretched languorously, like a cat, his words a contented slur.

She leaned forward and with her teeth, very delicately, nipped at his chest, and his hand went up to cup the back of her head, his fingers threading through her hair, which was already nearly dry.

"Nice," he murmured.

"You are beautiful, too," she whispered.

"Shh," he said rudely and sleepily, but she didn't mind.

He yawned mightily and looped his arm around her and pulled her into his body as he drifted off to sleep, as if she were the only thing anchoring him to earth, and he wanted to bring her with him into his dreams.

She followed him there moments later.

SHE STIRRED FROM a nap because the sun had traveled and was now beaming down on her bare belly.

She tilted her head.

And her heart skipped.

For there he was. Those eyes of his, and his increasingly bewhiskered face. Gazing warmly at her.

So like she'd imagined that day in Tingle's Bookshop years ago.

He reached for her hand and twiddled her fingers idly.

"What time is it?" she asked sleepily.

"Does it matter?" He sounded genuinely surprised.

His voice had that lovely fresh out of sleep rasp.

"No," she said, and stretched, pointing her toes.

Her leg was pressed against his hard furred one.

He was gazing at her with something like bemused awe.

She was basking in his admiration, feeling beautiful, until he said: "I had no idea your hair was so . . . enormous."

"I . . . what?" She clapped her hands to her head.

"It's gone very fluffy and tall and just vast. You could wear it into battle proudly and terrify your enemies."

She couldn't stop laughing. "Hush!" She smoothed it down frantically.

Her body was deliciously sore in so many places, but she now recognized an unfamiliar feeling about her rib cage, too.

It was from laughing until she ached.

She didn't think she'd done that since . . .

Since the last time she'd laughed until she ached with Lyon.

"It's splendid hair. Truly. It's very interesting." He captured it for her, skeined it around his hand idly. "And soft. Well done, growing such hair."

He was relentless, and now she was laughing helplessly.

"Here, have it back."

He unspooled her hair from his hand, and casually draped it instead across her face.

She pushed it away.

"Said the man who has a good deal more hair than he needs on his face at the moment. Not to mention a queue. As if you were a pirate."

Her second strategic use of the word that day.

Something flickered in his eyes then. He casually rolled away from her onto his back and looked thoughtfully up at the sky, hands folded behind his head.

Her heart gave a little lurch.

Lyon had something on his conscience. And she suspected she knew what it was.

"Would you like me to shave?" he said finally.

"Would you do it?"

"Of course. Tell me what else you'd like me to do for you. Or to you."

"Surprise me."

"Don't I always?" he murmured.

He leaned over and touched his tongue, very lightly, to her nipple, then drew it into his mouth and gently sucked.

"Will that do for a start?"

"Dear God," she rasped, as a white-hot shock of pleasure rayed through her limbs.

He drew leisurely hard circles around her nipple with his tongue, then introduced his teeth lightly into the surprise, while his hand wandered to cup and stroke her other breast. Drunk with the astonishing bliss, she sighed and arched into it.

He kissed a soft trail down, down the seam that divided her ribs, dragging his fingers in the wake of his lips, and he nudged up one of her thighs and without further preamble, delved his tongue into the hot, velvety, very damp core of her, and licked. Hard. Slowly. Deliberately. Again, and then again. His tongue darted, stroking, diving, his fingers playing delicately with that tender, excruciatingly sensitive skin on the inside of her thighs, and she arched to meet him, undulated to abet him, to greedily take in this extraordinary new pleasure.

"Lyon . . . Oh God . . . Oh God . . ."

And as she screamed his name, her fingers knit through his hair and she bowed upward, feeling as if she might break in two from the explosive pleasure.

He rose up over her, and as she was still pulsing with release, he seized her hips and lifted her so he could be inside her in one thrust.

Slowly, slowly, this time. Savoring every inch of her, torturing himself, teasing her. She watched him, and the sun behind him gave him a corona, and his face was all shadow apart from his eyes, first brilliant flashes of blue, then closed, as his head tipped back and his own release rocked through him.

Chapter 21

❧

THIS TIME HAD, INDEED, been humbling and surprising for both of them.

Somehow it was now definitive: their desire was bigger than both of them. There was an endless supply of it, and the more they indulged, the more there was of it.

He was still catching his breath, one hand absently, idly, stroking her hair as she lay burrowed somewhere between his shoulder and armpit.

"Lyon . . ."

He lifted his head when he heard the tone in her voice. Instantly wary.

"Are you Le Chat?"

He went absolutely rigid. Very like a sword in a scabbard, for that matter.

He rolled away from her, onto his side, and his hand went down as if he was indeed reflexively reaching for a sword.

He caught himself in time and then fixed her with an inscrutable stare that she could have sworn contained something of admiration for arriving at that conclusion.

"Why do you ask?"

"The simplest answer would have been no."

He was studying her shrewdly for signs of accusation or hysteria.

She thought perhaps she was too permanently sated for hysteria to ever take hold again.

Then he rolled over flat on his back and stared up at the sky.

She could say now, *I was jesting. Of course you're not a feared pirate.* She could release him from the question, so she wouldn't need to bear the burden of the knowledge.

But in the silence he was gathering his thoughts, and she could not go on without knowing.

She waited. A gull wheeled above them, and Olivia moved closer to him, pressing her thigh lightly against his. So he would feel safe telling her the truth.

He drew in a long breath, then blew it out at length. Clearly considering how to begin.

"Five years ago . . . I came, quite by happenstance—which means I charmed a drunk man into telling me at a dock pub one night—into possession of some sensitive knowledge. An investment group was engaged in the conversion of cargo into slaves. They owned a fleet of five ships."

She tensed at the idea of slave ships.

He sensed it. He took hold of her hand and threaded her fingers through it, comforting her, holding her fast.

"They had already made multiple trips, successfully eluding the law, bribing just the right authorities apparently, and getting wealthier and wealthier from the sale of human beings. My personal wealth as a merchant—I adopted another name as a merchant—was burgeoning and my reputation was growing. I was approached as a potential investor in this hideous practice through a third party—

exchanging cargo for humans and back again. As you may have guessed, I demurred. Diplomatically."

She held his hand tighter.

"But there existed—exists, I should say—people in all walks of life who find the slave trade as abhorrent as you or I. And to put it succinctly, I discreetly gathered a crew. And my crew and I boarded each of these ships in turn by night, removed their cargo, be it silks or spices or what have you, put their crews into boats, and set them adrift, and then we—"

"And then you blew the ships to smithereens." She breathed wonderingly.

Which would have essentially destroyed both the group's profits and eliminated any opportunity they might have to try again. Salting their earth, figuratively speaking.

And frightening the devil out of anyone who might want to traffic in slaves, ever, in European waters.

Very, very thorough. So much more thorough than merely alerting the authorities. And he had of course thought all of this through to this conclusion.

He turned to look at her. "Yes."

The word was gently delivered. But completely unapologetic.

"And by boarded, you mean wore a mask and used swords and guns. And removing the cargo, you mean stealing it. And by putting them into boats, you mean putting them into boats at sword and pistol point."

She couldn't believe she was uttering those words, in that order, to Lyon Redmond.

"Yes, to the mask. When necessary, regarding the use of swords and guns." He paused. "It frequently was necessary."

And then he actually smiled again. Albeit faintly.

And it was a very unnerving, yet strangely thrilling, smile indeed.

She couldn't breathe.

"I know it was madness," he said, thoughtfully. "But I needed madness. I *was* mad. So I sought madness. And I found a way to expend it in a way I could justify, and that was very, very satisfying indeed."

He had put himself in harm's way. Over and over.

Then again, he had won the Sussex Marksmanship Trophy three years running.

The fact that he still lived was testament to how entirely skilled and clever he was. But then, he'd always been a planner.

He had rigidly followed rules for the first part of his life. But oddly, he seemed to have been born to make his own laws. He'd done it the first time he'd stolen a waltz from Cambersmith.

She had, in some ways, set him on this course. She smiled slightly at this thought.

She waited, thinking she ought to decide how to feel about this revelation. But she already knew.

A surge of fierce, possibly unseemly, happiness took her.

"And yet no one ever knew it was you?" she said on a hush.

"As I said, merchants in Europe have come to know me under a different name. And they know me as a trader who drives a hard bargain, but who is fair and reliable and very, very prosperous indeed, and committed to making others prosperous as well. As well as a dazzling conversationalist, a fine dancer with exquisite manners, catnip for women, and a welcome addition to dinner parties all over the continent." He smiled faintly at this, and gave her hand another squeeze. "Only two men and one woman ever suspected the truth, and they in fact nearly cornered me. Two of these people are married to each other—my sister Violet and the Earl of Ardmay—and the third owes his life to me."

"*Violet?*"

"Oh yes. My sister is so much more than anyone realizes. Of my crew, only Digby and my first mate know I am Lyon Redmond."

She tensed as she recalled something.

"You said five ships . . . but more were said to have been destroyed by Le Chat . . ."

"Ah. A pirate, and not a very good one, decided to impersonate Le Chat and seized a few ships and caused some havoc. A bad man, indeed. He had nothing to do with me. And I know this strains credibility indeed, but my sister shot him to save the life of her husband."

She rolled over to stare down at him. "Violet shot a *pirate*? A real pirate?"

He smiled at this. She suspected he was enjoying, just a little bit, startling her.

"A story for another time. Everyone underestimates my sister. Then again, perhaps it's what families are for, and we all have to battle our way out of preconceptions, and some of us have to fight harder to be seen than others. And if we're fortunate, we find someone who sees us for who we are."

And that's where they both fell silent.

Olivia didn't need to say anything.

Because this is what they were for each other. And as he'd said earlier, it was a rare, rare luxury. She'd always wondered whether she even deserved to be loved the way he loved her. But now she knew he simply needed her.

They were quiet. She traced that white musket ball scar on his abdomen gently, then pressed her lips against it.

His chest rose and fell in a sigh, and he threaded his fingers through her hair, gently, stroking.

"I have, in fact, learned that people see what they want to see, and that context is everything," he said. "I said I was a merchant, and no one thought I was anything other than what I purported to be. As the Redmonds do not yet own the world, I've never been recognized. I've of course also been very careful. Interesting, but everything I ever learned, from shooting to fencing to investing, turned out to be very useful indeed."

He flashed a wicked little smile.

She absorbed this thoughtfully. "And so the houses, the land, the . . . you paid for it by . . ."

"We took the cargo the ships were carrying and intending to convert into slaves," he continued calmly. "We dispersed it, selling and trading it so that its origins couldn't be traced. After that, I paid my crew—very, very well, I might add—invested the money in legitimate cargos and other ventures, all quite orthodox and above-board . . . and anonymously donated the rest to the likes of Mr. Wilberforce and anyone else committed to abolitionism and reformation of laws."

She was frozen with what was likely an inappropriate admiration. She simply could feel only two things: she was glad he had done it, and she was glad he'd survived it.

"And now?" she said softly.

"And now I am done. I will be selling *The Olivia* to my first mate, and my crew and I . . . we shall all go our separate ways. I doubt I'll see any of them again."

She propped herself up on her elbow again so she could look down into his face. They were quiet for a time, his fingers tangling idly in her hair.

A question haunted her. She thought she knew the reason, but she needed to say it aloud.

"Why did you do it?" she whispered.

He was silent a moment, thoughtful.

And then his mouth quirked at the corner.

"Because you couldn't."

He said it gently. But deliberately. Ruefully. Laying those words out as if delivering a truth.

Just the way he'd done the night he'd left: *What if loving you is what I do best?*

It was indeed what he did best.

He had gone and proved it.

Her breath snagged in her throat.

She saw herself reflected in his eyes. And that was how both she and Lyon had seen the world for years: through the lens of each other.

He held her gaze evenly. She knew how she probably ought to feel.

And then there was the truth.

"Thank you." She gave him the words, slowly, fervently. Her voice frayed and thick. Tears burning at the backs of her eyes.

The hush that followed was profound and soft and humbling.

They remained silent, honoring a love so immense and pure and unapologetic words would have seemed like a desecration in the moment.

It had belonged to them once.

But she still didn't know whether it belonged to them now.

IT SEEMED A terrible pity to put their clothes back on, but they did, in order to walk to the house. But Olivia carried her shoes, so she could feel the sand between her toes all the way.

And then, just for fun, Lyon carried her on his back up the hill to the gate.

"Ho, Benedict! Faster, faster!" she cried.

"That's not what I said to my horse when I rode him," he said indignantly, which made her laugh.

She rewarded him by slowly hand-feeding him slices of oranges in the house as the sun lowered. They feasted on bread and cheese and fish and wine until they were sleepy and and sated, and then they curled up next to each other on the cream brocade settee, and the conversation meandered from topic to topic the way a bird flits from tree to tree, simply because it can, taking pleasure in flight. She told him about her cousin, the new vicar, and the uproar he had caused, and about Colin's return from the gallows, and about Genevieve and the duke. He told her about some of his travels, leaving out, she was sure, the violent parts and leaving in only the beauty.

He was her best friend. She was again reminded that every single thing, from the profound to the mundane, was better when Lyon was added to it.

But it was déjà vu, too. Once again they skirted the things they ought to talk about and avoided difficult questions. Once again their time was finite. Once again a marriage loomed over them, and this time it was Olivia's.

"How did you get a sugar plantation, of all things, in Louisiana?"

"I purchased it from a man who was up to his eyes in gambling debts. Naturally, I got it cheaply."

"And you've been to see it? What is Louisiana like?"

"Steamy. Green. Beautiful. Mysterious. Wild. *Very* different from Sussex. The funny thing is, there are alligators, but no crocodiles."

"Do you ride them?"

"Naturally. I've a stable full of them. All named after you."

She laughed. "You didn't arrange to have that awful song composed, too, did you? The way you orchestrated the various modistes?"

"I wish I could take credit, but it really was a matter of the stars aligning, and so forth. Didn't I tell you I would one day become a legend?"

"You did, indeed. The song was awful, but Rowlandson at least got your thighs right."

"Did he? How so?"

She dragged her hand along one to watch his eyes darken, stopping tantalizingly just shy of his cock. A wanton thing to do, but nothing had ever felt more natural.

"They *are* very hard and very beautiful."

He leaned forward and touched his lips to hers softly, lingeringly. As if they did indeed have all the time in the world.

"I remember when I could only touch you here," he murmured against her mouth, and skated a finger slowly, slowly along the neckline of her dress, leaving a trail of sparks in its path. "And here."

He tugged at the hem of her dress, and she raised her arms so he could lift it from her head. And when she was entirely nude, he pulled her across his lap and she hooked her arms around his neck. Her eyelids were growing heavier.

"And I dreamed of touching you like this." He skimmed his hand along the inside of her thigh and her legs slipped open to allow him, to tempt him closer. "And like this." He dragged his hand across her belly, and feathered his fingers open over her breast.

She wrapped her arms around his neck and they

met it in a kiss that left both of them breathless. His fingers trailed inside her thigh, and then glided through her damp curls, and lingered there, gliding slowly, circling softly, delving.

"Hurry, Lyon," she begged on a hoarse whisper. "Oh, please."

Her wish was his command. Soon she was arching in his arms, pulsing with the pleasure of release. And then she clung to him. They breathed together in silence for a time. They were both a little more tired than either wanted to admit, because they didn't want to waste a moment of the time they had together.

He stood and effortlessly carried her to his bed, and lowered her gently. He undressed casually.

And then he lay down alongside her, and pulled her into his arms. She murmured happily and drowsily, something that sounded like his name.

"I will *never* stop wanting you," he whispered.

But she was already asleep. And all was perfect, because holding Olivia Eversea while she slept felt like what he was born to do.

SHE WOKE THE next morning to his sleepy blue eyes and his slowly wandering hands, and she wrapped her limbs around him, pulling him close.

She took him into her body greedily, her fingers gripping his hard shoulders as he drove the two of them to release.

She fell asleep again. He woke her a few hours later with black, black coffee.

And then they walked, hand in hand, back down to the cove. They stripped entirely without modesty and waded into the water, idly through the pool, floating on their backs, meeting now and again to share a kiss. They were both sore and a bit weary, but the weariness was the peaceful, sated sort that required no conversation.

Before the sun was too high they flung on their clothes again and climbed back up to the beach, hand in hand.

He stopped suddenly. He went absolutely motionless. Then gently dropped her hand, shading his eyes.

She followed the direction of his gaze.

"It's *The Olivia*."

She was just a suggestion on the horizon, but her masts and sails were stark against the blue of the sky.

"You'd best pack your trunk," he said finally.

His voice was odd. A bit thick. And unnervingly, carefully neutral.

She turned to study him.

And unease settled in when he didn't meet her eyes.

"Lyon . . . what about you?"

He was silent so long her heart started a sickening hammering.

When he spoke again, he hadn't moved at all. He kept his eyes shaded, watching that ship as surely as if he was at the helm himself.

"I won't be returning to England with you," he said finally. Again, very evenly.

Her mind blanked in shock. "But . . . why?"

He turned to her then, his eyes so warm.

"I wanted a reckoning, Olivia," he said evenly. "So did you. I now know what I need to know in order for my life to go on. Do you?"

He was bloody testing her, she could tell.

Panic swept in. Damn him and his *tests*. She was suddenly tempted to kick sand at him.

"Every relative I have is descending upon Penny-royal Green. I have an immense trousseau. I'm to get married in less than a fortnight. There's a bloody *song* about it," she said desperately. "My family will be *devastated* if it doesn't happen."

"Well, if you've a trousseau, you've a legal obligation to be married, don't you? I think unwed women are only legally allowed to own two riding habits. And God only knows one mustn't disappoint the author of flash ballads."

"I don't like it when you're acerbic."

"I, on the other hand, love it when you use words like 'acerbic.'"

She wasn't going to smile, and then she did, and then the smile faded in the face of that inexorably approaching ship, and her inexorably approaching wedding.

They locked eyes as the breeze finished drying their skin. He reached out suddenly, and tucked a whipping lock of black hair behind her ear, and smiled faintly. It didn't stay there.

"*Do* you love him, Olivia?"

An enormous pressure was welling in her chest. She could tell her silence went on longer than he preferred. It wasn't deliberate. She wasn't playing a game, or attempting to punish him.

It was just that she very much wanted to tell the truth.

"I could one day. I might one day."

"In other words . . . no. You don't love him. But it would be easy, wouldn't it? Life with Landsdowne? And marrying him would make everyone around you happy?"

She stared at him, searching his face for what it was he wanted her to say, but both his tone and expression were ruthlessly neutral and unreadable.

She considered all manner of retorts.

"I don't know what could be easy about being without you," she said brokenly.

He drew in a long breath at that. And then he pulled her into him and wrapped his arms around her, almost too hard, and tucked his face into the crook of her neck. She held on to him as though she'd been cast into the sea and he was the only rock.

She thought her rib cage might break apart from the pounding of her heart.

She almost thought she could feel *his* heart beating against her chest, but then it could be her own, too.

There really was no difference.

They clung as if they could imprint themselves on each other forever.

"I will never, ever forget a moment of our time here, Olivia," he murmured. "I'll cherish it for the rest of my life."

She stiffened suddenly. *That* sounded very like a farewell.

She pushed away from him and stood back, icy with shock. She stared at him numbly.

And again, his expression betrayed nothing. And he said nothing.

And then her icy shock gave way to burning fury.

Lyon knew she was furious. As though he'd anticipated it.

He was as white-faced and tense as if he was enduring some sort of great physical pain. But his legs were planted apart and he appeared implacable and quite resolute.

"Get on the ship and go home," he said. "And as for what you should do after that . . . You should do whatever you think is right. Because as you've told me more than once, you do not like to be told what to do. You need to decide for yourself."

Fury swept through her. She was once again that wounded girl who had shoved a beautiful pair of kid gloves back at him and fled, because all she wanted was to be with him forever, and she wanted to know what she should do, and what he would do, and she wanted it to be simple, and she wanted to know *now*.

She quite simply didn't want to disappoint or hurt anyone, ever again.

She hated him for being one step ahead of her, always.

For making her race to catch up to him.

What if loving you is what I do best?

He'd said that to her the night he'd left.

But he'd loved her then.

And here on Cadiz, he hadn't said he loved her still.

Surely he must.

But as he stood there silently, it was this realization that finally made her turn her back on him and go to pack her trunk.

SHE DIDN'T SPEAK to him at all again until they were again on the beach, and his crew was loading her trunk into one of the longboats.

"This is not a game, Lyon. Please . . . *please* just tell me what you're thinking."

She had never begged for anything in her life until he'd introduced her to the pleasures of her body and his.

"Just remember your code, Olivia."

He turned and walked fifty feet away from her and stopped. As if releasing a captive bird and encouraging it to rejoin its flock.

Pain roiled through her. She wrapped her arms around herself tightly in an attempt to soothe it.

And then he blurred as hot tears scorched her eyes.

But he didn't move. He stood, legs planted firmly apart, wind filling his shirt and tossing his loose hair, so beautiful and so *him* it was torture to witness.

But if he could let her go again, she could let him go, too.

She spun about so quickly her skirts lashed her legs, like a punishment.

And she didn't look back.

LYON WATCHED, ABSOLUTELY motionless as his crew helped Olivia into the boats.

He recognized the rigid line of her spine. That delicate little chin angled like an axe blade. So proud, his Olivia. So furious. So palpably hurt and confused he nearly retched, for her pain was his, and hers, right now, was vicious.

He watched as they rowed her out.

And he watched her grow smaller and smaller.

And he prayed. And he held his breath.

But she did it.

She got on the ship.

She got on the bloody ship.

She never once looked back.

Ah, she certainly knew how to punish him.

He dropped to his knees on the sand and blew out a long breath, wrapping his folded hands across the back of his head.

But this was a calculated gamble. And if it paid off, he promised the Creator it was the last gamble he'd take in his entire life.

Because he did know what he'd wanted to know: he knew now he would be willing to follow her to the ends of the earth.

But he wasn't going to do that.

And he knew that she loved him.

But he wasn't going to lead her to that conclusion.

He wanted her desperately, in every way, forever.

But she needed to fight for him.

And in the end, *she* needed to unequivocally choose him.

For her own sake, and for his.

Oh, he would be damned if he'd chase her again.

He would, however, make it possible for her to catch him.

Chapter 22

❧

OLIVIA RETURNED FROM "PLYMOUTH" to find various relatives as thickly scattered about Eversea House as the birds in the trees outside.

"You do have a remarkable glow, Olivia. Talk of abolitionism must be more thrilling than we all thought. Or the waters in Plymouth were healing. Darling, perhaps we ought to go to Plymouth," her aunt Pauline called to her uncle Phillips, who grunted. "See how pretty Olivia looks!"

"She's going to be a bride, Pauline. All brides are pretty." He didn't look up from his newspaper. "I don't think Plymouth is going to help *you*."

"This is all marriage, eventually, my dear," Pauline said complacently to Olivia, gesturing to her husband, apparently not at all nonplussed, and not noticing or not caring that Olivia was horrified.

"Not all brides are pretty. You should have seen that Waltham chit who was married in our church. She had a tiny little beard." She gestured to her chin.

This was said by another aunt, her father's sister Araminta, who swooped in to kiss Olivia as she bustled through the room on the way out to criticize the garden.

"More aunts here than at a picnic." Ian was at her side, murmuring.

"Ha," Olivia said bleakly.

"At least they aren't all humming 'The Legend of Ly—'"

"Don't you dare say it!" She whirled on him.

And then stormed out of the room.

Leaving all of her relatives bewildered and even Ian blinking.

"Brides," her aunts said in unison. "Have to get them married quick. The longer between the proposal and the ceremony, the tetchier they get."

"We got married straight away, and it didn't sweeten your temper any," her uncle said.

"Oh!" her aunt swatted him playfully.

And just like that, Olivia's life closed in over her again. Rather like the Red Sea closed over the pharaoh after Moses and his entourage scooted across.

She could almost believe Cadiz had been a dream. But she still had faint bruises where she'd been gripped as she and Lyon had gone at each other like rutting wild animals.

She closed her eyes as desire roared through her at the very thought.

That had not been a dream.

That, and the fact that she'd returned with something of a golden glow, since she'd forgotten her bonnet for a day. She remembered what Lyon had said: people see what they want to see. And never in a million years would anyone look at her and conclude she'd been making mad love on a beach with a vanished heir.

You should do what you think is right.

What the bloody hell did that *mean*? If it meant anything at all.

I won't be returning to England with you, Olivia.

Her life was here. Her family was here. Everything she loved and ever wanted was here.

Except him.

Just remember your code.

She lay awake at night in her room, so little changed from the last time she'd seen him. Whenever she did fall asleep she'd inevitably awaken with a start, imagining she heard pebbles thrown against the window.

She leaped up and peered, but it had been nothing but a dream.

The same one she'd had countless times since he'd left.

He hadn't said he loved her. And surely he did. She knew it in her bones. They were born to love each other.

But how could he let her go again so easily if he did?

"DO YOU THINK Aunt Pauline and Uncle Phillips are in love?"

She wanted to ask her mother a different question entirely, but she needed to lead her into it without worrying her overmuch.

Her mother stopped poring over the menu for the wedding breakfast and looked up at Olivia in some surprise.

"I don't know that they're *in* love. I'm certain that they love each other." Her mother quirked the corner of her mouth. "There's all kinds of love, of course."

She sat down next to her mother.

"Lemon seedcakes, Olivia?" Her mother fretted. "Or perhaps a tart instead? For the breakfast?"

"Lemon seedcakes sound lovely." She doubted she'd eat anything at all.

"Excellent." He mother made a note.

"Mama . . . were you in love with Papa when you married him?"

"Oh my. Dear me. Yes. I was."

She knew it to be definitely true, because her mother's face took on a misty, reminiscent glow. She hadn't settled for Jacob Eversea instead of Isaiah Redmond. Olivia was glad.

"Was he very handsome when he was younger?"

"You should have seen him when he was a boy, Olivia. He rode his horse at breakneck speeds, but he was such a brilliant rider, it was a pleasure to see him. Very thrilling for a young girl, you know. It got so that every time I heard the thunder of hooves my heart would about jump from chest, because I knew it was him. To this day when I hear hooves my heart leaps. And your papa no longer thunders, as you know."

Olivia smiled. "A bit like Colin used to ride. Before Madeline."

Her mother's face went peculiarly still and she stood up abruptly and paced to the window and looked out. Perhaps imagining a young Jacob Eversea galloping out there on the green.

She didn't reply for some time.

"It's not as though love doesn't get tested over the years, on occasion, Olivia. When you were a little girl, your father went to sea for a time, as he did when he was younger. He was a little too fond of risks with money, though he is generally very good at it, but we lost a good deal at one time. And then he went out in search of more fortune. It was . . . it was a difficult time. But true love weathers those things, and only grows stronger."

It was interesting to hear this version of her parents. Similar to hearing what her father had told her years ago about her courting her mother.

He hadn't been trying to warn her about Lyon then, she understood now. He'd been trying to warn her about Isaiah.

"That was just before Colin was born, right? When Papa went to sea?"

"Yes," her mother said.

"And you and Papa . . ."

" . . . are on the whole very happy, and we congratulate ourselves on our successful match and splendid offspring quite often."

Olivia laughed.

"And I cannot speak for all of womankind, Olivia. I can speak from experience and observation. I think there's the kind of love you're *born* with. The kind you can't help, because it's like your eye color or anything else. There's the kind you fall into. And there's the kind that you find yourself enveloped in after years of familiarity and comfort and a family to bind you. Which I suppose is the kind that Pauline and your uncle now have. I don't know if they're in love, but of a certainty they love each other. I don't know that one is better than the other, ultimately. All love is a blessing. The opportunity to give it and receive may be what humans are born for. And I like to think that if you loved once . . . it only means you can love again."

The words "Lyon Redmond" were never mentioned, but of course, the last sentence was all about him, and they both knew it.

"I love you, Mama."

"I love you, too, my dear. Olivia, all your father and I want is for you to be happy and safe and loved. It is all we ever wanted for you. Never forget it."

She said this fervently. As though delivering a message.

But given the condition of Olivia's nerves, everything had begun to seem significant.

Olivia, who had long loathed being told what to do, still rather wished that someone would.

SHE SLIPPED FROM the house and walked alone to the vicarage, past the churchyard fence. She recalled the view of hems and boot toes when she'd dropped her prayer book, at the very spot she stood now, then looking up into Lyon's eyes. And even now it made her heart leap.

And how she had gone walking with Landsdowne in public past this very churchyard, knowing the town would see her. Signaling to everyone that she intended to move on and live her life.

On impulse she veered into the churchyard to prowl among the stones of her ancestors.

She paused before a newer one, Lady Fennimore's.

She was a curmudgeon, that one, and Olivia always smiled when she saw what was written on her headstone.

Don't think it won't happen to you.

Which could apply to anything in life, really. Olivia liked it. Quite a flexible message. A message of dread or hope, depending on what sort of day you were having and who you were. She would have to think of a similar one to amuse future generations of Everseas who might stroll through this churchyard.

Olivia, Lady Landsdowne.

That's what her headstone would say.

For she would be married tomorrow.

She drew in a long breath, and tried to decide how she felt about it.

If Lyon wanted to intervene in her wedding, now would be the time to do it.

But damn him to Hell, he was nowhere to be seen. And if she thought about it too much she nearly stopped breathing. The force of the longing

was too much to bear, and once she made a decision,
she could begin allowing it to ebb.

Love *could* happen.

She decided today that Lady Fennimore was delivering a message of hope.

She didn't feel uplifted by it. But the momentum
of her decision would carry her through, she supposed.

She glanced up toward the vicarage, and she
shaded her eyes, and went still.

And then her heart gave a little glad lurch.

Her cousin Adam, the vicar, was in front of the vicarage, in shirtsleeves. He'd been out cutting wood,
from the looks of things. And he was speaking to
the bandaged beggar from Madame Marceau's! He
ushered the beggar swiftly into the vicarage, but it
was unmistakably him: the same shabby, tattered
clothing, the bandages. The poor soul appeared to
be bent, too, and he dragged a foot, which was likely
why he'd spent so much time sitting.

And she was glad she could send him to Adam,
who seemed to have endless reserves of time and
goodness to give to those who needed it. And if
she'd been the means by which that man found help
and comfort, well then, that was the only wedding
present she needed.

It seemed like a sign.

Though she would have preferred to have one of
the beggar's blessings, just to be certain of it.

AN EXHAUSTED, ANTICIPATORY hush had finally
fallen over Eversea house.

Olivia's wedding dress was laid out on a bed in
a miraculously unoccupied Eversea bedroom. Her
relatives had all visited it in a hush, in turn, as if it

were a loved one lying in state, and pronounced it exquisite.

Tomorrow everyone would troop down to the church—Landsdowne and his party of mother, sisters, and an old friend who had agreed to stand up with him would meet the Eversea family there—and the last of all the Eversea siblings to get married (as more than one aunt had reminded Olivia) was finally going to do just that. Though it was worth it, everyone conceded. It seemed Clever Olivia had clearly been holding out for a viscount all along. It wasn't quite the same as a duke, but dukes were hardly thick on the ground and Landsdowne was indisputably a catch, and thankfully she could now put all that Lyon Redmond nonsense behind her once and for all.

And after that, there would be a great party and dancing, with Seamus Duggan and his merry band of players providing the music, and the doors of Eversea House would be open to the whole of the town to celebrate the event of a decade, an event no one had truly thought would ever occur.

"JOHN EDGAR, WILT thou have this woman to thy wedded wife, to live together after God's ordinance in the holy estate of matrimony? Wilt thou love her, comfort her, honor, and keep her in sickness and in health; and, forsaking all other, keep thee only unto her, so long as ye both shall live?"

Landsdowne's response was instant.

"I will."

The words filled the corners of the church like the triumphant notes of an organ.

The church was crammed full of bodies—everybody who had ever lived in Pennyroyal Green seemed to be in attendance, including all of the Redmonds, who never missed a church service if it could be helped, and perhaps had ulterior motives for being present at this one—and it was warmer than she could ever remember it being. But still Olivia shivered in her wedding dress.

She could scarcely remember how she'd gotten here.

She'd awakened at dawn, and her mother and her sister and aunts, in a reverent, understanding hush, had slid the beautiful, much-discussed, flawlessly lovely dress over her head.

She remembered answering questions in monosyllables. She remembered trembling; she still was. And as Mademoiselle Lilette-Digby had said, only two things were required of her today: that she look beautiful, and that she repeat the right words at the vicar's prompting.

She'd accomplished the first.

"Wilt thou, Olivia Katherine, have this man to thy wedded husband, to live together after God's ordinance in the holy estate of matrimony? Wilt thou obey him, and serve him, love, honor, and keep him in sickness and in health; and, forsaking all other, keep thee only unto him, so long as ye both shall live?"

So long as ye both shall live.

The words seemed to knell.

It was a simple question. Asked millions of times, likely, since the ancient, binding words were first written.

It required a simple two-word answer.

It suddenly seemed perilous that only two words could lie between a person and the rest of her life.

Two words.

And yet she'd forgotten how to speak.

She glanced over her shoulder.

The congregation was almost comically motionless. They knew something was awry. Her senses were suddenly exquisitely acute. The very silence seemed to ring a high clear note, and everyone she'd known her entire life suddenly seemed as distinct as a woodcut.

Her mother's face, so like her own. Her eyes shining with tears, a complexity of emotion, love and grief.

But strangely, not surprise.

Her father, leaning ever so slightly forward, as if to make it easier for him to run to her if she needed him.

Isaiah Redmond's face cold and drawn, his green eyes brilliant as stained glass.

A face so like Lyon's.

A man who had lost to Jacob Eversea. She wondered if he loved her mother, still.

And if her mother loved Isaiah.

And suddenly she felt a wayward tenderness toward Isaiah, for Olivia thought she now understood what could happen to a person who had endured a lifetime without his love.

His beautiful blond wife, Fanchette, motionless. Waiting. Her lips seemed to be moving in a silent prayer. And Olivia wondered if it was for the sudden reappearance of her son.

Violet Redmond, who had killed a pirate for the man she loved.

And the Earl of Ardmay, for whom she'd killed, and who had let Lyon go free for the love of Violet.

Lord Lavay and his new wife, Elise, and her little boy, Jack, who could not be counted on to remain still for long, but who seemed aware that something of moment was happening, judging from his wide eyes.

Ian, whom no one thought would ever marry, and who had plans to sail around the world. And beautiful American Tansy, who became his world. Who had upended all of Sussex, primarily because she was lonely and needed to be loved, and Ian, of all people, was the only one who'd seen her with love's eyes.

Colin, who had thought he was in love with Louisa Porter, but had returned from his infamous gallows escape to marry Madeline, a wife who seemed to know him right down to his soul and who had made a more peaceful, tender man of him.

Marcus and Louisa. Who were so very right together that merely being in their presence made everyone happy.

Genevieve with the Duke of Falconbridge. How dangerously close Genevieve had come to marrying Harry, the wrong man. How hurt Harry had been. How brave Genevieve had been to do something about it before it was too late.

Her cousin Adam, the vicar, who had been nearly pilloried by the people of the town for love. But he had stood in this very church and one unforgettable morning he'd fought for her, the former Evie Duggan, a countess with a notorious past.

And there, to her surprise, in the very last pew, on the very edge nearest the door, was the beggar. Hunched and abject, perhaps hoping not to be seen, but wanting to be part of something beautiful.

Only now that they were all arrayed before her did she see clearly.

She had been in the congregation when Adam had tossed away his sermon before a judgmental congregation and quoted Corinthians, then countered it with the Song of Solomon. He had claimed his woman, his love, Evie Duggan, the most unlikely woman, with those words. Love is fire and flood. Love is patient and kind.

It was, indeed, all of that.

But love was also a warrior. When it set out to conquer, it cared naught for residual casualties.

And when it chose you, you could either resist.

Or you could surrender.

She wanted it to be simple. Surrender made everything simple.

Remember your code, Lyon had said to her.

It was as though she heard him whispering it in her ear.

And her code was: She never lied.

She quite simply could not live a lie for the rest of her life.

Her cousin Adam was watching her as though he was willing strength into her. Adam was so good, so kind. And he would understand.

He began again, carefully.

"Will you, Olivia, take John to be your husband? Will you love him, comfort him, honor and protect him, and, forsaking all others, be faithful to him as long as you both shall live?"

She only had to open her mouth and say two words.

She tipped her face up to Landsdowne.

Tension was whitening the corners of his mouth, drawing his fine face tauter, as her silence stretched.

And before her eyes she saw the realization dawning in his own.

At last she opened her mouth to speak.

But only one word emerged.

"John . . ."

His head went back hard and he closed his eyes. And then he shook his head slowly.

"I'm sorry," she said gently. Apologetically. But unequivocally. "I can't."

More audibly now.

"It would be a lie."

Truth was flooding her, and truth was courage.

And truth was her code, after all.

In the silence, the sound of shifting wool and silk and nankeen over the polished pews soughed like the wind. Someone cleared a throat surreptitiously.

A beam of light fought through a cloud and poured through the window nearest the altar, the better to illuminate something the entire town of Pennyroyal Green would speak of for centuries to come.

At last, someone moved.

But it was only the beggar, raising his hand in yet another silent blessing.

She watched his hand rise as if it were a dove of peace rising up to Heaven. Everything now seemed dreamlike and significant.

And then she followed his hand down with her eyes.

Her breath caught sympathetically. Because this time it snagged on his bandages. It at first looked like an accident.

But then in a series of, slow, fluid motions, like watching origami in reverse, he dragged them away from his face, straightened his bent shoulders, shrugged the filthy, tattered coat from his shoulders.

And stood.

A few heads turned toward him.

He didn't seem to notice.

But then he was accustomed to eyes on him.

And they only had eyes for each other, anyway.

"Of course," Olivia said softly.

THERE WAS A thud as someone fainted and tipped out of a pew.

The poor unfortunate was left to roll in the aisle, as everyone was now staring at the church door, because Lyon had vanished out of it and no one was quite certain they'd actually seen him.

One person crossed himself and muttered a prayer.

"For God's sake, he's not a ghost, he's just been gone for a surprisingly long time," someone muttered irritably.

The vicar raised his voice.

"If you would all kindly remain seated."

Adam had a stentorian and compelling voice, and as no one seemed to know what else to do at the moment, everyone seemed inclined to obey.

Not everyone had yet realized that the beggar had just transformed into Lyon Redmond and all but vanished out the church door.

Olivia whirled toward Landsdowne. Then toward the door. Then back toward Landsdowne. Then back toward the door.

Absurdly like an opera dancer.

The whole event, as delighted onlookers would later declare, was quite a show.

"John—" she began. Apologetically. But, God help her, impatiently.

He shook his head roughly. "I couldn't bear it if you were *kind*, Olivia." He sounded faintly, ironically bitter. "Just go to—"

He was about to say "him," but she didn't hear it, because she'd already leaped like a stag and bolted down the aisle, her silver-trimmed wedding dress hiked in both fists, running for her life after Lyon Redmond.

Chapter 23

❧

SHE BURST OUT OF the church door, which closed with a resounding, very final-sounding thud behind her as she pushed through.

Two men appeared from seemingly nowhere and neatly barred it so no one could come after her.

She swiveled in some surprise.

Lyon's crew. They'd clearly had instructions.

As usual, he'd planned ahead.

But where the devil *was* he?

Then she whipped her head about like a weathervane, searching for him. Not in the churchyard, hidden among all the stones she knew so well.

He'd vanished.

She swore an oath that widened even the eyes of the men standing guard at the door. But perhaps they were under instructions not to tell her.

Then she saw the door to the bell tower open a few inches.

She dashed over to it, pushed it open and ran up the stairs, tripping once, tearing the silver-trimmed hem.

And when she was at the top, her lungs heaving like bellows she stopped.

He was leaning against the wall, arms crossed, opposite the bell, in a pool of sunlight.

One step ahead of her, as usual.

He would always know what she needed before she did.

For a time, her breathing was the only sound, and it echoed in the tower.

And then:

"Those were the worst few moments of my life."

His voice was husky.

She wasn't ready to forgive him. Or to speak. Or to do anything but keep him in sight, lest he disappear again.

Because she had come to claim him now.

"They were also the best moments of my life," he added.

She still couldn't speak. Her Lyon. Standing here in *Pennyroyal Green*, in Sussex.

Silence.

A long sunbeam sent the dust motes gyrating in a celebratory dance.

"If you're wondering about the disguise . . ." He gestured to the tattered beggar's coat, now crumpled on the ground. " . . . when I learned you were to be married, I wasn't certain if I even wanted to see you. I wasn't certain if I ever wanted to come back to England. I didn't know if you were the same person I left. I didn't know whether you were happy with Landsdowne, and your happiness was all I ever wanted. I should have known . . ."

He paused.

"I should have known I would go to the ends of the earth for you. I was born loving you. And no matter what, I would have fought for you."

She still couldn't speak. With him, words had always been either unnecessary or never enough.

"It nearly killed me to do it. But I was right to send you away."

It was both a question and a statement.

But his voice had a husked edge, betraying his uncertainty. He was beginning to worry about her silence.

And because she never lied, and because she couldn't bear his suffering, the first word she finally said was:

"Yes."

The word she should have said to him so many years ago. *Yes, I'll go with you. Yes, I'll be with you. Yes, I believe in you. Yes, you are my life and my love and my destiny. Of course.*

Then again, it had taken everything up to this moment to understand all of this.

But her voice was shockingly small and frayed and she knew she was going to cry.

"I love you," she added hurriedly. Because she'd longed to say it to him, and she couldn't wait a moment longer. "I always have. I always will."

Those ought to be the wedding vows, Olivia thought. No one would ever utter those words lightly.

Her words chimed in the room like a bell.

He drew in a long breath, like a man who'd been under water too long.

He strolled over to her, casually, easily, as if to say, "Look. Now we have all the time in the world." He gave her a handkerchief. She took it and rubbed her fingers gently over the corner where his initials were stitched.

She knew how her own handkerchiefs would be embroidered from now on: "OKR." Olivia Katherine Redmond.

"You knew what I would do today," she said, dabbing her eyes.

"Of course. Still, it shaved years off my life."

"We'd best make good use of the years you have left, then."

He sighed and pulled her into his arms, wrapping her tightly. She melted against his beloved body. He laid his cheek against her hair. And for a time they breathed together, savoring the luxury of simply holding each other. He kissed her forehead, her eyelids, her cheeks, her lips.

He murmured those words again. "My love. My heart."

Not reckless now. Not innocent. Earned and true words, from one battered heart to another.

INSIDE THE CHURCH, four people at last countermanded the vicar's order to stay seated, and rose one at a time.

Isaiah Redmond.

Jacob Eversea.

Isolde Eversea.

Fanchette Redmond.

And then the murmurs began to sough around them.

Lyon Redmond Lyon Redmond Lyon Redmond Lyon Redmond that was Lyon Redmond.

"My son . . ." Redmond said hoarsely. "Was that . . . was that my son . . ."

"Where is my daughter?" Jacob demanded. He was making ready to scramble over the pew and bolt out the door, followed by the rest of the men of his family.

"Friends!" Adam said. *"Please.* One moment please." He raised his hands for silence.

They obeyed.

They turned to look at Reverend Sylvaine. And then they froze in place.

The vicar nodded to Landsdowne, as if giving someone permission to give a eulogy.

Landsowne drew in a breath.

He stood before the congregation, one of love's casualties, his face white and stunned.

And despite a life lived faultlessly, destined to become part of a flash ballad and a legend, and, for a time, a verb ("I think she intends to Landsdowne him.").

Later everyone said he was the picture of graciousness, but then Landsdowne had always met life with equanimity, which was precisely the way life had met him, until he got mixed up with the likes of Olivia Eversea.

He turned to face the congregation, who were now utterly still and watching him avidly, hoping to hear why on earth Olivia Eversea had just run out the church door like she'd been set on fire.

But all he said, in an admirably steady voice, was:

"My deepest apologies to those of you who came to see a wedding. Miss Olivia Eversea and I will not be married today, or ever."

He nodded his thanks to the vicar.

Then he blew out a breath and retreated to behind the pulpit, to the shocked ministrations of the man who had stood up with him.

Adam said, "Ladies and gentleman, friends and family, you may now return to your homes. There will be no wedding today."

Isaiah Redmond raised his voice. "My son! Where the devil is my son? Was that my—"

"Isaiah."

He turned in surprise.

It was the first word Isolde Eversea had said to him directly in over a decade.

And his face, as it always did, softened, in a way he simply could not help.

And that no one else watching could miss.

And Isaiah loathed vulnerability.

"Leave them be," she said gently.

Jacob took his wife's arm. "We'll go home," he said tautly. "We'll all go home."

A daughter bolting from the altar was practically a day in the life for an Eversea.

"What if she . . ." Isolde Eversea looked desperately at her husband.

And out of instinct born of years of love, for he knew Isolde so very, very well, he gave her his handkerchief as her eyes began to tear.

"What would you have them do, Isolde?" Jacob said gently. But his jaw was granite. "She'll come home. I know she will."

With a look into Isaiah Redmond's eyes that, in another century, would have had the other man reaching for his sword to defend himself, Jacob Eversea led his wife away.

And their relatives followed. Not having a wedding was almost as entertaining as having a wedding, given the circumstances.

For nearly everyone who wasn't the mother or father of the bride, that was.

The usual rustle took place as everyone got up from their pews and filed for the door.

Except for Landsdowne, who was still near the altar, hoping to remain invisible until he was able to make his escape with his own relatives.

And Lady Emily Howell, who fought through the crowds to get to him.

WHEN THE CHURCH was empty, and the roads were clear for as far as Adam's eyes could see—he and his wife, Evie, even did a little search of the churchyard—he went to the bell tower and climbed to the top, careful to make a little extra noise the higher up he got. Just to warn them.

Olivia and Lyon sitting together on the floor, his arm slung about her, her head on his shoulder, and they were talking and laughing quietly, as if they'd been married decades. She was sitting on his ragged folded-up coat.

"Adam!" Olivia sat up guiltily with a start.

Lyon put his hand gently on hers to reassure her.

"I made his acquaintance before the ceremony," Lyon told her. "And asked him to keep everyone seated, should you bolt after me. And I asked him to send everyone home, if you *did* bolt after me."

Because Lyon, after all, was a planner.

Olivia sighed happily. "He knows me better than I know myself."

"Remarkable man, your Mr. Redmond, Olivia," Adam said. Almost ruefully.

Adam had fallen in love with an unlikely woman and he'd needed to fight for her, too. His methods were different from Mr. Redmond's, but he knew without question when he was in the presence of true love, and it was holy.

"Remarkable man, your cousin the Reverend Sylvaine." Lyon smiled at the vicar.

The two of them, each was certain, were destined to become friends.

"Will your own wedding be here in Pennyroyal Green?" Adam asked.

Olivia and Lyon looked at each other, and then turned to Adam, and together they said:

"Yes."

AFTER THE WEDDING—or rather, after what was nearly a wedding—Isaiah Redmond retreated to his great shining desk in his library, where he had made so many brilliant decisions in his lifetime and one or two extraordinarily poor ones. He was picturing Olivia Eversea's face this morning as she broke one man's heart and leaped, like some kind of fierce angel, down the aisle and bolted out the door, her face ablaze with the kind of love he'd seen only once before in his life.

In the face of Isolde Eversea when she'd looked at him.

Everyone present had said Olivia had bolted after Lyon.

Isaiah closed his eyes and breathed through the great, never-ending wound that was the loss of his oldest son.

He didn't know. He just didn't know.

His hands were shaking now. And it was too early to reach for the brandy and he didn't want to be that kind of man, but life had dealt one thing after another to him in the past few years, and Isaiah feared he was finally beginning to age.

A throat cleared politely at the entry of his office.

He turned absently, reluctantly from his reverie.

It was a footman. Whose eyes seemed unnaturally bright, and whose face was white.

"What is it?" Isaiah said tersely.

"Mr. Lyon Redmond here to see you, sir."

Isaiah froze.

His breath stopped.

He half stood.

And slowly, slowly, his oldest son walked into the same room where he'd last seen him five years ago.

An elegant man. Shockingly handsome. But a hard man. Isaiah could see that at once. His presence was both so peaceful and so uncompromisingly confident that Isaiah couldn't speak through the weight of it.

Lyon was here. Lyon.

His stood in the center of the room before that shining desk.

The silence rang.

And the clock as usual swung off minutes.

"Lyon . . ."

Isaiah's voice was a dry rasp.

"Please don't get up, Father." He said this almost kindly.

Isaiah sat down again.

He didn't ask Lyon to sit. It was very clear Lyon didn't intend to. And Isaiah did not want to hear the rejection.

And all was silence of an almost holy kind. The room had always had a hush thanks to dense carpets and velvet upholstery and curtains.

Lyon had sailed wild seas and fought wild fights and seen lands far more dangerous.

And even though this was home, it had lost its power to intimidate. For Lyon understood his father better now than nearly anyone else in the world.

Isaiah drew in a ragged breath.

And then another.

He covered his eyes with one hand.

His shoulders swelled and fell again as he released a huge sigh. And for a moment he seemed to be absolutely motionless.

Until Lyon noticed that his father's shoulders were shaking.

Isaiah Redmond . . . was weeping.

Lyon waited. He wasn't unmoved, not entirely.

But he could not and would not be the person to comfort his father.

He didn't know who truly would, for Lyon knew that true comfort was found only with someone who knows your very heart. Lyon loved his mother with a fierce protectiveness. But it was entirely possible

Isaiah was one of the loneliest men in the world. Which might be the great tragedy of Isaiah's life.

Isaiah finally sighed and took another deep breath.

He looked up at Lyon, his green eyes brilliant against the red now.

"You're an extraordinary man, Father. You always could bend nearly anything to your will. Except love."

"Lyon. Son." His voice was still raw.

"You once told me I had a choice," Lyon said thoughtfully. "And perhaps you did at one time, too. The thing is, when you make the wrong choice, love breaks you."

Isaiah simply breathed. Watching him as if he was an apparition.

"Father . . . I know about the investment you made under Jacob Eversea's name as part of the Dreieck group. The Triangle Trade."

His father was motionless now. Lyon recognized that stillness. It was both an admission of guilt and a reflection of the old Isaiah, who would immediately begin planning how to maneuver this to his advantage.

"I won't tell you how I learned it, but I undertook to seek out the source for the woman I love. As you know, it's one the things she feels most passionately about. It's as part of her heart as I am. I feel passionately about it as well. And I can't imagine that even you condone the practice of slavery, not even for profit."

Isaiah was absolutely silent and motionless.

"So what was the plan? To expose Jacob Eversea eventually to the authorities? Or to ultimately make sure this involvement came to light in order to destroy his reputation and tarnish him forever in the eyes of his wife and daughter?"

The damning silence stretched.

And then Isaiah spoke. "You don't know our story, Lyon." There was a hint of steel in that. A hint of warning. But Isaiah hadn't the right to it, completely, and he knew it.

"I am here to tell you," Lyon said slowly. "that you best not try anything like that ever again. Ever. I cannot be clearer than that."

His father pressed his lips together.

"I'm going to marry Olivia Eversea as soon as we can obtain a license. I should say next Sunday will be the day, here in Pennyroyal Green. You are welcome to be present. But neither she nor I have need of your money or approval."

Isaiah sighed, and merely nodded.

"Father, I've learned a bit over the past few years. I am the best of you. I am the worst of you. I never surrender. I have a magnificent knack for making money hand over fist. And for what it's worth, for better or for worse, I am the man I am today primarily because of you. So thank you."

"Lyon," his father said again.

Lyon waited.

Isaiah cleared his throat. "I am . . . just . . . so glad . . . you are home."

Lyon knew it to be true. He knew his father loved him, in his own way. And that everything he'd done to everyone in his family was his attempt to justify a choice he'd made years ago.

But it would never be right.

Lyon simply nodded.

The two men studied each other.

Lyon hesitated, then asked the question that had haunted him.

"Do you still love her?" his voice was soft.

He meant Isolde Eversea.

Isaiah simply looked at him. His eyes were still red, which made them seem even more brilliantly green.

And at last he made a soft sound. Almost a laugh. Far too rueful, too fatalistic to truly be a laugh.

And that was Lyon's answer.

"Does she still love you?" his voice was careful now. He was venturing into a place he was uncertain he wanted to go.

"What do you think?" Isaiah produced a bittersweet ghost of a smile.

Lyon held still, absorbing this.

Because of course she did. He was certain of that, too.

But she loved her own husband, too. That was clear to anyone who saw them together.

Lyon exhaled thoughtfully. He could feel the desolation of years. He could not imagine what it had been like for Isaiah Redmond and Isolde Eversea.

And now they would be members of the same family.

Which might very well be flinging a lit match into kindling.

So be it.

No one and nothing was going to stop Lyon and Olivia from being together.

"Lyon," his father said thoughtfully. "You may have acquired a certain amount of wisdom, but I am still older than you are. I think one day, perhaps far in the future, you may discover your heart can hold many different kinds and shades of love. When you have children, you'll begin to see what I mean. And you will be amazed at what you can learn to live with every day."

Lyon wasn't interested in the distant future at the moment. He wanted, very restlessly, to get back to Olivia, who was still with her cousin at the vicarage.

He didn't ask his father if he would still take Isolde from Jacob Eversea if he could.

He thought he knew the answer, and he didn't want to hear it.

LYON'S SIBLINGS AND their spouses were gathered in one of the drawing rooms, the room where he and his brothers had once leaped from settee to table to chair, pretending the carpet was lava, and where he'd once been fascinated by the nuts and vines carved into the mantel. He heard their voices, the cadences and timbres, the flow of conversation, all achingly familiar.

He hung back for a moment. A little uncertain.

He knew how relationships could shift and flow and change to fill in gaps left by someone lost. But he was unafraid of nearly everything now, and he could do this, too.

And then they all looked up and saw him.

And there was an almost comical hush.

They stared at him as if he were a rhinoceros. Shyly, with a little trepidation, and as if they all wanted to fling themselves at him and pet him but they weren't certain whether he was tame enough.

"Still ugly, I see," Jonathan said, finally.

"Are you talking to the mirror?" Lyon said mildly.

Everyone laughed. Brotherly communication and affection was reestablished, and the ice was broken and Violet hurled herself into his arms.

"Well, my brave girl," he murmured to her, and gave her a squeeze. "One day we shall have a chat."

He'd noted straight away that her husband, the Earl of Ardmay, also known as Captain Flint, was in the corner of the room, leaning back and cuddling the baby. Violet, being a girl, was allowed to weep all over Lyon, and everyone else, even his brothers, found the carpet or ceiling interesting or discovered they'd gotten dust in their eyes and needed to blink a good deal.

Except Lyon.

"Don't hog him, Violet!" Jonathan said irritably.

"Yes, don't be a Lyon hog, Violet!" Miles teased.

"Lyon hog! That sounds like some hybrid animal Miles would find in Lacao," Lyon said.

There was more laughter and his brothers hugged and thumped him in a manly fashion and he hugged and thumped them in return.

If anyone in the room had harbored any lingering resentment about Lyon's disappearance and the crushing confusion and pain of his loss, it was instantly drowned by the superior power of love and gratitude and the sheer rightness of having Lyon here again. And now that they were older, and each of them had fallen in love, they understood more fully why Lyon had to do what he'd done. And relationships could shift and flow to allow him back in.

Each of them had won their own loves the hard way, and had been transformed and softened and deepened in the process, whether they wanted to be or not.

Five years, and now Jonathan was a man, dashing and imposing, who could very nearly be Lyon's twin.

Five years, and now Miles was handsome and calmly, resolutely confident.

Both had gravitas and presence and Lyon was fiercely proud of them. He knew how hard they must have needed to fight for their happiness and independence. He half wondered if this was his father's plan from the very beginning, but surely not even Isaiah Redmond was that clever.

Though he also knew he had their wives to thank for giving them the courage.

He learned rather quickly, and to his great relief, that Thomasina and Cynthia, Jonathan's and Miles's wives, were lively and witty and charming and warm. And very pretty, a pleasure to have in any room. Tommy had dark red hair and green eyes; she was an exotic beauty. Cynthia was a lovely blonde with blue eyes.

"Beautiful" was the word he reserved for Olivia.

"You're both clearly better than Jonathan and Miles deserve," he pronounced, upon meeting the two wives. "I can see that at once."

"I won Tommy by smoldering at her," Jonathan claimed. "Which I learned from you."

"He did, rather," Tommy admitted. "Smolder at me."

"Then I insist upon being the godfather of your children."

"We already have one hundred of 'em," Jonathan said idly.

Everyone present had already heard this joke, but it was Lyon's first time, and they thoroughly enjoyed his reaction.

Though if he'd known how many times he would hear it in the years to come, he might have rolled his eyes.

He learned very quickly a little about Jonathan and Tommy's work on behalf of child labor laws.

"We need to talk at length later. You and Olivia will have much to say to each other," he told Tommy. "And I need to discuss projects in which to invest."

And there transpired an infinitesimal silence and a few strained smiles.

Olivia Eversea was synonymous with Beelzebub in the Redmond household. She'd long been blamed for his disappearance. Undoing that wouldn't happen precisely overnight.

"You will love her. And she will be part of our family, and we will be a part of hers, as soon as I can get a license. I imagine we can be married as soon as Sunday next. I'm quite looking forward to having Olivia and Violet in the same room."

Violet made a face at him.

"Then you're a braver man than I am, Lyon," Jonathan said.

"Well, that goes without saying." Lyon was moving, casually, toward the Earl of Ardmay, Captain Flint, who had judiciously kept his distance, because, remarkably, baby Ruby was still asleep in his arms.

"Did you smolder at Cynthia?" Lyon asked Miles. "As I recall, your techniques required some refinement."

"*She* smoldered at me," Miles teased.

"We'll have to compare notes on our techniques, Cynthia." Lyon winked at her.

And then he moved over and leaned against the wall next to the earl, who had once been charged with capturing Le Chat and bringing him to justice, and had refused to do it, for the love of a woman. The madness that drove a man into being a pirate was the same kind of madness that made another man let him go free: it was all for the love of a woman.

"Ardmay," Lyon said simply, by way of greeting.

The earl had nothing to say to Lyon except, "Welcome home, Redmond."

He handed the baby to him, and Lyon took her as if she were an egg.

He could tell Ruby was born to break hearts. A

tiny, snoozing, velvety pale thing with the most shockingly miniature eyelashes. He thought the first heart she might break would be his.

The Earl of Ardmay interrupted Lyon's reverie. "Do you want one of these?"

He sounded amused. He could see the expression on Lyon's face.

"Dozens," Lyon said absently, only just realizing it. He thought about how Olivia had been with the Duffys, and he knew that the two of them were going to be the best parents ever born.

"Lyon, did you smolder at Olivia?" Tommy wanted to know.

Lyon looked up from baby Ruby, his eyes still misty with reveries about babies that looked like Olivia.

"No," Miles answered for him. "He didn't. But I was there that night. And let me tell you what happened. When he clapped eyes on her, I could have sworn a gong went off . . ."

IT WASN'T UNTIL he met with his mother alone, and she folded him in her arms, that Lyon Redmond finally wept. For all that he knew, and all that he was certain she knew and understood, and because he loved and had missed his mother.

Chapter 24

❧

The next Sunday . . .

SOMETIME DURING THE FOLLOWING week, word reached Pennyroyal Green that the betting book at White's had disappeared.

A howl of outrage went up among the bloods of the *ton*.

Lyon claimed no knowledge of it.

And Olivia's brothers shrugged innocently.

Olivia didn't believe any of them.

They were going to protect her, and her wedding would not be a sport.

"Isn't it lovely to know that it's the last time anyone will speculate over the two of us?" Lyon said simply, bringing Olivia's hand to his mouth for a kiss. "We are not a sport. We're a man and a woman in love, and we'll be married and have a family to rival the Duffys. An entire cricket team."

"Or an orchestra," she said dreamily.

"Or an investment group."

She laughed.

They reveled in walking about Pennyroyal Green together, waving at everyone they saw, stopping to chat, startling the life out of some people, but then charming them so completely that everyone, even Mrs. Sneath, walked away convinced that Olivia and Lyon were meant to be, and poor Landsdowne was nearly forgotten.

They visited the elm tree, and he showed her the "O" he'd carved. She touched it tenderly, and kissed him just as tenderly to make up for the suffering he'd experienced that day, waiting in vain, alone but for a pair of squirrels and his own longing.

They found the little clearing again, and in a fit of nostalgia made love right there on the moss, on his spread-out coat, and got the job done very quickly, as they knew what they were doing and were now very, very good at it.

And then she gave him her gift:

A little gold pocket watch with his initials on it.

It had taken some doing to find the watch and get it engraved quickly, but Mr. Postlethwaite was a resourceful man, especially when a good deal of money was involved.

"Go ahead. Open it."

With great ceremony, he clicked it open.

Inside was the miniature she'd given him so many years ago, and which had found its way back to her.

"This time you get to keep both of them. The miniature and the real thing."

This was an occasion for another kiss. A lingering, drugging, tender kiss that left her sighing against his chest, longing for the day they would lie in bed next to each other forever.

"I thought we would go to Bristol for our wedding journey," he said.

"*Bristol?*"

And then she understood.

"I've manage to obtain an invitation for us to visit Mrs. Hannah More."

"Truly?" Olivia breathed.

And this was an occasion for a kiss that went on until the sun began to lower.

"Let's just look at the time, shall we? Not because we have to, because we want to."

Lyon delightedly clicked open his new watch.

AND THEN, AT last, it was Sunday.

From two directions the families walked to the church, and one witty observer claimed it looked rather like enemy armies convening upon a battlefield from separate encampments. The morning was misty, lending it portent and drama. But both the Redmonds and Everseas possessed exquisite manners, and history had seen more delicate armistices negotiated. In all likelihood, no Eversea would cleave a Redmond skull today over a stolen cow, which was how the trouble between them was rumored to have started back in 1066.

But one never knew.

Nearly the whole of Pennyroyal Green was crowded into the church, and those who couldn't fit waited outside, hands clasped in anticipation.

Olivia wore a simple white muslin dress.

Lyon wore a look of awe.

Genevieve stood up with Olivia, and both Miles and Jonathan stood up with Lyon. And the mothers of all these men and women, united by love of their children, wept quietly, and even the stoic fathers, enmeshed in rather complex thoughts of their own, may have gotten a bit misty-eyed.

And then Reverend Adam Sylvaine spoke the words.

"Lyon Arthur James, wilt thou have this woman to thy wedded wife, to live together after God's ordinance in the holy estate of matrimony? Wilt thou love her, comfort her, honor, and keep her in sickness and in health; and, forsaking all other, keep thee only unto her, so long as ye both shall live?"

"I will." Lyon's beloved voice was so solemn.

"Wilt thou, Olivia Katherine, have this man to thy wedded husband, to live together after God's ordinance in the holy estate of matrimony? Wilt thou obey him, and serve him, love, honor, and keep him in sickness and in health; and, forsaking all other, keep thee only unto him, so long as ye both shall live?"

"I will."

She'd never been more grateful that only two words separated her from this moment and forever with Lyon.

They added their voices and vows to the centuries of other words spoken in love, hope, and trepidation, and into the very timbers and stones of the little church they sank, to comfort and inspire the next century of worshippers and brides and grooms.

And it might have been a misty morning. The little church might have seemed as dark and soft as a womb.

But everyone said the bride's and groom's faces were so radiant they could have read aloud by them.

When the doors of the church were pushed open and they emerged, such a roar of celebration rose it was said that it flushed birds from trees all the way to the Scottish border, echoed through London, and rippled the very sea beneath a ship once called *The Olivia*, but now called *The Delphinia*, and the sun leaped high in the sky out of sheer surprise.

Seamus Duggan had composed a song for the occasion. Out of rebellion, he called it "The Legend of Lyon Redmond," and it had no words at all. But from his fiddle he coaxed a tune of wild yearning, of anger and love and soaring celebration, and its melodic leaps and rests told the story of Olivia and Lyon better than any words could. And it was said that centuries later birds in that part of Sussex still whistled the tune.

The song would one day make Seamus Duggan a rich man, but that was a story for another day.

Mrs. Olivia Katherine Redmond hooked her arm through her husband's, and they led the procession at a leisurely pace, so that children would have plenty of time to frolic in their wake. And because of the Duffys and the O'Flahertys and Evie Duggan's sister, there were a *lot* of children, and plenty of dogs, thank to the O'Flahertys' promiscuous dog Molly.

Arm in arm they proceeded. The matriarchs and patriarchs, Jacob and Isolde Eversea, Isaiah and Fanchette Redmond. Marcus Eversea and his wife, Louisa. Colin Eversea and Madeline. Violet Redmond and the Earl of Ardmay. Miles Redmond and Cynthia. Ian Eversea and Tansy. Phoebe Vale, once a schoolteacher at Miss Marietta Endicott's Academy, and the Marquess Dryden. Jonathan Redmond and Tommy. Adam Sylvaine and Evie Duggan. Most of them had fallen in love in Pennyroyal Green, and all joined the procession to celebrate their love.

Then came Ned Hawthorne arm in arm with his daughter Polly, who, unbeknownst to anyone, had at last transferred her abiding affection from Colin Eversea to Samuel Heron, a Gypsy boy who lived on the edge of town, and who, along with Leonora and Martha Heron, followed in the processing, cheering and leaping up for the coins Lyon turned every now and again to toss. Mr. Culpepper and Mr. Cooke, who kept the chessboard warm at the Pig

& Thistle. Mr. Tingle and Mr. Postlethwaite. Mrs. Sneath and the ladies of the Society for the Protection of the Sussex Poor, including Amy Pitney and Josephine Charing. Miss Marietta Endicott and a stream of little girls who all attended her esteemed academy.

And everyone in Pennyroyal Green who had ever admired, fallen in love with, been kissed by, lost a woman or bet or fight to, sung a song about, or simply seen an Eversea or Redmond.

To the sound of Seamus's fiddle and cheers and the jingle of coins Lyon rained down upon the crowd at intervals, they wound from the church through town, past the Pig & Thistle, past Tingle's Bookshop and Postlethwaite's Emporium, and finally, past the two ancient oaks twined round each other.

The ones long said to symbolize the Redmonds and Everseas, their destinies so entwined now that they both fought for supremacy and held each other up, and could not live without each other.

They were bursting with spring leaves.

"I confess, I half thought those trees would topple when we married. The legend is so instilled in all of us," Olivia said to Lyon, over the music.

"Those trees will outlive all of us by centuries," Lyon said complacently. "And besides, who's to say more drama isn't to come?"

He arched a brow, and kissed her hand again, lingeringly, which resulted in another roar of approval and shouted teasing.

Up high, hidden among the leaves, on a thick ancient branch, in a spot no one could see unless one was capable of acrobatically craning one's head, a single word was carved.

Isolde

Not a soul who paraded by noticed it.

Except Isaiah Redmond, who had carved it there almost thirty years ago one night, while he waited for a girl who never came. He was as aware of it as he was of the beating of his own heart.

Epilogue

October 2015
Pennyroyal Green

IT WASN'T UNTIL HER head grew light that Isabel realized she'd stopped breathing.

Nothing in her wild imaginings—and her imagination was *quite* the playground—had prepared her for the reality of the legendary oaks. They were so vast they nearly created their own atmosphere. Perhaps they were now like a great pin in a map, the only thing that kept the soft green folds of the Sussex downs from curling up at the edges and flapping away in a stiff wind.

The thought seemed almost heretically whimsical, in light of their majesty.

But then she'd always struggled with awe. It felt like a form of surrender.

And she'd always struggled with surrendering, period.

Isabel didn't know she had that in common with every single one of her ancestors. But she did know that one in particular had never truly given up on the man she loved. Her diary was the reason Isabel stood here today.

The lowering sun had begun its kind work of burnishing everything a nostalgic sepia. The crowds of shoppers and tourists *click click click*ing with their camera phones to capture the storied trees, the picturesque storefronts, the little ancient squat stone church surrounded by a yard crowded with tilting, lovingly tended stones, the pub, the view up the hill to that great brick academy, had thinned to a trickle.

Isabel, at least for the moment, had the trees to herself.

She managed to get her lungs moving in a steady rhythm again. She imagined the trees were as vast below as above, their roots reaching down, down through the earth, little tendrils stretching out to mingle with the roots of the crops that grew here and of the grass the cows and sheep feasted upon, part of everyone who had ever lived here from the time the first Eversea allegedly stole a cow from and was then bludgeoned by a Redmond (or perhaps it was the other way around?) back in 1066. Permanent, known, necessary, beloved.

In other words, the very opposite of Isabel.

Until recently.

It still took her a moment after she opened her eyes in the morning to remember this.

And then sunlight seemed to flood her veins. Followed by a pure swoop of vertigo that was as similar to panic as it was to joy.

And on her iPad now was an image of a family tree that fanned out for seemingly miles in every direction, all those names connected in fine lines, all of those lines connected to her.

Anyone strolling by would see (and they *would* look—turning heads was something else she had in common with the author of that diary) a petite, slim woman whose blond hair was twisted into (but plotting its escape from) an expert chignon. Her boots and jeans and black leather jacket had a slightly worn, singular quality that made them look expensive. They weren't. Once, long ago, nice bicycles or brand-name sneakers or families who roared with laughter while they played catch together out in their front lawns had hollowed her out with such yearning it was a wonder she didn't sound like a woodwind in a breeze.

She had learned not to want. She'd instead acquired a hard layer of watchful inscrutability, roughly the equivalent of the barrel one climbs into before going over Niagara Falls. Which was what basically it had felt like to be shunted from one foster home to another from the time she was eight.

She was nearly thirty now. She was thriving, if not yet *precisely* prospering, on her own terms. But she still felt uncomfortable owning too many things. Everything she acquired, from her cell phone to her sofa pillows to her thrift store leather jacket to her music collection, was thoughtfully, carefully, chosen and almost tenderly cared for.

One day, maybe, she'd take something for granted.

It was just that she'd lived inside that damned barrel for so long.

She snorted at herself when she realized her hands were trembling, as she really had no patience for ninnies of any kind. She slipped her hand in her jacket pocket and ran her fingers absently over the tiny crystals she'd glued painstaking to her hard phone case one night. Meticulous, painstaking work settled her nerves. They were in the shape of her name.

And then she fished out the phone and impulsively punched in a number.

It was nine in the morning in California.

"I'm having a cup of coffee and reading about that Stephanie Plum girl you told me about, Isabel, sweetie." Laura answered without preamble. "She certainly makes a lot of poor choices, doesn't she?"

Isabel laughed. "That's one way to describe her. Hey, Laura, I'm finally here."

She called her Laura because "Grandma" still didn't trip easily off her tongue.

Isabel's mother, perhaps the most zealous black sheep ever born, had disappeared with Isabel's feckless unknown father into the wilds of California and sundered all family ties before dying. Isabel's mother, like Isabel, never did anything by halves.

Neither did Laura. She'd paid someone to put together a family tree, which was how she'd learned of Isabel's existence, and then she'd tirelessly tracked her to San Francisco. (There were explorers in their bloodline, after all.) That was how Isabel had suddenly acquired aunts and uncles and cousins, all of whom she liked (eventually), and all of whom liked her (eventually), and all of whom were subsequently *mighty* pissed off when Laura had given Isabel the cherished family heirlooms, the diary and the gold watch.

"She needs them the most," Laura had told the rest of them, placidly, unmoved by fits of pique at her age. To Isabel she'd said: "Your Great-Great-Great-Aunt Olivia Redmond would have wanted *you* to have them. You'll know why when you read her diary."

Isabel could weather her pissed-off relatives with aplomb. She'd weathered significantly worse.

And she'd never wanted anything more than that diary and that pocket watch.

Because when she'd thumbed open the watch, inside was a miniature of a girl who was virtually her twin, apart from the dark hair.

And the diary, when she read it, had the compelling force of a trebuchet.

Two months, a few internet reservations, and a bewildered boyfriend later, she was in England. Alone.

"I'm so happy you made it safely, Isabel!" Laura's voice was suddenly faint. She sounded as if she was not only in another time zone, but another dimension. "What is it like? Where are you right now?"

"I'm actually already *in* Pennyroyal Green. In front of the trees, the ones in Olivia's diary. They're the size of an apartment building. They might even be bigger than Mark's ego. Or his venture capital funding." Mark was her on-again, off-again boyfriend. Laura had met him. She'd think this was pretty funny.

"Whoop! I didn't quite hear any of that, Isabel. You're crackling in and out now. Can you speak up?"

"I'm in PENNYROYAL. GREEN. By the TREES."

"You're . . . utting . . . out . . ."

"PENNYROY—"

Alas, the connection was toast.

"Americans," snorted a woman strolling by. "Always shouting about something."

She irritably flicked the sleekest sheet of blond hair Isabel had ever seen over her shoulder, so dangerously shiny she could have blinded fighter pilots with it, and Isabel stepped aside lest she be lashed like a lazy peasant.

She bit back a wicked urge to shout an apology after the woman.

Or perhaps she ought to yank her own hair from its chignon and give it a violent retaliatory flick: *En garde!* Surely a few of her forebears had dueled?

But her own hair was curly. It would likely merely snap back and hit her in the face. In her experience, surrendering to impulses generally did metaphorically just that. Which was how words like "irrepressible" (the magenta hair episode) and "alarming" (the self-administered tattoo) had ended up in her case file. Neither word was entirely fair or accurate, though she'd thought "irrepressible" was funny because it made her sound like a tap-dancing Broadway musical star: "the Irrepressible Isabel Redmond!"

In truth, incidents like those were a bit like exhaust from an internal combustion engine. The inevitable byproduct of ruthlessly stifling nearly everything she thought and felt. No mean feat, given that she was her mother's daughter.

She'd figured out by the time she was nine years old that she was to be at the mercy of subjectivity and other people's adjectives, and she would just have to wait it out.

Her jewelry designs now benefited from her years of ruthless self editing: She transmuted wildness into exquisitely simple shapes, seductive curves, startling materials, sharp points. (All words, coincidentally, Mark had used to describe *her*.) A number of exclusive boutiques in the Bay Area had begun to sell her work. She was now making enough money to get by without a day job.

The blonde woman tossed a final pretty, quelling frown over her shoulder at Isabel. She swished her tall, willow-switch slim self up the street, her hair swinging in metronome counterpoint to the little shopping bag swinging from her hand.

An *unmistakable* bag.

Isabel went still.

Only graphic design nerds (and Isabel was one of them) knew the narrow deep green stripe edged in hair-fine silver was meant to represent the view of the sea as you looked out over the Sussex downs. But everyone knew what those tiny silver letters— P-O-S-T-L-E-T-H-W-A-I-T-E-'-S—kerned across that green line really meant: *I am made of money.*

Postlethwaite's fifteen stores worldwide curated

the simple, the exquisite, the startling, the confusing (also words Mark had used to describe her), and catapulted artists and designers into stardom.

Olivia had bought the very gold watch now tucked into Iabel's pocket from the first Mr. Postlethwaite here in Pennyroyal Green.

And even though Isabel was certain she currently couldn't afford to buy a single thing in there, she intended to convince them to sell her jewelry.

Or her name wasn't Isabel Redmond.

She wanted to be brave. The way Olivia was brave.

Isabel had read that diary in one marathon sitting, awaking groggily the next morning, eyes sandy, fully intending to text Olivia to see if she was free for lunch. That's how vivid and familiar and endearing her voice was.

She was stubborn, very funny, self-righteous, fiercely smart, passionate.

A lot like Isabel.

But the differences between them where what bothered Isabel a good deal.

She might have in common with Olivia an urge to *leave* and the nerve to do it.

But Olivia's courage to leave everything she knew behind had been rooted in love. For her family. And for Lyon.

Her love for Lyon had all but set the pages of the diary on fire.

Whereas Isabel moved easily because she'd always been unmoored, and because she wanted to leave before she was left.

She wasn't certain this counted as courage.

She was somehow certain that diary held some secret she needed to know.

Either that, or it had given her yet another reason to leave.

She was suddenly absurdly conscious of her heart

knocking hard at her breastbone, like a door-to-door salesman who knows, just *knows* someone is home.

"Olivia," she whispered. "I'm here. You walked right on this spot on your wedding day. Remember?"

She felt a little foolish. But only a little.

She didn't have to edit anymore.

She transferred her phone into her left hand and looked about surreptitiously. She was utterly alone at least for the moment. So she surrendered to an impulse.

She cautiously, gently, laid a hand against the tree. As if feeling for its heartbeat.

She exhaled and closed her eyes. She couldn't decide whether she felt grounded or dizzied. Perhaps both.

She stood like that for perhaps thirty seconds before a motorcycle roared up the road.

She squeaked and leaped backward.

And her phone shot from her hand like a squeezed bar of soap.

She whirled to watch it sail through the air in what felt like excruciating slow motion, right on schedule to be run over and crushed to bits.

She hunched, as if she herself were about to be crushed, slapped her hands over her eyes, and waited.

The murderous crunch never came.

But over the hammering of her heart, she thought she heard the motorcycle cut its engine.

"You can open them."

She peeled her hands away from her eyes. Abashed.

A man stood between her and the glare of the lowering sun, which was giving him something of a red halo.

Good God, he was tall. Suddenly she fully understood the meaning of the word "rangy."

He was holding her phone out to her.

"I saw something leap into the road. Is this yours? I managed not to crush it."

The voice was amused. Solicitous. Baritone with a lovely scorched velvet edge. She'd once dated a guy who was perpetually hoarse from smoking and enthusiastically shouting "WOOOO!" at rock concerts. This was entirely different. This was something she could imagine whispering in her ear in the dark from the pillow next to hers.

Though of course that lovely rasp could be because he'd sucked in one too many insects while riding his motorcycle.

She saw it leaning on its kickstand behind him. A beautiful machine, somehow both sculptural and savage. A vintage Triumph.

He sounded refined and very English, an odd contrast to his helmet-smashed dark curls, the faint mauve circles of weariness under his eyes, the shadow of a beard, the battered leather jacket that hung gracefully from shoulders that went on for kilometers. He had a sort craggy, Tolkien-hero-on-a-quest face. Not pretty. Quite masculine. Compelling, in that she couldn't look away from it. Especially his eyes, deep set and very dark, and at the moment, not blinking

She just nodded mutely. Like a "looby," a word she'd learned from Olivia's diary.

"Were you aware your phone was suicidal?" he asked gravely. On a hush. When it seemed she would never speak.

She found her voice. "It was an accident. At least that's what I'll tell the police."

He laughed. Thankfully.

Because that had been awfully black humor.

He glanced down at the phone and squinted at the little crystals.

"Isabel . . . Redmond?"

When he lifted his face again it was slowly, wonderingly.

Speculation written all over his features.

It was her first taste of being known.

MALCOLM HAD SLOWED when he saw something fly toward him into the road, but he was only mildly curious. It wouldn't be the first time something had been chucked at him. Back in his university days he used to rev his motorcycle just before dawn, which was when he left for classes. Until the day his elderly neighbor Mrs. Gilly burst out her door in her bathrobe and hurled what turned out to be one of her prize hyacinth bulbs at him. It must have been the nearest projectile to hand. "I've 'ad enough of that bleeding racket ye bleeding useless git!"

It bounced off his helmet.

And he'd hadn't a clue he was being so obnoxious. But then it almost seemed the job of men that age to be oblivious and self-absorbed, which is why he now spent a good portion of his time setting the bones and stitching the wounds of men that age. Learning the hard way to be other than obnoxious was what built character.

So a tree-fondling woman hurling things at him was scarcely a blip on the radar of Malcolm's life, when one considered war, medical school, births, deaths, triumphs, failures, women (who counted as triumphs and failures), existential torment, and the granddaughter of a duke, who was expecting him for dinner, and would flay him with scathingly elegant irony if he was late again.

She was worth it, Jemima was.

Most of the time.

He managed not to run over whatever it was that had flown at him and would have been on his way.

But he glanced over his shoulder and saw a petite blonde woman next to the trees.

Her shoulders were hunched.

And she'd covered her eyes with her hands as if her heart had just been broken.

Oh, God.

And so he had to go back.

"The trouble with you, Coburn," his friend Geoff Hawthorne once said, "is that you always go *toward* the trouble, instead of away from it."

If Malcolm had a coat of arms, this is what it would say. In Latin.

Now, however, he was beginning to feel foolish holding out the phone to a strange silent woman.

She at last met his gaze head on.

His breathing hitched as though he'd literally been pierced with a needle.

He frowned, and surely this was unchivalrous, so he arranged his face in carefully neutral planes.

He just hadn't expected to have his equilibrium roughly jostled by a pair of blue eyes this evening.

He couldn't remember ever seeing eyes quite that color before. So achingly lovely they made him restless. He felt oddly as though he needed to *do* something about them.

He got his breath going again. He was hardly callow. He could cope with this.

She had fair hair but her eyelashes were black and she had a disconcertingly direct gaze. Some might say a *challenging* gaze. She had a compact little body, eloquently curved. Her posture was perhaps too straight. As though she'd spent a lifetime braced for the next stiff wind. She looked, as a matter of fact, like a walking dare.

But the rest of her—the spirals of hair slipping from her chignon, the pale pink curve of her lower lip, the heart-shaped face, were straight out of a pre-Raphaelite painting. Soft. Even dreamy. A pair of earrings in the purest dewdrop shape glittered in her ears and reflected him in miniature.

Finally her hand crept out, like a creature coaxed from a burrow, and she took the phone.

"Forgive me if this is presumptuous, but are you perhaps one of *the* Redmonds? Of the Redmonds of Pennyroyal Green? And so many other places now?" he asked.

Her face went slowly luminous. He watched, his breathing hitched again.

Then, like someone in command of a switch, she shut that light off.

Interesting.

"Oh, do you know the Redmonds?" Her accent was American and her casualness was studied. He suspected his answer meant a very good deal to her.

He smiled faintly. "Everyone knows them. They're legends. You've met the trees." He gestured. "And felt the trees."

She blushed.

He was immediately sorry he'd said that. He suspected she was the sort who would very much mind blushing.

"One *wants* to touch them," he was careful to add. "It's the closest we get to time travel isn't it? You're American, are you? Is this your first visit to Pennyroyal Green? I'm sorry. So rude of me. I've better manners than that, truly. My name is Malcolm Coburn."

She said nothing. But her face blanked peculiarly.

"Malcolm Coburn . . ." she repeated musingly, at last. "I think you're on my tree!"

On her *tree*? Oh, Hell. Through no fault of their own, these ancient oaks attracted all manner of nature loons and cultists and New Ageists and conspiracy theorists. The local police had once arrested a group of Druids for dancing naked around them at midnight.

But then she laughed. A fantastic, abandoned, musical sound, not a mad one.

"I'm so sorry. You should see your expression! I meant . . ." She reached into her purse and deftly extracted an iPad, and swiped at it a few times, then turned it around and tapped. "My *family* tree." She fanned the image wider with her fingers and then zoomed in on a portion of it.

Which was when he noticed the words on the inside of her index finger. He'd seen that kind of tattoo before, usually on prisoners and gang members and idiot teenage boys, which was how he knew she'd done it to herself with needle and thread. The letters were tiny, neat, and flawlessly proportioned. It had required determination, precision, and near preternatural patience and tolerance for pain.

It said: *made you look.*

He felt an interesting, not unpleasant little prickle at the back of his neck.

So. Isabel Redmond was a little dangerous.

It worried him that he liked this.

"And there are Coburns over here," she was saying, scooting the image across the iPad with her finger. "I thought I saw a Malcolm Coburn."

He leaned toward it and whistled low. "Look at what you have here. That is, indeed, my branch, and there I am. We're not really *directly* related, you and I, but tangentially, as you can see. I'm descended from John Fountain. If you don't mind?" She shook her head, and he dragged his finger lightly up the screen and landed it on John Fountain, son of Elise Fountain, adopted son of Philippe Lavay. "But he was known as Jack back then. One of John Fountain's and Ruby Alexandra's daughters married a Fitzwilliam, whose daughter married a Coburn. Two hundred or so years ago."

He looked up at her again.

"I feel I ought to warn you I'm a bit of a history geek. I know far more about Pennyroyal Green and the families here than you'd ever want to hear. And the Redmonds and Everseas *are* Pennyroyal Green."

"I actually *want* to hear everything. I know very little. I only have this tree, and Olivia Eversea's diary—she began keeping it shortly after she was married—*and* I have this."

She tucked the iPad under her arm and slipped something from her pocket.

It was a gold watch.

He didn't question that she would trust him, a stranger, to look at her gold watch and iPad. She didn't seem at all naïve. Somehow he was positive she could handle herself. Possibly she knew Krav Maga or some other exotic and violent martial art.

They looked down at Olivia in a hush.

"She's so pretty," he said, finally. "You look exactly like her."

He froze.

His head went up and he pressed his lips together.

He hadn't meant it to sound like that. He wasn't a flirt. It always felt too much like strategy, which to him had always seemed somewhat dishonest, and who had the time? He certainly didn't. When he wanted something from a woman he had no trouble letting it be known directly. He usually got what he wanted.

"You haven't any romance in you," Jemima had once sighed, draping her long, blond hair over his sweaty chest one evening.

Sex, love, and romance were all their own thing, and they only occasionally overlapped. He didn't say that out loud. In part because he could imagine the rousing ensuing argument. He wasn't even certain he knew how to explain it to her.

Isabel Redmond, judging from that wicked light in her eyes, was enjoying his discomfiture.

"I thought I looked like her, too," she said matter-of-factly.

She closed the watch gently on her Aunt Olivia's lovely face and turned it over, tracing the initial on the back with one finger. Absently.

A little silence fell.

"You probably already know this," he told her, "but it's clear to me that 'LAJR' stands for Lyon Arthur James Redmond. Were you aware that he's a legend in these parts?"

"I did know about his initials. I haven't heard about the legend. You're not teasing me?"

Yearning flashed, swift and bright and fleeting over her face.

Intriguing. She didn't want him to know how much it meant to her.

"I'm not, truly," he said gently. "Everyone in Pennyroyal Green still speak of Lyon and Olivia as if it were yesterday. But that's how the English feel about history in general. There's in fact an absolutely beautiful piece of music named for him called 'The Legend of Lyon Redmond.' A folk tune. There's a festival in a few weeks, a group that does a brilliant version of it. Perhaps you'll hear it during your visit."

Her hesitation told him that she knew he was fishing for how long she'd be staying.

"I love live music. And I've let a flat for next three months. In a charming old building behind Miss Marietta Endicott's Academy . . ." She gestured in the direction..

So she was staying for a while. He knew a surge of intense and wholly irrational relief and triumph that she had decided to tell him.

Speaking of staying, he'd kept very late clinic hours the evening before, and he should probably shave before he saw Jemima this evening. "It's just that it would be so refreshing to see your chin now and again, Malcolm," she'd said last time.

He should leave now.

Isabel slipped the watch back into her pocket and shifted her iPad into her hands again.

"The flat you let is the former Seamus Duggan Memorial Home for Unwed Mothers," he told her. "And Duggan, coincidentally, is the composer of 'The Legend of Lyon Redmond.' There are still Duggans in these parts, too."

She scrutinized him, faintly troubled, faintly hopeful, as if she were ascertaining whether he was teasing her again.

"Truly," he found himself saying firmly. As though it were some kind of promise.

Her face went closed, and she rubbed at her arm abstractedly, then caught herself and gave a short laugh. "It's just . . . I got goosebumps when you said that. It all seems rather . . ."

"Synchronistic?"

"I was going to say 'right.' Another way of saying synchronistic, I suppose."

Both words made him a little uneasy at the moment. Because everything from the hurtling cell phone up to this moment felt somehow right and synchronistic.

"While you're here, you can see where Olivia and Lyon lived when they were first married."

"I plan to. I plan to visit every place she mentioned. In her diary she writes about living between England and Cadiz. Their first child was born in England. They had five of them, three boys and—but maybe you know all of this?"

"I don't know it from Olivia's perspective. And it's fascinating. What do you know?"

She glowed gorgeously, delighted to have something to share. "Well, Olivia wanted to see the world, and Lyon wanted to show it to her. They went on to Louisiana—Lyon had had a plantation there and it was really prospering—and then they moved on to New York when her brother Ian and his wife Titania settled there. That's where they lived during the civil war. She writes about her brothers and sisters coming to visit. I saw a *statue* of my Great-Great-Great-Uncle Jonathan in London." She gave a short wondering laugh.

"Jonathan Redmond is one of my heroes. His wife was remarkable, too. They transformed the lives of poor children and helped transform manufacturing in this country. We learned about him in school."

"I touched *him*, too," she confessed, gesturing at the tree she'd just felt. "I patted his brass thigh."

Malcolm had a sudden inconvenient image of her hand on his own thigh.

Which briefly erased his ability to speak.

"So many brave people in my family, I've discovered." She said this shyly, and almost, carefully, searching his face again, perhaps worried about offending him in case his family was riddled with cowards. He found this amusing and unaccountably touching. "Olivia and Lyon were both involved in the abolitionist movement in America."

"They *were* remarkable, Olivia and Lyon Redmond. But there probably isn't an ordinary person on the whole of your family tree. For instance . . ." His finger landed on Lyon's brother, Miles Redmond. "Are you familiar with Redmond Worldwide?"

"The GPS and travel people?"

"The very same. They were radar and aviation pioneers, too, back in the early days of flight. Stop me if you already know all of this."

"I know some things, but please tell me anything you'd like."

"Miles Redmond—Lyon's younger brother—was a renowned explorer and naturalist. His series on the South Seas is still read today. My own copy is nearly worn threadbare. I read the devil out of it when I was younger. Still have it."

"Books like that are precious," she said firmly.

"What kinds of books do you like to read?" he tried, casually. He suddenly very much wanted to know.

"I'd like to read Miles Redmond's books."

Indicating that she'd reveal things about herself selectively and on her own terms, thank you very much.

A peculiar blend of amusement and irritation surged through him.

She didn't realize how very, very determined he could be.

"I'm sure you can find a set in Tingle's Bookshop," he said smoothly. "Which is . . ." he pivoted, then pointed up the street. " . . . right over there. You won't need GPS to find it. Miles did make it to Lacao one more time. But he remained in England when his wife Cynthia became pregnant with their first child. They had four sons, and a daughter, as you can see." He tapped each name gently. "It seemed his destiny was to continue to help the rest of the world *see* the world. One of them in particular was rather notorious. . . ." he touched a name. "Augustine Redmond."

"A little notoriety strengthens the bloodline, from what I understand."

"If you're basing strength on scoundrels, then you'll be delighted to know your blood is strong indeed."

Gratifyingly, she laughed.

"Redmond Worldwide has branched out into mountaineering equipment, travel gear—nearly everything travel related. Their headquarters are in London, but they have offices around the world."

"They sponsored an Everest climb a few years ago, didn't they? And weren't they in the America's Cup last year?"

Ah. So she read the newspapers, at the very least. Perhaps business journals.

"Yes. And they've recently partnered with Cole-Eversea for high-performance outdoor wear. Later in life Colin Eversea, Olivia's brother, and a Mr. Gideon Cole founded Cole-Eversea textiles after successfully breeding a sheep with the softest, most durable wool. The business has been in the family—your family—ever since. Colin Eversea and his wife Madeline had children later in life, four of them. Two boys, two girls, all rascals save one, or so I'm given to understand. One of their descendants heads the company."

"I found my Cole-Eversea sweater in a thrift store." She plucked at the tissue-fine cashmere cardigan she wore open beneath her jacket. "Otherwise I never would have been able to afford it."

He froze.

He'd caught a glimpse of something on her breasts when she'd plucked at her sweater.

He jerked his head up and all but glared at her.

"Are you . . . are you wearing a McLusky t-shirt?" He could barely get the words out.

"I . . . ah . . . Yes." She said this carefully. Startled.

"The band. McLusky." He said this abruptly.

"Is there . . . another McLusky?"

"I fuc . . . that is, I *love* McLusky." He said this almost accusingly.

McLusky was difficult to love, too. Noisy, obnoxious, visceral, clever, obscure. He couldn't think of anyone who remembered them.

Let alone a woman.

There ensued a fraught little silence.

She narrowed her eyes. Studying him in a way that meant: *Prove it.*

"I'm fearful I'm fearful I'm fearful of flying and flying is fearful of me," he quoted softly, like a soldier repeating a password to a sentry.

There was a short silence.

"Well." She said cryptically. Imbuing that word with a dozen shades of meaning.

He imagined describing her to his friend Geoff Hawthorne later: "She wore cashmere over McLusky."

An interesting moment zinged between them.

"What do you do for a living?" she asked suddenly.

"I'm a doctor."

She blinked. "Doctors, in my experience, usually *lead* with 'I'm a doctor.'"

He gave a short laugh. "I have a practice, a clinic, in the Sneath Building down the hill—you may have passed it on your way up. I've a partner, Finn O'Flaherty. A lot of local patients. We even do occasional house calls."

That was all he said. It was his turn to be circumspect.

She just nodded, taking this in. She didn't do what a few too many women did when they learned he was a doctor: fawn. He didn't know why they did that. Apart from the money, doctors often made terrible partners, for so many reasons. The ghastly long and unpredictable hours, for one.

He definitely wasn't the sort of doctor Jemima wanted him to be.

And he was as immovable as the bloody trees in front of him when it came to those reasons for doing what he did.

He looked abruptly down at her iPad again. "Ah . . . now as for the notorious. . . . you'll enjoy hearing about Ruby Alexandra, the daughter of Violet Redmond and the Earl of Ardmay. There are two famous portraits of her—or rather, one famous, one infamous—one at the Duke of Falconbridge's residence, and the other still hangs in Alder House. You can see that one for yourself whilst you're here. She was a spectacular beauty and scandal seemed to dog her. She married her best friend, ultimately. A boy she'd grown up with. John Fountain. *My* forebearer. He was adopted by Philippe Lavay, but he'd been born a bastard. Hardly a suitable match for the daughter of an earl, particularly back then. He sailed off to make his fortune. He did, and then some. You'll find quite a few buildings named for him around England. I understand it was quite the Wuthering Heights story of their day, with a much better ending."

"Every good story should have a little drama."

Hmmm. He wasn't certain he agreed. He also wasn't certain drama was something anyone could avoid. Destiny was like a tiger trap. Sometimes you just fell into the pit.

"Speaking of the Duke of Falconbridge. . . ." She

dropped her finger on Alexander Moncrieffe, bound to Genevieve Eversea. "What do you know about him?"

He knew that the current duke's granddaughter was expecting him for dinner, and would be disappointed he hadn't shaved.

But he didn't say it aloud. The omission felt like a lie. He didn't like himself for it, and he didn't understand it. There would be time to mull that later.

"Well, you *are* indeed indirectly related to the current duke. Let's see . . . Ah, Lord Anthony Argosy married the Duke and Duchess of Falconbridge's middle daughter, Grace. Nearly twenty years apart in age when that happened—his first marriage was *not* a success—and her parents weren't thrilled about this match. But the union proved spectacularly happy, and quite bountiful, as you can see."

He pointed to the abundance of girls and boys fanning out from Argosy's and Grace's little branch of the tree tree.

"Oh, good," she murmured. "It's always a relief when people go on to be happy."

Some peculiar emotion—it felt like anger—sizzled faintly on the periphery of his awareness. *Who made you unhappy, Miss Redmond*? He wanted to know. He suddenly wanted vengeance for her.

"I could close my eyes and drop a finger nearly anywhere here on this tree and we'd have a fascinating story. Explorers, actors, politicians, tycoons, soldiers, surgeons, rock stars, body guards . . . were you aware that Colin Eversea's oldest son founded a private investigation firm? It's huge now. Trains and employs bodyguards and the like . . . so if you're ever a visiting dignitary, or married to one, you can call upon them."

He'd dropped the word "married" into that sentence strategically.

From her brief crooked smile, she knew he was fishing.

And she didn't volunteer any information.

Fair enough.

"And here's an interesting Eversea . . . see, Clive Dunkirk? Drummer in the 70's band Heliotrope?"

"I bought all of Heliotrope's records at a thrift store one day," she said idly.

She looked up sharply when she noticed he'd fallen abruptly silent.

"You love Heliotrope, too, don't you?" she asked. Sounding almost resigned.

"I'm a fan," he said, noncommittally.

He passionately loved Heliotrope. Thunderous, complex, frightening, epic. And loud. Everything he'd been inside when he was younger, and he supposed, in some form or another, still was.

She hiked her eyebrows as if she knew the truth.

"You love visceral music," he hazarded a moment later. As if diagnosing her.

"I love visceral everything," she said instantly.

This sounded like a challenge.

Perhaps even an invitation.

Their eyes locked for an assessing moment, and then he dropped his again, uncertain, in truth, what to do about that.

He wasn't often nonplussed.

"Ah . . . and here's an infamous Eversea. Evangeline Moon."

"Evangeline Moon was an *Eversea*? The actress from the 30s?"

He was very much enjoying watching her face light up when he told her things. Malcolm dragged his finger up along the family tree and stopped it at Adam Sylvaine, then skated it down as he spoke. "She was born Eve Anna Talbot. Eve became a family name, beginning with Evie Duggan, who was married to Pennyroyal Green's vicar, Adam Sylvaine. The current vicar is a Sylvaine, by the way. But Adam was a contemporary of your Aunt Olivia, her cousin. Anyway, Reverend Sylvaine and Evie Duggan had four children. Long before that there was a rumor Evie Duggan killed her first husband, who was an earl. Which was likely nonsense. A few hundred years later, Evangeline Moon was born in poverty in San Francisco. She inherited both Evie Duggan's looks *and* the scandal-prone DNA."

"I knew she was from San Francisco. But Gabriel Graham was her true love," Isabel said firmly. "I had *such* a crush on him when I was younger. I was riveted by his movies. I couldn't believe anyone that charismatic had ever existed."

Malcolm was so suddenly irrationally jealous of the long-dead, effortlessly cool Gabriel Graham that his finger jerked like a record scratch up to another part of her family tree.

"Now Genevieve Eversea, Olivia's sister, married the Duke of Falconbridge. Their direct descendants still abound in England, all of Europe, really. You may even see them in town while you're here. Unless you blink, because the future duke is usually a blur in that Maserati."

"Do you know him well, then?"

He pressed his lips together. "He thinks *I'm* a Plebian. His brothers and sister are more tolerable."

He could imagine Jemima's reaction to being called "tolerable."

Isabel was studying him, a faint furrow between her brows.

It was perilously close to sunset. He should have left ten minutes ago.

A bird sang a glorious snatch of song, and Isabel

tipped her head back to see if she could find the singer in the tree.

"Do you see something carved there? It looks like an 'I' and maybe an 'S.'"

The lowering sun had indeed struck new angles and illuminated hidden nooks. And there it was.

He tipped his own head back. "I think you're right. I-S. I've never noticed it before. As though someone was trying to carve 'Isabel.'"

She drew in a long, audible breath.

And exhaled a shuddery one.

And suddenly, abruptly, she slipped her iPad back into her bag and folded her hands in front of her.

"I'm sorry," he said instantly. "Is all this history a bit much?"

"No . . . *I'm* sorry . . . I'm happy, actually." She glanced up at him quickly, then smiled swiftly, but the smile was wobbly. "That was my happy face, honestly. It's just. That I . . . I didn't really know my parents, so . . ."

This sentence trailed into nothingness as she pretended to be distracted by rummage through her handbag.

"Ah," he said instantly, neutrally, a universe of understanding in that syllable.

Isabel looked up at him again. He had doctor's eyes. A way of looking into you that implied you may as well tell him your secrets, because he knew them anyway.

She was certain *plenty* of women and patients had volunteered their secrets to him.

He wasn't going to find her quite as forthcoming.

She looked forward to his efforts, however.

The silence stretched a bit. She'd created an awkward moment and she regretted it.

He didn't really need to know a thing about her

in order for her to enjoy him, and she'd been so caught up in the momentum of the conversation she'd tripped on her own conversational thread.

"The reason I practice medicine in Pennyroyal Green . . ." he ventured. ". . . . where I was born . . . Sometimes I think it has a bit to do with Jack Fountain, who never knew his own father. Maybe a need to belong, to feel connected to something, is in my DNA."

She knew why he'd said it: so that she would recognize that her own untold story, however dark or difficult, was simply part of centuries of human experience.

She was very unaccustomed to insightful men.

She wasn't certain how much she liked it

"I wonder if someone might even stand beneath these trees a hundred years from now and tell the story of Isabel Redmond to someone else," she mused.

He gave a short laugh. "Given your bloodline, it almost seems inevitable. And a hundred years is like yesterday here in England. For example, Isaiah Redmond, Lyon's father, died later in life under mysterious circumstances. There's a faction here in England that maintains to this day that Jacob Eversea—Olivia's father—killed him."

"No!" she was perversely thrilled.

"Nothing was ever proven, of course. Nothing ever seems to be proved when it comes to the Everseas. They traditionally get away with everything, or so legend has it."

She smiled at him slowly. She loved knowing roguish blood flowed in her veins. And that her history contained mysteries.

"To this day, there's still a bit of tension between the Everseas and Redmonds," he added idly. "I thought I should warn you. In case you encountered a bit of tension during your visit."

She smiled slightly. She knew precisely why he'd said that.

They allowed the word "tension" to simmer there in silence.

"Thank you," she said finally.

When he smiled slightly a dimple winked briefly at the corner of his mouth. That dimple was more perfect than anything Postlethwaite's had ever stocked.

"My old school chum, Geoff Hawthorne, owns the Pig & Thistle, just a bit up the road," he said. "They have a splendid antique Rowlandson print of Lyon Redmond simmering in a pot presided over by two cannibals. If you're hungry."

She laughed, and then he laughed at himself when he realized how that had sounded.

"Sounds wonderful," she told him.

"Don't worry. I'm fairly certain there aren't any cannibals in your bloodline. Though Miles Redmond was nearly eaten by one."

He nudged up the kickstand of his motorcycle with the toe of a well-worn boot. He walked the bike gently, as though it were a beloved pet. She approved.

She fell into silent stride next to him.

"Speaking of rogues," he said suddenly, "did you know your Great-Great-Great-Uncle Colin Eversea escaped from the gallows?"

"No!"

"Oh, yes. There's even a song about him," Malcolm said. "And you wouldn't believe the number of verses it has now."

THE END

The Casebook of Barnaby Adair novels from
#1 *New York Times* bestselling author

Stephanie LAURENS

WHERE THE HEART LEADS
978-0-06-124338-7

Handsome, enigmatic, and deliciously dangerous, Barnaby
Adair has made his name by solving crimes within the
ton. When Penelope Ashford appeals for his aid in solving
the mystery of the disappearing orphans in her care, he is
moved by her plight—and captivated by her beauty.

THE MASTERFUL MR. MONTAGUE
978-0-06-206866-8

When Lady Halstead is murdered, Barnaby Adair helps her
devoted lady-companion, Miss Violet Matcham, and her
financial adviser, Montague, expose a cunning killer. But will
Montague and Violet learn the shocking truth too late to
seize their chance at enduring love?

LOVING ROSE
978-0-06-206867-5

Rose has a plausible explanation for why she and her children are residing in Thomas Glendower's secluded manor.
Revealing the truth would be impossibly dangerous, yet day
by day he wins her trust, and then her heart. But when her
enemy closes in, Rose must turn to Thomas to protect her
and her children.

LAU6 0814

THE SMYTHE-SMITH QUARTET BY
#1 *NEW YORK TIMES*
BESTSELLING AUTHOR

JULIA QUINN

JUST LIKE HEAVEN
978-0-06-149190-0

Honoria Smythe-Smith is to play the violin (badly) in the annual musicale performed by the Smythe-Smith quartet. But first she's determined to marry by the end of the season. When her advances are spurned, can Marcus Holroyd, her brother Daniel's best friend, swoop in and steal her heart in time for the musicale?

A NIGHT LIKE THIS
978-0-06-207290-0

Anne Wynter is not who she says she is, but she's managing quite well as a governess to three highborn young ladies. Daniel Smythe-Smith might be in mortal danger, but that's not going to stop the young earl from falling in love. And when he spies a mysterious woman at his family's annual musicale, he vows to pursue her.

THE SUM OF ALL KISSES
978-0-06-207292-4

Hugh Prentice has never had patience for dramatic females, and Lady Sarah Pleinsworth has never been acquainted with the words *shy* or *retiring*. Besides, a reckless duel has left Hugh with a ruined leg, and now he could never court a woman like Sarah, much less dream of marrying her.

THE SECRETS OF SIR RICHARD KENWORTHY
978-0-06-207294-8

Sir Richard Kenworthy has less than a month to find a bride, and when he sees Iris Smythe-Smith hiding behind her cello at her family's infamous musicale, he thinks he might have struck gold. Iris is used to blending into the background, so when Richard courts her, she can't quite believe it's true.

JQ4 0515

At Avon Books, we know your passion for romance—once you finish one of our novels, you find yourself wanting more.

May we tempt you with . . .

- **Excerpts** from our upcoming releases.

- Entertaining **extras**, including authors' personal photo albums and book lists.

- Behind-the-scenes **scoop** on your favorite characters and series.

- **Sweepstakes** for the chance to win free books, romantic getaways, and other fun prizes.

- Writing **tips** from our authors and editors.

- **Blog** with our authors and find out why they love to write romance.

- **Exclusive content** that's not contained within the pages of our novels.

Join us at
www.avonbooks.com

An Imprint of HarperCollins*Publishers*
www.avonromance.com